Praise for *Co*

"*Coastliners* is . . . tactile, sensory, imme

—*USA Today*

"[Harris] still knows how to create a multilayered story, even if she cooks it up on a wind-whipped beach instead of in a cozy kitchen."

—*San Francisco Chronicle*

"Harris is fast becoming one of the most reliable writers of appealing, idea-driven fiction. This affecting story about community resilience blends environmental and social themes with her signature wit and élan."

—*Christian Science Monitor*

"Impressively researched and filled to the brim with surprising plot twists, this deeply felt book is the best work yet of this prolific writer."

—*Book* magazine

"'Everything returns' is the thesis of Joanne Harris's latest effort. This time, the magic lies in the returning ocean tides rather than in food or drink."

—*Library Journal*

"This novel . . . flows as rhythmically as the waves that wash upon Le Devin, the tiny French island where the story takes place."

—*New York Daily News*

"Harris delivers the goods for readers who can't get enough."

—*Kirkus Reviews*

"[Harris] proves she doesn't need pantry ingredients to cook up a delectable story."

—*Boston Herald*

© Adine Sagalyn / Agence Opale

About the Author

JOANNE HARRIS is the author of three novels, the critically acclaimed *Chocolat; Blackberry Wine;* and *Five Quarters of the Orange.* Half French and half British, she lives in England.

ALSO BY JOANNE HARRIS

Five Quarters of the Orange

Blackberry Wine

Chocolat

Perennial

An Imprint of HarperCollins*Publishers*

Coastliners

A NOVEL

Joanne Harris

A hardcover edition of this book was published in 2002 by William Morrow,
an imprint of HarperCollins Publishers.

COASTLINERS. Copyright © 2002 by Joanne Harris. All rights reserved.
Printed in the United States of America. No part of this book may be used or
reproduced in any manner whatsoever without written permission except in the
case of brief quotations embodied in critical articles and reviews. For information
address HarperCollins Publishers Inc., 10 East 53rd Street, New York, NY 10022.

HarperCollins books may be purchased for educational, business, or sales
promotional use. For information please write: Special Markets Department,
HarperCollins Publishers Inc., 10 East 53rd Street, New York, NY 10022.

First Perennial edition published 2003.

Designed by Deborah Kerner / Dancing Bears Design

The Library of Congress has catalogued the hardcover edition as follows:
Harris, Joanne.
     Coastliners : a novel / by Joanne Harris.—1st ed.
         p.   cm.
     ISBN 0-06-019812-5
     1. Fishing villages—Fiction. 2. Islands—Fiction. 3. France—Fiction. I. Title.
PR6058.A68828 C63   2002
823'.914—dc21   2001059045

ISBN 0-06-095801-4 (pbk.)

03   04   05   06   07   ❖/ RRD   10   9   8   7   6   5   4   3   2   1

to my mother

JEANNETTE PAYEN SHORT

No man is an island, entire of itself;
every man is a piece of the Continent,
a part of the main.

—JOHN DONNE,
  "Devotions upon Emergent Occasions"

To see a world in a grain of sand,
And a heaven in a wild flower,
Hold Infinity in the palm of your hand,
And Eternity in an hour.

—WILLIAM BLAKE,
  "Auguries of Innocence"

Acknowledgments

No book is an island, and I should like to thank the following people, without whom none of this would have been possible. Heartfelt thanks to my agent, Serafina Warrior Princess; to Jennifer Luithlen, Howard Morhaim, and everyone else who has negotiated, cajoled, intimidated, and otherwise steered this book toward publication. Thanks also to my editor, Jennifer Hershey, and to all my friends at Avon Morrow; to Kevin and Anouchka for being (most of the time) a safe harbor; thanks to my e-correspondents Curt, Mary, Emma, Simon, and Jules for keeping me in touch with the rest of the world; to Stevie, Paul, and David for mint tea and pancakes; thanks to Charles de Lint—with apologies for the inadvertent theft of two crow feathers; and to Christopher Fowler, for holding the line. Thanks to the innumerable sales staff and booksellers who have worked to keep my books on the shelves, and, finally, thanks to the people of Les Salants, who I hope will forgive me in time. . . .

Prologue

Islands are different. The smaller the island, the more true this becomes. Look at Britain. Barely conceivable that this narrow stretch of land should sustain so much diversity. Cricket, cream teas, Shakespeare, Sheffield, fish and chips in vinegary newspaper, Soho, two universities, the beachfront at Southend, striped deck chairs in Green Park, *Coronation Street*, Oxford Street, lazy Sunday afternoons. So many contradictions. All marching together like boozy protesters who have not yet realized their main cause for complaint is one another. Islands are pioneers, splinter groups, malcontents, misfits, natural isolationists. As I said, different.

This island, for instance. Only a bike ride from one end to the other. A man walking on water might reach the coast in an afternoon. The island of Le Devin, one of the many islets caught like crabs in the shallows off the Vendée coastline. Eclipsed by Noirmoutier on the coastal side, by Ile d'Yeu from the south, on a foggy day you might miss it altogether. Maps hardly give it a mention. Indeed it scarcely deserves island status at all, being little more than a cluster of sandbanks with pretensions, a rocky spine to lift it out of the Atlantic, a couple of villages, a small fish-packing factory, a single beach. At the far end, home—Les Salants, a row of cottages—barely enough to call a village—staggering down through rocks and dunes toward a sea that encroaches closer at every bad tide. Home the inescapable place, the place to which the heart's compass turns.

Given the choice I might have preferred something different. Somewhere in England perhaps, where my mother and I were happy for nearly a year before my restlessness drove us on. Or Ireland, or Jersey, Iona, or Skye. You see that I seek out islands as if by instinct, as if trying to recapture the elements of *my* island, Le Devin, the single place for which there can be no substitute.

Its shape is rather like that of a sleeping woman. Les Salants is her head, shoulders turned protectively against the weather. La Goulue is her belly, La Houssinière the sheltered crook of her knees. All around lies La Jetée, a skirt of sandy islets, expanding and contracting according to the tides, slowly shifting the shoreline, nibbling one side, depositing on the other, rarely keeping their shape long enough to earn names. Beyond that is the total unknown, the shallow shelf beyond La Jetée dropping sharply into a rift of unsounded depth that locals call the Nid'Poule. A message in a bottle, thrown from any point on the island, will most often return to La Goulue—the Greedy One—behind which the village of Les Salants huddles against the hard sea wind. Its position east of the rocky head of Pointe Griznoz means that gritty sand, silt, and general refuse tend to accumulate here. High tides and winter storms exacerbate this, building battlements of seaweed on the rocky shore that may stand for six months or a year before another storm washes them away.

As you can see, Le Devin is no beauty. Like our patron saint, Marine-de-la-Mer, the hunched figure has a rough and primitive look. Few tourists come here. There is little to attract them. If from the air these islands are dancers with tulle skirts spread wide, then Le Devin is the girl in the back row of the chorus—a rather plain girl—who has forgotten her steps. We have fallen behind, she and I. The dance goes on without us.

But the island has retained its identity. A stretch of land only a few kilometers long, and yet it has a character entirely of its own, dialects, food, traditions, dress, all as different from the other islands as they are from mainland France. The islanders think of themselves as Devinnois rather than French or even Vendéen. They have no allegiance to politicians. Few of their sons bother to perform their military service. So far from the center of things, it seems absurd. And so far from the reaches of officialdom and the law, Le Devin follows its own rules.

Which is not to say foreigners are unwelcome. Quite the opposite; if we knew how to encourage tourism, we would. In Les Salants, tourism means wealth. We look across the water at Noirmoutier with its hotels and guest houses and shops and the great graceful bridge, which flies across the water from the mainland. There, the summer roads are a river of cars—with foreign plates and luggage straining from the racks—the beaches black with people, and we try to imagine what it would be like if they were ours. But little of it ever goes beyond fantasy. The tourists—the few who venture this far—stay stubbornly in La Houssinière on the near side of the island. There is nothing for them in Les Salants, with its rocky, beachless coast, its dunes of stones mortared together with hard sand, its gritty ceaseless wind.

The people of La Houssinière know this. There has been a feud for as long as anyone can remember between the Houssins and the Salannais, religious issues at first, then disputes over fishing rights, building rights, trade, and inevitably, land. Reclaimed land belongs by law to those who have reclaimed it and to their descendants. It is the Salannais' only wealth. But La Houssinière controls deliveries from the coast (its oldest family runs the only ferry) and sets the prices. If an Houssin can cheat a Salannais, he will. If a Salannais manages to get the better of an Houssin, the whole village shares in the triumph.

And La Houssinière has a secret weapon. It's called Les Immortelles, a sandy little beach, two minutes from the harbor and protected on one side by an ancient jetty. Here sailboats skim the water, protected from the westerly winds. This is the only safe place to bathe or to sail, sheltered from the strong currents that tear at the headland. This beach—this freak of nature—has made the difference between the two communities. The village has grown into a little town. Because of it La

Houssinière is prosperous by island standards. There is a restaurant, a hotel, a cinema, a discothèque, a campsite. In summer the small harbor is packed with pleasure boats. La Houssinière houses the island's mayor, its policeman, its post office, its only priest. A number of families from the coast rent houses here in August, bringing trade with them.

Meanwhile Les Salants is dead throughout the summer, panting and parching in the wind and heat. But to me, it's still home. Not the most beautiful place in the world, or even the most welcoming. But it's my place.

Everything returns. It's a maxim on Le Devin. Living on the gaudy rag-end of the Gulf Stream, it is an affirmation of hope. Everything returns eventually. Wrecked boats, messages in bottles, lifebuoys, jetsam, fishermen lost at sea. The pull of La Goulue is too strong for many to resist. It may take years. The mainland is alluring, with its money, cities, and antic life. Three out of four children leave at eighteen, dreaming of the world beyond La Jetée. But the Greedy One is patient as well as hungry. And for those like myself, with nothing else to anchor us down, return seems inevitable.

I had a history, once. Not that it matters now. On Le Devin no one cares about any history but our own. Objects wash up on these shores—wreckage, beach balls, dead birds, empty wallets, expensive training shoes, plastic cutlery, even people—and no one questions their origin. The sea removes what is not claimed. Sea creatures too will occasionally move along this highway, Portuguese men-of-war and nurse sharks and sea horses and brittle stars and the occasional whale. They stay or they go, brief curiosities to be gaped at and as rapidly forgotten as soon as they leave our waters. To the islanders, nothing exists beyond La Jetée. From that point onward there's nothing to break the horizon until you reach America. No one ventures farther. No one studies the tides or what they bring. Except me. Being jetsam myself, I feel entitled.

Take this beach, for example. It's a remarkable thing. One island, a single beach; a happy accident of tides and currents; a hundred thousand tons of ancient sand, stubborn as rock, gilded by a thousand envious glances into something more precious than gold dust. Certainly it has made the Houssins wealthy, although we both know—Houssins and Salannais alike—how easily, how arbitrarily things could have been different.

An altered current, drifting a hundred meters to the left or the right. A degree shift in the prevailing wind. Movement in the geography of the seabed. A bad storm. Any one of these things at any time could bring about a cataclysmic reversal. Luck is like a pendulum, swinging slowly across the decades, bringing the inevitable in its shadow.

Les Salants still waits patiently, expectantly, for its return.

PART ONE

Flotsam and Jetsam

<h1 style="text-align:center">1</h1>

 I returned after ten years' absence, on a hot day in late August, on the eve of summer's first bad tides. As I stood watching the approach from the deck of *Brismand 1*, the old ferry into La Houssinière, it was almost as though I had never left. Nothing had changed: the sharp smell of the air; the deck beneath my feet; the sound of the gulls in the hot blue sky. Ten years, almost half my life, erased at a single stroke, like writing in the sand. Or almost.

I'd brought scarcely any luggage, and that reinforced the illusion. But I'd always traveled light. We both had, Mother and I; there had never been much to weigh us down. And at the end it had been I who paid the rent for our Paris flat, working in a dingy late-night café to supplement the income from the paintings Mother hated so much, while she struggled with her emphysema and pretended not to know she was dying.

All the same I should have liked to have returned wealthy, successful. To show my father how well we'd managed without his help. But my mother's small savings had run out long ago, and my own—a few thousand francs in a Crédit Maritime; a folder of unsold paintings—amounted to little more than we'd taken with us the day we left. Not that it mattered. I was not planning to stay. However potent the illusion of time suspended, I had another life now. I had changed.

No one looked at me twice as I stood slightly apart from the others on the deck of the *Brismand 1*. It was high season, and there were already a good number of tourists aboard. Some were even dressed as I was, in sailcloth trousers and fisherman's *vareuse*—that shapeless garment halfway between a shirt and a jacket—town people trying too hard not to look it. Tourists with rucksacks, suitcases, dogs, and children stood crammed together on the deck among crates of fruit and groceries, cages of chickens, mailbags, boxes. The noise was appalling. Beneath it, the *hissshh* of the sea against the ferry's hull and the *screee* of gulls. My heart was pounding with the surf.

As *Brismand 1* neared the harbor I let my eyes travel across the water toward the esplanade. As a child I had liked it here; I'd often played on the beach, hiding under the fat bellies of the old beach huts while my father conducted whatever business he had at the harbor. I recognized the faded Choky parasols on the *terrasse* of the little café where my sister used to sit; the hot dog stand; the gift shop. It was perhaps busier than I remembered; a straggling row of fishermen with pots of crabs and lobsters lined the quay, selling their catch. I could hear music from the esplanade; below it, children played on a beach that, even at high tide, seemed smoother and more generous than I remembered. Things were looking good for La Houssinière.

I let my eyes roam along the Rue des Immortelles, the main street, which runs parallel to the seafront. I could see three people sitting there side by side in what had once been my favorite spot: the seawall below the esplanade overlooking the bay. I remembered sitting there as a child, watching the distant gray jawbone of the mainland, wondering what was there. I narrowed my eyes to see more clearly; even from halfway across the bay I could see that two of the figures were nuns.

I recognized them now as the ferry drew close—Soeur Extase and Soeur Thérèse, Carmelite volunteers from the nursing home at Les Immortelles, were already old before I was born. I felt oddly reassured that they were still there. Both nuns were eating ice creams, their habits hitched up to their knees, bare feet dangling over the parapet. The man sitting beside them, face obscured by a wide-brimmed hat, could have been anyone.

The *Brismand 1* drew alongside the jetty. A gangplank was raised into place, and I waited for the tourists to disembark. The jetty was as crowded as the boat; vendors stood by selling drinks and pastries; a taxi driver advertised his trade; children with trolleys vied for the attention of the tourists. Even for August, it was busy.

"Carry your bags, mademoiselle?" A round-faced boy of about fourteen, wearing a faded red T-shirt, tugged at my sleeve. "Carry your bags to the hotel?"

"I can manage, thanks." I showed him my tiny case.

The boy gave me a puzzled glance, as if trying to place my features. Then he shrugged and moved on to richer pickings.

The esplanade was crowded. Tourists leaving; tourists arriving; Houssins in between. I shook my head at an elderly man attempting to sell me a knot work key ring; it was Jojo-le-Goëland, who used to take us for boat rides in summer, and although he'd never been a friend—he was an Houssin, after all—I felt a pang that he hadn't recognized me.

"Are you staying here? Are you a tourist?" It was the round-faced boy again, now joined by a friend, a dark-eyed youth in a leather jacket who was smoking a cigarette with more bravado than pleasure. Both boys were carrying suitcases.

"I'm not a tourist. I was born in Les Salants."

"Les Salants?"

"Yes. My father's Jean Prasteau. He's a boatbuilder. Or was, anyway."

"GrosJean Prasteau!" Both boys looked at me with open curiosity.

They might have said more, but just then three other teenagers joined us. The biggest addressed the round-faced boy with an air of authority.

"What are you Salannais doing here again, heh?" he demanded. "The seafront belongs to the Houssins, you know that. You're not allowed to take luggage to Les Immortelles!"

"Who says?" demanded the round-faced boy. "It's not *your* esplanade! They're not *your* tourists!"

"Lolo's right," said the boy with dark eyes. "We were first."

The two Salannais drew a little closer together. The Houssins out-numbered them, but I sensed they were willing to fight rather than give up the suitcases. For a moment I saw myself at their age, waiting for my father, ignoring the laughter from the pretty Houssin girls at the *terrasse* of the café until at last it grew too much and I fled to my hideout under the beach huts.

"They were first," I told the three. "Now scat."

For a moment the Houssins looked at me resentfully, then left, mut-tering, for the jetty. Lolo gave me a look of pure gratitude. His friend just shrugged.

"I'll walk with you," I said. "Les Immortelles, was it?" The big white house stood only a few hundred meters down the esplanade. In the old days it had been a nursing home.

"It's a hotel now," said Lolo. "It belongs to Monsieur Brismand."

"Yes, I know him."

Claude Brismand; a thickset Houssin with a bombastic mustache, who smelled of cologne, who wore espadrilles like a peasant, whose voice was rich and expensive as good wine. Foxy Brismand, they called him in the village. Lucky Brismand. For many years I had believed him to be a widower, although there were rumors that he had a wife and child some-where on the mainland. I'd always liked him even though he was an Houssin; he was cheerful, talkative, his pockets bulging with sweets. My father had hated him. As if in defiance, my sister, Adrienne, had married his nephew.

"It's all right now." We had reached the end of the esplanade. Through a pair of glass doors I could see the lobby of Les Immortelles—a desk, a vase of flowers, a big man sitting near the open window smok-ing a cigar. For a moment I considered going in, then decided against it. "I think you can manage from here. Go on in."

They did; the dark-eyed boy without a word, Lolo with a grimace of apology for his friend. "Don't mind Damien," he said in a low voice. "He always wants to fight."

I smiled. I'd been the same. My sister, four years older than I, with her pretty clothes and beauty parlor hair, had never had any trouble fitting in; at the *terrasse* of the café, her laughter had always been loudest.

I made my way across the crowded street to where the two old Carmelites were sitting. I wasn't sure whether they would recognize me—a Salannaise they hadn't seen since she was a girl—but I'd always liked them in the old days. Coming closer I was unsurprised to notice that they had hardly changed at all: both bright-eyed, but brown and leathery like dried things on the beach. Soeur Thérèse wore a dark head scarf rather than the white *quichenotte* coif of the islands; otherwise I wasn't sure whether I could have told them apart. The man beside them, with a coral bead around his neck and a floppy hat shading his eyes, was a stranger. Late twenties or early thirties, a pleasant face without being striking; he could have been a tourist but for the easy familiarity with which he greeted me, the silent nod of the islands.

Soeur Extase and Soeur Thérèse looked at me keenly for a moment, then broke into identical beaming smiles. "Why, it's GrosJean's little girl."

Long companionship far from their convent had given them the same mannerisms. Their voices were similar too, quick and cracked as magpies. Like twins, they shared a peculiar empathy, carrying on sentences for each other and puncuating each other's words with encouraging gestures. Eerily, they never used either of their names, one always referring to the other as *"ma soeur,"* although as far as I know they were not related.

"It's Mado, *ma soeur*, little Madeleine Prasteau. How she's grown! Time passes—"

"—So quickly here in the islands. It doesn't seem more than—"

"—A couple of years since we first came and now we're—"

"Old and cranky, *ma soeur*, old and cranky. But we're pleased to see you again, Little Mado. So different you always were. So veryvery different from—"

"Your sister." They spoke the last words in unison. Their black eyes gleamed.

"It's good to be back." Until I spoke the words I hadn't known how good it was.

"It hasn't changed much, has it, *ma soeur*—"

"No, nothing changes much. It gets—"

"Older, that's all. Like us." Both nuns shook their heads matter-of-factly and returned to their ice creams.

"I see they've converted Les Immortelles," I said.

"That's right," nodded Soeur Extase. "Most of it, anyway. There are still a few of us left on the top floor—"

"Long-term guests, Brismand calls us—"

"But not many. Georgette Loyon and Raoul Lacroix and Bette Planc-pain. He bought their houses when they got too old to cope—"

"Bought them cheap and fixed them up for the summer people—"

The nuns exchanged glances. "Brismand only keeps them here because he gets charity money from the convent. He likes to keep in with the church. He knows what side *his* wafer's buttered."

A thoughtful silence as the pair of them sucked at their ice creams.

"And this is Rouget, Little Mado." Soeur Thérèse indicated the stranger, who had been listening to their comments with a grin on his face.

"Rouget, the Englishman—"

"Come to lead us astray with ice cream and blandishments. And at our age too."

The Englishman shook his head. "Ignore them," he advised, still grinning. "I only indulge them because otherwise they'd tell all my secrets." His voice was pleasantly, if strongly, accented.

The sisters cackled. "Secrets, heh! There isn't much we don't know, is there, *ma soeur*, we may be—"

"—Old, but there's nothing wrong with our ears."

"People forget about us—"

"Because we're—"

"Nuns."

The man they called Rouget looked at me and grinned. He had a clever, quirky face that lit up when he smiled. I could feel his eyes taking in every detail of my appearence, not unkindly, but with expectant curiosity.

"Rouget?" Most names on Le Devin are nicknames. Only foreigners and mainlanders use anything else.

He took off his hat with an ironic flourish. "Richard Flynn; philosopher, builder, sculptor, welder, fisherman, handyman, weatherman"—he gestured vaguely toward the sands at Les Immortelles—"and most important, student and comber of beaches."

Soeur Extase greeted his words with an apppreciative cackle suggesting that this was an old joke. "Trouble, to me and you," she explained.

Flynn laughed. I noticed that his hair was roughly the same color as the bead around his neck. *Red hair, bad blood*, my mother used to say, though it is an unusual color in the islands, generally held to be a sign of good luck. That explained it. Even so, a nickname confers a kind of status on Le Devin, unusual in a foreigner. It takes time to earn an island name.

"Are you living here?" Somehow I thought it unlikely. There was something restless about him, I thought; something volatile.

He shrugged. "It's as good a place as any."

That startled me a little. As if all places were the same to him. I tried to imagine not caring where home was, not feeling its ceaseless drag on my heart. His terrible freedom. And yet they'd given him a name. All my life I had simply been *la fille à GrosJean*, like my sister.

"So." He grinned. "What do you do?"

"I'm a painter. I mean, I sell my paintings."

"What do you paint?"

For a moment I thought of the little flat in Paris, and the room I used for my studio. A tiny space, too small for a guest room—and Mother had made even that concession with bad grace—my easel and folders and canvases propped up against the wall. I could have chosen any subject for my paintings, Mother was fond of saying. I had a gift. Why then did I always paint the same thing? Lack of imagination? Or was it to torment her?

"The islands, mostly."

Flynn looked at me but said nothing more. His eyes were the same slaty color as the cloud line at the horizon's edge. I found them curiously difficult to look at, as if they could see thoughts.

Soeur Extase had finished her ice cream. "And how's your mother, Little Mado? Did she come over with you today?"

I hesitated. Flynn was still looking at me. "She died," I said at last. "In Paris. My sister wasn't there."

Both nuns crossed themselves. "That's sad, Little Mado. So veryvery sad." Soeur Thérèse took my hand between her withered fingers. Soeur Extase patted my knee. "Are you having a service in Les Salants?" asked Soeur Thérèse. "For your father's sake?"

"No." I could still hear the harshness in my voice. "That's over. And she always said she'd never come back. Not even as ashes."

"A pity. It would have been better for everyone."

Soeur Extase gave me a quick look from beneath her *quichenotte*. "It can't have been easy for her, living here. Islands—"

"I know."

Brismand 1 was leaving again. For a moment I felt utterly lost. "My father didn't make things any easier," I said, still watching the retreating ferry. "Still, he's free of her now. It's what he wanted. To be left alone."

2

"Prasteau. That's an island name."

The taxi driver—an Houssin I did not recognize—sounded accusing, as if I had used the name without permission.

"Yes, it is. I was born here."

"Heh." The driver glanced back at me, as if trying to place my features. "You still got family on the island, heh?"

I nodded. "My father. In Les Salants."

"Oh." The man shrugged, as if my mention of Les Salants had ended his curiosity. In my mind's eye I saw GrosJean in his boatyard, saw myself watching him. A guilty stab of pride as I remembered my father's craftsmanship. I forced myself to look at the back of the driver's head until the feeling left me.

"Right then. Les Salants."

The taxi smelled musty, and the suspension was shot. As we drove along the familiar road out of La Houssinière, my stomach was filled with tremors. I remembered everything too well now, too clearly; a patch of tamarisks, a rock, a glimpse of corrugated roof over a shoulder of dune made me feel raw with memories.

"You know where you want to be, do you, heh?" The road was bad; as we turned a corner the taxi's back wheels caught for a moment in a slough of sand; the driver swore and revved viciously to free them.

"Yes. Rue de l'Océan. The far end."

"Are you sure? There's nothing here but dunes."

"Yes. I'm sure."

Some instinct had made me stop a short distance outside the village; I wanted to arrive on foot. The taxi driver took my money and left, his wheels spraying sand, his exhaust blatting. As the silence reasserted itself around me, I was conscious of an alarming sensation, and I felt another lurch of guilt as I identified the feeling as joy.

I had promised my mother I would never come back.

That was my guilt; for a moment I felt dwarfed by it, a speck beneath the enormous sky. My very presence here was a betrayal of her, of our good years together, of the life we had made away from Le Devin.

No one had written to us after we left. Once we had passed the boundaries of La Jetée we had become just so much more flotsam; ignored, forgotten. My mother had told me this often enough, on cold nights in our little Paris flat, with the unfamiliar sounds of traffic outside and the lights from the brasserie flicking from red to blue through the broken blinds. We owed nothing to Le Devin. Adrienne had done the right thing; married well; had children; moved to Tangiers with her husband, Marin, who dealt in antiques. She had two little boys, whom we had only seen in photographs. She rarely contacted us. Mother took this as proof of Adrienne's devotion to her family, and held her up as an example to me. My sister had done well; I should be proud of her.

But I was stubborn; though I had escaped, I was unable to completely grasp the bright opportunities offered by the world beyond the islands. I could have had anything I wanted—a good job, a rich husband, stability. Instead, two years of art school; two more of aimless traveling; then bar work; cleaning; makeshift jobs; my paintings sold on street corners to avoid paying gallery fees. Carrying Le Devin secretly inside me.

"Everything returns."

It's the beachcomber's maxim. I said it aloud, as if in reply to an unspoken accusation. After all, it wasn't as if I were planning to stay. I had paid a month's rent in advance for the flat; what little I owned remained just as I had left it, suspended, awaiting my return. But for now the fantasy was too beguiling to ignore; Les Salants, unchanged, welcoming, and my father. . . .

I began to run, clumsily, across the broken road toward the houses, toward home.

3

The village was deserted. Most of the houses had closed shutters—a precaution against the heat—and they looked makeshift and abandoned, like beach huts out of season. Some looked as if they had not been repainted since I left; walls that had once been freshly whitewashed each spring had been scoured colorless by the sand. A single geranium raised its head from a dry window box. Several houses were no more than timber shacks with corrugated roofs. I remembered them now, though they had never appeared in any of my paintings.

A few flat-bottomed boats or *platts* had been dragged up the *étier*—the saltwater creek that led into the village from La Goulue—and were beached on the brown low-tide mud. A couple of fishing boats were moored in the deeper water. I recognized them both at once; the Guénolés' *Eleanore*, which my father and his brother had built years before I was born, and on the far side the *Cécilia*, which belonged to their fishing rivals, the Bastonnets. Something high up on the mast of one of the boats tapped monotonously against metal—*ting-ting-ting-ting*—in the wind.

There was barely a sign of anyone. For a moment I caught sight of a face peering out from a shuttered window; heard a door slam on the sound of voices. An old man was sitting under a parasol outside Angèlo's bar, drinking *devinnoise*, the island liqueur flavored with herbs. I recognized him straightaway—it was Matthias Guénolé, eyes sharp and blue in a weathered face—but I saw no curiosity in his expression as I greeted him. Simply a flicker of acknowledgment, the brief nod that passes as courtesy in Les Salants.

There was sand in my shoes. Sand too had piled against the walls of some of the houses, as if the dunes had mounted an attack on the village. Certainly the summer storms must have taken their toll; a wall had collapsed by Jean Grossel's old house; several roofs were missing tiles; and behind the Rue de l'Océan, where Omer Prossage and his wife, Charlotte, had their farm and their little shop, the land looked waterlogged, broad patches of standing water reflecting the sky. A series of pipes at the side of the road gushed water into a ditch, which in turn drained into the creek. I could see some kind of a pump working by the side of the house, presumably to speed up the process, and heard the grind of a generator. Behind the farm, the sails of a small windmill revolved busily.

At the end of the main street, I stopped beside the well at the shrine of Marine-de-la-Mer. There was a hand pump there, rusted but still workable, and I pumped a little water to wash my face. In an almost forgotten ritual gesture I splashed water into the stone bowl by the side of the shrine, and in so doing I noticed that the Saint's little niche had been freshly painted, and that candles, ribbons, beads, and flowers had been left on the stones. The Saint herself stood, heavy and inscrutable, among the offerings.

"They say if you kiss her feet and spit three times, something you've lost will come back to you."

I turned so abruptly that I almost lost my balance. A large, pink, cheery woman was standing behind me, hands on hips, head slightly to one side. A pair of gilt hoops swung from her earlobes; her hair was the same exuberant shade.

"Capucine!" She'd aged a little (she had been pushing forty when I left), but I recognized her instantly; nicknamed La Puce, she lived in a battered pink trailer on the edge of the dune with her unruly brood of children. She'd never been married—*men are just far too tiresome to live with, sweetheart*—but I remembered late-night music on the dunes, and furtive men trying too hard not to notice the little trailer with its frilly curtains and welcoming light at the door. My mother had disliked her, but Capucine had always been kind to me, feeding me chocolate-covered cherries and telling me all kinds of scandalous gossip. She had the dirtiest laugh on the island; in fact she was the only adult islander I knew who ever laughed aloud.

"My Lolo saw you in La Houssinière. He said you were coming here!" She grinned. "I ought to kiss the Saint more often if this kind of thing is going to happen!"

"It's good to see you, Capucine." I smiled. "I was beginning to think the village was deserted."

She shrugged. "Luck turns, they say." Her expression darkened for a moment. "I was sorry to hear about your mother, Mado."

"How did you know?"

"Heh! It's an island. News and gossip are all we have."

I hesitated, conscious of my heart pounding. "And—and my father?"

For a second her smile flickered. "As usual," she said lightly. "It's never easy, this time of year." Then, regaining her cheery composure, she put her arm around my shoulders. "Come and have a *devinnoise* with me, Mado. You can stay with me. I've got a spare bed since the Englishman left—"

I must have looked surprised, because Capucine gave her rich and dirty laugh.

"Don't go getting any ideas. I'm a respectable woman now—well, nearly." Her dark eyes were bright with amusement. "But you'll like Rouget. He came to us in May, and caused such a stir! We'd not seen anything like it since that time Aristide Bastonnet caught a fish with a head at both ends. That Englishman!" She chuckled softly to herself, shaking her head.

"Last May?" That meant he'd only been there three months. In three months, they'd given him a name.

"Heh." Capucine lit a Gitane and inhaled the smoke with satisfaction.

"Turned up here one day, stone broke, but already doing deals. Talked himself into a job with Omer and Charlotte, till that girl of theirs started giving him the eye. I put him up in the trailer until he could fix up his own place. Seems he had a run-in with old Brismand, among others, back in La Houssinière." She gave me a curious look. "Your sister married Marin Brismand, didn't she? How are they doing?"

"They live in Tangiers. I don't often hear from them."

"Tangiers, heh? Well, she always said—"

"You were talking about your friend," I interrupted. "What does he do?"

"He has ideas. He builds things." Capucine gestured vaguely over her shoulder at the Rue de l'Océan. "Omer's windmill, for instance. He fixed that."

We had rounded the curve of the dune and I could see the pink trailer now, as I remembered it but slightly more battered and sunk deeper into the sand. Beyond that, I knew, was my father's house, though a thick hedge of tamarisks hid it from view. Capucine saw me looking.

"Oh no you don't," she said firmly, taking my arm and guiding me into the hollow toward the trailer. "We've got gossip to catch up on. Give your father a little time. Let the grapevine reach him before you do."

On Le Devin, gossip is a kind of currency. The place runs on it: feuds between rival fishermen, illegitimate children, tall stories, rumor and revelation. I could appreciate my value in Capucine's eyes; for the moment, I was an asset.

"Why?" I was still staring at the tamarisk hedge. "Why shouldn't I see him now?"

"It's been a long time, heh?" said Capucine. "He's got used to being alone." She pushed the trailer door, which was unlocked. "Come on in, sweetheart, and I'll tell you all about it."

Her trailer was oddly homelike, with its cramped, rose-painted interior, its clothes draped over every surface, its smell of smoke and cheap perfume. In spite of its obvious sluttishness, it invited confidences.

People seem to confide in Capucine as they never do with Père Alban, the island's only priest. The boudoir, it seems, even such an elderly one, has more appeal than the confessional. Age had failed to increase her respectability, but all the same there was a healthy regard for her in the village. Like the nuns, she knows too many secrets.

We talked over coffee and cakes. Capucine seemed to have an unlimited capacity for the little sugar pastries called *devinnoiseries*, supplementing them with frequent Gitanes, coffee, and chocolate cherries, which she took from an enormous heart-shaped box.

"I've been going over there to see GrosJean a couple of times a week," she told me, pouring more coffee into the doll-size cups. "Sometimes I bring a cake, or stick some clothes into the machine."

She was watching my reaction and looked pleased when I thanked her.

"He's all right, isn't he? I mean, can he manage on his own?"

"You know what he's like. He doesn't give much away."

"He never did."

"Right. People who know him understand. But he isn't good with strangers. Not that *you*—" She corrected herself at once. "He just doesn't like change, that's all. He has his habits. Comes to Angélo's every Friday night, has his *devinnoise* with Omer, regular as anything. He doesn't talk much, of course, but there's nothing wrong with his mind."

Insanity is a real fear in the islands. Some families carry it like a rogue gene, like the higher incidences of polydactyly and hemophilia that occur in these stagnant communities. Too many kissing cousins, say the Houssins. My mother always said that was why GrosJean chose a girl from the mainland.

Capucine shook her head. "He has his ways, that's all. And it's not easy, this time of year. Give him a little space."

Of course. The Saint's day. When I was a child my father and I had often helped repaint the Saint's niche—coral, with the traditional pattern of stars—in preparation for the annual ceremony. The Salannais are a superstitious lot. We have to be; though in La Houssinière, such beliefs and traditions are considered slightly ridiculous. But La Houssinière is sheltered by La Jetée. La Houssinière is not at the mercy of the tides. Here in Les Salants the sea is closer to home and needs to be pacified.

"Of course," said Capucine, interrupting my thoughts, "GrosJean's lost more than most to the sea. And on the Saint's day, the anniversary, so to speak . . . Well. You have to make allowances, Mado."

I nodded. I knew the story, although it was an old one, dating back to before my parents married. Two brothers, close as twins; island-fashion, they even shared the same name. But P'titJean had drowned himself at the age of twenty-three, needlessly, over some girl. Apparently they had managed to convince Père Alban that it had been a fishing accident. Time and frequent retelling had softened the harshness of the tale; now I found it difficult to believe that, thirty years later, my father still blamed himself. But I'd seen the gravestone, a single piece of island granite, in La Bouche, the Salannais cemetery beyond La Goulue.

JEAN-MARIN PRASTEAU

1949–1972

BELOVED BROTHER

My father had worked the inscription himself, a finger's length deep in the massive stone. It had taken him six months.

"Anyway, Mado," said Capucine, biting into another pastry. "You stay with me for now, just until the Sainte-Marine is over. You don't have to rush back straightaway, do you? You can spare a day or two?"

I nodded.

"There's more room in here than you think," said La Puce optimistically, indicating a curtain dividing the main compartment from the sleeping area. "You'd be comfortable back there, and my Lolo's a good lad, he wouldn't be poking his nose around the curtain every couple of minutes." Capucine took a chocolate cherry from her apparently endless supply. "He should be back by now. Can't think what he does all day. Hanging around with that Guénolé boy." Lolo, I understood, was Capucine's grandson; her daughter Clothilde had left him in her care while she looked for work on the mainland.

"Everything returns, so they say. Heh! My Clo doesn't seem in any

big hurry to come back. She's having too much of a good time."
Capucine's eyes darkened a little. "No, there's no point kissing the Saint
for *her*. She keeps promising to come back for the holidays, but there's
always some excuse. In ten years' time, perhaps—" She broke off, seeing
my expression. "I'm sorry, Mado. I didn't mean *you*—"

"That's all right." I finished my coffee and stood up. "Thanks for
your offer."

"You're going there now? Today?" Capucine frowned at me for a
moment, hands on hips, her pink wrap half falling from her shoulders.
"All right," she said at last. "But don't expect too much."

4

My mother was from the mainland. That makes me only half an islander. She was from Nantes, a romantic who fell out of love with Le Devin almost as quickly as she did with my father's bleak good looks.

She was ill-equipped for life in Les Salants. She was a talker, a singer, a woman who wept, ranted, laughed, externalized everything. My father had little to say even at the start. He was incapable of small talk. Most of his utterances were monosyllabic; his greeting was a nod. What affection he showed was given to the fishing boats that he built and sold from the yard at the back of our house. He worked outside in summer, moving his equipment into the hangar for winter, and I liked to sit close by, watching as he shaped the wood, soaking the clinkers to give them elasticity, turning the graceful lines of bow and keel, stitching the sails. These were always white or red, the island colors. A coral bead decorated the prow. Each boat was polished and varnished, never painted except for the name flying across the bow in black and white. My father favored romantic names, *Belle Ysolde, Sage Héloïse* or *Blanche de Coëtquen*, names from old books, although as far as I knew, he never read anything. His work was his conversation—he spent more time with his "ladies" than with anyone else, but he never named a boat after any of us, not even my mother, though I know she would have liked him to.

As I rounded the curve of the dune I could see that the boatyard was deserted. The hangar doors were closed, and from the height of the parched grasses that had grown up against them, appeared not to have been opened for months. A couple of hulks lolled, half buried in sand, by the gate. The tractor and its trailer were parked under a corrugated-plastic shelter and seemed to be in working condition, but the lifter, which my father had once used to winch boats onto the trailer, looked rusty and unused.

The house was no better. It had been untidy enough in the old days, littered with the remains of hopeful projects that my father had begun, and then abandoned. Now it looked derelict. The whitewash had faded; a pane of glass had been boarded up; the paint on doors and shutters was cracked and peeling. I could see a cable running across the sand to the outhouse where a generator hummed; it was the only sign of life.

The mailbox had been left unemptied. I removed the wedge of letters and brochures that protruded from the box and carried them through into the deserted kitchen. The door had been left unlocked. There was a pile of dirty dishes next to the sink. A pot of cold coffee on the stove. A sickroom smell. My mother's things—a dresser, a chest, a square of tapestry—were still in place, but now there was dust on everything and sand on the concrete floor.

And yet there were signs that someone had been at work. There were pieces of pipe and wire and wood in a toolbox at the corner of the room, and I noticed that the water heater, which GrosJean had always been about to repair, had been replaced by a copper-bellied contraption connected to a bottle of butane. Loose wiring had been tucked neatly behind a panel; repairs had been made to the fireplace and the chimney, which always used to smoke. These signs of activity contrasted with the dereliction of the rest of the house, as if GrosJean had been so absorbed in his other work that he had had no time for dusting or washing clothes.

I dropped the letters onto the kitchen table. To my annoyance I found I was shaking. I looked through the mail—there must have been six months' or a year's worth of it—and found my last letter to him in the pile, unopened. I looked at it for a long time, seeing the Paris address on the reverse, remembering. I'd carried it around for weeks before finally mailing it, feeling dazed and strangely free. My friend Luc from the café had asked me what I was waiting for. "Where's the problem? You want to see him, don't you? You want to help?"

It wasn't that easy. In ten years, GrosJean had not written to me. I had sent him drawings, photographs, school reports, letters, without ever receiving a reply. And yet I had continued to send them, year after year. Of course I never told Mother. I know exactly what she would have said.

I put down the letter, my hand trembling a little. Then I put in into my pocket. Perhaps, after all, it was better this way. It gave me time to think again. To consider the options.

As I had first thought, there was no one home. I tried not to feel like a trespasser as I opened the door into my old room, then into Adrienne's. Little had been moved. Our things were still there; my model boats, my sister's film posters. Beyond them was my parents' room.

I pushed the door into semidarkness; the shutters were drawn. The smell of neglect closed around me. The bed was unmade, showing striped ticking under a crumpled sheet. There was an overflowing ashtray to one side; dirty clothes were piled on the floor. A niche by the side of the door with a plaster statue of Sainte-Marine; a cardboard box containing oddments. Inside this box I spotted a photograph—I recognized it at once, although it had lost its frame. My mother had taken it on my seventh birthday, and it had shown the three of us—GrosJean, Adrienne, and myself—grinning at a big cake shaped like a fish.

Now, my face had been cut out of the picture—clumsily, with scissors—so that only GrosJean and Adrienne remained; she with her arm resting lightly on his. My father was smiling at her over the space where I had been.

Suddenly I heard a sound outside the house. I crumpled the picture quickly into my pocket and stopped to listen, my throat tightening. Someone passed softly under the bedroom window, so lightly that I almost missed it against the pounding of my heart; someone barefoot, or wearing espadrilles.

Wasting no time I ran into the kitchen. Nervously I pushed back my hair, wondering what he would say—what I would say—whether he would even recognize me. In ten years I had changed; my puppy fat vanished; my short hair grown to shoulder length. I'm not the beauty my mother was, although some people used to say we looked alike. I'm too tall, without her grace of movement, and my hair is an unremarkable brown. But my eyes are hers, heavy-browed and of the curious, chilly shade of gray-green which some people find ugly. Suddenly I wished that I had made more of an effort with my appearance. I could at least have worn a dress.

The door opened. Someone was standing on the threshold, wearing a heavy fisherman's jacket and carrying a paper sack in his arms. I knew him at once, even with a knitted cap hiding his hair; his quick, precise movements were nothing like my father's bearlike shamble. He was past me and into the room almost before I knew it, closing the door behind him.

The Englishman. Rouget. Flynn.

"I thought you might need some bits and pieces," he said as he dropped the paper bag on the kitchen table. Then, seeing my expression: "Anything wrong?"

"I wasn't expecting you." I managed at last. "You took me by surprise." My heart was still lurching. I clutched at the photograph in my pocket, feeling hot and cold, not knowing how much of it he could read in my face.

"Nervous, aren't you?" Flynn opened the bag on the table and began to take out the contents. "There's bread, milk, cheese, eggs, coffee, breakfast stuff. Don't worry about paying me back; it's all on his account." He put the loaf in the linen bread bag hanging from the back of the door.

"Thanks." I couldn't help noticing how very much at home he seemed in my father's house, opening cupboards without hesitation, putting the groceries away. "I hope it wasn't too much trouble."

"No trouble." He grinned. "I live two minutes away, in the old *block-haus*. I sometimes drop by."

The *blockhaus* stood on the dunes above La Goulue. Like the strip of land upon which it stood, it belonged officially to my father. I remembered it, a German bunker left over from the war, an ugly square of rusty concrete half swallowed by the sand. For years I'd believed it was haunted.

"I wouldn't have thought anyone could live in that place," I said.

"I fixed it up," said Flynn cheerily, putting the milk away in the fridge. "The worst part was getting rid of all the sand. Of course, it isn't finished yet; I need to dig a well, and put in some proper plumbing, but it's comfortable, it's solid, and it didn't cost me anything but time and the price of a few things I couldn't find or make for myself."

I thought of GrosJean, with his perpetual works in progress. No wonder he liked this man. Some kind of a builder, Capucine had said. I understood now who had carried out the repairs to my father's house. I felt a sudden pang in my heart.

"You know, you probably won't see him tonight," Flynn told me. "He's been restless these past few days. Hardly anyone's seen him."

"Thanks." I turned away to avoid meeting his eyes. "I know my father."

That much was true; after the procession on the night of the Sainte-Marine, GrosJean would always vanish in the direction of La Bouche, burning candles beside P'titJean's grave. The yearly ritual was sacrosanct. Nothing disturbed it.

"He won't even know you're back yet," continued Flynn. "When he finds out, he'll think the Saint answered all his prayers at once."

"That's nice of you," I said coolly. "But GrosJean never kissed the Saint for anyone."

5

The festival of Sainte-Marine-de-la-Mer occurs once a year, on the night of August's full moon. That night, the Saint is carried from her place in the village to the ruins of her church at Pointe Griznoz. It is a difficult task—the Saint is three feet tall, and heavy, for she is made of solid basalt—and it takes four men to carry her on a plinth to the water's edge. There, the villagers file past her one by one; some stop to kiss her head in the old ritual gesture, in the hope that something lost—or more likely someone—may return. Children decorate her with flowers. Little offerings—food, flowers, packets of rock salt tied with ribbon—even money—are thrown to the rising tide. Cedar and pinewood chips are burned in braziers on either side. Sometimes there are fireworks, bursting defiantly over the indifferent sea.

I waited until after dark before I left the house. The wind, always strongest on this part of the island, had veered southward, and rattled its *danse macabre* at the doors and windows. As I set off, my coat wrapped tightly around me, I could already see the glow from the braziers on the edge of the Pointe. A church once stood here, though it has been ruined and unused for almost a hundred years. Since then the sea has taken it, bite by bite, until now only a single piece stands—a piece of the north wall. The niche where once Sainte-Marine had her place is still visible against the weathered stones. In the little tower above the niche, a bell once hung—La Marinette, Sainte-Marine's own bell—but that has long since disappeared. One legend says it fell into the sea; others tell the story of how La Marinette was stolen and melted down for scrap by an unscrupulous Houssin, who was cursed by Sainte-Marine and driven mad by its ghostly ringing. It still rings sometimes; always on windy nights, always a herald of disaster. Cynics attribute the booming sound to the rush of the south wind through the rocks and crevices of Pointe Griznoz, but the Salannais know better; it is La Marinette, still ringing out her warnings, still watching Les Salants from below.

As I approached the Pointe I could see figures silhouetted against the firelit wall of the old church. Many of them, thirty at least, more than half the village. Père Alban, the island priest, was standing by the water, his chalice and staff in his hands. Looking gray and drawn in the firelight, he greeted me briefly and without surprise as I passed. I noticed he smelled vaguely of fish, his soutane tucked neatly into his fishing waders.

The old ceremony is a strangely moving sight, although the villagers of Les Salants are quite unaware that they are picturesque. They are a different race from myself and my mother—short and stocky for the most part, small featured, Celtic; black haired, blue eyed. These striking looks fade quickly, however, and they become gargoyles in old age, wearing the black of their ancestors and—for the women—the white *quichenotte*. At any time, three-quarters of the population appears to be over sixty-five.

I scanned the faces rapidly, hopefully. Old women in perpetual mourning, long-haired old men in fishing gaiters and black cloth coats or *vareuses* and boots, a couple of young men, the fisherman's gear brightened by the addition of a garish shirt. My father was not among them.

The celebratory atmosphere I remembered from childhood seemed to be missing this year; there were fewer flowers around the shrine, and little sign of the usual offerings. Instead I thought the villagers had a grim look, like people under siege, although perhaps this was merely the difference between a child's perception and that of the adult I had become.

Finally it came; a glow of lamplight from the dunes beyond Pointe Griznoz and the wailing sound of *biniou* players as Sainte-Marine's procession began. The *biniou* is a traditional instrument; played well, it sounds a little like bagpipes. In this case there was something feline in the sound, a keening note that cut across the drone of the wind.

I could see the plinth with the Saint perched on it; four men, one at each corner, struggled to carry it across the rough ground. As the procession came closer I could pick out details: the mound of red and white flowers below Sainte-Marine's ceremonial skirts, the paper lanterns, the fresh gilding on the old stone. Here too were the Salannais children, faces scubbed pink by the wind, voices shrill with exhaustion and nerves. I recognized Capucine's grandson, the round-faced Lolo, and his friend Damien, both carrying paper lanterns—one green, one red—running easily across the sand.

The procession rounded the last dune. As it did, the wind caught one of the lanterns and it burst into flames; and in the sudden brightness I recognized my father.

He was one of the bearers, and for a moment I was able to see him clearly without being observed. The firelight was kind; in its glow his face seemed scarcely to have changed, and it gave his features an uncharacteristic, animated look. He was heavier than I remembered; thickened by age; his big arms straining to hold the plinth level. There was a terrible concentration in his face. The Saint's other bearers were all younger men; I noticed Alain Guénolé and his son Ghislain, both fishermen, used to heavy work. As the procession came to rest in front of the group of expectant villagers, I was surprised to see that the last bearer was Flynn.

"Santa Marina." A woman from the crowd in front of me stepped forward and pressed her lips briefly to the feet of the Saint. I recognized her; it was Charlotte Prossage, who ran the grocery, a plump and birdlike woman with a look of perpetual anxiety. The others kept a respectful distance away, some fingering amulets or photographs.

"Santa Marina. Bring back our business. The winter tides always flood the fields. It took me three months to clear them last time. You're our Saint. Take care of us." Her voice managed to sound both humble and slightly resentful. Her eyes flicked restlessly here and there.

The moment Charlotte's prayer was over, others took her place. Her husband, Omer, nicknamed La Patate for his comic, shapeless face; Hilaire, the Salannais vet, with his bald head and round glasses. Fishermen, widows, a teenage girl with restless eyes, all speaking in the same rapid and slightly accusing mutter. I could not push through without giving offense; GrosJean's face was obscured once more behind the tide of bobbing heads.

"Marine-de-la-Mer. Keep the sea from my door. Bring the mackerel to my nets. Keep that poacher Guénolé from my oyster beds."

"Sainte-Marine, bring us good fishing. Keep my son safe when he goes out to sea."

"Sainte-Marine, I want a red bikini and some Ray-Ban sunglasses." The girl glanced briefly at me as she stepped away from the Saint. I recognized her now; it was Mercédès, daughter of Charlotte and Omer, who had been seven or eight when I left the island, now tall and leggy, with loose hair and a sullen, pretty mouth. Our eyes met; I smiled, but the girl merely shot me a look of dislike and pushed past me into the crowd. Someone else took her place; an old woman in a head scarf, her face bent pleadingly over a battered photograph.

The procession was on the move again; down toward the sea, where the Saint's feet would be lowered into the water to be blessed. I reached the far side of the crowd just as GrosJean was turning away; I saw his profile, now beaded with sweat, glimpsed the flash of a pendant around his neck, and failed once more to catch his eye. A moment longer and it was too late; now the bearers were struggling down the rocky incline toward the water's edge, Père Alban holding out a hand to keep the Saint from toppling. The *biniou* wailed forlornly; a second lantern caught fire, then a third, scattering black butterflies across the wind.

They reached the sea at last; Père Alban stood aside and the four bearers carried Sainte-Marine into the water. There is no sand at the

Pointe, only stones underfoot, and the going was bright and treacherous in the light that ricocheted from the water. The tide was almost high. Behind the squeal of the *biniou*, I thought I could hear the first sounds of the wind through the crevices, the hollow drone of the south wind, which would soon amplify to a booming almost like that of a drowned bell. . . .

"La Marinette!" It was the old woman in the head scarf, Désirée Bastonnet; her eyes dark with dread. Her thin, nervous hands still played on the photograph, from which the smiling face of a boy reflected the lamplight.

"No it isn't." That was Aristide, her husband, head of the fishing clan of the same name; an old man of seventy or more, with a big chieftain's mustache and long gray hair under his flat island hat. He lost a leg years before I was born, in the same fishing accident that had killed his eldest son. He gave me a sharp look as I passed him. "No more of that bad-luck talk, Désirée," he told his wife in a low voice. "And put that thing away."

Désirée averted her eyes and folded her fingers over the picture. Behind her, a young man of nineteen or twenty glanced at me with shy curiosity from behind small wire-framed glasses. He seemed about to say something, but at that moment Aristide turned around and the young man hurried to join him, his bare feet making no sound on the rocks.

The bearers were standing chest-deep now, facing the shore and holding the Saint with her feet in the water. Waves splashed against the base of the plinth, washing the flowers into the current. Alain and Ghislain Guénolé had taken the front position; Flynn and my father the back, bracing themselves against the swell. Even in August it must have been cold work; the chill from the flying spray numbed my face, and the wind cut through my woollen coat so that I shivered. And I at least was dry.

When all the villagers had taken their places, Père Alban lifted his staff for the final blessing. At that second GrosJean raised his head in the direction of the priest, and our eyes met.

For a moment my father and I existed inside a pocket of silence. He stared at me from between the feet of the Saint, mouth slightly open, a line of concentration between his eyes. The pendant around his neck burned red.

There was something in my throat, some kind of obstacle, which made it difficult for me to breathe. My hands felt as if they belonged to someone else.

Next to my father, I thought I saw Flynn make some gesture. Then a wave broke sharply behind them, and GrosJean, still looking at me, stumbled in its swell, lost his footing, held out a hand to steady himself . . . and dropped Sainte-Marine from the plinth into the deep water of Pointe Griznoz.

For a frozen second she seemed to float, miraculously, in the fiery sea; the silk skirt belling crimson around her. Then she was gone.

GrosJean stood helplessly, staring at nothing. Père Alban made a futile grab for the fallen Saint. Aristide gave a crack of surprised laughter. Behind him, the bespectacled young man took a step toward the water, then stopped. For a moment, no one moved. Then a moan came up from the Salannais, joining the moan of the wind. My father stood there for a second longer, the lantern lights absurdly festive on features that had lost all other animation. Then he fled, hauling himself out of the sea, slipping on the rocks, forcing himself upright once again, struggling in his heavy, waterlogged clothing.

"Father—" I called as he reached me, but he had already gone without a backward glance. As he reached the head of Pointe Griznoz I thought I heard him make a sound; a long, torn, moaning noise, but that might have been the wind.

6

 Traditionally, after the cliff-top ceremony everyone goes to Angélo's bar for a drink on the Saint. This year less than half the worshipers did; Père Alban went straight home to La Houssinière without so much as blessing the wine; the children—and most of their mothers—went to bed, and the usual exuberance was noticeably lacking.

Of course, the loss of Sainte-Marine was the principal reason. Without her, their prayers would go unanswered; the tide unchecked. My father's distress was clearly secondary to their superstitious fears, and I was annoyed at the ease with which his flight had been dismissed. Omer La Patate had suggested an immediate search for the missing Saint, but the tide was too high and the rocks too uneven for safety, and the operation was delayed until the morning.

For myself, I went straight to the house and waited for GrosJean to come home. He did not come. Finally, at about midnight, I went back to Angélo's, where I found Capucine restoring her nerves over coffee and *devinnoiseries*.

She stood up when she saw me, concern in her face.

"He's not there," I said, sitting next to her. "He hasn't come home."

"He won't. Not now," said Capucine.

People were looking at me; I sensed curiosity, and a coolness that made me feel stiff and strange. Capucine lit a cigarette and blew smoke through her nostrils and spoke matter-of-factly, though not without sympathy: "You always were stubborn. Never could take the easy way, could you? Always rushing at things head-on." She gave me a tired smile. "Give your father some space, Mado. Give him a chance."

"A chance?" It was Aristide Bastonnet, with Désirée on his arm. "After tonight, after what happened at the Pointe, what chance do we have?"

I looked up. The old man was standing behind us, leaning heavily on his stick, his eyes like flints. The young man with the glasses stood slightly to one side, his hair falling over his eyes, looking embarrassed. Now I knew him; it was Xavier, Aristide's grandson; he'd been a solitary boy in the old days, preferring books to games. Only a few years apart in age, we had rarely spoken.

Aristide was still glaring at me. "What did you come back for, heh?" he demanded. "There's nothing here anymore."

"Don't answer," said Capucine. "He's drunk."

Aristide showed no sign of having heard her. "You're all the same, you young people!" he said. "You only come back when you want something!"

"Grandfather—" protested Xavier, putting his hand on the old man's shoulder. But Aristide shook him aside. Though the old man was a head shorter, his rage made a giant of him, his eyes burning like a prophet's.

Beside him, his wife looked at me nervously. "I'm sorry," she said in a low voice. "Sainte Marine—our son—"

"Be quiet!" snapped Aristide, turning so sharply on his stick that, if Désirée had not been standing so close, he might have fallen. "Do you think *she* cares about that, heh?"

He left without a backward glance, his people in his wake, his wooden leg dragging on the concrete floor. Silence followed them.

Capucine shrugged. "Don't mind him, Mado. He's just had a *devin-noise* too many."

"I don't understand."

"Nothing to understand," said Matthias Guénolé. "He's a Bastonnet. Head full of rocks." This was less encouraging than it might have seemed; the Guénolés have hated the Bastonnets for generations.

"Poor Aristide. There always has to be some conspiracy." I turned and saw a tiny old woman in widow's black perched on the stool beside me. Toinette Prossage, Omer's mother and the village's oldest resident. "As far as Aristide's concerned people are always trying to get him put away, people after his savings—heh!" She gave a crow of laughter. "As if everyone didn't know he's spent so much on his house—*Bonne Marine!* Even if his boy came back after all these years, there'd be nothing left for him but an old boat and a strip of waterlogged land that even Brismand wouldn't take off his hands."

I fingered the letter, which was still in my pocket. "Brismand?"

"Of course," said Toinette. "Who else could afford to develop this place?"

According to Toinette, Brismand had plans for Les Salants. Plans that were as sinister as they were unclear. I recognized the Salannais' traditional dislike of a successful Houssin.

"He could do the job on Les Salants—*pfft!* Just like that," said the old woman, with an expressive gesture. "He's got the money and the machines. Drain out the marshes, raise some defenses at La Goulue—he could have it done in six months. No more floods. Heh! All for a price, mind you. He's not made his money doing favors."

"Maybe you should see what he has to suggest."

Matthias Guénolé looked at me sourly. "What, sell out to an Houssin?"

"Leave her alone," said Capucine. "The girl means well."

"Yes, but if he could stop the flooding—"

Matthias shook his head with finality. "You can't control the sea," he said. "It does as it likes. If the Saint wants to drown us, she will."

It had been a succession of bad years, I learned. Despite Sainte-Marine's protection, the tides had risen higher every winter. This year, even the Rue de l'Océan had been flooded, for the first time since the war. Summer too had been unusually troubled. The creek had swollen and sunk half the village under three feet of seawater, damage that had not yet been entirely repaired.

"We'll end up like the old village, at this rate," said Matthias. "Everything drowned, even the church." He filled his pipe and tamped down the tobacco with a grimy thumb. "I mean. A church. If the Saint can't help, who can?"

"Now *that* was a Black Year," declared Toinette Prossage. "1908 it was. My sister Marie-Laure died that year, of the influenza, the winter I was born." She stabbed the air with a crooked finger. "That was me, a Black Year baby; never expected to survive. But I did! And if we want to survive this one, we should do something more than snap at each other like gannets." She peered sternly at Matthias.

"Easy to say, Toinette, but if the Saint isn't behind us—"

"That's not what I meant, Matthias Guénolé, and you know it."

Matthias shrugged. "It wasn't me who started that business," he said. "If Aristide Bastonnet would just admit, for once, that he was wrong—"

Toinette turned to me, her eyes snapping. "You see what it's like? Grown men—*old* men—behaving like little children. No wonder the Saint shows her displeasure."

Matthias bristled. "It wasn't *my* boys who dropped the Saint—" Capucine glared at him. He looked abashed. "I'm sorry," he told me. "No one blames GrosJean for that. If anything, it's Aristide's fault. He wouldn't let his grandson carry the Saint because there would have been two Guénolés, and only one Bastonnet. Of course *he* couldn't help. Not with his wooden leg." He sighed. "I've told you before. It's going to be a Black Year. You heard La Marinette ringing, didn't you?"

"That wasn't La Marinette," said Capucine. Automatically, her left hand forked the sign against mischance. I saw Matthias do the same.

"I tell you, we've got it coming, it's been thirty years—"

Matthias forked the sign again. " '72. That was a bad year."

I knew it was; that year had seen the death of three villagers, one of them my father's brother.

Matthias took a drink of his *devinnoise*. "Once, Aristide thought he'd found La Marinette, you know. Early that spring, that was, the year he lost his leg. Turned out it was an old mine left over from the first war. Ironic, don't you think?"

I agreed it was. I listened as politely as I could, although this was a tale I'd heard many times as a child. Nothing had changed, I told myself with a kind of despair. Even the stories were as old and tired as the inhabitants, worked and reworked like worry beads on a string. Pity and impatience welled up inside me, and I gave a deep sigh. Matthias continued, oblivious, as if the incident had happened yesterday.

"The thing was half-buried in a bank of sand. It rang when you hit it with a stone. All the kids came around then with sticks and pieces of rock, trying to make it ring. Hours later, when the tide took it back out, it exploded, all on its own, a hundred meters from where La Jetée is now. Just about killed every fish from there to Les Salants. Heh!" Matthias sucked on his pipe with mournful gusto. "Désirée made a bucketload of bouillabaisse because she couldn't bear the thought of all those fish going to waste. Poisoned half the village." He looked at me from red-rimmed eyes. "I could never decide whether there'd been a miracle or not."

Toinette nodded in agreement. "Whatever it was, it turned our luck sour. Aristide's son Olivier died that year, and—well—you know." She looked at me as she said it.

"P'titJean."

Toinette nodded again. "Heh! Those brothers! You should have heard them in the old days," she said. "Such magpies they were, both of them. Talk, talk, talk."

Matthias took a mouthful of *devinnoise*. "The Black Year took Gros-Jean's heart then, just as sure as it took the houses at La Goulue. The tides *might* have been higher that year, but not by much." He let out a sigh of doleful satisfaction and gestured at me with the stem of his pipe. "I'm warning you, girl. Don't get comfortable here. Because one more year like that one—"

Toinette stood up and peered out of the window at the sky. Beyond the Pointe the dim orange horizon brooded, now leggy with distant lightning.

"Bad times coming our way," she observed, without apparent anxiety. "Just like '72."

7

I slept in my old room with the sound of the sea in my ears. When I awoke it was daylight, with still no sign of my father. I made coffee and took my time in drinking it, feeling absurdly low. What had I expected? A prodigal's welcome? But the sour atmosphere of the festival still hung over me, and the state of the house only made things worse. I decided to go out.

The sky was overcast, and I could hear gulls screeching over at La Goulue. I guessed the tide must be on its way out. I put on my coat and went for a look.

You can smell La Goulue before you see it. It's always stronger at low tide, a weedy, fishy smell that a stranger might find unpleasant, but which for me has complicated, nostalgic associations. Coming up from the island side I could see the deserted flats gleaming in the silvery light. The old German bunker, half-buried in the dune, looked like an abandoned building block against the sky. From the filament of smoke that escaped from its turret I guessed Flynn was cooking breakfast.

In all Les Salants, it was La Goulue that had suffered most over the years. The belly of the island had been badly eroded, and the path I remembered as a child had fallen into the sea, leaving a messy rockslide to mark its absence. A row of ancient beach huts I remembered as a child had been washed away; a single survivor remained, like a long-legged insect above the stones. The entrance to the creek had widened, although it was clear that some effort had been made to shelter it—a rough wall of stones mortared together still stood crookedly at the western side, although this too had shifted over time, leaving the creek vulnerable to the tides. I began to understand Matthias Guénolé's pessimism; a high tide with the wind behind it would race up the creek, spilling up over the dike that edged it and onto the road. But the main difference at La Goulue was something much more telling. The battlements of weed, always present even in summer, were gone now, leaving nothing but a bare stretch of stones with not even a layer of mud to cover them. That puzzled me. Had the winds changed? As I said before, everything always comes back to la Goulue. Today there was nothing; no weed, no jetsam, not even so much as a piece of driftwood. The gulls seemed to understand it too; yarking angrily at one another, they scrawled the air but never settling long enough to feed. In the distance, the ring of La Jetée showed pale frills against the dark water.

There was no sign of my father by the water's edge. Perhaps he had gone to La Bouche, I told myself; the cemetery was a little way up the creek from the village. I had been there a few times, although not often; on Le Devin, the dead are men's business.

Gradually I became aware of a presence close by. Something in the way the gulls moved, perhaps; certainly he made no sound. I turned to see Flynn standing a few yards behind me, looking out across the same stretch of sea. He was carrying two lobster pots, and there was a duffel bag slung across his shoulder. The pots were full, and both were painted with a red *B* for Bastonnet.

Poaching is the only crime taken seriously on Le Devin. Stealing from another man's pots is as bad as sleeping with his wife.

Flynn gave me an unrepentant smile. "Amazing, what the sea brings up," he remarked cheerily, gesturing with one of the pots toward the Pointe. "I thought I'd come early and check things over, before half the village turns up looking for the Saint."

"The Saint?"

He shook his head. "No sign of her yet at the Pointe, I'm afraid. She must have rolled with the tide. The currents here are so strong that she could be halfway to La Goulue by now."

I said nothing. I didn't know about the Saint, but it takes more than a bad tide to wash up a lobster pot. When I was a child the Guénolés and the Bastonnets used to lie in wait for one another in the dunes, armed with shotguns loaded with rock salt, each hoping to catch the others red-handed.

"Lucky for you," I said.

His eyes gleamed. "I manage."

But a moment later his attention was already elsewhere, and he was turning over with his bare feet the little pearls of wild garlic that grew in the sand. When he had a few of these, he bent down and put them into one of his pockets. I caught their pungent scent, fleetingly, on the salt air. I remembered collecting them myself for my mother's fish stew.

"There used to be a path here," I said, looking across the bay. "I used to follow it down to the flats. Now it's gone."

Flynn nodded. "Toinette Prossage remembers a whole street of houses here, with a jetty and a little beach and everything. All of it fell into the sea years ago."

"A beach?" I supposed it made sense; at low tide La Jetée's sandbanks had once been within walking distance of La Goulue; over the years they had migrated. I looked at the single beach hut, useless now, perched high above the rocks.

He grinned. "Nothing's safe on an island."

Once again I glanced at the two pots. He had pegged the lobsters so that they wouldn't fight.

"The Guénolés' *Eleanore* broke her moorings during the night," continued Flynn. "They think the Bastonnets did it. But it must have been the wind."

Apparently Alain Guénolé, his son Ghislain, and his father, Matthias, had been up since dawn looking for signs of the missing *Eleanore*. A solid, flat-bottomed fishing boat, she might have rolled with the surf and be lying, intact, somewhere out on the low-tide flats. It was optimistic thinking, but worth a try.

"Does my father know?" I asked.

Flynn shrugged. I could see from his expression that he already counted the *Eleanore* lost. "Maybe he hasn't heard. He didn't come home last night, did he?" My surprise must have shown on my face, because he smiled. "I'm a light sleeper," he said. "I heard him go down to La Bouche." A pause, during which Flynn played with the coral bead around his neck. "You haven't been there, have you?"

"No. It isn't one of my favorite places. Why?"

"Come on," he said, dropping the lobster pots and holding out his hand to me. "There's something you need to see."

La Bouche always takes the first-time visitor by surprise. The size of it, perhaps; the aisles and alleys of headstones, all marked with Salannais names, the hundreds—maybe thousands—of Bastonnets, Guénolés, Prossages, even our own Prasteaus, lounging side by side like tired sun-bathers, their differences forgotten.

The second surprising thing is the *size* of these stones; scarred and wind-polished giants of island granite, they stand like monoliths, anchored by sheer weight into the restless soil. Unlike the living, the Salannais dead are a sociable lot; they tend to visit from one grave to another as the sand shifts, unrestrained by family grievances. To keep them subdued, we use the heaviest stones we can. P'titJean's stone is a massive piece of gray-pink island granite that covers the grave completely, as if P'titJean can never be buried deep enough.

Flynn had refused to answer my questions as we made our way toward the old cemetery. I followed him reluctantly, picking my way over the stony ground. I could see the first of the old headstones now, standing taller than the brow of the dune that sheltered them. La Bouche had always been my father's private place. Even now I felt obscurely guilty, as if I were stealing secrets.

"Come to the top of the dune," said Flynn, seeing my hesitation. "You'll see everything from there."

For a long time I simply stood on the breast of the dune, looking down into La Bouche. "How long has it been like this?" I said at last.

"Since the spring storms."

Some attempt had been made to protect the graves. Sandbags had been laid along the footpath closest to the creek, and loose earth dug back around some of the stones, but it was clear that the damage was too extensive for such basic repairs to be effective. Gravestones stood clear of their sockets like sick teeth, some still erect, others canted at unhealthy angles into the shallow water where the creek had overflowed its low banking. Here and there an urn of dead flowers poked above the surface; otherwise for fifty meters or more, there was nothing but the stones and the smooth pale reflection of the sky.

I stayed for a long time, in silence, watching.

"He's been coming here every day for weeks," Flynn explained. "I've told him it's useless. He won't believe me."

I could see P'titJean's grave now, not far from the flooded path. My father had decorated it with red flowers and coral beads, in honor of Sainte-Marine. The little offerings looked oddly pathetic on their island of stone.

My father must have taken it badly. Deeply superstitious, even the ringing of La Marinette would not have held such a potent message for him as this.

I took a step toward the path.

"Don't," warned Flynn.

I ignored him. My father had his back toward me and was so absorbed in what he was doing that he did not hear me until I was almost close enough to touch him. Flynn stayed where he was, not moving, almost invisible among the grassy dunes but for the muted gleam of his autumn hair.

"Father?" I said, and he turned to face me.

Now, in daylight, I could see to what extent GrosJean had aged. He looked smaller to me than he had the other night, shrunken in his clothes; his big face scruffed with grayish old-man's stubble; his eyes bloodshot. His sleeves were spattered with mud, as if he had been digging, and there was mud right up to the cuffs of his fishing waders. A Gauloise drooped from his lip.

I took a step forward. My father watched me in silence; his blue eyes, permanently creased by the sun, shining. He did not seem to react to my presence; he might have been watching a fishing float as it spun into the water, or calculating the distance between a boat and the jetty, careful to avoid a spill.

"Father," I said again, my smile feeling strange and stiff on my face. I pulled back my hair to show him my face. "It's me."

Still GrosJean made no sign to indicate whether he had even heard. His eyes shone; whether in anger or pleasure I could not say. I saw his fingers move to his throat, to the pendant that hung there. No, not a pendant. A locket. The kind in which keepsakes are hidden.

"I wrote to you—I thought perhaps—if you needed—" My voice too did not seem to be my own. GrosJean watched me, expressionless. Silence, like black butterflies, over everything.

"You could try saying something," I said.

Silence. A beat of wings.

"Well?"

Silence. Behind him on the dune, Flynn watched, motionless.

"What?" I repeated. The butterflies were in my voice now, making it tremble. I could hardly breathe. "I came back. Aren't you going to say anything at all?"

For a moment I thought I saw a flicker in his eyes. I may have imagined it. In any case, it was gone in a second. Then, before I knew it, my father had turned and was heading back toward the dunes without a word.

8

 I should have expected it. In a way I *had* expected it, had lived through this rejection years before. Even so it burned me; with Mother dead and Adrienne gone, surely now I had a right to expect some response.

Things might have been different if I had been a boy. GrosJean, like most island men, had wanted sons: sons to work the boatyard, to tend the family grave. Daughters, with all the expense that entailed, were of no interest to Jean Prasteau. A first daughter had been bad enough; a second, four years later, had finally killed what little remained of my parents' intimacy. I grew up trying to atone for the disappointment I had caused, wearing my hair short to please him, avoiding the company of other girls to win his approval. To some degree it had worked; sometimes he would let me come fishing for sea bass in the surf, or take me with him to the oyster beds with pitchforks and baskets. These were precious moments for me; snatched at times when Adrienne and my mother went into La Houssinière together; hoarded and gloated over in secret.

He spoke to me at these times, even when he wasn't speaking to my mother. He would show me the gulls' nests and the sandy places off La Jetée where the seals returned year after year. Sometimes we would find things washed up on the beach and take them home. Very occasionally he would tell me stories and old sayings from the islands.

"I'm sorry." It was Flynn. He must have come up behind me silently as I stood by P'titJean's grave.

I nodded. My throat was sore, as if I had been shouting.

"He doesn't really talk to anyone," said Flynn. "Mostly he gets by on sign language. I don't think he's spoken to me more than a dozen times since I've been here."

There was a red flower floating in the water just off the path. I watched it, feeling sick. "He does talk to you, then," I said.

"Sometimes."

I could feel him at my side, troubled, waiting to offer comfort, and for a moment all I wanted to do was accept. I could turn toward him, I knew—he was just tall enough for me to rest my head on his shoulder—and he would smell of ozone and the sea, and the untreated wool of his jersey. Underneath, I knew, he would be warm.

"Mado, I'm sorry—"

I looked straight past him, expressionless, hating his pity, hating my own weakness even more. "The old bastard," I said. "Still playing his games." I took a long, shaky breath. "Nothing changes."

Flynn eyed me cautiously. "Are you all right?"

"I'm fine."

He walked me back to the house, picking up his lobster pots and bag on the way. I said little; he kept up a stream of patter, which I did not hear, but for which I was dimly grateful. From time to time I touched the letter in my pocket.

"Where will you go now?" asked Flynn as we joined the path to Les Salants.

I told him about the little flat in Paris. The brasserie in front. The café where we used to go on summer evenings. The avenues of lindens.

"It sounds good. Maybe I'll move there one day."

I looked at him. "I thought you liked it here."

"Maybe so, but I'm not planning to stay. No one ever made a fortune by burying themselves in the sand."

"To make a fortune? Is that what you're after?"

"Of course. Isn't everyone?" He gave me a mischievous smile.

There was silence. We walked together, he soundlessly, I making small crunching sounds with my boots on the pieces of shell that littered the dune.

"Don't you ever miss *your* home?" I said at last.

"God, no!" He made a face. "Why should I? There was nothing there."

"What about your parents?"

He shrugged. "My mother worked hard," he said. "My father wasn't there. And my brother—"

"Your brother?"

"Yeah. John." He seemed disinclined to pursue the subject, which made me all the more curious. "Didn't you get on?" I asked.

"Let's just say we were—different." He grinned. "Families. Who needs them, heh?"

I wondered if that was what GrosJean thought; if that was why he'd cut me out of his life. "I can't just leave him," I said quietly.

"Of course you can. It's obvious he doesn't want—"

"What does it matter what he wants? You've seen the boatyard, haven't you? You've seen the house? Where's the money coming from? And what happens to him when it runs out?"

There's no bank in Les Salants. *A bank*, says the island maxim, *lends you an umbrella when it's sunny, then takes it back when it starts to rain*. Instead, fortunes are hoarded in shoe boxes and under kitchen sinks. Loans are, for the most part, made through private agreement. I couldn't imagine GrosJean borrowing money; neither could I imagine a fortune hidden under the floor.

"He'll manage," said Flynn. "He's got friends here. They'll look after him."

I tried to see Omer La Patate looking after my father, or Matthias, or Aristide. Instead I saw GrosJean's face the day we left home; that look of blankness, which could equally well have been despair or indifference or something else altogether; the almost imperceptible nod of acknowledgment as he turned away. Boats to be built. No time for good-byes. Calling from the taxi window; *I'll write. I promise.* Mother, struggling with our cases, her face crumpled under the burden of unspoken words.

We were nearing the house. I could see its red tiled roof above the dunes. A thin filament of smoke came from the chimney. Flynn walked alongside me, head bent, not talking, his expression hidden behind the fall of his hair.

Then, suddenly, he stopped. There was someone in the house; someone standing at the kitchen window. I could not see his features, but his bulk was unmistakable; a big, bearlike figure with his face pressed against the glass.

"GrosJean?" I whispered.

He shook his head, his eyes wary. "Brismand."

9

He hadn't changed. He was older. Grayer. Broader around the waist but still wearing the espadrilles and fisherman's cap I remembered as a child, his thick fingers heavy with rings, his shirt stained with sweat under the armpits, although the day was cool. He was standing at the window as I came in, a steaming mug in one hand. A strong scent of Armagnac coffee filled the room.

"Ah, it's little Mado." His voice carried. It had a rich, rolling tone; his smile was frank and infectious. His mustache, though gray, now looked more bombastic than ever; that of a vaudeville comedian or a Communist dictator. He took three rapid steps forward and put his thickly freckled arms around me. "Mado, it's good, *good* to see you again!" His embrace, like everything else about him, was massive. "I made coffee. I hope you don't mind. And we're family, aren't we?" I nodded, half-stifled in his arms. "How is Adrienne? And the children? My nephew doesn't write as often as he should."

"Neither does my sister."

He laughed at that, a sound as rich as the coffee. "Youngsters, heh! But you—*you!* Let me see you. You've grown! You make me feel a hundred years old—but it's worth it to see your face, Mado. Your lovely face."

I'd almost forgotten that—his charm. It has a way of taking you by surprise, of leaving you without defenses. I could see the intelligence too behind the flamboyant exterior; his eyes were knowing, slaty, almost black. Yes, I'd liked him as a child. I still did.

"Still flooded in the village, is it? Bad business." He sighed hugely. "You must find it very different now. But it isn't for everyone, is it? Island life? Young people want more gaiety than the poor old island can give them."

I was conscious of Flynn, still standing just outside the door with his lobster pots. He looked reluctant to come in, though at the same time I sensed his curiosity, and his unwillingness to leave me alone with Brismand.

"Come inside," I told him. "Have some coffee."

Flynn shook his head. "I'll see you later."

Brismand barely glanced at Flynn as he left, then turned to me again, slinging an arm companionably over my shoulders. "I want to know all about you."

"Monsieur Brismand—"

"Claude, Mado, please." His enormous friendliness was slightly over-whelming, like that of a giant Santa Claus. "But why didn't you tell me you were coming? I'd almost given up hope—"

"I couldn't come before. My mother was ill."

"I know." He poured me a shot of coffee. "I'm sorry. And now this business with GrosJean—" He settled into a chair that creaked under his weight and patted the place next to him. "I'm glad you came, little Mado," he said simply. "I'm glad you trusted me."

The first years after leaving Le Devin were the hardest. It was lucky we were strong. But my mother's romantic nature had hardened to a tense, fearful practicality, which served us well. Unfit for any skilled job, she made a small income as a cleaner. Even so, we were poor.

GrosJean sent no money. Mother accepted this with bitter satisfac-tion, feeling vindicated. At school, a big Paris lycée, my shabby clothes made me even more of an outsider.

But Brismand had helped us in his way. We were family now, after all, even if we did not share his name. He sent no money, but there were parcels of clothes and books at Christmas, and boxes of paints for me when he discovered my interest. At school I had found refuge in the art department, which reminded me a little of my father's workshop with its small, busy sounds and its scent of fresh sawdust. I began to look forward to the lessons. I had a talent for the subject. I drew pictures of beaches and fishing boats and low-roofed whitewashed houses with brooding skies overhead. Of course, my mother hated them. Later, they became our main source of income, but she disliked the subject matter no less. She suspected, though she never said, that it was my way of breaking our agreement.

Throughout my college years Brismand continued to write. Not to my mother—she had embraced Paris in all its glitz and tawdriness and had no desire to be reminded of Le Devin—but to me. They were not long letters, but they were all I had, and I devoured every scrap of information. I concluded that his reputation in Les Salants was undeserved; the product of small-mindedness, prejudice, and jealousy. No one else had kept in touch with us; only he had shown any support. Sometimes I found myself wishing that he, not GrosJean, could have been my father.

Then, twelve months ago, came the first hint that all was not well in Les Salants. A passing reference to begin with—he had not seen Gros-Jean for some time—then more. My father's eccentricity, always present even during my childhood, was becoming more pronounced. There were rumors that he had been very ill, although he had refused to see the doctor. Brismand was concerned.

I did not reply to these letters. My mother was already taking up all of my attention. Her emphysema—made worse by the city pollution—had taken a downturn, and the doctor had tried to persuade her to move. Somewhere by the sea, he suggested, where the air would be healthier. But Mother refused to listen. She adored Paris. She loved the shops, the cinemas, the cafés. She was peculiarly unenvious of the rich women whose apartments she cleaned, taking vicarious pleasure in their clothes, their furniture, their lives. I sensed that was what she wanted for me.

Brismand's letters continued to arrive. He was still concerned. He had written to Adrienne, but received no reply. I understood that; I'd phoned when Mother had gone into the hospital, only to be told by Marin that Adrienne was pregnant again and couldn't possibly travel. Mother had died four days later, and a tearful Adrienne had told me on the phone that her doctor had forbidden her to exert herself.

❀

I took my time over the coffee. Brismand waited patiently, his big arm around my shoulder. "I know, Mado. It's been hard for you."

I wiped my eyes. "I should have expected it."

"You should have come to me." He looked around; I saw him taking in the dirty floor, the stacked plates, the unopened letters, the neglect.

"I wanted to see for myself."

"I understand." Brismand nodded. "He's your father. Family is everything."

He stood up, suddenly seeming to fill the room, and dug his hands into his pockets. "I had a son, you know. My wife took him away when he was three months old. For thirty years I waited, hoping—knowing—one day he'd come home."

I nodded. I'd heard the story. In Les Salants, of course, people assumed Brismand was to blame.

He shook his head, looking suddenly old, the theatrics put aside. "Foolish, isn't it? The way we delude ourselves. The barbs we leave in each other." He looked at me. "GrosJean loves you, Mado. In his way, he does."

I thought of my birthday photograph, and the way my father's arm had rested on Adrienne's shoulder. Gently, Brismand took my hand. "I could help you take care of your father," he said.

"I know."

"I could make arrangements. It's a nice place, Mado. Les Immortelles. Hospital facilities; a mainland doctor; big rooms; and he could see his friends anytime he liked."

I hesitated. Soeur Thérèse and Soeur Extase had already told me about Brismand's long-term residential care plan. It sounded expensive.

He shook his head dismissively. "I'd handle that. The sale of the land would cover all his expenses. Maybe more. I understand how you feel, Mado. But it might be for the best."

I promised to think about it. It was an idea at which Brismand had hinted before in his letters, although never so openly as this. It seemed a good offer; unlike Mother, GrosJean had never believed in medical insurance, and I could not afford to pay for his care on my small income. He needed help, that was certain. And I had a life in Paris to which I could—to which I *should*—return. For ten years I had idealized Les Salants, making an exile of myself for the sake of a place that no longer existed—if ever it had done so—except in memory. But whatever my dreams had once been, the reality was too bleak for me to retain them now. I didn't belong there anymore. Too many things had changed.

10

As I was leaving the house I met Alain Guénolé and his son Ghislain, coming the other way from the village. Both were out of breath. They looked very alike, but though his father wore the traditional sailcloth *vareuse*, Ghislain was wearing a toxic yellow T-shirt that glowed like neon against his brown skin. On seeing me, he grinned and began to run choppily up the big dune.

"Madame GrosJean," he gasped, pausing to catch his breath. "We need to borrow the tractor trailer from the boatyard. It's urgent."

For a moment I was sure he hadn't recognized me. This was Ghislain Guénolé, who was two years older than I was; with whom I'd played as a child. Had he really called me *Madame GrosJean?*

Alain nodded to me in greeting. He too was anxious, but it was clear that he considered no business urgent enough to make him run. "It's the *Eleanore*," he called over the dune. "We spotted her out at La Houssinière, just off Les Immortelles. We're going out there to bring her in, but we need your father's trailer. Is he home?"

I shook my head. "I don't know where he is."

Ghislain looked concerned. "It can't wait," he said. "We'll have to take it now. Perhaps *you*—if you tell him what it was for—"

"Of course you can take it," I said. "I'll come with you."

At this Alain, who had caught up, looked doubtful. "I don't think—"

"My father built that boat," I said firmly. "Years ago, before I was born. He'd never forgive me if I didn't help. You know how fond he is of her."

GrosJean was more than fond of her; I remembered that much. *Eleanore* had been the first of his "ladies," not the most beautiful of his creations, but maybe the most dear. The thought that she might now be lost filled me with dismay.

Alain shrugged. The boat was his livelihood. There was no place for sentiment when money was at stake. As Ghislain ran for the tractor I was conscious of a feeling of relief, as if this crisis were some kind of a reprieve.

"Are you sure you want to bother?" said Alain as his son fastened the trailer onto the old machine. "It's not exactly entertainment."

I was stung at his casual assumption. "I want to help," I said.

❀

The *Eleanore* had bottomed on some rocks about five hundred meters out of La Houssinière. She had become wedged in place by the rising tide, and though the sea was still quite low, the wind was brisk, crunching the damaged hull farther against the rock at every wave. A small group of Salannais—including Aristide, his grandson, Xavier, Matthias, Capucine, and Lolo—were watching from the shore. I scanned the faces eagerly, but my father was not among them. I saw Flynn though, in his fishing boots and jersey, carrying his duffel bag over his shoulder. They were soon joined by Lolo's friend Damien; now that I saw him next to Alain and Ghislain I could see he shared the Guénolé features.

"Stay back, Damien," said Alain, seeing him approach. "I don't want you getting in the way."

Damien shot his father a sullen look and sat down on a rock. When I looked back a few moments later I saw that he had lit a cigarette and was smoking it, his back turned defiantly. Alain, his eyes fixed on the *Eleanore,* seemed not to notice.

I sat down next to the boy. For a time he ignored me. Then, curiosity got the better of him and he turned to face me. "I've heard you were living in Paris," he said in a low voice. "What's it like?"

"Like any other city," I told him. "Big, noisy, crowded."

For a moment he looked downcast. Then, brightening; "European cities, maybe. American cities are different. My brother's got an American shirt. He's wearing it now."

I smiled, averting my eyes from Ghislain's luminous torso.

"They eat nothing but hamburgers in America," said Alain, who had been listening, "and all the girls are fat."

The boy looked indignant. "How would you know? You've never been there."

"Neither have you."

On the nearby jetty, which shelters the little harbor, a number of Houssins were also watching the damaged boat. Jojo-le-Goëland, an old Houssin with a sailorly manner and a lubricious eye, greeted us with a wave. "Come to watch?" He grinned.

"Out of the way, Jojo," snapped Alain. "Men have work to do here."

Jojo laughed. "You'll have your work cut out, trying to get to her from here," he said. "The tide's coming up, and there's a wind from the sea. I wouldn't be surprised if you ran into trouble."

"Ignore him," advised Capucine. "He's been talking like that ever since we arrived."

Jojo looked pained. "I could take her down to the beach for you," he suggested. "Haul her off the rocks with my *Marie Joseph*. Easy to bring a tractor down onto the sand. Load her up easy."

"How much?" said Alain with suspicion.

"Well, there's the boat. The labor. Access . . . Call it a thousand."

"Access?" Alain was incensed. "To where?"

Jojo smirked. "Les Immortelles, of course. Private beach. Monsieur Brismand's instructions."

"Private beach!" Alain glanced at the *Eleanore* and scowled. "Since when?"

Jojo carefully lit the stub of a Gitane. "Hotel patrons only," he said. "Can't have any old riffraff littering the place up."

It was a lie, and everyone knew it. I could see Alain measuring the possibilities of moving the *Eleanore* by hand.

I glared at Jojo. "I know Monsieur Brismand very well," I told him, "and I don't think he'd want to charge access to this beach."

Jojo smirked. "Why don't you go and ask him?" he suggested. "See what he tells you. Take your time; the *Eleanore* isn't going anywhere."

Alain looked at the *Eleanore* again. "Can we do it?" he asked Ghislain.

Ghislain shrugged. "Can we, Rouget?"

Flynn, who during this interchange had disappeared with his duffel bag in the direction of the jetty, now reappeared without it. He looked at the boat and shook his head. "I don't think so," he said. "Not without the *Marie Joseph*. Better do as he says before the tide gets any higher."

The *Eleanore* was heavy, a typical island oyster boat with her low bow and leaded underside. With the tide at her back it would soon be almost impossible to lift her from the rocks. Waiting for the tide—a wait of ten hours or more—would only mean further damage. Jojo's smirk widened.

"I think we could do it," I said. "We need to move the nose that way, toward the wind. We could use the trailer once we get it into the shallow water."

Alain looked at me, then at the other Salannais. I could see him measuring our endurance, calculating how many hands we needed for the task. I glanced back, hoping to see GrosJean's face among the rest, but there was no sign of him.

"I'm in," said Capucine.

"Me too," said Damien.

Alain frowned. "You boys stay clear," he said. "I don't want you getting hurt." He glanced at me again, then at the others. Matthias was too old to take part, but with Flynn, Ghislain, Capucine, and myself we might be able to manage. Scornfully, Aristide kept his distance, though I noticed Xavier watching with a wistful look in his eyes.

Jojo waited, grinning. "Well, what do you say?" The old sailor was obviously amused that Alain should consider a woman's opinion.

"Try it," I urged. "What is there to lose?"

Still, Alain hesitated.

"She's right," said Ghislain impatiently. "What? Are you getting old or something? There's more fight in Mado than there is in you!"

"Okay," decided Alain at last. "We'll give it a go."

I saw Flynn looking at me. "I think you've got an admirer." He grinned, jumping lightly down onto the wet sand.

※

It was almost evening, and the tide was three-quarters high when we finally admitted defeat, and by then Jojo's price had gone up by another thousand francs. We were freezing, numb, exhausted. Flynn had lost his jauntiness, and I'd come close to being crushed between the *Eleanore* and a rock during the struggle to shift her. At an unexpected surge from the rising tide, the nose veered sharply away with the wind, and *Eleanore*'s hull crunched sickly into my shoulder, knocking me sideways and sending a black flag of water into my face. I felt the rock behind me, and there was a moment of panic when I was sure I was going to be pinned, or worse. Fear—and relief at my narrow escape—made me belligerent. I turned on Flynn, who was just behind me.

"You were supposed to be holding the nose! What the hell happened?"

Flynn had dropped the ropes we were using to secure the boat. His face was a blur in the failing light. He was turned half away from me, and I could hear him cursing, very fluently for a foreigner.

There was a long squealing sound as *Eleanore*'s hull shifted once more on the rocks, then a lurch as she settled back. From the jetty came a mocking cheer from the Houssins.

Grimly, Alain called across the water to Jojo. "Okay. You win. Get the *Marie Joseph*." I looked at him, and he shook his head at me. "It's no good. We'll never do it now. Might as well get this over with, heh?"

Jojo grinned. He'd been watching the whole time, smoking a chain of cigarette ends, saying nothing. Disgusted, I began to make my way toward the shore. The others followed me, struggling in their wet clothes. Flynn was closest, head down and hands tucked under his armpits.

"We nearly had her," I told him. "It could have worked. If only we'd been able to keep the damn *nose* in place—"

Flynn muttered something under his breath.

"What was that?"

He sighed. "Perhaps when you've finished having a go at me you might like to bring the tractor around. They'll need it at Les Immortelles."

"I don't expect we'll be going anywhere for a while."

Disappointment made my voice harsh; Alain looked up briefly at the sound, then looked away. The little group of Houssin onlookers broke into ironic applause. The Salannais looked grim. Aristide, who had been watching from the jetty, gave me a look of disapproval. Xavier, who had stayed with his grandfather throughout the attempted rescue, gave me an uncomfortable smile over the wire rims of his glasses.

"I hope you think it was worth it," said Aristide.

"It could have worked," I said in a low voice.

"Because while you were busy proving you're as tough as everyone else, Guénolé was losing his boat."

"At least I made the effort," I said. "If one more person had joined us, we could have saved her."

The old man shrugged. "Why should we help a Guénolé?" And leaning heavily on his stick, he began the way back down the jetty, with Xavier following silent in his wake.

※

It took another two hours to bring *Eleanore* to the beach, another half hour for us to maneuver her from the wet sand onto the trailer. By that time the tide was at its highest, and night was falling. Jojo smoked his cigarette ends and chewed the loose tobacco from the butts, occasionally blurting juice onto the sand between his feet. At Alain's insistence, I watched the slow process of recovery from above the tide line and waited for the sensation to return to my bruised arm.

Eventually the job was done, and everyone took a rest. Flynn sat down in the dry sand, his back against the tractor's wheel. Capucine and Alain lit Gitanes. At this end of the island the mainland was clearly visible, backlit with an orange glow. Occasionally a *balise*—a warning beacon—blinked out its simple message. The cold sky was purple, milky at the rim and just beginning to show stars among the clouds. The wind from the sea knifed through my wet clothes, making me shake. Flynn's hands were bleeding. Even in the dim light I could see where the wet ropes had cut into his palms. I felt a little sorry at having shouted at him.

Ghislain came to stand beside me. I could hear his breathing close to my neck. "Are you okay? The boat hit you a hell of a bang back there."

"I'm fine."

"You're cold. You're shivering. Can I get—"

"Leave it. I'm fine."

I suppose I shouldn't have snapped at him. He meant well. But there was something in his voice—a kind of dreadful protectiveness. From the shadow of the tractor's wheel I thought I heard Flynn give a low laugh.

I'd been so certain that GrosJean would turn up eventually. Now, so late in the proceedings, I wondered why he'd stayed away. After all, he must have heard about the *Eleanore*. I wiped my eyes, feeling bleak.

Ghislain was still watching me over his Gitane. In the semidarkness his luminous T-shirt gave out a sickly glow. "Are you sure you're all right?"

I gave him a wan smile. "I'm sorry. We should have saved the *Eleanore*. If only we'd had more people." I rubbed at my arms for warmth. "I think Xavier might have helped if Aristide hadn't been there. I could tell he wanted to."

Ghislain sighed. "Xavier and I used to get on okay," he told me. "Obviously, he's a Bastonnet. But it didn't seem to matter as much then. But now Aristide won't let him out of his sight and—"

"That awful old man. What's his problem?"

"I think he's afraid," said Ghislain. "Xavier's all he has left now. He wants him to stay on the island and marry Mercédès Prossage."

"Mercédès? She's a pretty girl."

"She's all right." It was too dark to see, but from the tone of Ghislain's voice I was sure he was blushing.

※

We watched the sky darken. Ghislain finished his cigarette while Alain and Matthias looked over the damage to the *Eleanore*. It was worse than we'd feared. Like all oyster boats *Eleanore* was shallow-keeled, designed not for deep-sea fishing but for easy access to the beds. The rocks had peeled the bottom right off her. The rudder was in pieces—the lucky red bead that my father put onto each of his boats still dangling from the remains of the mast—the engine missing. I followed as the men hauled her up onto the road, feeling drained and sick. As I did, I noticed that the old breakwater at the far end of the beach had been reinforced with blocks of stone to form a broad dike that reached out toward La Jetée.

"That's new, isn't it?" I said.

Ghislain nodded. "Brismand had that done. Bad tides these past couple of years. They were washing away the sand. Those rocks give it some protection."

"It's what you need in Les Salants," I observed, thinking of the damage at La Goulue.

Jojo grinned. "Go see Brismand about it. I'm sure he'd know what to do."

"As if we'd ask *him*," muttered Ghislain.

"You're a stubborn lot," said Jojo. "You'd rather see the whole place washed into the sea than pay a fair price for repairs."

Alain looked at him. Jojo's grin widened momentarily, exposing his stubby teeth. "I always told your father he needed insurance," he remarked. "He never would listen." He glanced at the *Eleanore*. "Time that hulk was scrapped anyway. Get yourself something new. Modern."

"She's all right," said Alain, not rising to the bait. "These old boats are pretty much indestructible. It looks worse than it is. She needs a lit-tle patchwork, a new engine. . . ."

Jojo laughed and shook his head. "Go on, patch her up. It'll cost you ten times more than she's worth. What then? Want to know what I make in just one day during the season, selling rides?"

Ghislain gave him an ugly look. "You could have taken the engine yourself," he challenged. "Sell it yourself on one of your trips to the coast. You're always trading stuff. No one asks questions."

Jojo showed his teeth. "I can see you Guénolés still know how to run your mouth," he said. "Your grandfather was just the same. Tell me, whatever came of that lawsuit against the Bastonnets? How much did you make out of that, heh? And how much did it cost you, d'you think? And your father? And your brother?"

Ghislain dropped his gaze, abashed. It is a well-known fact in Les Salants that the Guénolé-Bastonnet lawsuit ran for twenty years and ruined both parties. Its cause—an almost-forgotten wrangle over oyster beds on La Jetée—became academic long before the end, as shifting sandbanks engulfed the disputed territory, but the hostilities never ceased, passing from generation to generation as if to compensate for the squandered inheritance.

"Your engine probably washed out across the bay," said Jojo, with a lazy gesture toward La Jetée. "That or you'll find it down by La Goulue, if you dig deep enough." He spat a wad of wet tobacco onto the sand. "I hear you lost the Saint last night too. Careless lot, aren't you?

Alain kept his calm with difficulty. "Easy for you to laugh, Jojo," he said. "But luck turns, they say, even here. If you didn't have this beach—"

Matthias nodded. "That's right," he growled. The old man's Devin-nois accent was so thick that even I had difficulty following his words. "This beach makes your luck. Don't forget that. It could have been ours."

Jojo cawed with laughter. "Yours!" he jeered. "If it had been yours you'd have pissed it away years ago, the way you piss away everything else—"

Matthias took a step forward, his old hands shaking. Alain put his own hand warningly on his father's arm. "Enough. I'm tired. And there's work to do tomorrow."

But something in that phrase had stuck in my mind. Something to do with La Goulue, I thought, and La Bouche, and the scent of wild garlic on the dunes. *It could have been ours.* I tried to identify what it was, but I was too cold and exhausted to think clearly. And Alain was right; none of this had changed anything. I still had work to do in the morning.

11

I arrived at the house to find my father in bed. In a way I felt relieved; I was in no state to begin a discussion then. I put my wet clothes by the fireplace to dry, drank a glass of water, and went to my room. I noticed as I turned out the night-light that a little jar of wildflowers had been placed at my bedside; dune pinks and blue thistle and rabbit-tail grasses. It was an absurdly touching gesture from my undemonstrative father, and I spent some time lying awake trying to make sense of it, until eventually sleep overtook me, and a moment later it was morning.

When I awoke, I found GrosJean had already gone out. Always an early riser, he would wake at four in the summertime and go for long walks along the shore; I dressed, had breakfast, and followed his example.

When I reached La Goulue at about nine o' clock, it was already crowded with Salannais. For a moment I wondered why; then I remembered the missing Sainte-Marine, briefly eclipsed the previous day by the loss of the *Eleanore*. This morning the search for her had begun again as soon as the tide permitted it, but so far there was no sign of the lost Saint.

Half the village seemed to have joined the search. All four Guénolés were there, combing the lowtide flats, and a group of onlookers had gathered on the pebble strip below the path. My father had gone far out beyond the tide line; armed with a long wooden rake, he was sweeping the seabed with methodical slowness, occasionally stopping to remove a stone or a clump of weed from the tines.

To one side of the pebble strip I saw Aristide and Xavier, watching the proceedings but not taking part. Behind them, Mercédès was sunbathing and reading a magazine while Charlotte looked on with her usual air of anxiety. I noticed that although Xavier's eyes avoided most people, they avoided Mercédès most assiduously. Aristide looked grimly cheerful, as if someone else had received bad news.

"Bad luck about the *Eleanore*, heh? Alain says they're quoting six thousand francs to repair her, in La Houssinière."

"Six thousand?" It was more than the boat was worth; certainly more than the Guénolés could afford.

"Heh." Aristide smiled sourly. "Even Rouget says she's not worth fixing."

I looked beyond him at the skyline; a yellow stripe between the clouds illuminated the bare flats with a sickly sheen. Across the mouth of the tidal creek, a few fishermen had spread out their nets and were laboriously picking them clean of seaweed. They had dragged the *Eleanore* farther up the banking and she lolled, her ribs showing like those of a dead whale, on the mud.

Behind me, Mercédès rolled elegantly onto her side. "From what I heard," she said in a clear voice, "it would have been better if *she*'d kept her nose out."

"*Mercédès!*" moaned her mother. "Such a thing to say!"

The girl shrugged. "It's true, isn't it? If they hadn't wasted so much time—"

"Stop that right now!" Charlotte turned to me in agitation. "I'm sorry. She's highly strung."

Xavier looked uncomfortable. "Bad luck," he told me in a low voice. "She was a good boat."

"She was. My father built her."

I looked across the flats to where GrosJean was still at work. He must have been nearly a kilometer out, his tiny, dogged figure almost invisible against the haze.

"How long have they been at it?"

"Two hours, maybe. Since the tide started to go out." Xavier shrugged, not meeting my eyes. "She could be anywhere by now."

The Guénolés, apparently, felt a responsibility. The loss of their *Eleanore* had delayed the search, and the crosscurrents from La Jetée had done the rest. It was Alain's opinion that Sainte-Marine had been buried somewhere across the bay, and that only a miracle could bring her back.

"La Bouche, the *Eleanore*, then this." It was Aristide, still watching me with an expression of dangerous good cheer. "Tell me, have you told your father about Brismand yet? Or is that another surprise?"

I looked at him, startled. "Brismand?"

The old man showed his teeth. "I wondered how long it would be before he came sniffing round. A place in Les Immortelles, in exchange for the land? Is that what he offered you?"

Xavier glanced at me, then at Mercédès and Charlotte. Both of them were listening attentively. Mercédès had abandoned all pretense of reading and was watching me over her magazine, her mouth slightly open.

I held the old man's gaze levelly, not wanting to be forced into a lie. "Whatever my business with Brismand, it's my own. I won't discuss it with you."

Aristide shrugged. "So I was right," he said with bitter satisfaction. "It's about what's best for GrosJean. That's what they say, isn't it? That it's all for the best?"

I've always had a temper. Slow to rise, but banked and burning, it can be fierce. I could feel it rising now. "What would you know about it?" I said harshly. "No one ever came back to look after you, did they?"

Aristide stiffened. "That's nothing to do with it," he said.

But I couldn't stop. "You've been sniping at me since I arrived," I said. "What you can't understand is that I love my father. You don't love anyone!"

Aristide flinched as if I had struck him, and at that moment I saw him as he was—no longer an evil troll, but a tired old man, bitter and afraid. I felt a sudden rush of pity and sorrow for him—for myself. I'd

come home so full of good intentions, I thought helplessly. Why had
they soured so fast?

But there was spirit in Aristide still; he faced me with a challenge in
his eyes, even though he knew I had won. "Why else would you come
back?" he said in a low voice. "Why would anyone, unless they wanted
something?"

"Shame on you, Aristide, you old gannet." It was Toinette, who had
come up quietly from the path behind us. Beneath the flaps of her
quichenotte, her face was almost invisible, but I could see her eyes, bright
as a bird's, shining. "Listening to silly gossip at your age? You should
know better."

Aristide turned, startled. Toinette was, by her own account, nearly a
hundred years old; he, at seventy, was a comparative youngster. I saw
grudging respect in his face, and a kind of shame. "Toinette, Brismand
was at the house—," he began.

"And why shouldn't he be?" The old woman took a step forward.
"The girl's family. What? Do you expect *her* to care about your old
feuds? Isn't that what's been tearing Les Salants apart for the last fifty
years?"

"I still say—"

"You'll say nothing." Toinette's eyes snapped like firecrackers. "And
if I find you've been spreading any more of that nasty talk, heh—"

Aristide looked sullen. "It's an island, Toinette. You can't help hearing things. It won't be my fault if GrosJean finds out."

Toinette looked across at the flats, then at me. There was concern in
her face, and I knew then that it was too late. Aristide's poison was sown.
I wondered who had told him about Brismand's visit, how he had
guessed so much.

"Don't you worry. I'll put him right. He'll listen to me." Toinette
took my hand between both of hers; they were dry and brown as
driftwood. "Come along, then," she said briskly, pulling me with her
up the path. "You'll do no good hanging around here. Come home
with me."

❀

Her home was a single-room cottage at the far end of the village. It was old-fashioned even by island standards, flint-walled and with a low roof of mossy tiles held up by smoke-blackened beams. Door and windows were tiny, almost child-size, and the toilet was a rickety shed at the side of the house, behind the woodpile. As we approached we could see a single goat cropping the grass that grew on the roof.

"You've gone and done it now, heh," said Toinette, pushing open the front door.

I had to duck my head to avoid touching the lintel. "I haven't done anything."

Toinette removed the *quichenotte* and gave me a stern look. "Don't try that game with me, girl," she said. "I know all about Brismand and his schemes. He tried the same thing with me, you know, a place in Les Immortelles in exchange for my house. He even promised to throw in funeral arrangements. Funeral arrangements!" She gave a cackle. "I told him I'm planning to live forever!" She turned to me, sober again. "I know what he's like. He'd charm the pants off a nun, if he had a buyer. And he has plans for Les Salants. Plans that don't include any of us."

I'd heard that before at Angélo's. "If he has, I can't think what they are," I said. "He's been good to me, Toinette. Better than most Salannais."

"Aristide." The old woman frowned. "Don't judge him too harshly, Mado."

"Why not?"

She prodded me with a sticklike finger. "Your father isn't the only one who's suffered here," she told me sternly. "Aristide lost two sons, one to the sea, the other to his own stubbornness. It's soured him."

His eldest son, Olivier, had died in a fishing accident in 1972. His youngest, Philippe, had spent the next ten years in a house that had become a silent shrine to Olivier. "Of course, he went off the rails."

Toinette shook her head. "He got involved with a girl—an Houssine—you can imagine what Aristide thought about that."

She had been sixteen. When Philippe had found out she was pregnant he had panicked and run away to the mainland, leaving Aristide and Désirée to face the girl's angry parents. All mention of Philippe had been forbidden in the Bastonnet house after that. Olivier's widow had died of meningitis a few years later, leaving Xavier, her only son, in the care of his grandparents.

"Xavier's their only hope now," explained Toinette, echoing Ghislain's words. "Anything Xavier wants, he gets. Anything, as long as he stays here."

I thought of Xavier's pale, expressionless face, his restless eyes behind the glasses. If Xavier married, Ghislain had told me, he would be sure to stay. Toinette read my thoughts. "Oh yes, he's been half-promised to Mercédès since they were children," she said. "But my granddaughter's a willful piece. She has ideas."

I thought of Mercédès; the note in Ghislain's voice when he spoke of her.

"And she'd never marry a poor man," said Toinette. "The minute the Guénolés lost their boat, their boy lost his chance with her."

I considered that. "You're not suggesting the Bastonnets had something to do with what happened to the *Eleanore*?"

"I'm saying nothing. I don't spread gossip. But whatever happened to her, you, of all people, shouldn't get involved."

Again I thought of my father. "He loved that boat," I said stubbornly.

Toinette looked at me. "Maybe he did, heh. But it was the *Eleanore* P'titJean took out on that last trip of his, the *Eleanore* that was found drifting the day he was lost, and every time your father's looked at her since he must have seen his brother there calling him. Believe me, he's better off without her."

Toinette smiled and took my hand, her small fingers dry and light as dead leaves. "Don't worry about your father, Mado," she said. "He'll be all right."

12

 I arrived at the house half an hour later to find that GrosJean had been there before me. The door was ajar, and as soon as I approached I knew something was wrong. A strong smell of alcohol reached me from the kitchen, and as I stepped into the room my feet crunched on glass from a broken bottle of *devinnoise*.

It was only the beginning.

He had smashed every piece of crockery and glassware he could lay his hands on. Every cup, plate, bottle, had been broken. My mother's Jean de Bretagne dishes, the tea service, the little row of liqueur glasses in the cabinet. The door to my room was open; my boxes of clothes and books scattered. The flower vase by my bedside had been trampled; the flowers trodden into the pulverized glass. The silence was eerie, still resonating with the force of his rage.

This was not entirely new to me. My father's frenzies had been infrequent but terrible and, always followed by a quietus that lasted days, sometimes weeks. My mother had always said that it was the silences that preyed on her most; the long intervals of blankness, the times when he seemed absent from everything but his rituals: his visits to La Bouche, his drinking sessions at Angélo's bar, his solitary walks by the seashore.

I sat down on the bed, my legs feeling suddenly weak. What had caused this new outburst? The loss of the Saint? The loss of the *Eleanore?* Something else?

I considered what Toinette had told me about P'titJean and the *Eleanore*. I had never known. I tried to imagine what my father must have felt when she was lost. Sadness, perhaps, at the loss of his oldest creation? Relief that P'titJean had finally been laid to rest? I began to understand now why he hadn't been at the rescue. He'd *wanted* her to be lost; and I, fool that I was, had tried to save her.

I picked up a book—one of the ones I had left behind—and smoothed out its cover. His rage had seemed to target books especially; some had had pages torn out; others had been trampled. I had been the only one of us who enjoyed books; Mother and Adrienne had preferred magazines and the television. I could not help thinking that this destruction was a direct attack at me.

It was only a few minutes later that I thought to try Adrienne's room. Of course, it was untouched. GrosJean did not even appear to have looked in. I put my hand to my pocket, checking the birthday photo inside. It was still there. Adrienne smiled at me across the space where I had been, her long hair half hiding her face. I remembered how she had always been given a present on my birthday. That year it had been the dress she was wearing in the picture, a white shift with red embroidery. I'd had my first fishing rod. I'd liked it, of course; but I'd sometimes wondered why no one ever bought *me* a dress.

I lay on Adrienne's bed for a long time with the smell of *devinnoise* in my nostrils and the faded pink bedspread against my face. Then I stood up. I saw myself in her wardrobe mirror: pale, puffy-eyed, lank-haired. I took a good look. Then I left the house, walking carefully over the broken glass. Whatever was wrong with GrosJean, I told myself—whatever was wrong with Les Salants—I was not the one to mend it. He'd made that very clear. This was where my responsibility ended.

※

I made for La Houssinière with more relief than I could admit to myself. I had tried, I repeated. I really had. If I had had any kind of support, but my father's silence, the undisguised hostility of Aristide, even the equivocal kindness of Toinette, showed me I was alone. Even Capucine, when she discovered my intentions, would most likely take my father's side. She'd always been fond of GrosJean. No, Brismand was right. Someone had to be reasonable. And the Salannais, clinging desperately to superstition and the old ways while the sea took more of them every year, were not likely to understand. It would have to be Brismand. If I could not make GrosJean see sense, then maybe Brismand's doctors would.

I took the long way round toward Les Immortelles, past La Bouche. I saw no one except Damien Guénolé, sitting alone on the rocks with his fishing bag and rods. I waved to him, and he nodded but said nothing. The tide was beginning to come back in with a distant rush of white noise. Beyond that, at the narrowest point of the island, you can watch the tide coming in from both sides at once. Someday, the waist that joins the two parts of Le Devin will be breached, cutting off Les Salants from La Houssinière for good. When that happens, I thought, it will be the end of the Salannais.

I was halfway to Les Immortelles when I met Flynn coming the other way. I had not expected to see anyone else—the shoreline path was narrow and infrequently used—but he seemed unsurprised to see me. And his manner seemed altered this morning: the cheery carelessness of the man replaced by a cautious neutrality, his eyes almost without light. I wondered if it was because of what had happened the night of the *Eleanore*, and I felt a tightening around my heart.

"No sign of the Saint, then?" Even to myself, my brightness rang false.

"You're going to La Houssinière." It wasn't a question, although I could see he expected a reply. "To see Brismand," he went on, in the same neutral tone.

"Everyone seems very interested in my movements," I said.

"They should be."

I heard the sharp note in my voice. "What does that mean?"

"Nothing." He seemed about to go on his way, stepping aside to give me space, his eyes already somewhere else. Suddenly it seemed very important to stop him from leaving. He, at least, should understand my point of view. "Please. You're his friend," I began. I knew he understood who I meant.

He paused for a moment. "So?"

"So maybe you can talk to him. Persuade him, somehow."

"What?" he said. "Persuade him to leave?"

"He needs special care. I have to make him see that. Someone has to be responsible." I thought about the house, the broken glass, the dismembered books. "He might harm himself," I said at last.

Flynn looked at me, and I was startled to see such a hard expression in his eyes. "It sounds reasonable," he said softly. "But you and I know better, don't we?" He smiled, not pleasantly. "It's about *you*. This talk of responsibility—that's all it comes to in the end. What suits you."

I tried to tell him it wasn't like that. But words that had seemed so natural when Brismand said them merely sounded fake and helpless coming from my mouth. I could tell Flynn thought so; that I was doing it for myself, for my own security, or even as a kind of revenge on Gros-Jean for all those years of silence. . . . It wasn't like that, I tried to tell him. I was sure it wasn't.

But Flynn was no longer interested. A shrug, a nod, and he was gone down the path as fast and as silent as a poacher, leaving me to stare after him in growing anger and bewilderment. Who the hell was he, anyway? What gave him the right to judge me?

❀

Arriving at Les Immortelles I found that my anger, instead of fading, had grown. I no longer trusted myself to speak with Brismand—half afraid that the first kind word might open the floodgates to the tears that had threatened since the day of my arrival. Instead I loitered by the jetty, enjoying the quiet sounds of the water and the little pleasure boats that winged across the bay. It was early yet for tourists; only a few lay at the top of the beach underneath the esplanade, where a row of freshly painted beach huts squatted on the white sand.

On the other side of the street I became aware of a young man watching me from the saddle of a flashy Japanese motorbike. Long hair over his eyes, cigarette held loosely between the fingers, tight jeans, leather jacket, and motorcycle boots . . . It took a moment for me to recognize him. Joël Lacroix—the handsome and much-indulged son of the island's only policeman. He left his bike standing by the curbside and made his way across the road toward me.

"You're not from here, are you?" he asked, taking a drag from his cigarette. It was clear he didn't remember who I was. Why should he, after all? The last time I had spoken to him we were at school, and he was a couple of years older than I.

He eyed me appreciatively, grinning. "I could show you around if you like," he suggested. "See some sights, what there is, anyway. There's not much."

"Some other time, thanks."

Joël flicked his cigarette across the road. "Where are you staying, heh? Les Immortelles? Or have you got relatives here?"

For some reason—perhaps that speculative gaze—I was reluctant to reveal who I was. I nodded. "I'm in Les Salants."

"You must like roughing it, heh? Out west among the goats and the salt marshes? Half of them have got six fingers to each hand over there, you know. *Clo-ose* families." He rolled his eyes, then looked at me more closely, with belated recognition. "I do know you," he said at last. "You're the Prasteau girl. Monique—Marie—"

"Mado," I said.

"I heard you'd come back. I didn't recognize you."

"Why should you?"

Joël flicked his hair back self-consciously. "So you came back to Les Salants? It takes all kinds." My indifference had cooled his interest. He lit up again, using a silver Harley-Davidson lighter almost as big as the packet of Gitanes. "Me, give me the city anytime. One day I'm just going to get on my bike and take off, heh. Anywhere but here. You won't see *me* hanging around Le Devin for the rest of my life." He pocketed his lighter and sauntered back across the street toward the waiting Honda, leaving me alone again in front of the beach huts.

I had taken off my shoes, and beneath my toes the sand was already warm. Once more I was conscious of its thickness. Last night's tractor tracks still marked it in one place; I remembered how the trailer's wheels had caught in it as we labored to push the crippled *Eleanore* toward the road; how it had given beneath our combined weight; and the scent of wild garlic on the dunes. . . .

I stopped. That scent. I'd thought of it then too. Somehow at the time I'd associated it with Flynn; and with something Matthias Guénolé had said, his hands shaking with rage at some comment by Jojo-le-Goëland, something about a beach.

That was it. *It could have been ours.*

Why? Luck turns, he'd said. But why mention the beach? Still it eluded me; smelling of thyme and wild garlic and the salt scent of the dunes. Never mind; it wasn't important. I walked as far as the water, coming in now but taking its time, trickling gently through the runnels in the sand, seeping up through the hollow places beneath the rocks. To the left of me, not far from the jetty, was the dike, newly reinforced with stone blocks to form a broad breakwater that reached over a distance of a hundred meters. Two children were already climbing there; I could hear their cries, so like those of the seagulls, in the clear air. I tried to imagine what a beach would have done for Les Salants: the trade it might have brought, the infusion of life. The beach makes your luck, Matthias had said. Lucky Brismand lived up to his name once again.

The rocks that formed the breakwater were still smooth and unmarred by barnacles or seaweed. On the near side it was maybe two meters high, from the far side the drop was much shorter. Sand had accumulated there, deposited by the current. I could hear the two children playing there, throwing handfuls of weed at each other in shrill excitement. I looked back at the beach huts. The single surviving hut at La Goulue had been perched high above the ground; I remembered its long legs, like an insect's, anchored into the rock. The huts at Les

Immortelles were snug to the ground, with barely a space beneath in which to crawl.

The beach had gained some sand, I told myself.

Suddenly I had it; the scent of wild garlic intensified, and I heard Flynn saying *a jetty and a beach and everything*. He'd been talking about La Goulue; I'd been looking at the beach hut and wondering where all the sand had gone.

The children were still throwing seaweed. There was a lot of seaweed on the far side of the breakwater; not as much as there had once been at La Goulue, but at Les Immortelles someone probably came to clear it every day. Moving closer I could see that there were dark red patches among the brown and green, a red that reminded me of something. I poked at it with my foot, removing the layer of seaweed that covered it.

And then I saw it. It had been badly treated by the tide; the silk had frayed and the embroidery unraveled, and the whole thing was clotted with wet sand. But it was impossible to mistake. Sainte-Marine's ceremonial skirt, torn from the statue on the night of the festival and washed up, not at the Greedy One, as we might have expected, but here, at Les Immortelles, the luck of La Houssinière. Washed up by the tide.

The tide.

Suddenly I found that I was shaking, but not with the cold. The Salannais had blamed the south wind for all their misfortunes, but in fact it was the *tides* that had changed; the tides, which had once brought the fish to La Goulue and which now stripped it of everything it had; the tides, which drove straight up the little creek into the village, where once Pointe Griznoz had protected us.

I stared at the piece of rotten silk for a long time, hardly daring to breathe. I thought of the beach huts, the sand, the original breakwater. When had it first been built? When had the beach and the jetty at La Goulue been washed away? And now this new construction, built onto the old one so recently that even the barnacles had yet to settle?

One thing leads to another; small connections, small changes. Tides and currents can change quickly on an island as small and sandy as Le

Devin; and the effect of any such change can be devastating. Bad tides washing the sand away, Ghislain had told me the night of *Eleanore*'s rescue. Brismand was protecting his investment.

Brismand had been kind to me, concerned about the flooding. And he had expressed interest in GrosJean's land. He had offered to buy Toinette's house too. How many others had he also approached?

13

My first impulse was to go and see Brismand straightaway. On second thought, however, I decided against it. I could see his look of astonishment, the gleam of humor; I could hear the rich sound of his laughter as I tried to explain my suspicions. And he'd been kind to me, almost a father. I felt hateful for even suspecting him.

Capucine and Toinette seemed less than interested when I tried to explain what I'd seen. There had been more flooding during the night, and there was even less good cheer than usual in Angélo's as the Salannais drowned their new sorrows in gloomy silence.

"Now if you'd found the Saint herself—" Toinette grinned, exposing peggy teeth. "*She's* the luck of Les Salants, not some beach that might have been here thirty years ago. And you're not saying Sainte-Marine made it all the way to Les Immortelles, are you? Now that *would* have been a miracle."

I tired to curb my exasperation. This talk of miracles and luck seemed only to reinforce their defeatism, their inactivity. It was as if they and I were speaking a completely different language.

Of course there was still no sign of the missing Saint at the Pointe, or even at La Goulue. More likely she was buried, said Toinette, sunk in the low-tide mud off La Griznoz, to be rediscovered in twenty years' time by some child digging for clams—that is, if she was discovered at all.

The general feeling in the village was that the Saint had abandoned Les Salants. The more superstitious ones spoke of a Black Year to come; even the younger villagers were dispirited by their loss. "The festival of Sainte-Marine was the only thing we did as a community," explained Capucine, pouring a generous measure of *devinnoise* into her coffee cup. "It was the only time we ever tried to pull together. Now everything's coming apart. And there's nothing we can do about it."

She gestured toward the window, but I did not need to look outside to understand what she meant. Neither the weather nor the fishing had improved. The August high tides were coming to an end, but September would bring worse, and October would bring storms that would sweep off the Atlantic and across the island. The Rue de l'Océan was churned mud. As well as the *Eleanore*, several of the flat-bottomed *platts* had been washed out to sea, even though they had been dragged far beyond the tide line. Worst of all, the mackerel seemed now to have completely disappeared, and fishing was at a standstill. To make matters worse, fishermen in La Houssinière were going through a period of unrivaled prosperity.

"I don't understand you!" I exclaimed. "What's happened to Les Salants? Everything's a mess, the road's half-flooded, boats washed away, houses falling down. Why isn't someone doing something about it? Why are you people just sitting around, watching it happen?"

Aristide replied over his shoulder, "What are we supposed to do, heh? Try to turn back the tide, like King Canute?"

"There's always *something*," I said. "What about sea defenses, like those in La Houssinière? Sandbags, if nothing else, to protect the road?"

"Useless," spat the old man, shifting his wooden leg impatiently. "You can't control the sea. Might as well spit in the wind as try."

❦

The wind felt good on my face as I walked dispiritedly across the Rue de l'Océan. What was the point of trying to help? It is this stubborn stoicism that characterizes the Salannais, a trait born not of self-assurance but of fatalism, even superstition. I picked up a rock from the road and flung it as far as I could against the wind; it dropped into a clump of *oyat* and was lost. For a moment I thought of my mother, how all her warmth and her good intentions had been eroded away, leaving her dry and anxious and filled with bitter thoughts. She had loved the island too. For a time.

But I have my father's stubbornness in me. She often remarked on it, on our evenings in the little Paris flat. Adrienne was more like her, she said; a loving, friendly girl. I had been a difficult child: withdrawn, sullen. If only Adrienne hadn't been obliged to move to Tangiers . . .

I did not respond to these complaints. There was no point in even trying. I had long since stopped pointing out the obvious: Adrienne hardly ever wrote or called, or even once invited us to stay. It was as if she and Marin wanted to put as much distance between themselves and Le Devin—and anything that reminded them of it—as possible. But to my mother, Adrienne's silence was simply proof of her devotion to her new family. The few letters we received were hoarded greedily; a Polaroid of the children took pride of place above the fire. Adrienne's new life in Tangiers—romanticized beyond recognition into a fairy tale of souks and temples—was the nirvana to which we should both aspire, and to which we would eventually be called.

❦

I returned to the house. It was the same alarming shambles as before, and for a moment I almost lost my courage. There was always room for me at Les Immortelles, Brismand had told me. All I had to do was ask. I imagined a clean bed, white sheets, hot water. I thought of my little flat in Paris with its parquet floor and reassuring smell of paint and polish. I thought of the café opposite, and *moules-frites* on a Friday night, and maybe the cinema later. What was I still doing here? I asked myself. Why was I putting myself through all this?

I picked up one of my books, smoothing the crumpled pages. A picture story, lavishly illustrated, about a princess transformed by evil magic into a bird, and a hunter . . . As a child I'd had a keen imagination, my inner life compensating for the quiet rhythms of the island. I'd assumed my father was the same. Now I wasn't sure I wanted to know what—if anything—lay behind his silence.

I picked up some more books, hating to see them so carelessly spread, crack-spined on the broken glass. My clothes were less important—I'd brought so few with me in the first place, and I'd been planning to buy some in La Houssinière anyway—but I picked them up and put them into the machine to be washed. My few papers, the drawing materials I'd had as a girl—a slab of cracked watercolors, a paintbrush—I replaced in their cardboard box next to the bed. It was then that I saw something by the foot of the bed, something shiny and half-trodden into the piece of carpet that covered the stone floor. Too bright to be glass, it shone with a mellow gleam in a stray fleck of sunlight from between the shutters. I picked it up. It was my father's locket, the one I'd noticed before, a little dented now and with the remains of its broken chain dangling from the catch. He must have lost it in his rampage, I thought; maybe dragging at his collar in an attempt to loosen it; releasing the chain and failing to notice it as it slithered from under his shirt. I looked at the object more closely. It was silver-gilt, about as large as a five-franc piece, and there was a little catch at the side to open and close it. A woman's thing, really. For some reason I was reminded of Capucine. A keepsake. I opened it, feeling absurdly guilty, as if I were spying on my father's secret business, and something fell out into my hand—a fluffy curl of hair. It was brown, like his had once been, and my first thought was that it might have been his brother's. GrosJean seemed uninclined toward romance, had never, as far as I knew, even remembered my mother's birthday or their wedding anniversary, and the thought that he might now be carrying a lock of my mother's hair around with him was so far-fetched as to make me smile uneasily. Then I opened the locket wider and saw the photograph.

It had been scissored from a larger one; a young face grinning toothily from the gilt frame, short hair spiked up at the front and big round eyes . . . I looked at it in disbelief, studying it, as if by so doing I could transform my own image into that of someone more deserving. But it was me all right; my own photograph from the birthday picture, one hand still frozen on the cake knife, the other reaching out of the frame toward my father's shoulder. I pulled out the original from my pocket, where it had begun to scuff with repeated handling. In it my sister's face looked sullen to me now, envious, her head turned away pettishly, like that of a child unused to being denied attention. . . .

I felt a burst of some emotion that made my cheeks flare and my heart beat more wildly. It was me he'd chosen after all; my picture he'd worn around his neck with a tuft of my baby hair beside it. Not Mother. Not Adrienne. Me. I'd imagined myself forgotten, but all this time I'd been the one he remembered in this way, carried with him in secret, like a lucky charm. What did it matter that he hadn't answered my letters? What did it matter that he wouldn't speak?

I stood up, holding the locket hard in my hand, my doubts forgotten. I knew now exactly what I had to do.

I waited for nightfall. The tide was almost high then, a good time for what I had in mind. I put on my boots and *vareuse* and made my way out over the windy dunes. Off La Goulue I could see the dull glow of the mainland, with the beacon flicking out its red warning every few seconds; elsewhere the sea was luminous with that glaucous light peculiar to the Jade Coast, occasionally flaring into harder brilliance as the clouds cleared over a fragment of moon.

On the roof of his *blockhaus*, I caught sight of Flynn, looking out into the bay; I could just see him outlined against the sky. I watched him for a moment, trying to make out what he was doing, but he was too far away. I hurried on toward La Goulue, where the tide would soon be turning.

In the bag slung over my shoulder I had brought a number of the orange plastic floats that island fishermen use for their mackerel nets. As a child I had learned to swim with the help of a life belt made from these floats, and we had often used them to mark lobster pots and crab baskets out off La Goulue, collecting them up from the rocks at low tide, and stringing them together like giant beads. It had been a game then, but a serious one; any fisherman would pay a franc each for the recovered floats, and this was often the only pocket money we received. The game—and the floats—would help me again tonight.

Standing on the rocks below the cliff, I threw them out to sea, thirty in all, making sure that I aimed past the swell line and into the open current. Once, not so long ago, at least half of the floats would have washed right back into the bay with the next tide. Now—But that was the experiment.

I stayed watching for a few more minutes. It was warm in spite of the wind; a final breath of summer, and as the clouds dispersed above me, I could see the broad field of the Milky Way across the sky. Feeling suddenly very calm, I waited, under a sky wild and enormous with stars, for the tide to turn.

14

From the light at the kitchen window I knew GrosJean was back. I could see him outlined there, a cigarette to his lips, his hunched figure like a monolith against the yellow glow. I felt a stir of trepidation. Would he speak? Would he rage?

He did not look around when I came in. I had not expected him to; instead he remained unmoving among the wreckage he had caused, a cup of coffee in one hand and a Gitane cupped between his yellowed fingers.

"You dropped your locket," I said, putting it down on the table beside him.

I thought I sensed some change in his posture, but he did not look at me. Stolid and heavy as the statue of Sainte-Marine, he seemed unmovable.

"I'll make a start on the place tomorrow," I said. "It needs a little work, but I'll soon make it comfortable for you again."

Still, no answer. As a child I had known how to interpret the signs, reading his gestures like entrails. I'd expected this too; and instead of anger I felt a vast and sudden pity for him, for his sorry silence, his tired eyes.

"It's all right," I said. "You'll be all right." And I went to him and put my arms around his neck, smelling his old scent of salt and sweat and paint and varnish, and we sat there like that for about a minute until the cigarette end had burned down to a stub and fell from his hand onto the stone floor in a gaudy splash of sparks.

I got up early the next morning and went off in search of my fishing floats. There was no sign of them either at La Goulue or farther up the creek into Les Salants; not that I had expected any.

I was in La Houssinière before six; the sky was clear and pale, and there were only a few people—fishermen, mostly—in sight. I thought I saw Jojo-le-Goëland digging out on the flats, and a couple of figures far out on the tide line with the big square nets Houssins use for shrimping. Apart from that, the place was deserted.

I found the first of my orange floats under the jetty. I picked it up and moved on toward the breakwater, stopping occasionally to turn over a stone or a clump of seaweed. By the time I reached it I had picked up a dozen more of the floats, and spotted three more wedged between rocks, just out of reach.

All told, sixteen floats. A good catch.

"Is it a game?"

I turned too quickly, and my bag dropped onto the wet sand, spilling its contents. Flynn looked at the floats curiously. His hair caught the wind like a warning flag.

"Well, is it?"

I remembered his previous day's coolness. Today he looked relaxed, pleased with himself, the explosive look gone from his eyes.

I did not reply at once. Instead, I forced myself to pick up the floats and return them, very slowly, to the bag. Sixteen of thirty. A little more than half. But it was enough to confirm what I had already known.

"I didn't see you as a beachcomber, somehow," said Flynn, still watching me. "Found anything interesting?

I wondered how he *had* seen me. A city girl on vacation? An interference? A threat?

Sitting at the foot of the seawall, I told him what I had found, with the aid of drawings in the sand. I was still shaking—the morning wind was cold—but my mind was clear. The proof was there, so easy to spot once you began looking. Brismand would have to pay attention, now that I had found it. He would have to listen to me.

Flynn took it all with a maddening lack of surprise.

"Doesn't it matter to you? Don't you even care what's happening here?"

Flynn was watching me with a curious look. "This is a turnaround for you, isn't it? Last time I heard you'd just about washed your hands of everybody in Les Salants. Including your father."

I felt my face grow hot. "That's not true," I said. "I'm trying to help."

"I know. But you're wasting your time."

"Brismand will help me," I said doggedly. "He'll have to."

He smiled without humor. "You think so?"

"If he won't, then we'll think of something ourselves. There'll be plenty of people in the village wanting to help. Now I've got proof—"

Flynn sighed. "You can't prove anything to these people," he said patiently. "Your logic's beyond them. They'd rather just sit tight and pray and complain until the water goes over their heads. Can you really see any of them putting their differences aside to help the community? Do you think they'd listen to you if you suggested it?"

I glared at him. He was right, of course. I'd seen as much myself. "I can try," I said. "Someone has to."

He grinned. "You know what they're calling you in the village? La Poule. Always clucking over something."

La Poule. For a moment I stood silently, too angry to speak. Angry at myself, for caring. At his cheery defeatism. At their stupid, bovine indifference.

"Look on the bright side," said Flynn maliciously. "At least you've got an island name now."

I should never have spoken to him, I told myself. I didn't trust him; I didn't like him; why had I expected him to understand? As I marched across the deserted beach toward the big white house of the same name I felt alternate ripples of hot and cold move over me. Foolishly, I'd sought his approval because he was a stranger; a mainlander, a man who found solutions to technical problems. I'd wanted to impress him with my own conclusions; to prove to him that I wasn't the busybody he thought me to be. And all he'd done was laugh. Sand slewed beneath my boots as I climbed up the steps toward the esplanade; there was sand under my fingernails. I should never have talked to Flynn, I told myself. I should have gone straight to Brismand.

I found Brismand in the lobby of Les Immortelles, going through some records. He seemed delighted to see me, and for a moment my relief was such that I found myself dangerously close to tears. His arms engulfed me; his eau de cologne was overwhelming; his voice was a cheery roar. "Mado! I was just thinking about you. I bought you a present." I had dropped my bag of floaters on the tiled floor. I tried to breathe in his giant embrace. "Just a moment. I'll get it for you. I think it's your size."

For a minute I was left alone in the lobby while Brismand vanished into one of the back rooms. Then he reemerged carrying something wrapped in tissue paper. "Go on, *chérie*, open it. Red's your color. I can tell."

Mother had always assumed that, unlike Adrienne and herself, I simply wasn't interested in pretty things. I'd led her to believe it with my scornful remarks and apparent unconcern for my appearance; but the truth was that I had despised my sister and her pinups and her beauty products and her giggling girlfriends because I'd known it was pointless to take an interest. Better to pretend I didn't want those things. Better not to care. The tissue paper made small, brittle sounds beneath my fingers. For a moment I was unable to speak.

"You don't like it," said Brismand, his mustache drooping like a sad dog's.

Surprise made me inarticulate. "I do," I managed at last. "It's lovely."

He had guessed my size with perfect accuracy. And the dress was beautiful; bright red crepe de chine that gleamed in the cool morning sunshine. I saw myself wearing it in Paris, perhaps with high-heeled sandals and my hair loose. . . .

Brismand looked comically pleased with himself. "I thought it might take your mind off things. Give you a lift." His eyes went to the bag of floaters at my feet. "What's this, Little Mado? Beachcombing?"

I shook my head. "Research."

I had found it easy to tell Flynn of my conclusions. I found it much less so with Brismand, although he listened with no trace of amusement, occasionally nodding in an interested way as I outlined my findings with the aid of many gestures.

"This is Les Salants. You can see the direction of the main currents from La Jetée. This is the prevailing wind from the west. This is the Gulf Stream, here. We know La Jetée shelters the eastern side of the island, but the sandbank *here*"—punctuating the word with a tap of the finger—"diverts this current *here*, which goes past Pointe Griznoz and finishes up *here* at La Goulue."

Brismand nodded silent encouragement.

"Or at least, it did once. But now that's changed. Instead of stopping here it moves past La Goulue—and stops *here*—"

"At Les Immortelles, yes."

"That's why the *Eleanore* missed the cove and ended up on the other side of the island. That's why the mackerel have moved on!"

Again, he nodded.

"But that isn't all," I continued. "Why are things changing now? *What's* changed?" He seemed to consider that for a moment. His eyes drifted across the seafront, reflecting the sunlight. "Look." I pointed across the beach toward the new defenses. From where we were sitting we could see them clearly—the snub nose of the dike poking out toward the east; the breakwater at either end.

"You can see how it's happened. You've extended the dike just enough to make a sheltered place here. The breakwater helps keep the sand from being washed away. And the dike protects the beach and moves the current just a bit *this* way, bringing sand from la Jetée—from *our* side of the island—toward Les Immortelles."

Brismand nodded again. I told myself he couldn't have understood the full implications.

"Well don't you see what's happened?" I demanded. "We have to do something. It has to be stopped before the damage goes any further."

"Stopped?" He raised an eyebrow.

"Well yes. Les Salants—the flooding—"

Brismand put his hands on my shoulders in a sympathetic way. "Little Mado. I know you're trying to help. But Les Immortelles has to be protected. That's why the breakwater was put there in the first place. I can hardly remove it now, just because some currents have shifted. For all we know, they might have shifted anyway." He gave one of his monumental sighs. "Imagine a pair of Siamese twins," he said. "Sometimes it's necessary to separate them so that one may survive." He peered at me to make sure I understood what he was saying. "And sometimes a difficult choice has to be made."

I stared at him, feeling suddenly numb. What was he saying? That

Les Salants had to be sacrificed so that La Houssinière could survive? That what was happening was somehow inevitable?

I thought of all the years he had remained in contact with us; the chatty letters, the parcels of books, the occasional presents. Keeping his options open; staying in touch. Protecting his investment.

"You knew, didn't you?" I said slowly. "You've known this was going to happen all along. And you never said a word."

His posture, shoulders bent and hands sunk into his pockets, managed to convey his deep feeling of hurt at the cruel accusation. "Little Mado. How could you say that? It's a misfortune, certainly. But these things happen. And if I may say so, it merely goes to reinforce my concern for your father, and my firm belief that he will ultimately be happier somewhere else."

I looked at him. "You said my father was ill," I said clearly. "What's wrong with him exactly?" For an instant, I saw him hesitate. "Is it his heart?" I persisted. "His liver? His lungs?"

"Mado, I don't know the details, and frankly—"

"Is it cancer? Cirrhosis?"

"As I said, Mado I don't know the details." He was less jovial now, and there was tension around his jaw. "But I can call in my doctor whenever you like, and he'll give you his balanced, professional opinion."

My doctor. I looked down at Brismand's gift in its cocoon of tissue paper. The sunlight lapped the fiery silk. He was right, I thought; red was my color. I could leave it all in his hands, I knew. Go back to Paris—the new season at the gallery was just beginning—work on my new portfolio. Some cityscapes this time, maybe some portraits. After ten years, perhaps I was ready for a change of subject.

But I knew I wouldn't do it. Things had changed; the island had changed, and something in me with it. The nostalgia I had felt for Les Salants during all my time away had become something more visceral, something harder. And my homecoming—the illusions, the sentiment, the disappointments, the joy—I realized now that none of that had really happened. Until this moment I had not come home at all.

"I was sure I could count on you." He had taken my silence for agreement. "You know, you could move into Les Immortelles until we sort things out. I hate to think of you in that place with GrosJean. I'll give you my nicest suite. On the house."

Even now, though I was sure he was hiding the truth from me, I was conscious of an absurd feeling of gratitude. I shook it aside. "No thank you," I heard myself saying. "I'll stay at home."

16

 The week that followed brought another spate of troubled weather. The salt flats behind the village flooded, obliterating two years' reclamation work. The search for the Saint had to be postponed due to high tides, though only a handful of optimists still held out any hope of her retrieval. A second fishing boat was lost; Matthias Guénolé's *Korrigane,* the oldest working boat on the island, ran aground in high winds just off La Griznoz, and Matthias and Alain were unable to retrieve it. Even Aristide said it was a waste.

"Hundred years old, she was," mourned Capucine. "I remember her going out when I was a girl. Lovely red sails. Course, Aristide had his *Péoch ha Labour* in those days, and I remember their going out together, each one trying to get to the wind first so he'd cut the other off. That was before his son Olivier was killed, of course, and Aristide lost his leg. After that the *Péoch* went to ruin in the *étier* until one winter the tides took it, and he never even made a move to save her." She shrugged her plump shoulders. "You wouldn't have recognized him in those days, Mado. He was a different man then, in his prime. Never got over Olivier's death. Never mentions him now."

It was a stupid accident. It always is. Olivier and Aristide were investigating a wrecked trawler on La Jetée at low tide; it shifted suddenly, trapping Olivier underneath the waterline. Aristide tried to reach him in the *Péoch* but slipped between his boat and the wreck, crushing his leg. He called for help, but nobody heard. Three hours later Aristide was picked up by a passing fisherman, but by then the tide had turned and Olivier had drowned.

"Aristide heard everything," said Capucine, chasing her coffee with a splash of crème de cassis. "Said he could hear Olivier screaming for help in there, screaming and crying as the water came up."

They never recovered the body. The tide dragged the trawler down into the Nid'Poule before they could search it, and it sank too far too fast. Hilaire, the local vet, amputated Aristide's leg (there was no doctor in Les Salants, and Aristide refused to be treated by an Houssin), but he claims to feel it even now, itching and aching in the night. He puts this down to the fact that Olivier was never buried. They buried the leg, though—Aristide insisted—and you can still see the grave, at the far end of La Bouche. A wooden post marks the spot, upon which someone has written: HERE LIES OLD BASTONNET'S LEG—MARCHING AHEAD TO GLORY!! Underneath it someone has planted what looks like flowers, but which on closer examination reveals itself to be a row of potatoes. Capucine suspects a Guénolé.

"Then his other son, Philippe, ran away," she continued. "And Aristide threw himself into the court case with the Guénolés, and Désirée, with no children left of her own, looked after Xavier. Poor old Aristide was never the same after that. Not even when I told him it wasn't his leg that mattered to me." She snickered with tired lewdness. "Another café-cassis?"

I shook my head. Outside the trailer I could hear Lolo and Damien yelling at each other in the dunes.

"He was a handsome man then," remembered Capucine. "They were all of them handsome, I suppose, in those days, all my special boys. Cigarette?" She lit up deftly, dragging in the smoke with a growl of pleasure. "No? You should, you know. Calms you down."

I smiled. "I don't think so."

"Please yourself." She shrugged, her plump shoulders wriggling under the silk of her dressing gown. "I need my little vices." She jerked her head at the box of chocolate cherries standing by the window. "Pass me another, won't you, love?"

The box was new, heart-shaped, still half full.

"An admirer," she said, popping one of the sweets into her mouth. "I've still got what it takes, even at my age. Have one."

"No, I think you enjoy them more than I do," I told her.

"Sweetheart, I enjoy *everything* more than you do," said Capucine, rolling her eyes.

I laughed. "I see you're not letting the floods get you down."

"Bof." She shrugged again. "I can always move if I have to," she said. "Take a bit of doing to move this old thing after so many years, but I could manage it." She shook her head. "No, it's not me that needs to worry. As for the rest of them—"

"I know." I'd already told her about the changes at Les Immortelles.

"But it seems such a small thing," she protested. "I still don't see how a few meters of breakwater can make such a difference."

"Oh, it doesn't take much," I told her. "Divert a current by a few meters. It hardly looks like anything. And yet it can cause changes all around the island. It's like dominoes falling. And Brismand knows. He may even have planned it that way."

I told her about Brismand's Siamese twins analogy. Capucine nodded, sustaining herself with several more of the chocolate cherries as she listened. "Sweetheart, I'd believe anything of those bloody Houssins," she said comfortably. "Hm. You should try one of these. Plenty more where they came from." I shook my head impatiently. "But why should he want to buy flooded land?" went on Capucine. "It's no more use to him than it would be to us."

I had already tried to inform the Salannais, in spite of Flynn's warnings, throughout that long week. Angélo's café seemed to be the best place to spread the word, and I went there often, hoping to raise interest among the fishermen. But there were always card games, chess tournaments, football matches on satellite television, all taking precedence, and when I persisted there were blank looks, polite nods, comical glances, which froze my good intentions and left me feeling ridiculous and angry. Voices fell silent when I walked in. Backs hunched. Faces fell. I could almost hear them whispering, like boys at the arrival of a strict schoolmistress.

"Here's La Poule. Quick. Look busy."

Aristide's hostility toward me had not altered. It was he who had nicknamed me La Poule; and my efforts to educate the Salannais about the movements of the tides had merely intensified his antagonism. Now he greeted me with grim sarcasm every time I crossed his path.

"Here she is, La Poule. Got another idea to save us all, have you, heh? Going to lead us to the Promised Land? Going to make us all into millionaires?"

"Heh, it's La Poule. What's today's plan? Going to turn back the tide? Stop the rain? Raise the dead?"

His bitterness, Capucine told me, was in part due to his grandson's apparent lack of success with Mercédès Prossage, in spite of his rival's setbacks. Xavier's crippling shyness in the girl's presence seemed to be even more of a handicap than the loss of the Guénolés' livelihood, and Aristide's habit of watching Mercédès all the time and scowling if she as much as spoke to any man but Xavier did nothing to improve things. I often noticed her sitting by the side of the *étier* when the boats came in. She seemed to pay no attention to either of her young admirers, merely filing her nails or reading a magazine, clad in a variety of revealing outfits.

Ghislain and Xavier were not alone in their worship of her. I noticed with some amusement that Damien too spent an unusual amount of time by the creek, smoking cigarettes, his collar turned up against the wind. Lolo played alone in the dunes without him, looking forlorn. Mercédès, of course, completely failed to notice Damien's infatuation, or if she did, she gave no sign. Watching the children arrive from school in the little minibus from La Houssinière I saw that Damien often sat alone, keeping silent even among his friends. Several times I noticed bruises on his face.

"I think the Houssin children are giving ours a rough time at school," I remarked to Alain, that night in Angélo's. But Alain was unsympathetic. Ever since the loss of his father's *Korrigane* he had been sour and uncommunicative, ready to take offense at the slightest comment.

"The boy has to learn," he said shortly. "There's always been bullying among the kids. He'll just have to live with it, that's all, the way the rest of us did."

I said I thought that was a rather hard line to take with a boy of thirteen.

"Nearly fourteen," said Alain. "It's the way things are. Houssins and Salannais. It's a basket of crabs. It always has been. My father had to thrash me to make me go to school, I was so scared. I survived, didn't I, heh?"

"Maybe surviving isn't enough," I told him. "Perhaps we should be fighting back."

Alain smirked, not pleasantly. Behind him, Aristide looked up and made flapping movements with his arms. I felt my face grow hot but ignored him.

"You know what the Houssins are doing. You've seen the defenses at Les Immortelles. If there had been something like it at La Goulue, then perhaps—"

"Heh! That again!" snapped Aristide. "Even Rouget says it wouldn't work!"

"Yes, that again!" I was angry now, and several people looked up at the sound of my voice. "We could have been safe, if we'd done what the Houssins did. We can still be safe, as long as we do something now, before it's too late—"

"Do something? Do what? And who's going to pay for it?"

"All of us. We could pull together. We could pool our resources—"

"Rubbish! It can't be done!" The old man was standing now, looking at me over Alain's head with ferocious eyes.

"Brismand did it," I said.

"Brismand, Brismand—" He stabbed the ground with his stick. "Brismand's rich! And he's lucky!" He gave a harsh cough of laughter. "Everyone on the island knows that!"

"Brismand makes his own luck," I told him levelly. "And we could do it too. You know it, Aristide. That beach—it could have been ours. If we could find a way to reverse what's been done—"

For a moment Aristide's eyes met mine, and I thought something passed between us, something almost like understanding. Then he turned away again.

"We're Salannais," he snapped, the harshness back in his voice. "What the hell would we do with a beach?"

17

Discouraged and angry, I concentrated my energies upon finishing the repairs to the house. I had phoned my landlady in Paris to warn her that I was staying away for a few weeks longer, and transferred some funds from my savings account, and I spent a long time cleaning, repainting. GrosJean seemed to have mellowed a little, although he still hardly spoke; he would watch me in silence as I worked, sometimes helping with the dishes or holding the ladder when I painted or replaced the missing roof tiles. He tolerated the radio sometimes; conversation, rarely.

Once more I had to learn to interpret the quality of his silences, to read his gestures. As a child I'd had that skill; I picked it up again, like an almost forgotten musical instrument. The small gestures—inconspicuous to outsiders but filled with secret meanings. The throaty sounds, indicating pleasure or fatigue. The rare smile.

I realized that his silence was in fact a deep and quiet depression. It was as if my father had simply removed himself from the ordinary run of life, sinking, like a foundered boat, through deeper and deeper layers of indifference until he was almost impossible to reach. Nothing I could do for him penetrated that indifference; and his drinking sessions at Angélo's only seemed to make it worse.

"He'll come around eventually," said Toinette, when I voiced my concern. "He gets like this sometimes—for a month, six months, longer. I only wish some other people could do the same."

I had found her in her garden, collecting snails from the woodpile into a big pan; alone of all the Salannais, she seemed to prefer the bad weather.

"I'll say this for the rain," she declared, bending so low that her spine crackled. "It brings the snails out." She reached painfully behind the woodpile and pinged a snail into her pan with a grunt. "Ha! Got the little bastard." She held out the pan to show me. "Best meal in the world, that. Just crawling about, waiting to be picked up. Salt 'em for a while to get the slime out. Then put 'em in a pan with some shallots and red wine. Live forever. Tell you what"—she held out the pan to me—"take a few to your father. Bring him out of his shell, heh?" She cackled delightedly.

I only wished it could be so easy. GrosJean still went to La Bouche every day, though the flooding had barely subsided. Sometimes he stayed there until nightfall, digging runoff ditches around the waterlogged graves, or most often merely standing at the head of the creek and watching the levels rise and fall.

Wet August crashed into blustery September, and although the wind veered westward again, conditions at Les Salants did not improve. Aristide caught a bad cold collecting shellfish in the shallows off La Goulue. Toinette Prossage fell ill too, but refused to see Hilaire about it.

"I'm not having that vet telling me what to do," she wheezed irritably. "Let him see to the goats and the horses. I'm not that desperate yet."

Omer pretended to joke about it, but I could tell he was concerned. Bronchitis at ninety can be a serious matter. And the worst of the weather was still to come. Everyone knew it, and tempers were short.

La Bouche, it was felt, was the least of our problems.

"It's always been a bad spot," said Angélo, who was from Fromentine and therefore had no relatives at La Bouche. "What can you do about it, heh?"

Only the older people showed real distress at the flooded cemetery; among them Désirée Bastonnet, Aristide's wife, who visited her son's memorial with touching punctuality every Sunday after mass. Though sympathetic to Désirée's feelings, the consensus was that the living deserved priority over the dead.

Since my arrival I had spoken to Désirée only in greeting, and she had been barely polite in her haste to get away, although I thought her shyness came more from a fear of displeasing Aristide than a real reluctance to speak to me. This time she was alone; coming down the road from La Houssinière on foot, dressed in her customary black. I smiled at her as she passed me, and she greeted me with a startled look, then, with a furtive glance to either side, smiled back. Her small face bobbed beneath the black island hat. She was carrying a bunch of yellow flowers in one hand.

"Mimosa," she said, seeing me looking. "It was Olivier's favorite. We always had it on his birthday—such a cheerful little flower, with such a lovely scent." She smiled awkwardly. "Aristide says it's all nonsense, of course, and so expensive out of season. But I thought—"

"You're going to La Bouche."

Désirée nodded. "He would have been fifty-six."

Fifty-six; perhaps a grandfather. I glimpsed it in her eyes, something bright and unutterably sad; the vision of the grandchildren that might have been.

"I'm buying a plaque," she continued. "For the church in La Houssinière. BELOVED SON. LOST AT SEA. I can put the flowers under it, Père Alban says, when I'm in Les Immortelles." She gave me her sweet and painful smile. "Your father's a lucky man, Mado, whatever Aristide says," she said. "He's lucky you came home."

This was the longest speech I had ever heard from Désirée Bastonnet. It astonished me so much that I could hardly speak a word; and by the time I had decided how to answer, she had passed me by, still carrying her bunch of mimosa.

I found Xavier by the *étier*, hosing down some empty lobster pots. He looked even paler than usual, his glasses making him look like an academic who has lost his way.

"Your grandmother doesn't look well," I told him. "You should tell her to ask me for a lift in the tractor next time she wants to go into La Houssinière. She shouldn't be going there on foot, not at her age."

Xavier looked uncomfortable. "It's a chill, that's all," he said. "Spending all that time at La Bouche. She thinks that if she prays for long enough, there'll be a miracle." He shrugged. "I reckon that if the Saint was going to give us a miracle, she'd have done it by now."

On the other side of the creek I could see Ghislain and his brother by the wreck of the *Eleanore*. Predictably, Mercédès was sitting close by, filing her nails and wearing a hot-pink T-shirt bearing the words: GET IT HERE. Xavier's eyes were on her all the time he spoke.

"I've been offered a job in La Houssinière," he said. "Packing fish. Good money."

"Oh?"

He nodded. "Can't stay here forever," he said. "Got to go where the money is. Everyone knows Les Salants is finished. Might as well take what's offered before someone else does."

Over the water I heard Ghislain laughing, a little too loudly, at something Damien had said. A big string of mullet was slung negligently over the *Eleanore*'s bow.

"He buys those fish from Jojo-le-Goëland," remarked Xavier quietly. "He pretends he gets them from La Goulue. As if *she* cares how many fish he catches, anyway."

As if aware we had been discussing her, Mercédès took out a mirror and reapplied her lipstick.

"If only my grandfather would see sense," said Xavier. "The house is still worth something. The boat too. If only he wasn't so dead set against selling to Houssins—" He looked awkward then, as if aware he had given himself away.

"He's an old man," I said. "He doesn't like change."

Xavier shook his head. "He's been trying to drain La Bouche," he said, lowering his voice a little. "He thinks nobody knows."

That's how he had fallen ill, Xavier told me; a cold caught while digging trenches around his son's memorial. Apparently the old man had dug ten meters of trench all along the cemetery path before collapsing. GrosJean had found him there and had fetched Xavier. "The old idiot," he said, not without affection. "He really thought he could make a difference."

My surprise must have shown on my face, because Xavier laughed. "He's not as tough as he pretends," he said. "And he knows how Désirée feels about La Bouche."

That surprised me. I had always thought of Aristide as a patriarch who never considered anyone's feelings. Xavier continued, "If he'd been alone, he would have gone into Les Immortelles years ago, when he could have got a decent price for the house. But he wouldn't do that to my grandmother. He's responsible for her too."

I thought about that as I made my way back home. Aristide, a protective husband? Aristide, a sentimentalist? I wondered whether my father had that too, whether, beneath his passivity, there had once been fire.

During the past few days I had found Flynn more approachable, closer to the way he had been when I first met him in La Houssinière with the two sisters. Perhaps this was because of GrosJean; since my decision to refuse Brismand's offer to place my father in Les Immortelles I had sensed a lessening of the hostility toward me in Les Salants, in spite of Aristide's mockery. I realized that Flynn had been genuinely fond of my father, and felt slightly ashamed at having misjudged him. He had done a great deal of work to pay for the use of the *blockhaus;* even now he called round every few days with a fish he'd caught (or poached), or a few vegetables, or to do a job he'd promised GrosJean. I began to wonder how my father had coped at all before Flynn's arrival.

"Oh, he would have been all right," said Flynn. "He's tougher than you think." I'd found him that evening at his *blockhaus*, working on his water supply. "The sand beneath the rock filters the water," he explained. "Capillary action brings it to the surface. All I have to do then is to pump it up through this pipe."

It was a typically ingenious idea. I'd see signs of his work everywhere in the village: in the old windmill, which had been rebuilt to drain the water from the fields; in the generator in GrosJean's house; in a dozen damaged or broken things that had been fixed, polished, oiled, adapted, rebuilt, and put back into working order using little but skill and a few spare parts.

I explained about my talk with Xavier, and asked him if something similar could be built to drain water from La Bouche.

"You might be able to drain it," said Flynn, considering the suggestion, "but you couldn't keep it clear. It floods every time there's a high tide."

I thought about that. He was right; La Bouche needed something more than drainage. We needed something like the breakwater at La Houssinière—a solid barrier of rocks to protect the mouth of La Goulue and prevent the tides from attacking the creek. I said as much to Flynn.

"If the Houssins can build a dike," I said, "then so can we. We could build it from rocks taken off La Goulue. We could make it safe again."

Flynn shrugged. "Maybe. Assuming you can get the money somehow. And persuade enough people to help. And work out exactly where it has to go. A few meters wrong in either direction and the whole thing becomes a waste of time. You can't just pile a hundred tons of rock off the end of the Pointe and hope that works. You'd need an engineer."

I was not discouraged. "But it could be done?" I insisted.

"Probably not." He peered at the mechanism of the pump and made an adjustment. "It would only send your problem elsewhere. And it wouldn't reverse the erosion, either."

"No, but it might save La Bouche."

Flynn looked amused. "An old cemetery? What's the point?"

I reminded him of GrosJean. "All this has hit him hard," I said. "The

Saint, La Bouche, the *Eleanore* . . ." And, of course, I told myself silently: my own arrival and the upheavals it had brought.

"He blames me," I said at last.

"No. He doesn't."

"He dropped the Saint because of me. And now what's happened to La Bouche—"

"For God's sake, Mado. Do you always have to take responsibility? Don't you ever just let events take their course?" Flynn's voice was dry, although he was still smiling. "He doesn't blame you, Mado. He blames himself."

18

Disappointed by my failure to persuade Flynn, I went straight to La Bouche. It was low tide, and the water level was down; but even so, many graves remained submerged, and there were deep puddles across the path. The damage ran deeper close to the creek; sea mud dribbling over the broken lip of the reinforced banking.

That, I could see, was the vulnerable point, an area of no more than ten or fifteen meters in length. As the tide rushed up the creek, it spilled over, much as it did in Les Salants, before settling into the salt flats beyond. If only the banks could be raised a little, to give time for the water to clear—

Someone had already tried, using sandbags stacked up against the rim of the creek. My father or Aristide, probably. But it was clear that sandbags alone were not enough; it would take hundreds of them to provide any kind of protection. Again I considered a barrier of rocks; not at La Goulue, but here; a temporary measure, perhaps, but a means of drawing attention; alerting the Salannais to the possibilities. . . .

I thought of my father's tractor and the trailer in the abandoned boatyard. There was a lifter too, if only I could get it to work: a winch designed to move boats into position for inspection or repairs. It was slow, but I knew it could take the weight of any fishing boat, even something like Jojo's *Marie Joseph*. Using the lifter, I thought, I might even be able to drag loose rocks toward the creek to create a kind of barrier—one that might then be reinforced with dug earth and held in place with stones and sheets of tarpaulin. It might work, I told myself. In any case, it was worth a try.

It took me nearly two hours to bring the tractor and the lifter to La Bouche. By that time, it was midafternoon, but the sun was ghostly behind a haze of clouds, and the wind had shifted once again, sharply to the south. I wore my fishing boots and *vareuse*, with a knitted cap and gloves, but even so it was getting cold, and there was moisture on the wind; not rain, but the kind of spray that comes off the rising tide. I checked the sun's position; I guessed I had four or five hours. Little enough to do what needed to be done.

I worked as fast as I could. I had already located a few big loose rocks, but they were not as loose as I had first thought, and I needed to dig them clear of the dune. Water welled up around them, and I used the tractor to pull them out of their sockets. The lifter moved with exasperating slowness, maneuvering the rocks into place with its stubby crane arm. I had to move them several times before I got the position right, each time fixing the big chains into place around the rock and returning to the lifter, then lowering the arm so that the rock touched the lip of the creek in the correct position for me to remove the chains. I was soaked early on, in spite of my fishing gear, but hardly noticed it. I could see the level of the water rising; the level on the damaged banking was already perilously high, and little cat's-paws of wind ruffled the water. But the rocks were now in position, the piece of tarpaulin covering them, and all I needed to make that secure was a selection of smaller rocks and some earth to anchor the whole thing into place.

It was at this point that the lifter broke down. I'm not sure whether it was the crane arm, which had been tried beyond its capacity, or something in the engine, or maybe even the shallow water through which I had taken it, but it froze and refused to move anymore. I wasted time trying to find the cause of the fault, then, when it proved impossible, began to move the stones by hand, choosing the largest I could manage and cementing them in with spadefuls of earth. The tide was rising glee-

fully, cheered by the south wind. From a distance I could hear the breakers coming in across the flats. I continued to dig, using the tractor trailer
to bring the loose earth to the banking. I used all the tarpaulin I had
brought, using more stones to anchor it down so that the earth would
not be washed away.

I had covered less than a quarter of the necessary distance. Even so, my
makeshift defenses were holding; if only the lifter hadn't broken down—

It was getting dark now, though the clouds had dispersed a little.
Toward Les Salants the sky was red and black and portentous. I stopped
for a moment to stretch my aching back, and saw someone standing
above me on the dune, outlined against the sky.

GrosJean. I could not see his face, but I knew from his posture that
he was watching me. For a second he continued to do so, then, as I
began to move toward him, splashing clumsily through the muddy
water, he simply turned and vanished over the brow of the dune. I followed, but exhausted, too slowly, knowing that when I reached the spot,
he would be gone.

Below me, I could see the current advancing up the creek. The tide
was not yet high, but from my vantage point I could already make out
the weak spots in my defenses; the places where sly fingerlings of brown
water would work at the loose earth and stones, opening the way. The
tractor was already belly deep in water; any more, and the engine would
be flooded. I swore and ran back down toward the creek, started the tractor, stalled twice, then finally brought it around, noisy and protesting, in
a cloud of oily fumes, to a safer spot.

Damn the tide. Damn the luck. Angrily I threw a stone into the
water. It fell against the sides of the banking with an ironic splash. I
pulled up the remains of a dead azalea and threw that too. I was conscious of a sudden, apocalyptic rage ready to explode within me, and in
seconds I was reaching for any missiles that I could throw, stones and
dead wood and pieces of debris. The spade I had used was still lying on
the trailer; I grabbed it and started digging furiously at the soggy ground,
throwing up impossible showers of earth and water. My eyes were
streaming; my throat sore. For a time, I lost myself.

"Mado. Stop it. *Mado*."

I must have heard him, but I did not turn around until I felt his hand on my shoulder. My palms were blistered beneath my gloves. My breath was burning. My face was caked with mud. He was standing behind me, ankle deep in water. His usual ironic expression was absent; now he looked angry and concerned.

"For God's sake, Mado. Don't you ever give up?"

"Flynn." I stared at him blankly. "What are you doing here?"

"I was looking for GrosJean." He frowned at me. "I found something washed up off La Goulue. Something I thought he might be interested in."

"More lobsters," I suggested tartly, thinking of that first day at La Goulue.

Flynn took a deep breath. "You're as crazy as GrosJean," he said. "You'll kill yourself out here."

"Someone has to do something," I said, picking up the spade, which I had dropped when he interrupted me. "Someone has to show them."

"Show who? Show what?" He was trying to keep his temper but managed it badly; there was a dangerous light in his eyes.

"Show them how to fight back." I glared at him. "How to pull together."

"Pull together?" He was scornful. "Haven't you tried that already? Did you get anywhere?"

"You know why I didn't get anywhere," I said. "If only *you'd* got involved—they would have listened to you—"

He lowered his voice with an effort. "You don't seem to understand. I don't *want* to be involved. Why stick your hand in a basket of crabs? It won't work, and it will probably make things worse in the long run."

"If Brismand could protect Les Immortelles," I insisted between clenched teeth, "then we could do the same here. We could rebuild the old seawall, reinforce the cliffside at La Goulue—"

"Sure," said Flynn ironically. "You and two hundred tons of rock, an earthmover, a coastal engineer, and—oh, about half a million francs."

For a second I was shaken. "That much?" I said at last.

"At least."

"You seem to know a lot about it."

"Yes, well. I take notice of these things. I saw the work at Les Immortelles. It wasn't easy, I can tell you. And Brismand was building on foundations built over thirty years ago. You're talking about starting this from scratch."

"You could think of something if you wanted to," I repeated, shivering. "You understand how things work. You could find a way."

Flynn stared at the horizon as if there was something there to see. "You never give up, do you?"

Flatly: "No."

He did not look at me. Behind him the low clouds were almost the same ocher color as his hair. The salt smell from the rising tide stung my eyes.

"And you won't leave it alone until you get results?"

"No."

A pause. "Is it really worth it?" said Flynn at last.

"It is to me."

"I mean. Give them a generation and they'll all be gone. Look at them, for God's sake. Anyone with any sense left years ago. Wouldn't it be better just to let nature take its course?"

I just looked at him and said nothing.

"Communities die all the time." His voice was quiet and persuasive. "You know that. It's a part of life here. It might even be a good thing for people. Force them to think for themselves again. To build new lives for themselves. Look at them; interbreeding to death. They need new blood. They're just clinging onto nothing here."

Stubbornly: "That isn't true. They have a right. And too many of them are old. Too old to start again anywhere. Think about Matthias Guénolé or Aristide Bastonnet, or Toinette Prossage. The island is all they know. *They'd* never move to the mainland, even if their children did."

He shrugged. "There's more to the island than Les Salants."

"What? To be second-class citizens in La Houssinière? To rent a house from Claude Brismand? And where would the money come from? None of these houses is insured, you know that. They're all too close to the sea."

"There's always Les Immortelles," he reminded me gently.

"No!" I suppose I was thinking about my father. "That's not acceptable. This is *home*, it isn't perfect, it isn't easy but that's the way it is. This is home," I repeated. "And we're not going to leave."

I waited. The rich smell of the rising sea was overwhelming. I could hear the waves like the sound of blood in my head, in my veins. I watched him and waited for him to speak, feeling suddenly very calm.

He sighed. "Even if I could think of a way, you know, it might not work. It's one thing rebuilding a windmill, but this is something else. There can be no guarantees. We'd have to make them pull together. We'd need everyone in Les Salants working flat out. It would take a miracle."

That *we*. It made my cheeks flame and my heart pitch madly.

"So it can be done?" I sounded breathless, absurd. "There's a way to stop the flooding?"

"I'll need to think about it. But there is a way to make them pull together."

He was looking at me in that curious way again, as if I amused him. But now there was something else, an intent, arrested look, as if he were seeing me for the first time. I wasn't sure I liked it. "You know," he said finally, "it's not certain anyone will thank you for this. Even if it works, they might resent it. You've already got a reputation."

I knew that. "I don't care."

"Plus we'll be breaking the law," he continued. "You're supposed to apply for permission, submit documents, plans. Obviously that won't be possible."

"I told you. I don't care."

"It would take a miracle," he repeated, but I could tell he was close to laughter. His eyes, so cool a moment before, were full of lights and reflections.

"So?"

He laughed outright then, and I realized that although the Salannais often smile, snigger, or even chuckle under their breath, few of them ever laugh aloud. It sounded exotic to me, strange, a sound from a distant place.

"All right," said Flynn.

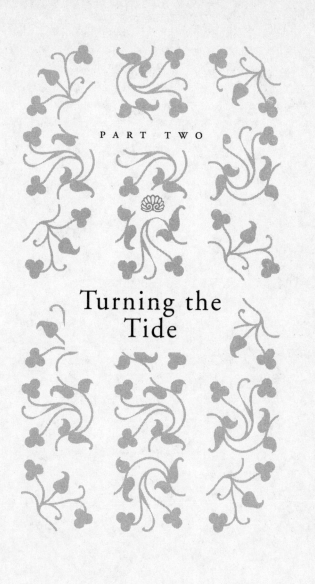

PART TWO

Turning the
Tide

1

Omer's house flooded overnight. The rains had swollen the creek, which, as high tide approached, had breached its defenses once again, and as Omer's house was the closest, it had been the first to suffer.

"Nowadays they don't even bother moving the furniture anymore," explained Toinette. "Charlotte just opens all the doors and lets the water run out the back. I'd have them here, but there's no room. And besides, that girl of theirs runs me ragged. I'm too old for girls."

Mercédès was at her most difficult. No longer content with Ghislain and Xavier, she had begun to spend time at Le Chat Noir in La Houssinière instead, queening it over a number of Houssin admirers. Xavier blamed Aristide's possessive behavior. Charlotte, who could have used the extra help, was at wits' end. Toinette predicted disaster.

"She's playing with fire," she declared. "Xavier Bastonnet's a good lad, but deep down he's as stubborn as his grandfather. She'll end up losing him—and knowing my Mercédès, that'll be the moment she realizes he was the one she wanted all along."

Certainly, if she had expected her absence to provoke a reaction, Mercédès was disappointed. Ghislain and Xavier continued to eye each other from either side of the *étier*, as if they were the lovers. Small malicious incidents occurred, for which they blamed each other—a slashed sail on the *Cécilia*, a bucketful of angleworms that mysteriously found its

way into one of Ghislain's boots—although neither could prove anything. Young Damien had disappeared from Les Salants altogether, and
now spent most of his time hanging around the esplanade, picking
fights.

I too was drawn to the place. Even out of season, there was a vitality
there, a sense of potential. Les Salants was deader than ever, stagnant. It
hurt me to look at it. Instead I went to Les Immortelles with a sketch
pad and pencils, though my fingers were clumsy, and I could not draw. I
waited; for what—for *whom*—I did not know.

❀

Flynn had given me little idea of what to expect. It was better, he said,
for me not to know. My reactions would be more spontaneous. He had
vanished from sight for several days after our conversation, and although
I knew he was planning something, he refused to tell me what it was
when I eventually tracked him down.

"You'd only disapprove." He seemed infused with energy today, his
eyes like gunpowder, gray and glittering and volatile. Behind him the
door of the *blockhaus* stood slightly ajar, and I could see something
wrapped in a sheet standing inside, something large. A spade stood
against the wall, still black with mud from the flats. Flynn saw me looking and kicked the door shut. "You're so suspicious, Mado," he complained. "I told you, I'm working on your project."

"How will I know it's started?"

"You'll know."

I glanced again at the *blockhaus* door. "You haven't stolen anything,
have you?"

"Of course not. There's nothing in there but a few bits and pieces I
found at low tide."

"Poaching again," I said with disapproval.

He grinned. "You'll never let me forget those lobsters, will you?
What's a little poaching between friends?"

"Someone's going to catch you at that one day," I told him, trying
not to smile, "and it serves you right if they shoot you."

Flynn just laughed, but the next morning I found a large gift-wrapped parcel outside the back door, tied with a scarlet ribbon.

Inside, a single lobster.

❀

It began not long after that, a hot and blustery night. On these windy nights GrosJean was often restless. He got up to check the shutters, or to sit drinking coffee in the kitchen while he listened to the sea. I wondered what he was listening for.

That night, I too was restless. The wind had risen again from the south, and I could hear it scratching at the doors and squealing at the windows like a plague of rats. Around midnight I dozed and dreamed brokenly of my mother, dreams I forgot almost instantly, but which had to do with the sound of her breathing as we lay side by side in one of a series of cheap rented rooms; her breathing, and the way it would sometimes stop for half a minute or more before wheezing back into life. . . .

At one I got up and made coffee. Through the shutters I could see the red light of the beacon on the far side of La Jetée, and beyond it, a sullen burnt orange skyline stitched with heat lightning. The sea was throaty, the wind not gale force but enough to make the cables on the moored boats sing, gusting occasional sprays of sand onto the glass. As I listened I thought I heard a single bell ring once—*boom!*—its note plaintive against the sound of the wind. It might have been my imagination, I told myself, a trick of the night, but then I heard it a second time, then a third, ringing out above wave and wind with increasing clarity.

I shivered.

The sound of the bell grew louder, brought from the Pointe by the gusting wind. It sounded eerie, unnaturally hollow, the bell of a sunken church tolling disaster. As I looked out toward the rocky Pointe I thought I could see something—a dancing, bluish glow—from the sea. It streaked upward from the ground—once, twice—breaking against the clouds in a sullen splurge of pale fire.

Suddenly I became aware that GrosJean had left his bed and was standing behind me. He was fully dressed, even to his *vareuse* and boots.

"It's all right," I said. "There's nothing to worry about. It's a storm, that's all."

My father said nothing. He stood stiffly at my side, a wooden figure, like the toys he used to make for me in the old days with the scraps from his workshop. There was no sign in his manner that he had even heard me. I could feel some strong emotion coming from him, though; something that caught at me like a cat snagging nylon. His hands were trembling.

"Everything is going to be fine," I repeated foolishly.

"La Marinette," said my father.

His voice sounded rusty and unused. For a moment the syllables chased one another in my mind, indecipherable.

"La Marinette," said GrosJean again, more insistently this time, putting one hand on my arm. His blue eyes pleaded.

"It's only the church bell," I repeated reassuringly. "I can hear it too. It's the wind bringing the sound from La Houssinière, that's all."

GrosJean shook his head impatiently. "La—Marinette," he said.

Flynn—I was sure this was his doing—had chosen an apt symbol at an apt time. But my father's reaction to the sound of the bell chilled me. There he stood, straining forward like a leashed dog, his hand gripping my arm hard enough to bruise. His face was white.

"Please, what is it?" I asked, disengaging my arm gently. "What's wrong?"

But GrosJean was once again beyond speech. Only his eyes spoke, dark with emotion, like the eyes of a saint who has spent too long in the wilderness and finally lost his mind.

"It's all right," I said again. "I'll go and see what's going on. I'll be back soon." And leaving him standing there with his face against the window, I pulled on my waterproof jacket and stepped out into the sullen night.

2

The sound of the waves was enormous, but the bell remained audible above it, a heavy, doom-ridden tolling that seemed to shiver through the ground. As I approached, another spray of light shot up from behind the dune. It scrawled across the sky, illuminating everything, then died just as quickly. I could see lights at windows, shutters opening, figures—barely recognizable in their overcoats and woollen caps—standing curiously at doors and leaning over fences. Already I could make out Omer's bulky figure under the road sign, flanked by a fluttering, dressing-gowned person who could only be Charlotte. There was Mercédès at the window in her nightdress. There were Ghislain and Alain Guénolé, with Matthias close behind. A straggle of children—Lolo and Damien among them. Lolo was wearing a red cap and leaping exuberantly in the small light from the open doorway. His shadow capered. His voice reached me thinly over the *doomdoom* of the bell.

"What the hell's going on over there?" It was Angélo, muffled to the eyes in his fishing cape and balaclava. He was carrying a flashlight in one hand, and he shone it briefly into my face, as if to check for intruders. He seemed reassured when he recognized me.

"Oh, it's you, Mado. Have you been up to the Pointe? What's going on there?"

"I don't know." The wind snatched at my voice and made it small and uncertain. "I saw the lights—"

"Heh, who could miss them?" The Guénolés had reached the dune by then, both carrying fishing lanterns and shotguns. "If some bastard's playing tricks out on the Pointe . . ." Alain made a suggestive gesture with his shotgun. "I wouldn't put it past those Bastonnets to pull a stunt like this. I'm going to the Pointe all right, to see what's going on—but I'm leaving the boy to keep watch. They must think I was born yesterday if they think I'd fall for a trick like that."

"Whoever's behind it, it isn't the Bastonnets," declared Angélo, pointing. "I can see old Aristide back there with Xavier holding his arm. Looks in a hurry too."

Sure enough the old man was hobbling along the Rue de l'Atlantique as quickly as he could, using his stick for balance on one side and his grandson's arm on the other. His long hair flapped wildly under the fisherman's cap.

"Guénolé!" he roared as soon as he came into earshot. "I should have known you bastards were behind this! What the hell do you think you're playing at, waking everyone up at this time of night?"

Matthias laughed. "Don't think you can throw sand in my eyes," he said. "Guilty conscience always crows the loudest. Don't say *you* don't know anything about this, heh? Why come out so quickly otherwise?"

"My wife's gone," said Aristide. "I heard the door slam. Out on the cliffs in this weather—at her age—she'll catch her death!" He raised his stick, his voice cracking with rage. "Can't you leave her out of this?" he shouted hoarsely. "Isn't it enough that your son—your *son*—" He lashed out at Matthias with his stick, and would have fallen over if Xavier hadn't held him up. Ghislain lifted his shotgun. Aristide cackled. "Go on then!" he yelled. "Shoot me, see if I care! Shoot an old man with only one leg, go on, it's all anyone would expect from a Guénolé, go on, I'll stand closer if you like then even you won't be able to miss—*Santa Marina*, won't that bloody bell stop ringing?" He took a shaky step forward, but Xavier held him back.

"My father says it's La Marinette," I said.

For an instant Guénolés and Bastonnets looked at me. Then Aristide shook his head. "It's not," he said. "It's just someone fooling about. No one's heard La Marinette ring since—"

Some instinct made me look back then, toward the dune. A man was standing there against the troubled sky. I recognized my father. Aristide saw him too, and bit off what he was about to say with a grunt.

"Father," I said gently. "Why don't you go home?"

But GrosJean did not move. I put my arm around him, and felt him trembling.

"Look, everyone's tired," said Alain in a softer voice. "Let's just go and see what's going on, heh? I've got an early start in the morning." Then, turning to his son with unexpected vehemence: "And you—for Christ's sake put the bloody gun away. Where d'you think you are, the Wild West?"

"It's only rock salt—" began Ghislain.

"I said put it away!"

Ghislain lowered the gun, looking sullen. Off the Pointe two more flares went off, crackling blue fire into the troubled air. I felt GrosJean flinch at the sound.

"Saint Elmo's fire," declared Angélo.

Aristide looked unconvinced. We walked on toward Pointe Griznoz. Omer and Charlotte Prossage joined us, then Hilaire with his walking stick, Toinette, and a trail of others. *Doom-doom* went the drowned bell, the blue fire crackled, and voices were high in an excitement that could quite quickly turn to anger, fear, or worse. I scanned the crowd for Flynn, but there was no sign of him anywhere. I felt a prickle of anxiety; I hoped he knew what he was doing.

I helped GrosJean up the dune while Xavier ran on ahead carrying the lantern, and Aristide followed us, dragging his wooden leg and leaning heavily on his stick. People overtook us rapidly, loping unevenly across the drifting sand. I saw Mercédès, her long hair loose and her coat buttoned over her white nightgown, and understood why Xavier had run on ahead.

"Désirée," muttered Aristide.

"It's all right," I said. "She'll be fine."

But the old man was not listening. "I heard it myself once, you know," he said, speaking almost to himself. "La Marinette. Summer of the Black Year, the day Olivier drowned. Fooled myself it was the sound of the trawler's hull then, popping and banging as the sea took it out. Later I understood. That was La Marinette I heard ringing that day. Ringing disaster, as she always does. And Alain Guénolé"—his voice changed tone abruptly—"Alain was his friend, you know. They were of an age, both of them. Went fishing together sometimes, even though we disapproved."

He was beginning to tire, still leaning heavily on his stick as we rounded the curve of the big dune. Beyond lay the rocks of Pointe Griznoz, the remaining wall of Sainte-Marine's ruined chapel standing against the sky like a megalith.

"He should have been there," continued Aristide in a hectoring tone. "They'd arranged to meet at twelve to bring in any salvage from the old ship. If he'd come he could have saved my son. *If* he'd come. But instead he was in the dunes with his girl, wasn't he? Evelyne Gaillard, as it was, Georges Gaillard's girl from La Houssinière. He lost track of time. Lost track of time!" he repeated, almost gleefully. "Fucking his brains out—and with that Houssine—while his friend—my son—"

He was panting by the time we topped the dune. A group of Salannais were already there, their faces illuminated by the light of their flashlights and lanterns. The Saint Elmo's fire—if that's what it had been—had disappeared. The bell too had ceased ringing.

"It's a sign," cried someone—I think it was Matthias Guénolé.

"It's a trick," muttered Aristide.

More people were arriving even as we watched. I guessed that half the village was here already, and by the way they were coming, there would soon be more.

The wind slashed at our faces with salt and sand. A child began to wail. Behind me, I could hear the sound of praying. Behind them Toinette was yelling something about Sainte-Marine, a prayer or a warning.

"Where's my wife?" Aristide was shouting above the noise. "What's happened to Désirée?"

"The Saint," cried Toinette. "The Saint—"

"Look!"

We looked. And there was the Saint, standing above us, in the little niche, high up against the chapel wall. A primitive figure, barely visible in the dim light, her blunt features etched in fire. The movement of the flashlights and lanterns made her shift on her impossible perch, as if she were considering flight. Her festival robes belled out around her, and on her head was Sainte-Marine's gilded crown. Beneath her, the two old nuns, Soeur Thérèse and Soeur Extase, in attitudes of devotion. Behind them I saw that something had been scratched or drawn on the bare wall of the ruined chapel; some kind of graffiti.

"How the hell did *she* get up there?" It was Alain, staring up at the teetering saint as if he couldn't believe what he was seeing.

"And what are those two magpies here for?" growled Aristide, glaring at the nuns. But then he stopped. A figure in a nightgown was kneeling on the grass next to the two sisters, hands clasped. "Désirée!" Aristide limped as fast as he could toward the kneeling figure, who, seeing him approach, turned her wide eyes toward him. Her wan face was radiant. "Oh, Aristide, she's come back!" she said. "It's a miracle—"

The old man was shaking. His mouth opened, but for a few seconds nothing came out. His voice was gruff as he held out his hand to his wife and said, "You're freezing, you crazy old trout. What d'you want to come out here for without a coat, heh? I suppose I'll have to give you mine." And, removing his fishing jacket, he slung it around her shoulders.

Désirée accepted it, almost without noticing. "I heard the Saint," she said, still smiling. "She spoke—oh, Aristide, she *spoke* to me."

Little by little, the crowd was gathering around the foot of the wall.

"My God," said Capucine, forking the sign against malchance. "Is that really the Saint up there?"

Angélo nodded. "Though God only knows how she got there—"

"Sainte-Marine!" wailed someone from below the dune. Toinette

dropped to her knees. A sigh went through the crowd—*aiiii!* The surf
beat against the ground like a heart.

"She's ill," said Aristide, trying to pull Désirée to her feet. "Somebody
help me."

"Oh, no," said Désirée. "I'm not ill. Not anymore."

"Heh! You!" Aristide addressed the two Carmelites, still standing
beneath the Saint's niche. "Are you going to help me with her, or what?"

The two nuns stared at him, unmoving. "We had a message," said
Soeur Thérèse.

"In the chapel. Like Joan of Arc."

"Nono, nothing like Joan of Arc, that was voices, *ma soeur*, not
visions, and look where it got her in the end—" I strained to understand
what they were saying above the sound of the wind.

"Marine-de-la-Mer, dressed all in white with her—"

"Crown and lantern, and a—"

"Veil over her face."

"A veil?" I thought I was beginning to understand.

The sisters nodded. "And she spoke to us, little Mado—"

"Spoke. To us."

"You're sure it was her?" I couldn't stop myself from asking the
question.

The Carmelites looked at me as if I were simple. "Well of course it
was, little Mado. Who—"

"Else could it be? She said she'd come back tonight, heh—and—"

"Here she is."

"Up there."

They spoke this last in unison, their eyes bright as birds'. Beside
them, Désirée Bastonnet listened, rapt. GrosJean, who had been listening to this without moving, looked up, his eyes filled with stars.

Aristide shook his head impatiently. "Dreams. Voices. None of that's
worth leaving a warm bed on a cold night. Come on, Désirée—"

But Désirée shook her head. "She spoke to them, Aristide," she said
in a firm voice. "She told them to come. They came here—you were

asleep—they knocked on the door—they showed me the sign on the chapel wall—"

"I knew they were behind it!" exploded Aristide furiously. "Those magpies—"

"I don't think he should call us magpies," said Soeur Extase. "They're a bad-luck bird."

"We came here," said Désirée. "And the Saint spoke to us."

Behind us, necks craned. Eyes slitted against the gritty wind. Slyly, fingers flicked out in the sign against disaster. I could hear the sound of breath being caught, kept, held close.

"What did she say?" asked Omer at last.

"She wasn't very saintly," said Soeur Thérèse.

"Nono," agreed Soeur Extase. "Not very saintly at all."

"That's because she's a Salannaise," replied Désirée. "Not a mealy-mouthed Houssine." She smiled and took Aristide's hand. "I wish you'd been there, Aristide. I wish you'd heard her speak. It's been too long since our son drowned, thirty years too long. Since then, there's been nothing but bitterness and rage. You couldn't cry—you couldn't pray—you drove our other son away with your anger and your bullying—"

"Shut up," said Aristide, his face stony.

Désirée shook her head. "Not this time," she said. "You pick fights with everyone. You even pick on Mado when she suggests that life might go on instead of stopping here. What you really want is to see everything go down with Olivier. You. Me. Xavier. Everyone gone. Everything finished."

Aristide looked at her. "Désirée, please—"

"It's a miracle, Aristide," she said. "It's as if he'd spoken to me himself. If only you'd seen it . . ." And in the rosy light she raised her face toward the Saint, and at that moment I saw something falling gently down toward her from the high dark alcove, something like scented snow. Désirée Bastonnet kneeled on Pointe Griznoz, surrounded by mimosa blossoms.

At that all eyes turned to the Saint's alcove. For a second it seemed that something moved—a jumping shadow, perhaps, cast by the lamps.

"There's someone up there!" snapped Aristide, and snatching the rifle from his grandson's hands, he took aim and shot both barrels at the Saint in her alcove. There was a loud crack, shocking in the sudden silence.

"Trust Aristide to fire at a miracle," said Toinette. "You'd fire at the Virgin of Lourdes if you could, you halfwit, wouldn't you?"

Aristide looked abashed. "I was *sure* I saw someone—"

Désirée had stood up at last, her hands still full of flowers. "I know you did."

🌸

The confusion lasted several minutes. Xavier, Désirée, Aristide, and the nuns were at the center of it, each trying to stem the wave of questions that broke upon them. People wanted to see the miraculous flowers, to hear the Saint's words, to inspect the signs on the wall of the chapel. Looking beyond the Pointe I thought for a moment I saw something bobbing against the waves far below, and in a lull of the turning tide I might even have heard a splash, like something hitting the water. But that could have been anything. The figure in the alcove—if it had been there at all—was gone.

3

 A round of drinks in Angélo's bar—reopened for this exceptional occasion—did much to calm us. Apprehensions and suspicions were forgotten, the *devinnoise* poured freely, and half an hour later the scene had swung into what was almost a carnival mood.

The children, delighted at this excuse to stay up, played at pinball in one corner of the bar. There would be no school in the morning, and that was in itself cause enough for celebration. Xavier eyed Mercédès shyly, and for the first time was eyed in return. Between drinks, Toinette cheerily insulted as many people as she could. The nuns had finally persuaded Désirée to go back to bed, but Aristide was there, looking oddly subdued. Flynn came in at the tail end of the crowd, wearing a black knitted cap that covered his hair. He winked briefly at me, then settled himself discreetly at a table behind me. GrosJean sat beside me with his *devinnoise*, smoking a Gitane, smiling incessantly. From being afraid that the strange ceremony might have distressed him in some way, I realized that for the first time since my return, my father seemed truly happy.

He remained by my side for over an hour, then left so quietly that I barely saw him go. I did not try to follow him; I didn't want to tip the delicate balance between us. But from the window I watched him as he made his way home, only the glow of his cigarette faintly visible above the dune.

The discussion went on; Matthias, sitting at the largest table with the most influential Salannais gathered around him, was utterly convinced that the appearance of Sainte-Marine had indeed been a miracle.

"What else could it be?" he demanded, sipping a third *devinnoise*. "History is filled with examples of the supernatural interceding in daily life. Why not here?"

Already there were as many variations to the story as there were witnesses. Some declared they had actully seen the Saint *fly* to her perch in the ruined tower. Others had heard ghostly music. Toinette, given pride of place alongside Matthias and Aristide and greatly enjoying the attention, sipped her drink and explained how she had been the first to notice the signs on the church wall. There was no doubt it was a miracle, she said. Who could have found the missing Saint? Who could have carried her all the way across to La Griznoz? Who could have lifted her to the niche? No one human, certainly. It simply wasn't possible.

"Plus there's the bell," declared Omer. "We all heard that. What else could it have been but La Marinette? And the marks on the chapel wall—"

Certainly, it was agreed, something supernatural had been at work. But what did it mean? Désirée had taken it as a message from her son. Aristide did not speak of this but stayed unusually thoughtful over his drink. Toinette said it meant our luck was on the turn; Matthias hoped for better fishing. Capucine left, taking Lolo with her, but she too seemed subdued, and I wondered if she was thinking of her daughter on the mainland. I tried to catch Flynn's eye, but he seemed happy to let the discussion take its course. I took my cue from him and waited.

"You're losing your touch, Rouget," Alain told him. "I thought you at least would be able to tell us how the Saint flew up La Griznoz on her own."

Flynn shrugged. "Search me. If I knew how to work miracles, I'd be off this dump and drinking champagne in Paris."

The tide had dropped, and the wind with it. The clouds were dispersing, and beyond them the sky was red raw with the approach of dawn. Someone suggested we go back to the chapel and inspect the scene in daylight. A small group volunteered; the rest made their way back home, swaying a little, across the uneven road.

But after close inspection of the marks on the chapel wall, we were still no more enlightened. They looked *scorched*, somehow, burned into the stones; but there were no letters that anyone could make out, simply some kind of primitive drawing and some numbers.

"It looks like—a sort of plan," said Omer La Patate. "Those could be dimensions written there."

"Maybe it has some religious significance," suggested Toinette. "You should ask the sisters." But the nuns had gone with Désirée, and no one wanted to be the one to miss out by fetching them.

"Perhaps Rouget knows," suggested Alain. "He's supposed to be the *intello,* isn't he, heh?"

Heads nodded in agreement. "Yes, let's have Rouget here. Come on, let him through."

Flynn took his time. He looked at the burned marks from every angle. He narrowed his eyes, squinted, tested the wind, walked out to the edge of the cliff and looked out to sea, then returned to touch the marks again with his fingertips. If I hadn't known better I would have believed he had never seen them before in his life. Everyone watched him, awed and expectant. Behind him, the dawn.

At last he looked up.

"Do you know what it means?" said Omer, unable to control his impatience any longer. "Is it from the Saint?"

Flynn nodded, and though his face remained serious, I could tell he was grinning inside.

4

Aristide, Matthias, Alain, Omer, Toinette, Xavier, and I listened in silence as Flynn explained. Then Aristide exploded.

"An ark? You're saying she wants us to build an *ark?*"

Flynn shrugged. "Not exactly. It's an artificial reef, a floating wall. Whatever you call it, you can see how it works. The sand here"—he pointed to a far point out on La Jetée—"instead of being pulled away from the coast, returns here, to La Goulue. A plug, if you like, to stop Les Salants from leaking away into the sea."

There was another long, astonished silence.

"And you think the Saint left this?" said Alain.

"Who else?" said Flynn innocently.

Matthias concurred. "She's our Saint," he said slowly. "We asked her to save us. This must be her way of doing it."

More nods. It made sense. Obviously the Saint's disappearance had been misconstrued; she'd needed the time for research.

Omer looked at Flynn. "But we don't have anything to build a wall with," he protested. "Look what I paid just to bring over the stone for the windmill, heh? Cost me a fortune."

Flynn shook his head. "We won't need any stone," he said. "This has to be something that floats. And this *isn't* a seawall. A seawall might stop erosion—for a while, anyway. But this is much better. A reef—properly positioned—builds its own defenses. Given time."

Aristide shook his head. "You'll never get it to work. Not in ten years."

But Matthias looked intrigued. "I think you could," he said slowly. "But what about materials? You can't build a reef out of spit and paper, Rouget. Even you can't do that."

Flynn thought for a moment. "Tires," he said. "Car tires. They float, don't they? You can get them for nothing at any junkyard. Some places even pay you to take them away. You ship them over, chain them together—"

"*Ship* them over?" interrupted Aristide. "What with? You'd need hundreds—maybe thousands—of tires for what you're suggesting. What—"

"There's the *Brismand 1*," suggested Omer La Patate. "Maybe we could hire it."

"Pay through the nose to an Houssin!" exploded Aristide. "Now that would be a miracle!"

Alain looked at him for a long time in silence. "Désirée was right," he said at last. "We've lost too much already. Too much of everything."

Aristide turned on his stick, but I could tell he was still listening.

"We can't get back everything we've lost," went on Alain in a low voice. "But we can make sure we don't lose anything more. We can try to make up for lost time." He was looking at Xavier as he spoke. "We should be fighting the sea, not one another. We should be thinking of our families. Dead's dead; but *everything returns*. If you let it."

Aristide looked at him without speaking. Omer, Xavier, Toinette, and the others watched expectantly. If the Guénolés and the Bastonnets accepted the plan, then everyone else would follow. Matthias looked on, inscrutable behind his chieftain's mustache. Flynn smiled. I held my breath.

Then Aristide gave the brief nod that passes as a mark of respect on the island. Matthias nodded back. They shook hands.

We toasted their decision under the stony gaze of Marine-de-la-Mer, patron saint of things lost at sea.

5

 It was morning by the time I got home. GrosJean was nowhere to be seen, and his shutters were still closed, so I assumed that he had returned to bed and followed his example. I awoke at twelve-thirty to the sound of knocking at the door, and stumbled half-asleep into the kitchen to answer it.

It was Flynn.

"Rise and shine," he urged mockingly. "This is where the hard work *really* starts. Are you ready?"

I looked briefly at myself. Barefoot, still half-dressed in last night's damp and crumpled clothes, my salty hair dried stiff as a broom. He, on the other hand, seemed as cheery as ever, his hair tied back neatly at the collar of his overcoat.

"No need to look so pleased with yourself," I said.

"Why not?" He grinned. "I think it went well. I've got Toinette going around collecting donations, plus I've commandeered some crates from the fish-packing factory to build the reef modules. Alain's getting in touch with the garage. I thought perhaps you could supply some cables and chains for the anchoring. Omer's going to make the concrete. He's still got some supplies left over from the windmill. If the weather holds out, I think we could finish by the end of the month." He paused, seeing my expression. "Now then," he said carefully, "something tells me I'm about to get my head snapped off. What is it? D'you need a coffee?"

"You've got a nerve," I told him.

His eyes widened in amusement. "What now?"

"You could at least have warned me. You and your miracles. What if it had gone wrong? What if GrosJean—"

"Now I thought you'd be pleased," said Flynn.

"It's ridiculous. Before we know it there'll be a shrine on the Pointe—people coming to see the site of the miracle—"

"Good thing for business if they did," said Flynn.

I ignored him. "It was cruel. The way they all fell for it—poor Désirée, Aristide, even my father. Such easy conquests, all of them. Desperate, superstitious people. You really made them believe in it, didn't you? And you *enjoyed* it."

"So? It worked, didn't it?" He was looking rather hurt. "That's what it is, isn't it? This has nothing to do with the Salannais and their dignity. It's because I did what you couldn't. A foreigner. And they listened to me."

I suppose it might have been true. I didn't like him any better for pointing it out.

"I notice you had no objections last night," said Flynn.

"I didn't know what you were going to do then. That bell—"

"La Marinette." He grinned. "Nice touch, I thought. A tape loop and some old speakers."

"And the Saint?" I hated to add to his conceit, but I was curious.

"I found it the day I found you at La Bouche. I was going to tell GrosJean, remember? You assumed I'd been poaching."

I did remember. The theater of it must have appealed to him; the poetry. The Saint's festival: the lanterns, the hymns; the Salannais love of the picturesque.

"I took the ceremonial robes and the crown from the vestry in La Houssinère. Père Alban nearly caught me at it, but I managed to get away in time. The nuns were a pushover."

Of course they were. It was what they had been waiting for all their lives.

"How did you get the statue up there in the first place?"

He shrugged. "I fixed the boatyard lifter. Drove up onto the wet sand at low tide and winched her into place. Once the sea was in it looked impossible. Instant miracle. Just add water."

It was obvious, really, once I thought about it. As for the rest, a bunch of flowers, a few distress flares—climbing crampons hammered into the back of the chapel wall, his canoe moored close by for a hasty exit. Everything was so easy when you had the solution. So easy it was almost an insult.

"The only tricky bit was when Aristide spotted me on the wall," he said, grinning. "Rock salt won't do much harm, but it stings. Lucky most of it missed me."

I didn't return his smile. He already looked far too pleased with himself.

He wouldn't speculate about the result, of course. It was a tricky enough business already. By rights there should have been calculations to make, complicated mathematical formulae based on the falling speed of sand grains and the angle of the shore and the phase velocity of the breakers. Most of it would have to be guesswork. A few meters in the reef's position might change everything. But it was the best we could do at such short notice.

"I'm not promising anything," warned Flynn. "It's a stopgap. Not a permanent solution."

"But if it works—"

"At worst it should slow the damage for a while."

"And at best?"

"Brismand has been harvesting sand from La Jetée. Why shouldn't we?"

"Sand from La Jetée—" I repeated.

"Certainly enough for a castle or two. Maybe more."

"More," I said greedily. "More."

6

 It must be difficult for a mainlander to understand. After all, sand is not usually a metaphor for permanence. Writing in the sand is washed away. Lovingly built castles are leveled. Sand is stubborn and elusive. It scours rock and swallows walls beneath its dunes. It is never same twice. On Le Devin, sand and salt are everything. Our food grows ready-salted in a soil barely worthy of the name: from grazing on the dunes our sheep and goats have a delicate, salty flesh. Sand makes our bricks and mortar. Sand builds our ovens and our kilns. This island has changed shape a thousand times. It staggers on the brink of the Nid'Poule, shedding pieces of itself every year. Sand restores it, washing from La Jetée, curling around the island like a mermaid's tail, moving imperceptibly from one side to the other in curds of slow foam, turning on itself, sighing, rolling over. Whatever else may change, there will always be sand.

I say this so that mainlanders will understand the excitement I felt during those few weeks and afterward. For the first week it was planning. Then work, and more work: we woke at five in the morning and finished late into the night. When the weather was fine we worked solidly into the next day; when the wind was too strong, or when it rained, we brought the business indoors—into the boat hangar, Omer's windmill, a deserted potato shed—rather than waste time.

Omer went with Alain to La Houssinière to hire the *Brismand 1*, claiming to need it for deliveries of building materials. Claude Brismand was willing: it was out of season, and barring emergencies, the ferry was only used once a week for food deliveries and collections from the fish factory. Aristide knew a tire yard on the road to Pornic, and arranged delivery to the *Brismand 1* using the same haulers who normally delivered the tins of mackerel from the plant. It was decided that Père Alban should be in charge of the accounts—he was the only person to whom neither the Bastonnets nor the Guénolés had any objection. Besides, said Aristide, even a mainlander might think twice about cheating a priest.

Financing came from the unlikeliest quarters: Toinette revealed thirteen gold Louis sovereigns hidden in a stocking under her mattress, money of which even her family knew nothing. Aristide Bastonnet donated two thousand francs of his savings. Not to be outdone, Matthias Guénolé offered two and a half thousand francs. Others gave more modest sums: a couple of hundred francs from Omer, plus five sacks of cement; five hundred from Hilaire; another five hundred from Capucine. No money from Angélo, but a promise of free beer for all workers for the duration of the project. This ensured a steady increase in the workforce, though Omer had to be reprimanded several times for spending more time in the café than he did on the modules.

I phoned my landlady in Paris, and told her that I would not be returning. She agreed to put my furniture into storage and to send the few things I might need—clothes, books, and artist's materials—by rail into Nantes. I transferred the last of my funds from my savings account and closed it. I wouldn't need an account in Les Salants.

The reef, said Flynn, had to be built in pieces. Each piece comprised 150 car tires, secured together with airplane cables—ordered from the mainland—and stacked together. There were to be twelve of these modules in all, assembled on land, then erected at low tide by La Jetée. Concrete slabs very like those used as moorings for the island's boats were to be sunk into the seabed as anchors, with more cable to secure the modules. With only the lifter from the boatyard to carry the heavy materials, the work was laborious, and several times progress had to be suspended because of failure to get hold of the right materials in time. But everyone did what he could.

Toinette brought hot drinks to the workers on the Pointe. Charlotte made sandwiches. Capucine donned overalls and a knitted cap and joined the cement-mixing contingent, shaming several of the more reluctant menfolk into action. Mercédès sat for hours on the dune, supposedly as a message bearer, though in reality she seemed more interested in watching the men at work. I drove the lifter. Omer stacked tires while Ghislain Guénolé welded them into their crates. At low tide a contingent of children, women, and older men dug deep holes to house the anchor slabs, and we used the trailer to drag the slabs out onto La Jetée at low tide, marking the site with buoys. The Bastonnet boat—the *Cécilia*—went out at high tide to monitor the drift of the modules. And throughout it all Flynn moved among us with a sheaf of papers in his hands, measuring distances, calculating angles and wind speeds, frowning over the currents that crossed and curved toward La Goulue. The Saint watched over us from her niche on Pointe Griznoz, the rock below her splattered with white candle wax. Offerings—salt, flowers, cups of wine—littered the stones at her feet. Aristide and Matthias circled each other, their truce holding, each seeking to outdo the other in the race for completion. With his wooden leg, old Bastonnet was unable to do any of the heavy work, and instead urged his luckless grandson—already twice outnumbered by the Guénolés—to greater and greater efforts.

As the job progressed, I saw my father's condition improve beyond measure. He no longer spent so long at La Bouche; instead he watched the building work, although he rarely took active part. I often saw him, a boulderlike shape against the top of the dune, stolid and unmoving. At home he smiled more often and spoke to me several times in monosyllables. I sensed a change even in the nature of his silences, and there was less of a blankness in his eyes. Sometimes he stayed up in the evenings, listening to the radio or watching me as I drew quick little sketches in my notebook. Once or twice I thought I noticed a small disarray among my drawings, as if someone had looked through them. After that I left my sketch pad where he could look at it whenever he liked, although he never did so when I was there. It was a start, I told myself. Even with GrosJean, something seemed almost ready to resurface.

And, of course, there was Flynn. It happened before I knew it, insidiously, little by little, a gradual erosion of my defenses, which found me baffled and unaware. I found myself watching him without knowing why, studying his expressions as if I were planning a portrait, looking for him in crowds. There had been little more said since the morning after the miracle, but all the same, things seemed changed between us. I thought so, anyway. It was a combination of circumstances. I noticed things I had never noticed before. We were thrown together by the task at hand; we sweated together stacking tires, were drenched together by the rising tide as we struggled to fix the modules into place. We drank together at Angélo's. And we had a secret. It linked us. It made us conspirators, almost friends.

Flynn was a good listener when it was required, and was himself a rich source of amusing anecdotes and tall stories, tales of England and India and Morocco. Much of it was nonsense, but he had traveled; knew places and people, dishes and customs, rivers and birds. Through him I too traveled the world. But I never felt that I had reached that hidden part of him, the closed section of him into which I was not invited. It should not have troubled me. If he'd asked what I wanted of him I might have been hard put to answer.

The home he had made for himself in the old *blockhaus* was comfortable, but makeshift. A large inner chamber, cleaned and whitewashed, a window facing the sea, chairs, table, bed, everything built from shoreline bric-a-brac. The effect was gaudy but somehow pleasing, like the man himself. Shells stuck into the putty around the window. Chairs made from car tires covered in sailcloth. A hammock, once an old fishing net, hung from the ceiling. Outside, the generator hummed.

"I can't believe what you've done with this place," I remarked when I saw it. "It used to be a concrete cube filled with sand."

"Well, I couldn't stay with Capucine forever," he said. "People were begining to talk." Reflectively, he traced a pattern of seashells with his foot on the concrete floor. "I made a good castaway, though, didn't I?" he remarked. "All the comforts of home."

I thought there was a wistful note in his voice as he said it. "Castaway? Is that how you see yourself?"

Flynn laughed. "Forget it."

I didn't forget it; but I knew it was impossible to make him talk when he didn't want to. His silence did not prevent me from speculating, however. Had he come to Le Devin to escape some kind of trouble with the law? It was possible; people like Flynn always end up sailing a little too close to the wind, and I had often wondered why he had ended up on Le Devin in the first place, an island so small it barely shows up on maps.

"Flynn," I said at last.

"Yes?"

"Where were you born?"

"A place like Les Salants," he said carelessly. "A little village on the Irish coast. A place with a beach, and not much else."

So he wasn't English after all. I wondered what other wrong assumptions I'd made about him. "Don't you ever go back?" I suppose I still found it difficult to imagine not caring where my own birthplace was, imagined some counterpart in him to my homing instinct.

"Go back? God, no! What's to go back to?"

I looked at him. "What's to come here for?"

"Pirate treasure," Flynn told me in a mysterious voice. "Millions of francs—a fortune—in doubloons. Once I dig it up, I'll be out of here—*Pfft!*—like that. Hello Las Vegas." He grinned hugely. And yet again I thought I heard the note of wistfulness—almost of regret—in his voice.

I glanced around the room once more, and for the first time I realized that in spite of its cheeriness there was not a single personal item to be seen; not a photograph, not a book, not a letter. He could walk out of there tomorrow, I told myself, and leave no trace of who he had been or where he was going.

7

The next couple of weeks brought higher tides and stronger winds. Three days' work was lost to the heightened weather. The moon ripened from a sliver to a slice. Full moon at the equinox brings the storms. We knew it, and we raced its turning profile without a word.

Since my visit to him at Les Immortelles, Brismand had been unusually silent. I sensed his curiosity, though; his watchfulness. He had sent me a little note with some flowers the week after my visit, and an open-ended invitation to stay at the hotel if things became too difficult in Les Salants. He seemed to know nothing about our work but assumed that I had been spending my time making the house more habitable for GrosJean. He commended my loyalty in this, while managing to convey his deep hurt and regret at my lack of trust in him. Finally, he hoped I was wearing his gift, and expressed his desire to see me in it sometime soon. In fact the red dress was lying unwrapped at the bottom of my wardrobe. I hadn't dared try it on. Besides, now that the reef was approaching completion, there was far too much work to do.

Flynn had thrown himself wholeheartedly into the project. However hard the rest of us worked, Flynn was always in the thick of things—shifting loads, running tests, studying his diagrams, haranguing recalcitrant workers. He never flagged; even when the tides began to swell almost a week early, he did not lose heart. He might have been a Salannais himself then, fighting the sea for his patch of land.

❀

"When did you get so enthusiastic about this, anyway?" I asked him late one evening as once again he stayed behind at the boat hangar to secure the couplings on the completed modules. "You once told me it was pointless."

We were alone in the hangar, the stuttering light of a single neon tube insufficient for the task in hand. The smell of grease and rubber from the tires was overwhelming.

Flynn squinted down at me from the top of the module he was checking. "Is that a complaint?"

"Of course not. I just wondered what made you change your mind."

Flynn shrugged and pushed his fringe away from his eyes. The neon illuminated him starkly, coloring his hair an impossible red and making his face even paler than usual. "You gave me an idea, that was all."

"I did?"

He nodded. I felt ridiculously pleased at the thought that I had been the catalyst. "I realized that with a little direction, GrosJean and the others could manage in Les Salants for a long time," he said, using a pair of industrial pliers to close the fastenings on a piece of airplane cable. "I just thought I'd give them a push."

Them. I noticed he never said *we*, even though he'd been accepted more readily than I had. "What about you?" I asked suddenly. "Will you stay?"

"For a while."

"And then?"

"Who knows?"

I looked at him for a moment, trying to fathom his indifference. Places, people; nothing seemed to make much of an impression on him, as if he could move through life like a stone through water, clean and untouched. He climbed down from the module, wiped the pliers clean, and put them back into the toolbox.

"You look tired."

"It's the light." He pushed his hair aside again, leaving a smudge of grease across his face. I wiped it off.

"When we first met I had you down as a bit of a layabout. I was wrong."

"Nice of you to say so."

"I never really thanked you, either. Everything you did for my father—"

He was beginning to look uncomfortable. "That was nothing. He let me live in the *blockhaus*. I owed him." There was a note of finality in his voice that suggested that any further expressions of gratitude would not be welcome. And yet for some reason I felt unwilling to let him leave.

"You don't talk much about your family," I said, pulling one end of the tarpaulin back over the completed module.

"That's because I don't think about them much."

A pause. I wondered if his parents were dead; if he mourned them; if there was anyone else. He'd mentioned a brother once, with a casual dislike that had made me think of Adrienne. Maybe he liked it this way, I thought; to have no ties, no responsibilities. To be an island.

"Why did you do it?" I repeated at last. "What made you change your mind?"

He shrugged again, looking impatient. "Who knows? It was a job; it needed doing. Because it was there, I suppose. Because I could."

Because I could. It was a phrase that would return to haunt me, much later; at that moment I took it as a sign of his affiliation to Les Salants, and I felt a sudden surge of affection for him; for his apparent indifference, for his lack of temperament, for the methodical way he replaced the tools in the box even though he was half-dead with fatigue. Rouget, who never takes sides, was on ours.

8

We finished the modules in the hangar, preparing to put them into place. The concrete anchorings were already there by La Jetée, along with six of the completed modules, and now all that was needed was to haul the remaining modules by trailer onto the flats, then by boat to the appointed positions to be chained onto the moorings. Some experimentation would then be necessary, some shortening and lengthening of cables, some shifting of the modules. It might take time to determine the best way of doing it. After that, however, said Flynn, the reef would find its own position according to the wind direction, and all we could do would be to wait and see if the experiment had succeeded.

For almost a week the sea was too high to reach La Jetée, and the wind too strong to work. It tore at the dune, lifting sheets of sand into the air. It broke shutters and latches. It brought the tide almost into the streets of Les Salants and whipped the waves at Pointe Griznoz into a mad froth. Even the *Brismand 1* did not set out to sea, and we began to wonder whether there would be enough of a lull to finish the half-assembled reef.

"It's starting early," announced Alain pessimistically. "Full moon in eight days. The weather won't lay off before then. Not now."

Flynn shook his head. "We don't need more than one good day to finish," he said. "Haul the stuff out at low tide. It's all ready and waiting. After that the reef should look after itself."

"But the tides are all wrong," protested Alain. "The water doesn't go out far enough this time of year. And the sea wind doesn't help, heh? It pushes the tide right back."

"We'll manage," declared Omer stoutly. "We're not going to give up now, when we're so close to the end."

"The work's done," agreed Xavier. "This is just the finishing off."

Matthias looked cynical. "Your *Cécilia* won't take it," he said shortly. "You saw what happened to the *Eleanore* and the *Korrigane*. These boats just aren't up to this kind of sea. We should wait for a lull."

And so we waited in Angélo's, glumly, like old mourners at a wake. A few of the older men played cards. Capucine sat in a corner with Toinette and feigned interest in a magazine. Someone put a franc into the jukebox. Angélo supplied beer, but few of us wanted to drink. Instead we watched the weather reports in gruesome fascination; cartoon thunderheads chased one another across a map of France while a cheery weather girl advised caution. Not so far away, on Île de Sein, the tide had already leveled houses. Outside the horizon growled and flashed. It was night: the tide was at its lowest. The wind smelled of gunsmoke.

Flynn came away from the window, where he had been standing. "We should start work straightaway," he said. "Soon it may be too late."

Alain looked at him. "You're not saying we should do it tonight?"

Matthias reached for his *devinnoise* and laughed, not pleasantly. "You've seen it out there, have you, Rouget?"

Flynn shrugged and said nothing.

"Well, you won't get me out there tonight," said the old man. "Out on La Jetée in the dark, with a storm coming and the tide nearly on the turn. A good way to get yourself killed, heh? Or do you think the Saint will save you?"

"I think the Saint has done all the work she's going to," said Flynn. "From now on, it's up to us. And I think if we're going to finish the job at all, then it should be now. If we don't secure those first modules soon, then we'll lose the chance."

Alain shook his head. "Only a madman would go out tonight."

Aristide gave a dirty chuckle from his corner. "Too comfortable here, are you, heh? You Guénolés were always the same. Stay in the café making plans, while real life goes on outside. I'll come," he said, standing up with difficulty. "I'll hold the lamp if I can't do anything else."

Matthias was on his feet in an instant. "You'll come with me," he flung at Alain. "I won't have a Bastonnet saying a Guénolé was afraid of a little work and water. Get ready, and quick! If only I had my *Korrigane* the job would be done in half the time, but it can't be helped. Why—"

"My *Péoch* made your *Korrigane* look like a beached whale," challenged Aristide. "I remember a time when—"

"Are we going?" interrupted Capucine, getting to her feet. "*I* remember a time when you two were good for something more than just talk!"

Aristide glanced at her and flushed beneath his mustache.

"Heh, La Puce, this is no job for you," he said gruffly. "Me and my boy—"

"It's a job for all of us," said Capucine, pulling on her *vareuse*.

We must have made a strange procession as we made our way through the shallow water toward La Jetée. I drove the lifter on its caterpillar tracks, its single headlight fanning widely across the flats, making dancing shadows of the volunteers in their waders and *vareuses*. I drove as far as the water's edge, bringing the *Cécilia* behind me on the trailer. The flat-bottomed oyster boat could float easily in the shallow water, making it simple to load from the sand. We used the lifter to position a module onto the boat. It sagged and dipped beneath the weight but bore the burden. A man positioned at each side kept the cargo stable. More volunteers helped drag and push the *Cécilia* into deeper water. Slowly, using the long oars to steer and the small engine for power, the oyster boat moved away toward La Jetée. We repeated the slow, painful process four times, and by then the tide had turned.

I saw little of the work after that. My job was to deliver the pieces of the reef, then to bring the lifter and the trailer back to shore. Farther out I could just see their light, the shape of the *Cécilia* against the livid ring of the sandbank, and in the lull between the gusts of wind I could hear raised voices.

The tide was coming in fast by now. Without a boat I could not join the rest of the volunteers, but I watched with binoculars from the dune. I knew that time was running out. On Le Devin the tide comes in quickly—not as quickly perhaps as under Mont-Saint-Michel, where the waves come in faster than a galloping horse, but certainly faster than a man can run. It's easy to become stranded, and on that stretch of water between the Pointe and La Jetée the currents are fast and dangerous.

I bit my lips. It was taking too long. There were six people out on La Jetée: the Bastonnets, the Guénolés, and Flynn. Too many, really, for a boat the size of the *Cécilia*. They would be out of their depth by now. I could see moving lights along the sandbanks, dangerously far from the shore. A prearranged signal. *Blink-blink*. Everything was going according to plan. But it was taking too long.

Aristide told me about it later: the chain controlling the placement of one of the modules had caught under the boat, immobilizing the screw. The sea was rising; a job that would have been simple in shallow water had become next to impossible. Alain and Flynn struggled in the water with the trapped chain, using the still-unfinished reef for leverage. Aristide sat hunched in the bow of the *Cécilia*, watching.

"Rouget!" he snapped as Flynn surfaced after another unsuccessful attempt to loosen the chain. Flynn looked at him inquiringly. He had shed his *vareuse* and cap for ease of movement. "It's no good," advised Aristide gruffly. "Not in this weather."

Alain looked up and caught a wave full in the face. Coughing and cursing, he went under.

"You could get trapped under there," insisted Aristide. "The wind could push *Cécilia* onto the reef and you—"

Flynn simply took a breath and went under again. Alain hauled himself up into the boat. "We'll have to get back soon, or we won't have anything but rocks left to land the boats," called Xavier above the wind.

"Where's Ghislain?" asked Alain, shaking himself like a dog.

"Over here! Everyone's back on board now—except for Rouget."

The waves were rising. A swell had begun from beyond La Jetée, and by the light of their lanterns they could see the current that crossed toward La Griznoz gaining momentum as the water rose. What had been shallows was becoming open sea, and the storm was moving closer. Even I could feel it. The air was furred with static. A lurch shook the *Cécilia*— a submerged piece of unsecured reef—and Matthias swore and sat down hard. Alain, peering into the dark water for a sign of Flynn, almost fell.

"This isn't working," he said anxiously. "If we don't get the last couple of cables into place this reef is going to pull itself to pieces."

"Rouget?" called Aristide. "Rouget, are you all right?"

"The screw's free," called Ghislain from the stern. "Rouget must have got it after all."

"Then where the hell is he?" snarled Aristide.

"Look, we have to go soon," insisted Xavier. "It's going to be bad enough getting back as it is. *Pépé*"—this to Aristide—"we really should get back now!"

"No. We'll wait."

"But *Pépé*—"

"I said we'll wait!" Aristide glanced across at Alain. "I'll not have anyone saying a Bastonnet left a friend in trouble."

Alain held his gaze for a second, then turned to coil a length of rope at his feet.

"Rouget!" called Ghislain at the top of his voice.

Flynn surfaced a second later, on the wrong side of the *Cécilia*. Xavier saw him first. "There he is!" he shouted. "Pull him in!"

He needed help. He had managed to free the chain from under the boat, but now the module needed to be fitted into place. Someone had to hold the modules together long enough for the fastenings to be snapped on, which was a dangerous job. You could easily be crushed between the modules if a strong wave brought them together. Also the reef was underwater now; a five-foot gap over black and rocking sea made it haphazard work at best.

Alain took off his *vareuse*. "I'll do it," he volunteered. Ghislain would have taken his place, but his father stopped him. "No. Let me," he said, and dropped feet first into the water. The remaining volunteers craned their necks to see, but already the *Cécilia*, freed of its restraint, was drifting away from the reef.

The tide was gaining now; only a thin strip of mud flat was left on which to land. After that there would be nothing but rocks, and with the wind behind it, the boat would be trapped between them and the oncoming storm. I heard an eerie keening sound from the watchers aboard the *Cécilia;* the lantern *blink-blinked* in alarm, and through my binoculars I watched as two figures were hauled aboard. From this distance there was no way to know whether or not all was well. No signal followed the cry.

Impatiently I watched from La Goulue as the *Cécilia* dragged shoreward. Behind it, lightning walked the skyline. The moon, only a few days off full, slid behind a wall of cloud.

"They'll not make it," commented Capucine, with an eye to the dwindling flats.

"They're not trying for La Griznoz," said Omer. "I know Aristide. He always said that if you ever get stranded you ought to make for La Goulue. It's farther, but the currents aren't as strong, and it's a safer landing when you get there."

He was right. The *Cécilia* rounded the Pointe half an hour later, rocking a little but still steady enough, and turned her nose toward La Goulue. We raced her, still not knowing whether the reef had been completed or left to the elements.

"Look! There she is!"

The *Cécilia* had passed the ring of the bay. Beyond it the waves were high and pale-crested, reflecting the lurid sky. Inside the ring it was relatively calm. A beacon shone redly, illuminating them briefly in its light. In a lull of the wind we could hear voices raised and singing.

A strange and eerie sound, there in the cold with the promise of the storm so close behind them. The light from Aristide's lantern illuminated the six people in the boat, and now that they were closer I could see individual faces, flushed with a campfire glow. There was Alain and Ghislain in their long coats and Xavier standing at the stern with Aristide Bastonnet and Matthias Guénolé sitting beside him. They made a dramatic picture, something by John Martin, perhaps, with that apocalyptic sky: the two old men with their long hair and warlike mustaches, their profiles turned toward the land in grim triumph. Only later did I realize that this was the first time I had ever seen Matthias and Aristide together side by side in that way, or heard their voices raised in song. For an hour the two enemies had become—if not friends, then something like allies.

As I waded out to meet the *Cécilia* they saw me coming. Several people jumped into the water to help bring the boat ashore. Flynn was among them. He gave me a rough hug as I dragged at *Cécilia's* bow. In spite of his exhaustion, his eyes were alight. I flung my arms around him, shivering in the cold water.

Flynn laughed. "What's this?"

"You did it then." My voice was shaking.

"Of course."

He was icy, and he smelled of wet wool. Relief made me weak; I clung to him wildly, and we almost fell together. His hair whipped at my face. His mouth tasted of salt, and was warm.

In the bow of the boat Ghislain was telling anyone who would listen how Alain and Rouget had taken turns diving under the module to fasten the last set of cables. On the cliffside a number of villagers were waiting—I recognized Angélo, Charlotte, Toinette, Désirée, and my father among them. A group of children carrying flashlights started to cheer. Someone set off a distress flare, which skittered exuberantly across the stones toward the water. Angélo shouted down, "Free *devinnoise* for all the volunteers! Drink a toast to Sainte-Marine!"

The distant cry was taken up. "Long live Les Salants!"

"Down with La Houssinière!"

"Three cheers for Rouget!"

That was Omer, pushing past me toward the boat's nose. With

Omer on one side and Alain on the other, Flynn was hoisted above the water. Ghislain and Xavier joined them. Flynn rode on their shoulders, grinning.

"The engineer!" yelled Aristide.

"We don't even know if this reef is going to work yet," said Flynn, still laughing. Thunder drowned his protests. Someone called out something cheery and defiant at the sky. As if in answer, the rain began to fall.

9

Now came a time of uncertainty, for me as much as for the rest. Exhausted by intensive weeks of building we fell into an awkward respite, tired, too anxious for celebration. Weeks drifted by in the same disquieting way. We waited.

Alain was talking about investing in another boat. The loss of the *Korrigane* had brought fishing to a standstill for the Guénolés, and although they put a brave face on their troubles, it was fairly well known in the village that the family was deeply in debt. Ghislain alone seemed optimistic; I caught sight of him several times in La Houssinière, hanging around the Chat Noir café in a variety of psychedelic T-shirts. If Mercédès was impressed, however, she gave no sign of it.

No one mentioned the reef. So far it had held, finding its own position, as Flynn had predicted, but it was felt that it might be pushing our luck to speak of it outright. Few dared to hope too much. But flooding in La Bouche was down; Les Salants was clear to the lower marshland, and as the November tides came and went, there was no further damage either to La Bouche or to La Goulue.

No one voiced their hopes too loudly. To an outsider Les Salants would have seemed quite unchanged. But Capucine got a card from her daughter on the mainland; Angélo began to repaint his bar; Omer and Charlotte salvaged the winter potatoes; and Désirée Bastonnet went to

La Houssinière and spent over an hour on the phone long-distance to her son Philippe in Marseille.

None of it was of great significance. But there was *something* in the air: a sense of possibility, the beginnings of momentum.

GrosJean too was changed. For the first time since my arrival he took an interest in the long-disused boatyard, and I came home one day to find him in his overalls, listening to the radio and sorting through a box of rusty tools. Another day he began to tidy out the spare room. Once we both went out to P'titJean's grave—the flooding had mostly subsided by then—and raked new gravel around the stone. GrosJean had brought some crocus bulbs in his pocket, and we planted them together. For a time it was almost like the old days, when I helped my father in the boatyard and Adrienne went to La Houssinière with Mother, leaving us alone. That was our time, stolen and therefore precious; and sometimes we would leave the boatyard and go fishing on La Goulue, or sail little boats down the *étier*, like the boys he should have had.

Only Flynn seemed completely unchanged. He continued his routine as if the reef had nothing to do with him. And yet, I told myself, he'd risked his life for it that night on La Jetée. I didn't understand him at all. There was an ambiguity in him, in spite of his easy ways, a place at the center of him to which I was never invited. It was unsettling, like a shadow under deep water. Nevertheless, like all deeps, it drew me.

⁂

Our tide turned on the twenty-first of December, at eight-thirty in the morning. I heard the sudden lull as the wind changed, the last and highest of the month's tides giving up finally on the reef by La Jetée. I had walked out alone to La Goulue, as I did every day, to look for signs of change. The weed-green cobbles lay uncovered in the pale dawn, with the flats just visible beyond as the sea ebbed. A few *bouchots*—the wooden stumps that marked the old oyster beds—that had survived the winter weather intact protruded from the water with their necklaces of rope trailing. As I came closer I could see the waterline littered with tide-borne debris: a piece of rope, a lobster pot, a discarded sneaker. In a pool at my feet clung a single green limpet.

It was alive. That was unusual. The troubled tides at La Goulue rarely encouraged sea creatures to settle. Urchins, sometimes. Stranded jellyfish, like plastic bags left to dry on the shore. I bent to examine the stones at my feet. Embedded in the mud, they formed a broad cobbled stretch, treacherous to walk on. But today I could see something new. Something coarser than the silt of the flats, something lighter, which sprinkled the submerged heads of the cobbles with mica dust.

Sand.

Oh, hardly enough in all to cover my palm. But it *was* sand; the pale sand of La Jetée, which gleams from the bright ring of the bay. I'd know it anywhere.

I told myself that it was nothing; a thin film washed in by the tide, that was all. It meant nothing.

It meant everything.

I scraped as much of it as I could into my hand—a pinch, just enough to close my fingers over—and ran up the cliffside path toward the old *blockhaus*. Flynn was the only person who would understand the significance of those few grains. Flynn, who was on my side. I found him half-dressed, drinking coffee, his beachcombing bag ready at the door. I thought he looked tired and unusually cheerless as I came in out of breath.

"We did it! Look!" I began, holding out my open hand.

He looked at it for a long time, then shrugged and began pulling on his boots.

"A pinch of sand," he said in a neutral voice. "You might notice if you got some in your eye."

My excitement died inside me as suddenly as if it had been doused. "But it shows it's working," I said. "It's started."

He did not smile.

"The sand proves it," I insisted. "You've turned it around. You've saved Les Salants. You've turned back the tide."

Flynn gave a vicious crack of laughter. "For God's sake, Mado!" he said. "Can't you think of anything else? Is this really all you've ever wanted, to be a part of this—this drab little circle of losers and degenerates, no money, no life, growing old, hanging on, praying to the sea and sliding closer to extinction every year—I suppose you think I should be grateful to be stuck in this place, that it's some kind of privilege—" He broke off, his anger falling away abruptly, and looked past me out of the window. The vicious look had gone as completely as if it had never been there.

I felt numb, as if he had punched me. And yet hadn't I always sensed that in him, that readiness, that threat of something about to explode? "I thought you liked it here," I said. "Among the losers and degenerates."

He shrugged, looking ashamed now. "I do," he said. "Maybe too much."

There was a silence, during which he looked past me again at the window, reflecting the dawn in his slaty eyes. Then he looked back at me, and opening my fingers, smoothed sand across my palm.

"The grains are small," he commented at last. "There's a lot of mica in there."

"So?"

"So it's light. It won't settle. A beach needs a firm base—stones, pebbles, things like that—to anchor it. Otherwise it just washes away. As this will."

"I see."

"The flooding's over. Isn't that what you wanted? Why are you pushing for more?"

I said nothing, but he saw my expression.

"It means that much to you, does it?" he said at last.

Still I said nothing.

"A beach won't make this place into La Houssinière."

"I know that."

He sighed. "Okay. I'll try."

He put his hands on my shoulders. For a moment I felt that sense of possibility intensify, like static in the air. I closed my eyes, smelling thyme on him, and old wool, and the smell of the dunes in the morning. A slightly musty smell, like the smell of the space beneath the beach huts in La Houssinière, where I used to hide and wait for my father. I saw Adrienne's face then, watching me and grinning from her broad lip-sticked mouth, and I opened my eyes in a hurry. But Flynn had already turned away.

"I have to go." He picked up his bag and began pulling on his coat.

"Why? Did you think of something?" I could still feel the ghosts of his hands on my shoulders. They were warm ghosts, and something in the pit of my stomach seemed to respond to that heat, like flowers to the sun.

"Maybe. I'll think about it." He moved quickly toward the door.

"What is it? Why the hurry?"

"I need to get to town. There's something I want to order from Pornic before the ferry leaves." He paused then and shot me his careless, sunny grin. "See you later, heh, Mado? I've got to run."

I followed him out, puzzled. His sudden shifts of mood—passing from one extreme to the other as fast as autumn weather—were nothing new. But something had troubled him, something more than my sudden arrival. There was little chance, however, that he would tell me what it was.

Suddenly, as Flynn closed the door, a small movement caught my eye, a flash of white shirt some distance across the dunes. A figure on the path. His body obscured it almost at once, and when he stepped aside the figure was gone. However, even though I saw it only for a second, and only from the back, I thought I recognized him by his walk, his bulk, and by the angle of his fisherman's cap.

It made no sense; that way led to nowhere but the dunes. But later, going back along the same path, I found the tracks of his espadrilles on the hard sand, and I was sure I'd been right. Brismand had been there before me.

10

As soon as I reached the village I knew something had happened. Something in the air: a subtle charge, a whiff of elsewhere. I had run all the way from La Goulue with my handful of sand, clutching it so hard that it tattooed my palm with mica. As I came over the big dune toward GrosJean's abandoned boatyard I felt something cold inside me clutch at my heart in the same way.

There were five people standing there in front of the house—three adults and a couple of children. Dark-complexioned, all of them, the man wearing a long, vaguely Arabic robe under a heavy winter overcoat. The children—both boys, tawny-skinned but with hair bleached almost white by the sun—looked about eight and five years old. As I watched, the man opened the gate, and the women followed him through.

One was small and drab, with a yellow burnous over her hair. She followed after the two children, fussing in a language I didn't understand.

The second woman was my sister.

"Adriennee?"

The last time I'd seen her she had been nineteen, just married, slim and pretty in the sulky, gypsyish style affected by Mercédès Prossage. She was still the same, though I thought the years had hardened her a little, making her watchful, angular. Her long hair was lank and hennaed. Her brown wrists jangled with gold bracelets. But as she turned at the sound of my voice I knew immediately who it was.

"Mado, you've grown! How did you know we were coming?" Her embrace was brief and patchouli scented. Marin too kissed me on both cheeks. He looked like a younger version of his uncle, I thought, but downy-chinned and willowy, without any of Claude's flamboyant, dangerous charm.

"I didn't know."

"Well, you know our father. . . ." She scooped up the younger of her two boys in her arms and held him out to me. The child wriggled to escape. "You haven't seen my little soldiers, have you, Mado? This is Franck. And this—this is Loïc. Say hello to your *tata* Mado, Loïc."

The boys stared at me from identical brown faces, but said nothing. The small woman in the burnous—who I took to be the nanny—clucked at them frantically in Arabic. Neither Marin nor Adrienne introduced her, and she looked startled at my greeting.

"You've done some work here," said Adrienne, glancing at the house. "The last time we came it was a disgrace. Everything falling to pieces."

"The last time?" As far as I knew, she and Marin had never returned.

But Adrienne had already opened the door into the kitchen. GrosJean was standing at the window, looking out. Behind him, the remains of the breakfast things—bread, cold coffee, an opened jar of jam—awaited my arrival like a reproach.

The children looked at him curiously. Franck whispered something to Loïc in Arabic, and both boys giggled. Adrienne went up to him. "Papa?"

GrosJean turned slowly. His eyelids drooped.

"Adrienne," he said. "Good to see you."

And then he smiled and poured himself a bowl of cold coffee from the pot on the table beside him. Adrienne showed no surprise that he had greeted her, of course. Why should she? She and Marin embraced him dutifully. The two boys hung back and giggled. The nanny bobbed and smiled, her eyes respectfully lowered. GrosJean gestured for more coffee, and I made it, glad of the excuse to busy myself. My hands were clumsy with the water, the sugar. The cups slid from between my hands like fish.

Behind me Adrienne was talking about her children. The boys were playing on the rug beside the fire.

"We named them after you, Papa," explained Adrienne. "After you and P'titJean. We christened them Jean-Franck and Jean-Loïc, but we've been shortening them for the moment, until they grow into their real names. You see, we never forgot we were Salannais."

"Heh."

Even that half-word was a kind of miracle. How many times since my return had GrosJean spoken to me directly? I turned with the coffeepot, but my father was staring at the boys as they rolled and struggled on the rug, his face rapt. Franck saw him staring and poked out his tongue. Adrienne laughed indulgently. "Little monkey."

My father chuckled.

I poured coffee for everyone. The boys ate slices of cake and stared at me with their wide brown eyes. They are almost identical but for the difference in age, with long brown-blond bangs, thin legs, and round bellies beneath their brightly colored fleeces.

"I've wanted to come home for such a long time," sighed Adrienne, sipping her coffee. "But the business, Papa, and the children—there never seemed to be the time."

GrosJean listened. He drank his coffee, his big hand almost covering the bowl. He gestured for another slice of cake. I cut it and passed it to him across the table. There was no acknowledgment. And yet while Adrienne spoke my father nodded from time to time, occasionally giving the island affirmative—*heh*—as he did. For my father, this was being garrulous. Then Marin spoke of the business in Tangiers, of antique ceramic tiles, which were the current rage in Paris, of the export possibilities, tax, the amazing cheapness of labor, the circle of French expatriates to which they belonged, of the ruthlessness of their rivals, of the clubs they frequented. The tale of their life unfolded before us like a roll of bright silk. Souks, swimming pools, beggars, spas, bridge evenings, peddlers, sweatshops. A servant for every chore. My mother would have been impressed.

"And they do welcome the work, Papa. It's the standard of living over there. So low, it's ridiculous. We give them far more than they'd earn among their own."

I glanced at the little nanny, busily wiping Franck's face with a damp cloth. I wondered whether she had family of her own, back in Morocco, whether she missed home. Franck wriggled and complained in Arabic.

Adrienne took up the tale. "Of course, there have been problems."

A fire at a warehouse, started by a discontented rival. Millions of francs lost. Pilfering and fraud by unscrupulous employees. Antiwhite graffiti on the walls of their villa. The fundamentalists were gaining power, she said, trying to make life difficult for foreigners. And then there were the children to think of. It was time to think of moving on.

"I want my boys to have the best education, Papa," she declared. "I want them to know who they are. It's worth the sacrifice to me. I only wish Maman could have seen—" She broke off to look at me. "You know what she was like," she said. "You couldn't tell her what to do. You couldn't even give her money. She was too headstrong."

I stared at my sister without smiling. I remembered how proud Mother had been of her cleaning jobs; how she used to tell me about the Hermès shirts she'd ironed and the Chanel suits she'd collected from the dry cleaners; how when she found loose change behind the cushions of the sofa she had always left it in the ashtray, because to have taken it would have been stealing.

"We helped her all we could," continued Adrienne, glancing at Gros-Jean. "You know that, don't you? We've been so worried about you, all on your own here, Papa."

He gestured imperiously: *more coffee*. I poured.

"In any case, we'll be on the island for a couple more weeks, then staying over in Nantes for a little while. To make arrangements. Marin has an uncle there, Claude's cousin Amand. He's in the antiques business too, an importer. He's going to put us up until we can find something more permanent."

Marin nodded. "It's worth it to know the boys are at a good school.

Little Jean-Franck hardly speaks any French at all. And they both need to read and write."

"What about the new baby?" She'd been pregnant when Mother died, I remembered. And yet she didn't look like someone who had just given birth. Adrienne had always been very slim; now she was even more so. I noticed the brittle, bony look of her wrists and hands; the little cups of shadow under her cheekbones.

Marin shot me an accusing look. "Adrienne had a miscarriage at three months," he said in his nasal voice. "We don't talk about it." He spoke as if I had directly contributed to this.

"I'm sorry," I mumbled.

Adrienne gave me a tight-lipped smile. "It's all right," she said. She reached out a thin brown hand and touched one of the boys' heads. "I don't know where I'd be without my angels," she said.

The boys giggled and murmured to each other in Arabic. GrosJean watched them as if he could never see enough. "We could bring them again, during the holidays," suggested Adrienne in a brighter voice. "We could come for a nice long visit."

11

They stayed for two hours. Adrienne went over the house from top to bottom, Marin inspected the derelict boatyard, and GrosJean lit a Gitane, drank coffee, and watched the boys, his butterfly-blue eyes shining.

Those boys. It should not have surprised me. Sons were what he'd dreamed of, and the arrival of Adrienne, a mother of sons, had thrown the beginnings of our comfortable coexistence into sudden disarray. GrosJean followed the boys intently; occasionally ruffling their long hair; edging them away from the open fire when their game took them too close; picking up their discarded fleeces and folding them onto a chair. I felt restless, awkward, sitting opposite the nanny with nothing to do. The handful of sand—now in my pocket—itched to get out. I would have liked to go back to La Goulue, or on the dunes where I could be alone, but the look on my father's face fascinated me. That look, which should have been for me.

At last I could no longer remain silent. "I went to La Goulue this morning."

No reaction. Franck and Loïc were play-fighting, rolling like puppies on the floor. The nanny smiled shyly, but obviously didn't understand a word.

"I thought the tide might have brought something up."

GrosJean lifted his bowl, and for a moment his face disappeared into it. A faint slurping sound emerged. He deposited the empty bowl in front of him and nudged it toward me in the gesture that meant "more."

I ignored it. "See this?" I pulled my hand from my pocket and held it out in front of him. Sand clung to the palm.

Insistently GrosJean nudged the bowl again.

"Do you know what this means?" I heard my voice rise sharply. "Do you care?"

Again, that nudge. Franck and Loïc were staring at me open-mouthed, their game forgotten. GrosJean looked past me, blank and unmovable as an Easter Island statue.

Suddenly I was angry. Everything was going wrong; first Flynn, Adrienne, and now GrosJean too. I slapped the pot back onto the table in front of him, spilling coffee onto the cloth. "You want it?" I demanded. "*You* pour it! Or if you want me to do it for you, then say so. I know you can. Go on. *Tell* me!"

Silence. GrosJean simply stared at the window again, dismissing me, dismissing everything. He might have been his old self again, all our progress forgotten. After a moment, Franck and Loïc resumed their game. The shy nanny looked at her knees. Outside I heard Adrienne's voice raised in laughter or excitement. I began to clear the breakfast things, slamming the pots into the sink. I poured the rest of the coffee away, hoping for a protest, which never came. I washed the dishes and dried them in silence. My eyes burned. There was sand among the crumbs as I swept the table clean.

12

My sister and her family boarded at Les Immortelles. They came for lunch on Christmas Day, then dropped by almost every morning for an hour or so before leaving for La Houssinière again. On New Year's Day Franck and Loïc left with new bicycles, ordered especially from the mainland by my father. I didn't inquire where he got the money to pay for them, though I knew them to be expensive.

It was on the gangplank of *Brismand 1*, as GrosJean helped the nanny carry their cases on board, that Adrienne finally took me aside. I'd been expecting it, wondering how long it would take her to get to the point.

"It's Papa," she confided. "I haven't said anything in front of the boys, but I'm very concerned."

"So am I." I kept my voice neutral.

Adrienne looked aggrieved. "I know you don't believe me, but I'm very fond of Papa," she said. "I'm worried about him living here so isolated, so dependent on a single person. I don't think it's good for him."

"Actually," I said, "he's improved."

Adrienne smiled. "No one's saying you haven't done your best," she said. "But it's too much for one person to cope with. He needs more help than you can give him."

"What kind of help?" I could hear my voice rising. "The kind he'd get at Les Immortelles? Is that what Claude Brismand says?"

My sister looked hurt. "Mado, don't be like that."

I ignored that. "Did Brismand tell you to come back?" I demanded. "Did he tell you I wasn't cooperating?"

"I wanted Papa to see the boys."

"The boys?"

"Yes. To show him life goes on. It doesn't do him any good, living here when he could be near his family. It's selfish—and dangerous—of you to encourage him like this."

I stared at her, astonished and stricken. *Had* I been selfish? Had I been so wrapped up in my plans and imaginings that I had overlooked my father's needs? Could it really be that GrosJean didn't need the reef, or the beach, or any of the things I had done for him—that all he had ever wanted, in fact, was the grandsons Adrienne had brought with her?

"This is his home," I said at last. "And I'm a part of his family."

"Don't be naive," said my sister, and for a moment she was the old Adrienne completely, the scornful elder sister, sitting at the *terrasse* of the Houssin café and laughing at my boyish hair and cast-off clothes. "Maybe *you* think it's romantic living out here in the middle of nowhere. But it's the last thing poor Papa needs. Look at the house: everything put together out of odds and ends; there isn't even a proper bathroom. And what if he falls ill? There's no one to help him but that old vet, what's-his-name. What if he needs to go to a hospital?"

"I'm not forcing him to stay," I said, hating the defensive note in my voice. "I've been looking after him, that's all."

Adrienne shrugged. She might as well have said it aloud: *The way you looked after Mother.*

"At least I tried," I said. "What did you ever do for either of them? Living in your ivory tower. How do you know what it was like for us, all those years?"

I don't know why Mother had always insisted that *I* was the most like GrosJean. Adrienne merely smiled at me in that impenetrable way, serene as a photograph and as silent. Her smug silences had always enraged me. Anger crawled over me like an army of ants. "How many times did you visit us? How many times did you promise to call? I phoned you, Adrienne, I told you Mother was dying—"

Her stricken look silenced me. I felt my face grow red. "Look, Adrienne, I'm sorry, but—"

"Sorry?" Her voice was shrill. "How can you know what it was like for me? I lost my baby—my father's *grandchild*—and you think you can just say sorry?"

I tried to touch her arm, but she pulled away with a nervous, hysterical gesture that somehow reminded me of Mother. She glared at me, her eyes like knives. "Shall I tell you why we didn't visit, Mado? Shall I tell you why we stayed at Les Immortelles instead of at Papa's house, where we could have seen him every day?" Her voice was a kite now, light and brittle and soaring.

I shook my head. "Please, Adrienne—"

"It was *you*, Mado! Because *you* were there!" She was half-crying now, breathless with rage, though I thought I sensed a trace of self-satisfaction too; like Mother, Adrienne had always enjoyed histrionics. "Always nagging! Always bullying!" She gave a loud sob. "You bullied Maman, you were always trying to get her to move from Paris, the place she *loved*—and now you're doing the same to poor Papa! You're obsessed with this island, Mado, that's what it is, and you just can't understand when other people don't want what you want!" Adrienne wiped her face with her sleeve. "And if we don't come back, Mado, it won't be because we don't want to see Papa, it'll be because I can't face being near *you!*"

The ferry's whistle blew. In the silence that followed I heard a small shuffling noise behind me and turned around. It was GrosJean, standing silently on the gangplank. I held out my hands.

"Father—"

But he had already turned away.

13

January brought more sand at La Goulue. By midmonth it was easily visible; a thin fringe of white against the rocks, nothing so ambitious as a beach, but sand nevertheless, speckled sand flecked with mica flakes, which dried to powder at low tide.

Flynn kept his word. With the help of Damien and Lolo, he brought sacks of gritty rubble from the dunes and dumped them onto the mossy pebbles at the foot of the cliff. Tufts of coarse *oyat* grass were planted in this gray dirt to keep the sand from being washed away, and seaweed was spread out between the layers of rubble, anchored down with stakes and lengths of discarded fishing net. I watched the progress with curiosity, and a reluctant hopefulness. La Goulue, with its accumulation of rubbish, earth, seaweed, and netting looked even less like a beach than it had before.

"This is only the foundation," Flynn reassured me. "You don't want your sand to blow away, do you?"

He had been oddly diffident during Adrienne's stay, only calling once or twice instead of almost every day. I missed him—more so given GrosJean's behavior—and I began to understand how deeply his presence had affected all of us over the past weeks; how much he had colored us all.

I had told him about my quarrel with Adrienne. He listened with no trace of his habitual levity, a line between his eyes. "I know she's my sister," I said, "and I know she's had a tough time, but—"

"You can't choose your family," said Flynn. He had met Adrienne only once, in passing, during her stay, and I remembered he had been unusually silent. "There's no reason you and she should get along just because you're sisters."

I sighed. If only I could have made Mother understand that. "Gros-Jean wanted a boy," I said, picking a stem of dune grass. "He wasn't ready for two daughters." Now, I supposed, Adrienne had made up for that. All my efforts—the short hair, the boy's clothes, the hours in my father's workshop just watching him, the fishing, the scraps of time—all eclipsed, all stripped of meaning. Flynn must have seen something in my face, because he stopped working and looked at me with an odd expression.

"You're not here to live up to GrosJean's expectations, or anyone else's. If he can't see that what he's got is worth a thousand times more than—" He broke off, shrugging. "You have nothing to prove," he said with unusual gruffness. "He's lucky to have you."

It was what Brismand had said. But my sister had accused me of self-ishness, of using my father. I wondered now whether she had been right, whether my presence might not be doing more harm than good. What if all he wanted was to be near Adrienne and see the boys every day?

"You've got a brother, haven't you?"

"A half-brother." He was pinning down a piece of netting that had come loose from the dune. I tried to imagine Flynn as someone's brother; to me, he seemed the epitome of the only child.

"You don't like him much."

"He should have been an only child."

I thought of myself and Adrienne. She should have been an only daughter. Everything I tried to do, my sister had done it first, and done it better.

Flynn was inspecting the new growth of *oyat* grass on the dune. To anyone else he might have looked expressionless, but I could see the strain around his mouth. I suppressed the urge to ask him what had happened to his brother; to his mother. It had hurt him, whatever it was. Maybe almost as much as Adrienne and I had hurt each other. I felt a tremor run through me, something deeper than tenderness. I reached down and touched his hair.

"So we do have something in common," I said lightly. "Tragic families."

"No way," said Flynn, looking up at me with his sudden brash and brilliant smile. "You came back. I escaped."

In Les Salants few people seemed particularly interested in the growth of the beach. As winter drew to its end they were too busy noticing other things; how the changed current was bringing back the mullet, even more numerous than before; how nets were more often full than empty; how lobsters and sea spiders and the fat *dormeur* crabs loved the sheltered bay and virtually fought to crawl into the pots. The winter tides had brought no floods, and even Omer's flooded back fields had begun to recover, after almost three years underwater. The Guénolés finally put into operation their plan to buy a new boat. The *Eleanore 2* was built on the mainland, at a boatyard near Pornic, and for several weeks we heard nothing from them but reports on her progress. She was to be an island boat, like her predecessor; fast and high-keeled, with two masts and the quadrangular sail of the islands. Alain did not reveal how much she would cost, but with the changing currents he seemed optimistic that she would quickly earn her way. Ghislain seemed less enthusiastic— apparently they'd had to drag him away from the displays of speedboats and Zodiacs—but remained cheered by the prospect of money to be made. I hoped this new boat would have no nostalgic associations for my father, in spite of its name; secretly I had been hoping that the Guénolés would choose something different. GrosJean, however, seemed unmoved by reports of the *Eleanore 2*'s progress, and I began to think I was being too sensitive about the matter.

The reef had gained a name of its own: Le Bouch'ou, and two lighted beacons, one at either end, to show its position at night.

The Bastonnets, still flying the white flag with the Guénolés but watching their backs, made record catches. Aristide announced triumphantly that Xavier had taken sixteen lobsters that week and sold them to an Houssin—the mayor's cousin and owner of La Marée, a seafood restaurant by the beach—for fifty francs apiece.

"They'll be expecting the big rush of holiday people by July," he told me with grim satisfaction. "Soon that restaurant of his will be heaving. He can shift half a dozen lobsters in one evening during the season—thinks he can buy them up now, put them in his *vivier* and just wait until the prices rocket." Aristide chuckled. "Well, two can play that game. I'm having the boy build one of our own, up there on the creek. It's cheaper than tanks, and with the right kind of mesh the lobsters won't get out. We can keep them in there alive, even the little ones—that way we don't have to throw any of them back—and sell them at top prices when the time comes. Peg them so they don't fight. The tide brings their food right up the *étier* for us. Good thinking, heh?" The old man rubbed his hands together.

"It is," I said in surprise. "Why, this is downright enterprising of you, Monsieur Bastonnet."

"Isn't it, heh?" Aristide looked pleased. "Thought it was time we started to think for ourselves for a change. Make a little money for the boy. You can't expect a boy like that to live on nothing, especially if he's thinking about settling down."

I thought of Mercédès, and smiled.

"And that isn't the only thing," said Aristide. "You'll not guess who's going into business with me when his boat's ready." I looked at him expectantly. "Matthias Guénolé." He grinned at my surprise, his old blue eyes gleaming. "I thought that might give you a start," he said, reaching for a cigarette and lighting it. "I'll bet there aren't many people on the island who'd have thought they'd see Bastonnets and Guénolés working together in my lifetime. But this is business. Working together—two boats, five men—we could clean up on mullet, oysters, and lobsters. Make a fortune. Working alone all we do is steal the wind from one another, and give a good laugh to the Houssins at our expense." Aristide took a drag from his cigarette and leaned back, shifting his wooden leg to a more comfortable position. "Surprised you, heh?" he said.

More than that. To abandon the feud the families had waged for years, as well as radically altering the way he did business—six months ago I would not have believed either of these things possible.

That, if anything, was what finally covinced me that the Bastonnets had had nothing to do with the loss of the *Eleanore*. Toinette had suggested it; Flynn had reinforced my suspicions—though I had never for a moment believed that GrosJean could have colluded in any way—and it had remained an uncertain area in my mind ever since. But now I could put it to rest at last. I did so with pleasure and a sense of deep relief. Whatever had caused the loss of the *Eleanore*, it had not been Aristide. I felt a sudden liking for the gruff old man, and slapped him affectionately on the shoulder. "You deserve a *devinnoise*," I told him. "I'll buy."

Aristide stubbed his cigarette out in the ashtray. "I'll not say no."

❧

My sister's visit over Christmas had caused some excitement. Not least because of the boys, who had been duly admired from Pointe Griznoz to Les Immortelles, but mostly because it gave hope to those—like Désirée and Capucine—who were still waiting for long-lost relatives to make contact. Whereas my own return had brought suspicion, hers— coming when it did, with her boys and the promise of better things— brought only approval. Even her marriage to an Houssin was approved; Marin Brismand was rich—at least his uncle was, and in the absence of any other family, Marin was set to inherit everything. It was generally held that Adrienne had done very well for herself.

"You could do worse than follow her example," advised Capucine, over cakes in her trailer. "Do you good to settle down. That's what keeps the island going, marriage and children, never mind fishing and trade."

I shrugged. Though I had not heard from my sister again, ever since the conversation on the gangplank of the *Brismand 1* I had felt uneasy, questioning my own motives and hers. Was I using my father as an excuse to hide myself away? Was Adrienne's way the best?

"You're a good girl," said Capucine, lolling comfortably on her chair. "You've already helped your father a lot. Les Salants too. Now it's time to do something for yourself." She sat up and looked at me critically. "You're a nice-looking girl, Mado. I've seen the way Ghislain Guénolé looks at you, and some of the others—" I tried to interrupt her, but she flapped her hands at me in good-humored irritation. "You don't snap at people the way you used to," she continued. "You don't walk around with your chin stuck out, like you expected someone to pick a fight. People don't call you La Poule anymore."

That was true enough, even I'd noticed that.

"Plus, you've started your paintings again. Haven't you?"

I looked at the crescents of ocher paint beneath my fingernails, feeling absurdly guilty. It wasn't a great matter, after all; a few bits and pieces, a half-finished larger canvas in my room. Flynn is an unexpectedly good subject to paint. I find I remember his features better than others. Of course that was natural; I had spent rather a long time in his company.

Capucine smiled. "Well, it's doing you good," she declared. "Think of yourself, for a change. Stop carrying the whole world on your shoulders. The tide turns without your permission."

14

By February the changes at La Goulue were beginning to be visible to all of us. The diverted current from La Jetée continued to bring sand from there, a gentle process that only the children and I followed with any degree of interest. A thin layer of it now covered much of the rubble and grit that Flynn had brought in from the dunes, and the *oyat* and rabbit-tail grasses he had planted were doing a good job of keeping the sand from being blown or washed away. One morning I went down to La Goulue to find Lolo and Damien Guénolé trying gamely to build a castle. Not an easy business; the sand layer was too thin, with nothing but mud below it, but with a little ingenuity it could be done. They had built a kind of dam from driftwood and were pushing wet sand from it through a channel dug into the mud.

Lolo grinned at me. "We're going to have a proper beach," he said. "Bringing sand from the dunes and everything. Rouget said so."

I smiled. "You'd like that, would you? A beach?"

The children nodded. "There's nowhere to play, 'cept here," said Lolo. "Even the *étier*'s out of bounds now, with the new lobster thing."

Damien kicked at a stone. "That wasn't my dad's idea. It was those Bastonnets." He gave me a challenging look from beneath his dark lashes. "My dad might have forgotten what they did to our family, but I haven't."

Lolo made a face. "You don't care about that," she said. "You're just jealous because Xavier's going out with Mercédès."

"She is not!"

Certainly, it was not official. Mercédès still spent much of her time in La Houssinière, where, as she said, the action was. But Xavier had been seen with her at the cinema and in the Chat Noir, and Aristide was decidedly more cheerful, and spoke freely of investments, and of building for the future.

The dour Guénolés too were unusually optimistic. At the end of the month, the long-awaited *Eleanore 2* was finally completed and ready for collection. Alain, Matthias, and Ghislain went to Pornic by ferry to collect her, planning to sail her back to Les Salants from there. I went along for the ride, and to collect a trunk of my things—mostly art materials and clothes—which my landlady had sent me from Paris. I told myself I was curious to see the new boat; in fact, I had been feeling rather oppressed in Les Salants. Since Adrienne's departure GrosJean had reverted to an earlier, less responsive self; the weather had been dull; even the prospect of sand at La Goulue had lost some of its novelty. I needed a change of scene.

Alain had chosen the Pornic boatyard because it was closest to Le Devin. He knew the owner slightly, who was a distant relative of Jojo-le-Goëland, though as a mainlander he was not included in the Houssin-Salannais feud. His place was by the sea, next to the little marina, and as we entered, I was struck by the unforgettable, nostalgic smell of a working boatyard: the paint, the sawdust, the reek of burned plastic and welding and clinkers soaked in chemicals.

It was a family place; nowhere near as small as GrosJean's business had been, but small enough for Alain not to be overwhelmed. As he and Matthias went off with the owner to discuss payment, Ghislain and I remained in the boatyard, looking at the dry dock and the jobs in progress. The *Eleanore 2* was easy to spot, the only wooden boat in a line of plastic-hulled craft over which Ghislain lingered enviously. She was slightly bigger than the original *Eleanore;* but Alain had had her built in the same style, and though this builder lacked my father's careful crafts-manship, I could see that she was a fine boat. I looked all around her while Ghislain wandered off toward the water, and I was just looking underneath the *Eleanore 2* to inspect the keel when he came running back, a little breathless, his face alight.

"Over there!" he said, pointing behind him into the main storage area. Here parts were stored in the secure hangar, as well as lifting and welding machinery. Ghislain pulled at my hand. "Come and see!"

Rounding the corner of the hangar I could see that something large was under construction. It was not half-finished, but even so I could tell that it was the largest thing by far in the yard. The smell of oil and metal was sharp in the air.

"What d'you think it is? A ferry? A trawler?"

It was about twenty meters long, with two decks, surrounded by scaffolding. A blunt nose, a square stern; when I was a child GrosJean had called boats like this "metal pigs" and had despised them thoroughly. The small ferry we had taken to Pornic was just such a metal pig: square, ugly, and very functional.

"It's a ferry." Ghislain grinned at me, pleased with himself. "Want to know how I know? Look around the other side."

The other side was incomplete; large panels of metal had been riveted together to form the outer hull, but many of them were missing, like an incomplete and very dull jigsaw. The panels were dark gray, but on one of them someone had written the metal pig's name in yellow chalk; the *Brismand 2*.

I looked at it for a moment without speaking.

"Well?" said Ghislain impatiently. "What d'you think?"

I frowned. "I think if he can afford this," I said, "then Brismand must be doing even better than we thought."

15

 I returned alone, having detoured via Nantes to pick up my trunk. Perhaps it was because it had been some time since I really gave any attention to La Houssinière, but when I looked around I thought there seemed to be something unusual about the place. I couldn't quite put my finger on what it was, but the town seemed unfamiliar, oddly out of tune with itself. The streets shone with a different light. The air smelled different, more salty somehow, like La Goulue at low tide. People stared at me as I walked by, some nodding briefly in recognition, some averting their eyes, as if too busy to talk.

Winter on the island is always the dead season. Many of the younger people move to the mainland out of season to find work, only returning in June. But this year La Houssinière looked different, its sleep somehow unhealthy, closer to death. Most of the shops on the street were closed and shuttered. The Rue des Immortelles was deserted. The tide was low, the flats white with gulls. Whereas on a day like this there would normally have been dozens of fishermen digging for cockles and clams, a single figure with a long-handled net stood at the water's edge, poking aimlessly at a clump of seaweed.

It was Jojo-le-Goëland. I climbed over the wall and made my way across the *grève*. There was a brisk wind blowing across the flats that blurred my hair around my face and made me shiver. The ground was pebbly, and walking was painful. I wished that, like Jojo, I was wearing boots instead of thin-soled espadrilles.

From across the sand I could see Les Immortelles, a white cube on the seawall a few hundred meters away. Below it, the slim wedge of the beach. More rocks farther in. I hadn't remembered so many rocks, but from where I was standing it looked different, smaller and more remote, the beach foreshortened by the angle so that it seemed barely a beach at all, the breakwater standing out starkly against the sand. A lettered sign, too far away to read, stood under the wall.

"Hello, Jojo."

He turned at the sound of my voice, net in hand. At his feet his wooden collecting bucket contained only a clump of weed and a few angleworms. "Oh. It's you." He gave me a toothy grin around the wet stub of a cigarette.

"How's the fishing?"

"All right, I suppose. What are you doing so far out, heh? Digging worms?"

"I just wanted a walk. It's pretty out here, isn't it?"

"Heh."

I could feel him watching me as I made my way across the flats toward Les Immortelles. The wind was mild, the shore pebbly underfoot. As I came closer to the beach I found it more stony than I had remembered, and in some places I could see the exposed patches of a cobbled area where the sand had been swept away, revealing the foundations of an ancient dike.

Les Immortelles had lost some sand.

This became more apparent to me as I reached the tide line: here I could see how the wooden posts of the beach huts had been left bare, standing out like bad teeth. How much sand? I couldn't begin to guess.

❀

"Well, hello again!"

The voice came from behind me. In spite of his bulk his footsteps were barely audible on the sand. I turned, hoping he hadn't seen me flinch.

"Monsieur Brismand?"

Brismand tutted and lifted a finger in reproach. "Claude, please." He smiled, apparently delighted to see me. "Enjoying the view?"

That charm of his. I found myself responding to it without even meaning to. "It's very nice. Your residents must appreciate it."

Brismand sighed. "Inasmuch as they appreciate anything, I'm sure they do. Sadly, heh, we all have to age. Georgette Loyon grows especially frail. Still, one does one's best. After all, she is over eighty." He clapped an arm over my shoulders. "How's GrosJean?"

I knew I would have to be careful. "He's fine. You wouldn't believe the improvement."

"That's not what your sister says."

I tried to smile. "Adrienne hasn't been living here. I don't see how she can know."

Brismand nodded sympathetically. "Of course. It's so easy to be judgemental, isn't it? But unless one is willing to stay there indefinitely—"

I did not rise to the bait. Instead I looked away toward the deserted esplanade.

"Things look a little slow at moment, don't you think?"

"Well, it's a slow time of year. I have to admit I like the slow times better nowadays; I'm getting too old for the tourist business. I should be planning my retirement in a few years' time." He smiled benevolently. "But what about you? I've been hearing all kinds of things about Les Salants recently."

I shrugged. "We manage."

His eyes glittered. "I hear you've been doing more than that, though. Real enterprise in Les Salants, for a change. A lobster vivarium down on the old *étier*. Any more of this, and I might begin to think you were aiming at my own trade." He chuckled. "Your sister's looking well," he remarked. "Life off the island must be good for her."

Silence. Across the sand, a string of gulls rose from the tide line, squalling.

"And Marin, and the little ones! GrosJean must have been happy to see his grandchildren, after all this time."

Silence.

"I sometimes wonder what kind of a grandfather I would have made." He gave a giant sigh. "But I never really got the chance to be a father."

This talk of Adrienne and her children was making me uneasy, and I knew Brismand sensed it. "I hear you're building a new ferry," I said abruptly.

For a moment I saw real surprise in his face. "Really? Who said that?"

"Someone in the village," I said, not wanting to reveal my visit to the boatyard. "Is it true?"

Brismand lit a Gitane. "I've considered it," he said. "I like the idea. But it's hardly practical, is it? There's little enough space here as it is." He had recovered completely, his slate-colored eyes bright and amused. "I wouldn't encourage these rumors," he advised me. "You'll only cause disappointment."

He left shortly afterward, with a gleam of a smile and a hearty exhortation to come and see him more often. I wondered whether I had imagined that moment of discomfort, of genuine surprise. If he was building a ferry, I wondered, why would he keep it secret?

I was halfway back to Les Salants when I realized that neither he nor Jojo had made any mention of the eroded beach. Perhaps it was natural, after all, I told myself. Perhaps this always happened in winter.

Perhaps not. Perhaps we had *made* it happen.

The thought was nauseating, disquieting. There were no certainties in any case; my hours of study, my trials with the floaters, the days spent watching Les Immortelles meant nothing. Even the Bouch'ou, my mind protested, might have nothing to do with this. It takes more than a little amateur engineering to reshape a shoreline. More than a little envy to steal a beach.

16

Flynn was dismissive of my suspicions. "What else could it be but the tide?" he asked as we followed the coast from Pointe Griznoz. The wind was coming smack from the west, the way I like it, with a thousand kilometers of open sea as its runway. As we climbed down the coastal path I found I could already see the pale crescent of sand from the top of the little cliff, thirty meters long and maybe five across.

"There's a lot of new sand here," I shouted over the wind.

Flynn bent down to inspect a piece of driftwood sticking up between two rocks. "So? That's good, isn't it?"

But as I left the path and went down onto the shore I was amazed to notice how the dry sand gave under my boots, as if there were not a skim of sand over packed stones, but a generous layer. I dug a hand in and found a depth of three or four centimeters—not a great deal, maybe, for a long-established beach, but in our circumstances almost miraculous. It had been raked too, from shore to dune, like a neat seedbed. Someone had been hard at work.

"What's the problem?" asked Flynn, seeing my surprise. "It's just happened a little faster than we said, that's all. Isn't this what you wanted?"

Of course it was. But I wanted to know *how*.

"You're too suspicious," said Flynn. "You need to relax a little. Live for the moment. Smell the seaweed." He laughed and gestured with the piece of driftwood, looking so like an absurd magician with his wild hair and flapping black coat that I felt a rush of affection for him, and found myself laughing too.

"Look at it," he shouted above the sound of the wind, and pulled me by the sleeve so that I was facing the bay, looking out toward the pale unbroken horizon. "A thousand miles of ocean; nothing else between here and America. And we beat it, Mado. Isn't that fine? Isn't that worth just a little celebration?"

His enthusiasm was catching. I nodded, still breathless from laughter and the wind. His arm was around my shoulder now; his coat flapped against my thigh. The smell of the sea, that ozone smell spattered with salt mist, was overwhelming. The joyous wind swelled my lungs so that I felt like shouting. Instead I turned impulsively toward Flynn and kissed him; a long, breathless kiss that tasted of salt, my mouth clinging to his like a limpet. I was still laughing, although I no longer knew why. For a moment I was lost; I was someone else. My mouth burned; my skin prickled. I felt static in my hair. This is what it feels like, I thought, a second before being hit by lightning.

A wave rushed up between us, soaking me to the knees, and I sprang back, gasping with surprise and cold. Flynn was looking at me curiously, apparently unaware of his soaked boots. For the first time in months I felt uncomfortable in his presence, as if the ground between us had shifted, revealing something I hadn't even known about until this moment.

Then, quite suddenly, he turned away.

It was as if he'd struck me. Heat crawled all over me in a rush of embarrassment and mortification. How could I have been such a fool? How could I have misread him so badly?

"I'm sorry," I said, trying to laugh, though my face was burning. "I don't know what came over me just now."

Flynn glanced back. The light seemed quite gone from his eyes. "It's okay," he said in a neutral voice. "Everything's fine. We'll just forget it, right?"

I nodded, wishing I could shrivel up and blow away.

Flynn seemed to relax a little. He gave me a brief, one-armed hug, the way my father sometimes did when I'd pleased him. "Right," he said again. And the conversation returned to safer ground.

❀

As spring approached, I took to watching the beach every day again, to check for signs of damage or change. I was especially concerned as March began; the wind was veering south again, with the promise of bad tides to come. But the bad tides caused little harm in Les Salants. The creek held fast, La Bouche stayed dry, boats were for the most part stored securely away. Even La Goulue seemed unaffected, except for the mounds of unappealing black weed washed up by the tides, which Omer removed every morning to use on his fields. The Bouch'ou was stable. During a lull between high tides, Flynn went out to La Jetée in his boat and declared that the reef had suffered no serious damage. Our luck had held.

Little by little, optimism continued to return to Les Salants. It wasn't a simple matter of our improving fortunes. It was more than that. It was in the way the children no longer dragged their feet on their way to school, it was in Toinette's jaunty new hat, in Charlotte's pink lipstick and loosened hair. Mercédès no longer spent as much time in La Houssinière. Aristide's diminished leg no longer ached as much on rainy nights. I worked on restoring the boatyard for GrosJean; clearing out the old hangar, putting aside any usable materials, digging up hulks half-buried in the sand. And in houses all over Les Salants beds were aired, gardens dug, spare rooms refurbished in preparation for long hoped-for visitors. No one spoke of them—deserters are rarely mentioned in the village, less so even than the dead—but all the same, photographs were removed from drawers, letters reread, telephone numbers memorized. Capucine's daughter Clo was planning to come over at Easter. Désirée and Aristide had received a card from their youngest son. It was as if spring had come early, bringing new shoots from dusty corners and salty cracks.

My father too was caught up in it. The first I suspected was when I returned home from La Goulue to find a stack of bricks in front of the porch. There were breeze blocks behind them too, and sacks of concrete mix.

"Your father's planning to do a little building work," said Alain, when I saw him in the village. "A shower block, I think, or some kind of extension."

The news did not surprise me; in the old days, GrosJean had always been absorbed in one building project or another. It was when Flynn turned up with a loader, a concrete mixer, and a new delivery of bricks and breeze blocks that I began to pay attention.

"What's this?" I demanded.

"A job," said Flynn. "You father wants a few things doing."

He seemed oddly reluctant to speak of it; a new bathhouse, he said, to replace the one at the back of the boat hangar. Perhaps a few other things. GrosJean had asked him to do the work according to his own plans.

"But that's good, isn't it?" asked Flynn, seeing my expression. "It means he's taking an interest."

I wondered. The Easter holidays would be on us in a couple of months, and there had been talk of a visit from Adrienne, to coincide with the boys' school holidays. This might be a ploy to attract her. And there was the cost—materials, hire of machinery, labor. GrosJean had never given me any indication that he had money hidden away.

"How much?" I asked.

Flynn told me. It was a fair price, but higher, I was sure, than my father could afford. "I'll pay," I said.

He shook his head. "You won't. It's been arranged. Besides," he added, "you're broke." I shrugged. That wasn't true; I still had some savings left. But Flynn was adamant. The supplies had been paid for. The work, he said, was free.

❦

The building supplies took up most of the space in the boatyard. Flynn was apologetic, but as he said, there really wasn't anywhere else to put them, and it would be only for a week or two. So I abandoned my work there for the time, and went, sketchbook in hand, to La Houssinière. On arriving, however, I found Les Immortelles covered in scaffolding—a damp problem, perhaps, brought on by the high tides.

The tide was coming in; I went down to the deserted beach and sat with my back to the seawall to watch it. I had been sitting there for a few minutes, allowing my pencil to move, almost idly, across the paper, when I noticed a sign hammered into the rock high above me—a white board lettered in black, which read:

> LES IMMORTELLES. Private beach.
> It is an OFFENSE to remove SAND from this beach.
> Anyone doing so will be liable to PROSECUTION.
> *Order signed by P. Lacroix (Gendarmerie Nationale)*
> *G. Pinoz (Mayor)*
> *C. Brismand (Proprietor)*

I stood up and stared at the words. Of course, there had been instances of sand harvesting before: a few sacks here and there, usually for building, or for cleaning up the garden. Even Brismand turned a blind eye. Even so, the beach had lost a lot of sand. Far more than could be accounted for by the occasional theft.

The beach huts that had survived the winter were teetering on their wooden supports, a meter or more above the level of the beach; in August their bellies had touched the sand. I began to sketch rapidly: the leggy beach huts, the curve of the tide line; the row of cobbles behind the breakwater; the rising tide with its vanguard of cloud.

I was so absorbed in my work that it was some time before I became aware of Soeur Extase and Soeur Thérèse, sitting just above me on the seawall. No ice creams, this time; but Soeur Extase was carrying a bag of sweets, which she occasionally passed to Soeur Thérèse. Both sisters looked delighted to see me.

"Why, it's Mado GrosJean, *ma soeur*—"

"Little Mado with her drawing book. Come to watch the sea, heh? Smell the south wind?" asked Soeur Thérèse.

"That's what did for our beach the first time. The south wind," declared Soeur Extase. "That's what Claude Brismand says."

"Clever man, Claude Brismand."

"Veryvery clever."

I was always entertained at the way their voices echoed each other, one carrying on seamlessly from the other like those of twittering birds.

"Too clever by half, I'd say," I said, smiling.

The nuns laughed. "Or not clever enough," said Soeur Thérèse. They got down from their perch on the seawall and began to make their way toward me, hitching up their habits as they reached the sand. "Are you watching for someone?"

"There's no one out there, Mado GrosJean, no one at all."

"Who'd be out there now, in all weathers? That's what we used to say to your father—"

"*He* was always looking out to sea, you know—"

"But she never came back."

The old nuns settled on a flat rock nearby and peered down at me with their birdy eyes. I looked back at them, startled. I knew there was a vein of romance that ran through my father—the names of his boats proved it—but the thought that he might have waited here, watching the horizon for my mother's return, was unexpected and oddly moving.

"All the same, *ma soeur*," said Soeur Extase, reaching for a sweet. "Little Mado came back, didn't she—"

"And things are looking better for Les Salants. Thanks to the Saint, of course."

"Ah yes. The Saint." The nuns chuckled.

"Not so good at our end, though," said Soeur Extase, looking at the scaffolding at Les Immortelles. "Not so lucky here."

The tide was coming in fast. It always does on Le Devin, racing across the flats with deceptive speed. More than one fisher after oysters or shrimps has been obliged to abandon his catch and swim for it when caught out by that silent sweep of water. I could see a current, a strong one by the look of it, fingering its way toward the beach. Not an unusual feature on an island built on sandbanks: the smallest shift can divert a current, turning a sheltered inlet into bleak headland in the space of a winter, turning shallows to silt, to beach, and then to dunes in the space of only a few years.

"What's this for?" I asked the sisters, pointing at the sign.

"Oh, that was Monsieur Brismand's idea. He thinks—"

"Someone's been poaching sand."

"Poaching?" I thought of the new layer of sand at La Goulue.

"By boat, maybe; or with a tractor." Soeur Thérèse smiled happily from her perch. "He's offered a reward."

"But that's stupid," I said, laughing. "He must know that no one could have moved so much sand. It's the tides. The tides and the currents. That's all."

Soeur Extase had returned to her bag of sweets. Seeing me watching her, she held it out. "Well, Brismand doesn't think it's stupid," she said placidly. "Brismand thinks someone's been stealing his beach."

Soeur Thérèse nodded. "Why not?" she chirped. "It's been done before."

17

March left us a gift of high tides but fair weather. Business was good: Omer had made an excellent profit on his winter vegetables and was planning a more ambitious crop for next year; Angélo, after some renovations to his bar, had reopened and was doing a brisk trade even with Houssins, with the Guénolé-Bastonnet alliance supplying his oysters; Xavier had begun repairs on a little abandoned cottage near La Bouche and had been seen several times hand in hand with Mercédès Prossage; even Toinette was turning a good profit from visits to the Saint's shrine on La Griznoz, which had become popular with some of the older Houssins since the floods.

The changes were not all for the better, however. The Guénolé-Bastonnet alliance suffered a temporary setback when Xavier was waylaid on his way from La Houssinière with the money for a consignment of lobsters. Three men on motorbikes stopped him just outside the village, broke his glasses and his nose, and got away with a fortnight's takings. Xavier had not recognized any of his attackers, as they had been wearing motorcycle helmets.

"Thirty lobsters at fifty francs apiece," moaned Matthias to Aristide. "And your grandson let them get away!"

Aristide bristled. "Would *your* grandson have managed any better?"

"At least my grandson would have put up a fight," said Matthias.

"There were three of them," murmured Xavier, shyer than ever, looking odd and rabbity without his glasses.

"So?" said Matthias. "You can run, can't you?"

"From a motorbike?"

"It had to be Houssins," said Omer peaceably, sensing a fight brewing. "Xavier, did they say anything to you? Anything that might help you recognize them?"

Xavier shook his head.

"What about the bikes? You'd recognize *them*, wouldn't you?"

Xavier shrugged. "Maybe."

"Maybe?"

At last Xavier, Ghislain, Aristide, and Matthias went into La Houssinière to talk to Pierre Lacroix, the only policeman, neither side trusting the other to tell the story correctly. The policeman appeared sympathetic but showed little optimism.

"There are so many motorbikes on the island," he said, with an avuncular pat on Xavier's shoulder. "They might even have been mainlanders come over for the day on *Brismand 1*."

Aristide shook his head. "They were Houssins," he said stubbornly. "They knew the boy was carrying cash."

"Anyone from Les Salants would have known that," said Lacroix.

"Yes, but in that case he would have recognized the bikes—"

"I'm sorry." The tone was final.

Aristide looked at Lacroix. "One of the bikes was a red Honda," he said.

"A common make," said Lacroix, without returning his gaze.

"Doesn't your son Joël have a red Honda?"

There was a sudden, dangerous silence. "Are you suggesting, Bastonnet, that my son—that *my son*—" Lacroix's face flared beneath his mustache. "That's a malicious accusation," he said. "If you weren't an old man, Bastonnet, and if you hadn't lost your own son—"

Aristide leaped from his chair, clutching his stick. "My boy has nothing to do with this!"

"Neither has mine!"

They faced each other, Aristide white, Lacroix red, both shaking with rage.

Xavier took the old man's arm to stop him falling. "Pépé, it's no use—"

"Get *off* me, heh!"

Gently, Ghislain took his other arm. "Please, Monsieur Bastonnet, we have to go."

Aristide glared at him. Ghislain held his gaze. There was a long, furious silence.

"Well," said Aristide at last. "It's been a while since a Guénolé called me *monsieur*. The younger generation can't have deteriorated as much as I thought."

❀

They left La Houssinière with as much dignity a they could muster. Joël Lacroix watched them from the doorway of the Chat Noir café, a Gitane between his teeth and a little smile on his lips. The red Honda was parked outside. Aristide, Matthias, Ghislain, and Xavier walked past without a glance.

Xavier looked longingly toward the café entrance, but Matthias gripped his arm and hissed in his ear, "Don't you dare, son!"

Xavier looked at Matthias in stupefaction. Perhaps it was being called "son" by his grandfather's rival, or perhaps it was the expression on the old man's face, but it stopped him for just long enough to bring him to his senses. None of them doubted now that Joël had been behind the attack and the theft, but now was certainly not the time to say so. They made their way slowly back to Les Salants, and by the time they finally got home the unthinkable had happened: for the first time in generations, Bastonnets and Guénolés were in wholehearted agreement over something.

This time, they agreed, it was war.

By the end of the week the village was buzzing with rumor and speculation; even the children had got to hear the story, and it had been passed from mouth to mouth, with many contradictions and embellishments, until it had reached epic proportions. On one thing everyone stood fast, however: enough was enough.

"We would have let bygones be bygones," said Matthias over a friendly game of belote in Angélo's. "We were happy enough to trade with them. But they stacked the deck."

Omer nodded. "They've had it their way far too long," he agreed. "It's time we fought back."

18

 There followed a rigorous campaign against the Houssins. Our newfound sense of community demanded it. The price of lobster and crabs rose sharply; Angélo began to charge extra whenever an Houssin dropped in at the café; the minimarket in La Houssinière received a consignment of moldy vegetables from the Prossage farm (Omer blamed the weather); and one night, someone broke into the hangar in which Joël Lacroix kept his precious Honda and put sand in his petrol tank. Everyone waited for the policeman to make an outraged appearance, but he never did. To an outsider such things might have seemed trivial, even childish; but to the Salannais, who have so little, it was deadly serious. I understood that, and although I didn't always approve of their methods, I never said so aloud.

"Those Houssins have had everything their way too long," declared Omer. "They think just because they've been lucky for a while, nothing will ever change."

It was a measure of exactly how much progress we had made that no one contested this.

"We should advertise to bring the tourists to our end," suggested Capucine. "Set up on the quay at La Houssinière with a sandwich board when the tourists get here. That would bring the business in. And put one in the eye of those Houssins!"

Six months ago such a far-fetched idea—and from a woman—would have provoked laughter and scorn. Now Aristide and Matthias looked interested. Others followed suit.

"Why not, heh?"

"It sounds good to me."

The rest considered it for a moment. It wasn't the first time anyone had voiced that thought, but the idea of competing with the Houssins on any kind of equal footing had always seemed absurd. Now, for the first time, it seemed possible.

Matthias spoke for us all. "Charging extra for fish is one thing," he said slowly. "But what you're suggesting would mean—"

Aristide snorted. "La Houssinière isn't somebody's oyster bed, Guénolé," he said with some of his old ire. "The tourists are fair game."

"And we deserve them," added Toinette. "We owe it to ourselves to at least try."

Matthias shook his head. "I just wonder if we're ready."

The old woman shrugged. "We could be ready. The season starts in four months' time. Then there'll be half a dozen trippers a day until September, just waiting to be pulled in."

"We'd need somewhere for the people to stay," said Matthias. "We've got no hotel. No campsite to speak of."

"That's just Guénolé cowardice talking, heh," retorted Aristide. "Let a Bastonnet show you a bit of lateral thinking. You've got a spare room, haven't you?"

Toinette nodded. "Heh! Everyone has a room or two going begging. Most of us have a patch of land that can be used for camping. Add onto that a few breakfasts and dinner with the family, and you're as good as anyplace on the coast. Better, even. Those city people would give good money to stay in a typical island house. Light a log fire, hang some copper pans on the walls—"

"Make some *devinnoiseries* in a claybake oven—"

"Bring the island costumes out of storage—"

"Traditional music—I've got my *biniou* in the attic somewhere—"

"Handcrafts, needlework, fishing trips—"

Once begun, the ideas were difficult to stop. I tried to stop myself from laughing as the general excitement rose, although in spite of my amusement, something in me was moved. Even the skeptical Guénolés were getting carried away now, everyone shouting out suggestions, banging on the tabletops, rattling the glasses. The consensus was that summer people would buy anything they considered to be typical or artisan. For years we had deplored Les Salants' lack of modern facilities, jealously watching La Houssinière with its hotel, its gaming arcade, and cinema. For the first time, we saw how our apparent weakness could be turned to good profit. All we needed was some initiative, and a little investment.

※

As Easter approached, my father threw himself into his building project with renewed enthusiasm. He was not alone; all over the village there were signs of activity. Omer began to convert his disused barn; others planted flowers in bare yards or hung pretty curtains in windows. Les Salants was like a plain woman in love who, for the first time, begins to see in herself the potential for beauty.

Since her departure in January we had heard no further news of Adrienne. I was relieved; her return had brought with it a flotilla of uncomfortable memories, and her parting comments still troubled me. If GrosJean was disappointed, he showed little sign of it. He seemed utterly absorbed in his new project, and for that I was grateful, although he remained aloof. For that I blamed my sister.

Flynn too had seemed more remote in recent weeks. Part of it was because he was working hard: as well as GrosJean's building job he had also helped out in the village; he had installed a washhouse at Toinette's to be used by campers; and helped Omer convert his barn into a holiday flat. He made the same wisecracks, played cards and chess with the same killer accuracy, flattered Capucine, teased Mercédès, awed the children with unlikely tales of his travels abroad, and by turns charmed, cajoled, and perjured himself deeper into the heart of Les Salants. But to long-term plans and changes he remained indifferent. He ventured no more ideas or inspirations. Perhaps, now that the Salannais had learned to think for themselves, he didn't need to.

I was still troubled by the memory of what had happened between us at La Goulue. Flynn, however, seemed to have forgotten it completely, and, having played and replayed the episode in the part of my mind reserved for such things, I finally decided to do the same. I found him attractive; yes. The realization had taken me by surprise, and I had made a fool of myself. But his value as a friend was of more importance to me, especially now. I would never have admitted it to anyone else, but since the transformation of Les Salants and the development of my father's building plans, I had been feeling strangely left out.

It was nothing I could put my finger on. People were friendly and kind. There was no house in the village—not even Aristide's—where I would not immediately be made welcome. And yet in subtle ways I remained an outsider. There was a formality behind their dealings with me that I found strangely oppressive. If I called by for a cup of tea, it would be served in the best crockery. If I bought vegetables from Omer, he would always include a little more than I had paid for. It made me feel uncomfortable. It made me different. When I voiced this to Capucine, she only laughed. Flynn, I felt, was the only person who might understand.

As a result I spent more time with him than ever. He was a good listener, and he had the ability to put my problems into perspective with nothing but a grin or a flippant comment. More important, he understood my other life, my years in Paris, and when I talked to him I never needed to search my vocabulary for a simpler word, or struggle to explain a difficult concept, as I often had to with some of the Salannais. I would never have admitted it, but sometimes my friends in the village made me feel like a schoolteacher with a boisterous class. They charmed and exasperated me by turns; they had moments of extreme childishness toward one another, and moments of peculiar wisdom. If only they could expand their horizons . . .

"We've got a real beach now," I said to Flynn one day at La Goulue. "We might even get some real tourists."

Flynn was lying on his back on the sand, looking up at the sky.

"Who knows," I persisted, "we might become a fashionable resort." It was a lighthearted remark, but he didn't even smile. "At least we get to give Brismand a bit of his own. After the run he's had over the years it's time Les Salants had its turn."

"You think that's what's happening, do you?" he said. "You're having your turn?"

I sat up. "What's wrong? What haven't you told me?"

Flynn continued to stare at the sky. His eyes were filled with clouds.

"Well?"

"You're all so pleased with yourselves. One or two small victories and you think you can do anything. We'll have walking on water next."

"So?" I didn't like his tone of voice. "What's wrong with a little enterprise?"

"What's wrong, Mado, is that it's all been a little too successful. Too much, too quick. How long before word gets out, do you think? How long before everyone wants a slice?"

❧

But we were too busy to waste time with that kind of pessimism. Three months until the beginning of the tourist season, and the whole village worked harder and more willingly than we had when we were building the Bouch'ou. Success had made us bold; besides, we had begun to enjoy the sense of possibility the project had created among us.

Flynn, who could have lived on his triumph for the next year if he had chosen, calling in favors from everyone in Les Salants and never having to pay for a drink, kept his distance. The Saint took the credit in his place, and the shrine erected by Toinette was crammed with offerings. On April Fools' Day Damien and Lolo caused a minor scandal by embellishing the altar with a dead fish, but on the whole there was real reverence toward the reinstated Sainte-Marine, and Toinette enjoyed her share.

The previous year no Salannais would have even considered investing money, let alone borrowing any. There is no bank on Le Devin, and no collateral for a loan if there were. But now things were different. Savings could be brought out of boxes and wardrobes. We began to see possibilities where none had existed before. The phrase "short-term loan" was spoken for the first time by Omer, and was greeted with cautious approval. Alain revealed that he too had been thinking along the same lines. Someone had heard of an organization on the mainland—someone connected with the Ministry of Agriculture, perhaps—who might be approached for a grant.

As momentum gained, preparations grew more ambitious. I was commissioned to make several signs out of clinkers and artistic pieces of driftwood:

LOCAL SEA SALT (50F PER 5 KILO BAG)
BASTONNET ISLAND ROPEWORK
ANGÉLO'S CAFÉ-RESTAURANT (PLAT DU JOUR 30F)
CHAMBRE-D'HÔTE—ROOMS TO LET—FRIENDLY
FAMILY ATMOSPHERE
SHRINE OF SAINTE-MARINE-DE-LA-MER
(10F, GUIDED VISIT)

I even painted one for myself—GALERIE PRASTEAU: LOCAL ARTIST—thinking uncomfortably about my dwindling savings. For a while I too was hard at work, preparing canvases to sell when finally the tourists arrived.

For weeks the village was frenzied with hammering, weeding, shouting, raking, painting, whitewashing, drinking (thirsty work, this), and arguments.

"We should send someone out to the mainland, to Fromentine, to publicize," suggested Xavier. "Hand out leaflets, spread the word around."

Aristide agreed. "We'll both go. I'll stand on the quay and keep an eye to the ferry. You can do the rest of the town. Mado can make you a sandwich board, maybe some leaflets too, heh? We can stay at a bed-and-breakfast for few days. Easy as shooting hens in a barn!" He gave a cackle of satisfaction.

Xavier was less enthusiastic. Perhaps it was the thought of leaving Mercédès, even for a few days. But Aristide's enthusiasm, once fired, was unquenchable. He packed a few things, including the sandwich board, and spread rumors of family business to attend to.

"It won't do for those Houssins to know about things too early," he remarked.

I hand-lettered a hundred little posters, not having the facilities to print them off. Xavier was under instruction to put one in every shop window, every café in Fromentine.

> VISIT LES SALANTS
> UNCHANGED IN 100 YEARS
> OUR DELICIOUS LOCAL ISLAND COOKING
> OUR UNSPOILT GOLDEN BEACH
> OUR WARM AND FRIENDLY HOSPITALITY
> LES SALANTS—DISCOVER THE DIFFERENCE!

The wording had been pondered and reworked by the Bastonnets, the Guénolés, and the Prossages until they were all satisfied. I corrected the spelling. We put it about that the Bastonnets were going to the coast to help out a struggling relative in Pornic, and made sure the information was overheard in the right place. Tell Jojo-le-Goëland anything, and it's around La Houssinière quicker than you can blink. Opinion in Les Salants had it that the Houssins wouldn't know what had hit them until it was too late.

By summer, the war would be over.

19

Easter came, and the *Brismand 1* began to run twice weekly again. It was a good thing for Les Salants that it did, for all the rebuilding and redecorating work had left us short of supplies. Aristide and Xavier had met with an excellent reception in Fromentine, distributing all their leaflets and leaving details at the local tourist offices. A couple of weeks later they went back, traveling as far as Nantes this time, with twice as many leaflets to distribute.

The rest of us waited anxiously for news, putting the finishing touches to our handiwork and keeping a close watch for Houssin spies. For there *were* spies; Jojo-le-Goëland had been spotted several times lurking around La Goulue, motorcycles had been heard around the village, and Joël Lacroix had taken to strolling around the dunes in the evenings—or at least until someone shot him with a double barrel of rock salt. A halfhearted investigation was begun, but—as Alain pointed out to Pierre Lacroix, with an expression of deep sincerity—so many islanders have salt rifles that it would be impossible to find the culprit, even assuming it was a Salannais.

"It could just as easily have been someone from the coast," agreed Aristide. "Or even an Houssin—"

Lacroix's mouth thinned in displeasure. "Be careful, Bastonnet," he warned.

"Who, me?" said Aristide, shocked. "Surely you don't think *I* had anything to do with the attack on your son?"

There were no reprisals. Perhaps Lacroix had spoken to his son, or perhaps the Houssins were too busy preparing for their own season, but La Houssinière was eerily silent for the time of year. Even the motorcycle gang dropped momentarily out of sight.

"Good thing, too, heh!" said Toinette, who had her own salt rifle tucked behind her front door, next to the woodpile. "Let any of those hoodlums come sniffing around here and I'll give them both barrels of the best sea salt up the arse."

At this point Aristide's triumph lacked only one thing: the official announcement of the engagement between his grandson and Mercédès. There was some reason to anticipate it: the two were always together, Xavier inarticulate with admiration, the object of his affection coolly flirtatious in a series of eye-catching outfits. This was in itself enough to fuel supposition in the village. More to the point, however, was the fact that Omer favored the match. A jealous parent, he made no secret of this. The boy had prospects, he declared complacently. A Salannais, with his heart in the right place. Respect for his elders. And enough money to start up on his own. Aristide had already given Xavier an unknown sum—rumor flew wildly, but it was rumored the old man must have had savings hidden away—to begin independently, and Xavier had made extraordinary progress in restoring the abandoned cottage—once little more than a shell—into which he was planning to move.

"Time he got settled, heh," said Aristide. "We're none of us getting any younger, and I'd like to see some great-grandchildren before I die. Xavier's all I have left of my poor Olivier's blood. I'm counting on him to keep the name going. Without him—"

Mercédès was a pretty girl, and a Salannaise. Omer and the Bastonnets had been friends for years. And Xavier was stem over stern in love with her, said Aristide with a lascivious gleam in his eye: there would be grandchildren.

"I'm counting on a dozen," he would say complacently, making an hourglass gesture with his hands. Broad hips, good hocks; Aristide knew his livestock as well as any islander. Devinnois, he was fond of saying, should choose their wives like broodmares. And if she was pretty too—all the better.

"A dozen," he repeated happily, rubbing his hands. "Maybe more."

In spite of everything, however, there was a kind of desperation to our high spirits. It takes more than fighting talk to sustain a war, and our opponents in La Houssinière seemed too cool, too disinterested for comfort. Claude Brismand was seen on a number of occasions out by La Goulue, with Jojo-le-Goëland and Mayor Pinoz. If he was disturbed by what he had seen, he certainly gave no indication of it. He remained unconcerned, meeting all comers with the usual benevolent, fatherly smile. All the same, a number of rumors had already reached us. Business, it seemed, was not wonderful in La Houssinière. "I've heard Les Immortelles has had to cancel some bookings." said Omer. "Damp in the walls."

By the end of the week my curiosity about Les Immortelles got the better of me. I went over there on an excuse—art supplies to order from the mainland—but mostly to check out the rumors—now increasingly wild—about the purported damage to the hotel.

They had, of course, been exaggerated. All the same, Les Immortelles had deteriorated since my last visit. The hotel itself looked unchanged, except for the scaffolding on one side, but the sand layer had thinned still farther, with a steep drop to the stony shore.

I could see how it had happened. The chain of events that had led us to this point, all our work in Les Salants, the combination of inertia and arrogance in the Houssins, which obscured the truth, even though they were looking right at it. The scale—the audacity—of our deception made it impossible to envisage. Even Brismand, in spite of his probing, still failed to see what was beneath his nose.

Once begun, the deterioration would be fast, and final. The waves against the seawall would drag the remaining sand far into the slipstream, exposing rocks and cobbles until nothing but the smooth incline of the ancient dike was left. A few years might finish it altogether. A couple of summers, if the winds obliged.

I looked around for Jojo, Brismand, or anyone else who might give me news, but there was no one in sight. The Rue des Immortelles was almost deserted. I saw a couple of tourists buying ice creams from a stand where a bored-looking girl chewed gum under a faded Choky parasol.

As I moved closer to the seawall I noticed a single group of early tourists on the meager beach, a family by the look of it, with a tiny baby and a dog, all huddled and shivery beneath a flapping parasol. April is an uncertain month in the islands, and that day there was a scouring sea wind that stripped the warmth from the air. A small girl of about eight, all curls and round pansy eyes, was climbing rocks at the far end of the beach. She saw me watching and waved. "Are you on holiday here?" she called.

I shook my head. "No. I live here."

"Have you *been* on holiday, then? Do you go to the city for your holiday when we come here? Do you swim in the sea on weekends and go to the *piscine* for special?"

"Laetitia," chided the father, twisting around to see what was going on. "Don't ask rude questions."

Laetitia looked at me appraisingly. I winked at her. She needed no further encouragement; in a second she had clambered up the path onto the esplanade and was sitting precariously next to me on the seawall, one foot drawn up beneath her.

"Have you got a beach near your house? Is it bigger than this one? Can you go onto the beach anytime you want to? Can you build a sand castle on Christmas Day?"

I smiled. "If you like."

"*Zen!*"

Gabi was her mother, I learned. Philippe was her father. Pétrole was the dog. He was always sick on boats. Laetitia had a big brother, Tim, at university in Rennes. She had another brother, Stéphane, but he was only a baby. She made a little moue of disapproval.

"He never does anything. Sometimes he sleeps. He's so bo-oring. I'm going to go to the beach every day," she announced, brightening. "I'm going to dig down till I find clay. Then I'm going to make things with it. We did that last year in Nice," she explained. "It was *zen*. Super*zen*."

"Laetitia!" A distant voice called from the beach. "Laetitia, what did I say?"

Laetitia gave a theatrical sigh. "Bof. Maman doesn't like me climbing this far. I'd better go back."

She slid down the seawall with blithe unconcern for the drift of broken glass that had accumulated at its foot.

"Bye!" A moment later she was at the water's edge, throwing seaweed at the seagulls.

I waved back and continued my investigation of the esplanade. Since my last visit a few of the shops had reopened along the Rue des Immortelles, but apart from Laetitia and her family, there seemed to be no likely takers. Soeur Thérèse and Soeur Extase, severe in their ancient black habits, were sitting on a bench overlooking the sea. Joël Lacroix's motorbike was parked carelessly opposite, but there was no sign of its owner. I waved at the two nuns and came to sit beside them.

"Why it's little Mado again," said one of the sisters—they were both wearing their white *coiffes* today, and I found I could barely tell them apart. "No sketching today?"

I shook my head. "Too windy."

"Bad winds, heh, for Les Immortelles," said Soeur Thérèse, swinging her feet.

"Not so bad for Les Salants," added Soeur Extase. "We get to hear—"

"—All kinds of things. You'd be surprised at—"

"The things we get to hear about."

"They think we're like the poor old residents here, too old and dotty to know what's going on. And we are, of couse, *soeur*, old as the hills, that is if there—"

"—Were any hills here but there aren't here, only dunes—"

"Though not as much sand as there used to be, *ma soeur*, no, not nearly as much."

A silence while the two nuns peered at me, birdlike, from beneath their white *coiffes*. "I heard Brismand was having to cancel bookings this year," I said carefully. "Is that true?"

The sisters nodded in unison. "Not all the bookings. But some—"

"Yes, some. He was veryvery annoyed. There was a flood, wasn't there, *ma soeur*, must have been just after the—"

"—Spring tides. Flooded the cellars and through into the front. The architect says there's damp in the wall, because of the—"

"Sea wind. There'll be work to be done on that come winter. Till then—"

"There'll only be back rooms for the tourists now, no sea view, no beach. It's—"

"Veryvery sad."

Rather uncomfortably, I agreed.

"Still, if the Saint wills it—"

"Oh yes. If the Saint wills it—"

I left them waving after me, even more birdlike at a distance, their *coiffes* transformed into a pair of gulls riding the patient wave.

As I crossed the road I caught sight of Joël Lacroix watching me from the doorway of the Chat Noir. He was smoking a Gitane, its tip cupped fisherman-style into the palm of his hand. Our eyes met, and he acknowledged me curtly—*heh*—but said nothing. Just behind him in the café doorway I could make out the smoke-obscured form of a girl— long black hair, red dress, coltish legs in high-heeled sandals—whose outline seemed vaguely familiar. But even as I watched, Joël stepped away from the door, and the girl with him. I thought at the time there was something furtive about the way he turned away, shielding the girl from view.

It was only later, as I walked back toward Les Salants, that I remembered why the girl had seemed so familiar.

It was—I was almost certain of it—Mercédès Prossage.

20

Of course I said nothing to anyone about it. Mercédès was free to go where she pleased. But I felt uneasy; Joël Lacroix was no friend of Les Salants, and I didn't like to think of how much Mercédès might innocently be giving away.

I returned from La Houssinière to find my father at the kitchen table with Flynn, looking at some drawings on sheets of butcher's paper. For a moment I caught their faces unguarded—my father's alight with excitement, Flynn's with that look of absorption, like a boy with an ant farm—before they looked up and saw me watching them.

"It's another job," explained Flynn "Your father wants me to help with a conversion. The boat hangar."

"Really?" GrosJean must have sensed my disapproval, because he made a gesture of impatience. My interference, it seemed, was not appreciated. I turned to Flynn, who shrugged his shoulders.

"What can I do?" he said. "It's his house. I didn't encourage him."

It was true, of course. GrosJean could do what he liked with his own house. But I wondered where the money was coming from. And the boatyard, derelict as it was, was still a link with the past. I hated to lose it.

I looked more closely at the drawings. They were good; my father had a keen eye for detail, and I could see quite clearly what he intended; a summerhouse or a studio perhaps, with a living space, a small kitchen, and a bathroom. The hangar was large; put in a floor, a trapdoor, and a ladder to reach it, and there could be a pleasant bedroom under the eaves.

"It's for Adrienne, isn't it?" I said, knowing it was true. That bedroom with the trapdoor; the kitchen; the broad living room with its long window. "Adrienne and the boys."

GrosJean just looked at me, his eyes as flat as blue china, then returned to his drawings. I turned stiffly and went back outside, feeling sick. A moment later I sensed Flynn standing behind me.

"Who's going to pay for all this?" I asked, without looking at him. "GrosJean doesn't have any money."

"He might have savings you don't know about."

"You used to be a better liar than that, Flynn."

Silence. I could still feel him at my back, watching me. From the dune a volley of gulls rose in a great clap of wings.

"Perhaps he's borrowed the money," he said at last. "Mado, he's an adult. You can't run his life."

"I know."

"You've done everything you could. You've helped him—"

"And what for?" I turned around angrily. "What use was any of it? All he cares about is playing house with Adrienne and those boys."

"Welcome to the world, Mado," said Flynn.

Silence. With my foot I traced a line in the hard sand. "Who lent him the money, Flynn? Was it Brismand?"

Flynn looked impatient. "How should I know?"

"Was it Brismand?"

He sighed. "Probably. Does it matter?"

I walked away without looking at him.

❦

I expressed no further interest in the work to the hangar. It began nevertheless; Flynn brought a truckload of supplies from La Houssinière and spent a weekend stripping out the hangar; GrosJean was with him all the time, watching and consulting diagrams. In spite of myself I began to feel envious of all the time he spent with Flynn; it was as if, sensing my disapproval, my father had begun to avoid me.

I learned that Adrienne planned to return for the summer holidays, bringing the boys with her. The news caused excitement in the village, where several families were expecting long-delayed visitors of their own.

"I really think she'll hold to it this time," said Capucine. "She's not a bad girl, my Clo. Not a thinker, but a good heart."

Désirée Bastonnet too was looking hopeful; I saw her on the road to La Houssinière with a new green coat and a hat with flowers on the band. I thought she looked younger in her spring clothes, her back straight, her face unaccustomedly rosy, and she smiled at me as I passed. It was so surprising that I turned and caught up with her again, just to make sure I hadn't mistaken her for someone else.

"I'm going to meet my son Philippe," she told me in her quiet voice. "He's been visiting La Houssinière with his family."

For a moment I thought of Flynn, and wondered whether he too had a mother like Désirée, waiting for him to return. "I'm glad you're meeting him," I told her. "And I hope he can make peace with his father."

Désirée shook her head. "You know how stubborn my husband is," she said. "He pretends he doesn't know I've been in touch with Philippe; he thinks the only reason Philippe would want to come back after all these years is because he's after money." She sighed. "Still," she said in a determined tone, "if Aristide wants to waste this chance, that's his business. I heard the Saint speak, that night on the Pointe. From now on, she said, we make our own luck. And I intend to."

I smiled. Fake miracle or not, it had certainly transformed Désirée. Flynn's deception had at least accomplished this, and I felt a sudden warmth for him, in spite of my anger at the work he was doing for my father. Despite his pretended cynicism, I thought, Flynn was not indifferent.

I wished I could feel more positive about my sister's arrival. As the conversion of the hangar progressed, I could feel GrosJean gaining momentum with every day. It was in everything he did—his renewed energy, his alertness, the way he no longer sat in the kitchen staring dully out to sea. He began to speak more often too, although much of it was about Adrienne's return, and it did not cheer me as much as it might otherwise have done. It was as if someone had hit a switch in him, bringing him to life. I tried to feel happy for him, but found I could not.

Instead I flung myself with fierce enthusiasm into my painting. I painted the beach at La Goulue, the whitewashed houses with their red tiled roofs, the *blockhaus* at Pointe Griznoz with the pink tamarisks shaking flossily in the sea wind, the dunes bobbing with rabbit-tail grassses, the boats at low tide, sheets of birds riding the waves, long-haired fishermen in their pink-faded *vareuses*, Toinette Prossage in her white *coiffe* and widow's blacks, looking for snails under the woodpile. I told myself that when the tourists arrived there would be buyers for my work, and that my expenses—canvas, paints, and other materials—represented an investment. I hoped so; my savings were running dangerously short, and although GrosJean and I had relatively few household expenses, the cost of the building work made me anxious. I made inquiries locally and contacted a small gallery in Fromentine, where the owner agreed to sell some of my paintings for a percentage. I would have preferred something closer to home, but it was a start. I waited cautiously for the season to begin.

It was not long before I spotted the tourist family again. I was out at La Goulue with my sketchbook, trying to capture the look of the water at low tide, and they came up on me out of nowhere, Laetitia running on ahead with the dog Pétrole, her parents Gabi and Philippe a little farther behind with the baby in a carrier. Philippe was carrying a picnic basket and a beach bag full of toys.

Laetitia waved at me madly. "*Salut!* We've found a beach!" She ran to me breathlessly, her face shining. "A beach, and there's nobody here at all! It's just like a desert island. It's the *zen*-est desert-island beach *ever!*"

Smiling, I had to admit that it was.

Gabi greeted me with a friendly wave. She was a short, plump, brown woman, wearing a yellow *paréo* over her swimsuit. "Is it safe here?" she asked. "For swimming, I mean? There isn't a green flag or anything."

I laughed. "Oh, it's safe," I told her. "It's just that we don't usually get many visitors around this side of the island."

"We like this side best," announced Laetitia. "We like it best for swimming. And I *can* swim," she added with dignity, "but I have to keep my foot on the floor."

"Les Immortelles isn't safe for children," explained Gabi. "There's a steep drop and a current—"

"This is better, though," said Laetitia, beginning to scramble down the cliffside path. "There are rocks and everything. Come *on,* Pétrole!"

The dog followed her, barking excitedly. La Goulue rang with the unaccustomed sounds of childish exuberance.

"The water's a little cold," I said, looking at Laetitia, who had now reached the tide line and was poking around at the sand with a stick.

"She'll be all right," said Philippe. "I know this place."

"Really?" Now that I could see him more closely, I saw that he looked almost Devinnois, with the black hair and blue eyes of the islands. "I'm sorry, but do I know you? You look—familiar."

Philippe shook his head. "You don't know me," he said. "But maybe you know my mother." His eyes moved to a point behind me, and he smiled—a very familiar smile. Automatically I turned round.

"Mamie!" yelled Laetitia from the water's edge, and began to run toward the beach. Water sprayed everywhere. Pétrole began to bark.

"Mado," said Désirée Bastonnet, her eyes shining. "I see you've met my son."

He had come back for the Easter holidays. He, Gabi, and the children had been staying at a holiday cottage behind the Clos du Phare, and since our meeting on the road to La Houssinière, Désirée had called several times.

"It's *zen,*" declared Laetitia, comfortably biting into a pain au chocolat from the picnic basket. "All this time I had a *mamie* and I didn't even know about her! I've got a *papi* too, but I haven't seen him yet. We'll see him later."

Désirée looked at me and gave a little shake of her head. "Stubborn old fool," she said, not without affection. "He still hasn't forgotten that old business. But we won't give up."

21

In the first week of June, school broke up for the summer holidays. This traditionally marked the beginning of the season, and we watched the arrival of the *Brismand 1* with renewed interest. Lolo could always be counted upon to keep a lookout at the harbor, and he and Damien took turns to watch the esplanade with exaggerated nonchalance. If anyone noticed their scrutiny, they failed to comment. La Houssinière baked quietly under a sun grown scorching; the once-flooded Clos du Phare cracked fiercely underfoot, making walking painful and bicycles hazardous. *Brismand 1* arrived daily with barely a handful of trippers at a time, and Les Salants fretted and fussed like a bride kept waiting too long at the church. We were ready, more than ready; at last we realized how much time and money we had invested in the rebuilding of Les Salants, and how much we had at stake. Tempers frayed.

"You can't have given out enough leaflets," snapped Matthias to Aristide. "I knew we should have sent someone else!"

Aristide snorted. "We gave out every one! We even went to Nantes—"

"That's right, taking in the bright lights instead of seeing to our business—"

"You old goat, heh! I'll show you where to put your leaflets—"

Aristide stood up precipitously, stick at the ready. Matthias made as if to pick up a chair. It might have turned into the world's most elderly brawl if Flynn had not stepped in, suggesting another trip to Fromentine.

"Perhaps you'll find out what's going on there," he said mildly. "Or maybe the tourists could use a little persuasion."

Matthias looked skeptical. "I'm not having those Bastonnets living it up in Fromentine at my expense," he snapped. Clearly he imagined the harmless seaside town as a pit of vice and temptation.

"You could both of you go," suggested Flynn. "Keep an eye on each other."

The uneasy alliance was regained. It was decided that Matthias, Xavier, Ghislain, and Aristide would all take the Friday morning ferry to Fromentine together. Fridays were good days for tourists, said Aristide, because of the weekend crowd. Sandwich boards were well and good, but nothing could beat a caller on the gangplank. On Friday evening, they promised, all our problems would be over.

That gave us almost a week to kill. We waited impatiently, the older ones over chess and beers in Angélo's, the younger ones fishing over at La Goulue, where pickings were always richer than out on the Pointe.

Mercédès took to sunbathing there on hot days, her generous curves encased in a leopard-print swimsuit. I caught Damien several times watching her through binoculars. I suspected he was not the only one.

On Friday afternoon half the village was waiting at the quayside to welcome the *Brismand 1* home. Désirée. Omer. Capucine. Toinette. Hilaire. Lolo and Damien. Flynn was there, slightly aloof as always, and winked at me as I caught his eye. Even Mercédès was there, ostensibly to welcome Xavier home, in a short orange dress and impossibly high-heeled sandals. Omer watched her closely with a mixture of alarm and approval. Mercédès pretended not to notice.

Claude Brismand was watching too, sitting above us at the *terrasse* of Les Immortelles. I could see him from the jetty, monolithic in his white shirt and fisherman's cap, a glass of something in one hand. His posture was relaxed, expectant. It was too far for me to see his face. Capucine saw me watching him and grinned jauntily.

"He won't know what's hit him when the ferry comes in."

I wasn't so sure. Brismand knows most things on the island, and though he might not be able to change anything, I was fairly certain that whatever happened, it wouldn't take him by surprise. The thought made me uncomfortable, like a feeling of being watched—in fact the more I considered the stillness of that figure on the *terrasse* the more convinced I became that he was indeed observing me, with a peculiar, knowing intensity. I didn't like it at all.

Alain looked at his watch. "She's late."

Fifteen minutes, that was all. But as we waited, sweating and blinking in the glare from the water, it felt like hours. Capucine reached in her pocket for a chocolate bar and ate it in three quick, nervous bites. Alain looked at his watch again.

"I should have gone myself," he grumbled. "Trust them to blow it on their own."

Omer scowled. "I didn't hear *you* volunteering to go, heh?"

"I see something!" yelled Lolo from the water's edge.

Everyone looked. Against the milky horizon, a trail of white.

"The ferry!"

"Don't push like that, heh!"

"It's there! Just behind the *balise*."

It was another half hour before we could see well enough to make out details. Lolo had a pair of binoculars, which we took turns borrowing. The floating jetty rocked beneath our feet. The little ferry moved toward Les Immortelles in a wide arc, leaving a flume of white behind her. As she drew closer still we could see that the deck was busy with people.

"Summer people!"

"And so many—"

"*Our* people—"

Leaning out over the parapet, dangerously close to falling, was Xavier. His thin, distant voice reached out to us across the harbor as he waved madly from his precarious railing.

"We did it, heh! We did it! Mercédès! We did it!"

From the *terrasse* of Les Immortelles, Claude Brismand watched impassively, occasionally lifting the glass to his lips. *Brismand 1* finally lowered its gangplank, and the tourists began to mill onto the jetty. Aristide, leaning heavily on his grandson but triumphant, stumped down the gangway to be lifted by Omer and Alain to shoulder height as they too joined the chorus. Capucine unfolded a sign that read THIS WAY TO LES SALANTS. Lolo, never at a loss for a way of making money, pulled out a wooden bicycle-trailer from behind the wall and began to shout, "Luggage! Your luggage conveyed to Les Salants at a premium rate!"

There must have been thirty people aboard the ferry, maybe more. Students, families, an old couple with a dog. Children. I could hear laughter from the jetty, raised voices, some in foreign languages. Between embraces and back slappings, the heroes explained the mysterious failure of our first attemps at publicity: the disappearance of our posters, the perfidy of the tourist information officer in Fromentine (now revealed as an Houssin collaborator) who, while appearing to take our side, had in fact reported every detail of our plans to Brismand and done his best to dissuade tourists from visiting Les Salants.

From the street I could see Jojo-le-Goëland, openmouthed, a forgotten cigarette butt dropping from his fingers. Shop owners too had gathered to see what the fuss was about. I could see Mayor Pinoz standing in the doorway of the Chat Noir, and Joël Lacroix astride his red motorbike, both peering at our little crowd with growing amazement.

"Cycles for hire!" announced Omer Prossage. "Just down the road, cycles for Les Salants!"

Xavier, flushed with triumph, made his way down the gangplank toward Mercédès and spun her into his arms. If there was little warmth in her embrace, at least Xavier didn't seem to notice. Both he and Aristide were brandishing double handfuls of papers.

"Deposits!" yelled Aristide from Omer's shoulders. "Your house, Prossage—and yours, Guénolé—and five campers for you, Toinette, and—"

"Eleven deposits, heh! And more on the way!"

"It worked," said Capucine in awe.

"They did it!" crowed Toinette, flinging her arms around Matthias Guénolé and giving him a resounding kiss.

"*We* did it!" corrected Alain, spinning me into his arms with sudden exuberance. "Les Salants!"

"Les Salants, heh!"

"Les Salants!"

I don't know why I looked back then. Curiosity, perhaps, or the desire to preen a little. It was our triumph, our moment. Maybe I simply wanted to see his face.

I was the only one. As my friends moved on, singing, shouting, calling, chanting, I turned back—just for a moment—to look up at the hotel *terrasse*, where Brismand was sitting. A trick of the light showed his face very clearly. He was standing now, holding out his glass in a silent, ironic toast.

"*Les Salants!*"

And he was looking straight at me.

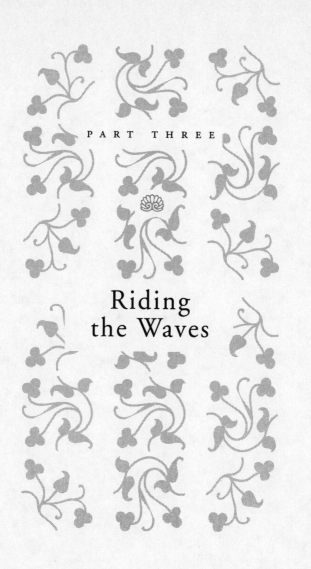

PART THREE

Riding
the Waves

1

My sister and her family turned up three days later. The hangar (now referred to as "the studio") was almost ready, and GrosJean was sitting on a bench in the yard, overseeing the final touches. Flynn was inside, looking at the wiring. The two Houssins who had been working on the conversion had already gone.

The boatyard, now separated from the studio by a broom fence, had been cut in two. Half of it now served as a garden, and GrosJean had embellished it with a few benches, a table, and some pots of flowers. The rest of the boatyard was still taken up by building materials. I wondered how long it would be before GrosJean decided to clear out his old work space altogether.

It should not have troubled me as much as it did. But I could not help myself; the boatyard had been our place, his and mine, the only place from which my mother and Adrienne had been excluded. There were ghosts there: myself, sitting cross-legged under the trestle; GrosJean shaping a piece of wood on the lathe; GrosJean humming along to the radio as he worked; GrosJean and I sharing a sandwich while he told one of his rare stories; GrosJean asking me, a long paintbrush in his hand, "What shall we call her? *Odile* or *Odette?*"; GrosJean laughing at my attempt at sail stitch; GrosJean standing back, admiring his work. . . . No one else had shared those things; not Adrienne, not Mother. They had never understood. Instead Mother had nagged him incessantly for jobs left undone, the half-finished projects, the shelves to be built, the gutter to be mended. At the end she had seen him as a bitter joke: a builder who began things but never completed them; a craftsman who managed only one boat a year; an idler who hid all day in a maze of clutter then emerged expecting to find his meal on the table. Adrienne was ashamed of his paint-marked clothes and lack of social graces, and avoided being seen with him in La Houssinière. I was the only one of us who saw him at work. Only I was proud of him. The ghost of myself lingered trustingly in the boatyard, secure in the knowledge that here, at least, we could both be what we dared not be elsewhere.

The morning of my sister's arrival, I was in the yard, painting my father's portrait in gouache. It was one of those cloudless summer mornings when everything is still green and damp, and my father was mellow and ready to be pleased, smoking and drinking coffee in the sun, the peak of his fisherman's cap pulled down over his eyes.

Suddenly, there came the sound of a car in the road behind the house, and I knew, with a sinking certainty, who it was.

My sister was wearing a white blouse and a flowing silk skirt, which made me feel grubby and underdressed. She kissed me on the cheek while the boys, identically clad in shorts and T-shirts, hung back, whispering, dark eyes wide. My father remained where he was, but his eyes were shining.

Flynn was at the hangar door, still in his overalls. I hoped he would stay—for some reason the thought of him working close by cheered me a little—but at the sight of Adrienne and her family he stood very still, keeping almost instinctively to the shadow of the doorway. I made a small gesture with my hand, as if to keep him there, but by then he had already stepped forward into the yard and, bypassing the gate, vaulted over the wall and onto the road. He gave me a little wave without turning around, climbed to the top of the dune, then began to run lightly back along the path toward La Goulue.

Marin followed the retreating figure with his eyes. "What's he doing here?" he asked. I looked at him, surprised by the sharp note in his voice. "He's been working for us. Why, do you know him?"

"I've seen him in La Houssinière. My uncle—" He stopped, his mouth crimped to a tight little line. "No, I don't know him," he said, and turned away.

❀

They joined us for lunch. I'd made lamb stew, and GrosJean ate with his usual silent enthusiasm, chasing each large, sloppy spoonful with a piece of bread. Adrienne picked delicately at her food, but ate little.

"It's so nice to be home again," she said, beaming at GrosJean. "My boys have been looking forward to it so much. They've been mad with excitement since Easter—"

I glanced at the boys. Loïc was playing with a piece of bread, crumbling it into his plate. Franck was staring out of the window.

"And you've made such a pretty holiday flat for them, Papa," went on Adrienne. "They'll have a wonderful time."

However, Adrienne and Marin, we soon learned, were to stay at Les Immortelles. The boys could stay at the studio with their nanny, but Marin had business with his uncle and was unsure how long their dealings would take. GrosJean seemed unmoved by the news and continued to eat in his slow, reflective way, his eyes fixed on the boys. Franck whispered something to his brother in Arabic, and both boys giggled.

"I was surprised to see that red-haired Englishman here," said Marin to GrosJean, helping himself to wine. "Is he a friend of yours?"

"Why, what's he done?" I asked, disliking his sour tone.

Marin shrugged and said nothing. GrosJean seemed not to hear at all.

"He's made a good job of the holiday flat, anyway," said Adrienne brightly. "What fun we can all have here!"

We finished the meal in silence.

❀

With the arrival of the boys, GrosJean was in his element. He sat in the yard and watched their games in silence, or showed them how to make little boats out of oddments of wood and sailcloth, or walked with them to the dunes and played hide-and-seek in the long grass. Adrienne and

Marin came by occasionally but rarely stayed long; Marin's business, they said, was more complicated than they had expected, and likely to take time.

❦

Meanwhile, Les Salants had begun to blossom. Gardens had been tidied, with hollyhocks and lavender and rosemary shooting up from the sandy soil; newly painted shutters and doors, streets swept and borders raked, houses bright with their ocher roof tiles and freshly whitewashed walls. Already the spare rooms and hastily converted outhouses were filling up. A group of tourists had arrived at the campsite near La Houssinière but gravitated to Les Salants for the dunes and the scenery. Philippe Bastonnet and his young family were back for the summer and came to La Goulue almost every day. Though Aristide still kept his distance, Désirée met them there, and could often be seen in the shade of a big parasol while Laetitia splashed exuberantly in the rock pools.

Toinette had opened up the land behind her little house as an unofficial campsite at half the Houssin prices, and a young couple from Paris had already pitched their tent there. The facilities were primitive—Toinette's outside toilet and washhouse, plus a hose and tap for fresh water—but there was food from Omer's farm, there was Angélo's—and of course there was the beach, still a little thin on sand but building with every tide. With the stones covered over, the ground was smooth and flat. Rocks beyond the tide line provided relief and shelter. There were inlets and pools for the children to exclaim over. I found that Laetitia made friends quite easily with the Salannais children. There was a little suspicion at first—it was rare for them to see tourists, and they were wary—but her engaging manner soon thawed their reserve. Within a week it became a common sight to see them together, running barefoot through Les Salants, poking sticks at the *étier*, rolling and rollicking in the dunes with Pétrole in frenzied pursuit. Round, earnest Lolo was especially taken with her and amused me by adopting her city speech and mimicking her accent.

My nephews didn't join them. Instead, in spite of my father's efforts to keep them close by, they spent most of their time in La Houssinière. There was a games arcade there, next to the cinema, where they liked to play. They were easily bored, said Adrienne apologetically.

The only other child who seemed uninterested in the beach was Damien. The eldest of the Salannais youngsters, he was also the most reserved; I had seen him alone on more than one occasion, smoking cigarettes and hanging about on the clifftop. When I asked him if he had quarreled with Lolo, he simply shrugged and shook his head. Kid's stuff, he declared dismissively. Sometimes he just needed to be on his own.

I half believed him. He had his father's surliness and his resentful nature: not naturally sociable, he must have found it galling that Lolo, formerly his most loyal companion, should have switched allegiance so quickly, and to Laetitia, a mainlander barely eight years old. With some amusement I noticed Damien adopting increasingly adult mannerisms, affecting the nonchalant turned-collar slouch of Joël Lacroix and his Houssin cronies. Plus Charlotte commented that young Damien seemed to have more money than a boy of his age should. There were rumors in the village that the motorcycle gang had been seen with a new member riding pillion. A youngster, by all accounts.

My suspicions were confirmed when I saw him in La Houssinière later that week, hanging around the Chat Noir café. I had gone to meet the *Brismand 1* with some new paintings for my gallery in Fromentine, and I saw him with Joël and some other young Houssins, smoking in the sun by the esplanade. There were girls there too, leggy young things in short skirts. Once again, I recognized Mercédès.

She caught my eye as I passed the little group, and bridled a little at my scrutiny. She was smoking—she never did at home—and I thought she looked a little pale in spite of her red lipstick, her dark eyes tired and smudgy. She laughed—too shrilly—as I went by, and dragged at her cigarette with a look of defiance. Damien looked away awkwardly. I did not speak to either of them.

La Houssinière was quiet. Not dead, as some Salannais had gleefully predicted, but somnolent. Cafés and bars were open but mostly half empty; there were maybe a dozen people on the beach at Les Immortelles. Soeur Extase and Soeur Thérèse were sitting in the sun on the hotel steps, and waved as I went past.

"Why, Mado!"

"What have you got there?"

I sat down next to them and showed them my folder of paintings. The sisters nodded appreciatively. "You should try to sell some to Monsieur Brismand, little Mado."

"We could do with something nice to look at, couldn't we, *ma soeur*—we've been staring at the same old—"

"—Martyrdoms for far too long." Soeur Thérèse ran her fingers over one of the paintings. It was a view of Pointe Griznoz, with the ruined church standing out against a late-evening sky.

"Artist's eyes," she said, smiling. "You've got your father's gift."

"Give him our love, Mado."

"And talk to Monsieur Brismand. He's in a meeting now but—"

"He's always had a soft spot for you."

I considered the idea. It might well be true; but I did not like the idea of doing business with Claude Brismand. I'd been avoiding him since our last meeting; I already knew he was curious about the length of my stay, and I did not want to open myself up to his questioning. I already had an idea that he knew more about what was going on in Les Salants than we guessed, and although he had never managed to catch anyone stealing sand from Les Immortelles, he remained certain that it was going on. The beach at La Goulue was not a thing that could be kept secret from the Houssins, and I knew it was only a matter of time before someone let slip the secret of our floating reef. When that happened, I thought, I wanted to be as far away from Brismand as possible.

I was about to go when suddenly I spotted a small object on the ground in front of me. It was a red coral bead like the ones my father put on his boats. Many islanders still wear them; someone must have lost his.

"You've got sharp eyes," observed Soeur Extase, seeing me pick it up.

"Keep it, little Mado," said Soeur Thérèse. "Wear it—it'll bring you luck."

I said good-bye to the sisters and had stood up to go (the *Brismand 1* had sounded its ten-minute warning call, and I did not want to miss it), when I caught the sound of a door slamming, and a sudden splurge of voices from the lobby of Les Immortelles. I could not make out what was being said; but I could hear anger in the tones, and a rising volume, as if someone were leaving in a temper. There were several voices, Brismand's deep tones counterpointing the others. Then a man and a woman emerged from the lobby almost on top of us with identical expressions of stone-faced rage. The sisters moved aside to let them pass, then drew together like curtains, grinning.

"Everything okay?" I said to Adrienne.

But neither she nor Marin deigned to reply.

2

Summer sailed in. The weather stayed good as it usually does at this time in the islands, warm and sunny but with the sea breeze from the west keeping temperatures pleasant. Seven of us now had tourists—including four families—staying in spare rooms and converted buildings. Toinette had a full complement of campers. That made thirty-eight people so far, with more arriving every time *Brismand 1* came in.

Charlotte Prossage got into the habit of making paella once a week, using crabs and langoustines from the new vivarium. She would make it in a huge pot and carry it to Angélo's, who would sell it in take-out foil containers. The tourists loved the idea, and soon she was having to enlist Capucine to help. She suggested a rotation where each of them prepared a dish once a week. Soon we had: paella on Sundays, *gratin devinnois* (baked red mullet, white wine, and sliced potatoes with goat's cheese) on Tuesdays, and bouillabaisse on Thursdays. Other people in the village virtually stopped cooking altogether.

On midsummer's day, Aristide finally announced the engagement between his grandson and Mercédès Prossage, and took the *Cécilia* on a lap of honor around the Bouch'ou to celebrate. Charlotte sang a hymn while Mercédès sat in the bow in a white dress, complaining under her breath about the seaweed smell, and the way the spray splashed her every time the *Cécilia* pitched.

The *Eleanore 2* had exceeded expectations. Alain and Matthias were delighted; even Ghislain took the news of Mercédès's engagement with surprising good grace and designed several elaborate and improbable plans of his own, most of which involved entering the *Eleanore 2* in regattas up and down the coast, and winning a fortune in prize money.

Toinette had started her own little business, selling dozens of little salt-scrub sachets (scented with wild lavender and rosemary) from her trailer. "It's so simple," she said, her black eyes gleaming. "Those tourists will buy anything. Wild herbs tied with ribbon. Sea mud, even." She cackled, hardly believing it herself. "You just put it into little jars and write THALASSOTHERAPEUTIC SKIN FOOD on the label. My mother put it on her face for years. It's an old island beauty secret."

Omer La Patate found a mainland buyer for his surplus vegetables at a greatly increased price to what he had been used to in La Houssinière. He set some of his reclaimed land aside for autumn flowers, after having believed for years that such frivolous things were a waste of time.

Mercédès often disappeared to La Houssinière for hours, ostensibly to the beauty parlor. "The time you spend in there," Toinette told her, "you must fart perfume by now. Chanel Number Five." She cackled.

Mercédès tossed her hair pettishly. "You're so coarse, *Mémé*."

Aristide stubbornly continued to ignore the presence of his son in La Houssinière and threw himself more deeply—and with a kind of desperation—into his plans for Xavier and Mercédès.

Désirée was saddened, but unsurprised. "I don't care," she repeated, sitting under her parasol with Gabi and the baby. "We've all lived too long in the shadow of Olivier's grave. What I want now is the company of the living."

Her eyes went to the top of the cliff, where Aristide often sat to watch the fishing boats come in. I noticed that his binoculars were pointing, not out to sea, but toward the tide line, where Laetitia and Lolo were building a fort.

"He sits up there every day," said Désirée. "He hardly says a word to me anymore." She picked up the baby and straightened his sun hat. "I think I'll go and have a stroll by the water," she said brightly. "I could do with some air."

∞

Still the tourists continued to come. An English family with their three children. An elderly couple with their dog. An elegant old lady, always in pink and white. A number of camping families with children.

We had never seen so many children. The whole village was screaming with them, shouting, laughing, bright and brash as their beach toys, dressed in lime and turquoise and fuchsia pink, smelling of suntan lotion and coconut oil and cotton candy and life.

Not all the visitors were tourists. I saw with some amusement that our own youngsters—Damien and Lolo, among others—had gained an unexpected status by association, and were even accepting bribes from the young Houssins in exchange for access to the beach.

"Enterprising young things," remarked Capucine, as I commented on this. "Nothing wrong with a bit of business. Specially when it means taking money off an Houssin." She chuckled placidly. "It's nice to have something they want, for a change, heh? Why shouldn't we make them pay?"

For a while, the black market flourished. Damien Guénolé collected filter-tipped cigarettes, which he smoked with, I suspected, secret distaste, but Lolo wisely took all his bribes in cash. He was saving up, he confided, to buy a moped.

"You can make all sorts of money with a moped," he told me seriously. "Odd jobs, errands, all kinds of stuff. You'll never be short if you've got transport."

Amazing, the difference a dozen children can make. Suddenly Les Salants was alive. Old people were no longer in the majority.

"I like it," declared Toinette when I mentioned it to her. "It makes me feel young."

She was not the only one. I found gruff Aristide on the top of the cliff, teaching a couple of small boys how to tie knots. Alain, usually so stern with his own family, took Laetitia out fishing in his boat. Désirée handed out sweets in secret to eager, grubby hands. Everyone wanted the summer people, of course. But the children fulfilled a more primal need. We bribed and spoiled them relentlessly. Dour old women were sweetened. Dour old men rediscovered boyhood pleasures.

Flynn was the children's favorite. He had always attracted our own children, of course, perhaps because he never made any attempt to do so. But with the summer people he was the Pied Piper; there were always children around him, talking to him, watching him as he built driftwood sculptures or sorted rubbish from the beach. They dogged him mercilessly, but he didn't seem to mind. They brought him their trophies from La Goulue and their tales of one another. They vied shamelessly with one another for his attention. Flynn accepted their admiration with the casual cheeriness he showed to everyone.

Since the arrival of the tourists, however, I thought Flynn seemed more withdrawn behind his good humor. He always had time for me, however, and we spent many hours sitting on the roof of the *blockhaus* or down by the water's edge, talking. I was grateful for it; now that Les Salants was on the road to recovery I had begun to feel strangely superfluous, like a mother who sees her children begin to grow away from her. Of course it was absurd—no one could have been happier at the change in Les Salants—and yet several times I found myself almost wishing for some interruption to our tranquillity.

Flynn laughed when I told him about it. "You were never made to live on an island," he said cheerily. "You need to live in a state of perpetual crisis to survive."

It was a flip comment, and at the time it made me laugh. "That's not true! I love the quiet life!"

He grinned. "There's no such thing when you're around."

Later I thought about what Flynn had said. Could it be that he'd been right? That what I needed was a sense of danger, of crisis? Was this what had first drawn me to Le Devin? And to Flynn himself?

That night at low tide I felt restless, and I went out on La Goulue to clear my head. There was a generous half moon; I could hear the muted *hisshhh* of the waves on the dark *grève*, and feel the mild turning wind. As I looked back from the edge of La Goulue I could see the *blockhaus*, a dark hulk against the starry sky, and for a moment I was sure I saw a figure detach itself from the block of darkness and slip away into the dunes. By the way he moved, I recognized Flynn.

Perhaps he'd gone fishing, I told myself, though he had not been carrying a lantern. Sometimes, I knew, he still poached oysters from Guénolé's beds, to keep his hand in. That was a job better suited to darkness.

After that single glimpse I saw no more sign of him, and feeling chilly, I began to make my way back toward the house. In the distance I could still hear the sound of singing and shouting from the village, and see yellow light spilling out across the road from Angélo's and beyond. Below me on the path, a couple of figures stood, almost invisible in the shadow of the dune. One was broad and round-shouldered, hands digging nonchalantly into the pockets of his *vareuse*, the other lighter on his feet, a whisker of light from the café just touching his hair into sudden flame.

I only saw them for a moment. A blur of lowered voices, a raised hand; an embrace. Then they were gone, Brismand into the village, his shadow stretching immensely across the dune, and Flynn back up the path in long, smooth strides toward me. I had no time to avoid him; he was on me before I knew it, his face bleakly moonlit. I was glad mine was in shadow.

"You're out late," he said cheerily. Evidently he didn't realize I had seen him with Brismand.

"So are you," I said. My thoughts were scrambled; I didn't trust myself with what I'd seen—or thought I'd seen. I needed to think about what it meant.

He grinned. "Belote," he said. "I left on a winning streak, for a change. Won a dozen bottles of wine from Omer. Charlotte's going to kill him when he sobers up." He ruffled my hair. "Sweet dreams,

Mado." And at that he was off, whistling between his teeth, back the way I had come.

I found it unexpectedly difficult to challenge Flynn about his meeting with Brismand. I told myself that it could have been an entirely chance meeting; Les Salants was not out-of-bounds to Houssins, and Omer, Matthias, Aristide, and Alain all confirmed that Flynn had indeed played belote that evening at Angélo's. He had not lied to me. Besides, as Capucine was fond of pointing out, Flynn wasn't a Salannais. He didn't take sides. Perhaps Brismand had simply asked him to do some work. All the same, a suspicion remained; a fragment in an oyster's shell, a small unease.

My mind kept returning to the lobby of Les Immortelles, to Brismand's noisy meeting with Marin and Adrienne; to the coral bead I had found on the steps of the hotel. Many islanders still wear them; my father often carried one, as do many fishermen.

I wondered whether Flynn still wore his.

3

As July ended I began to feel a growing concern for my father. With my sister and her family spending so much time in La Houssinière, GrosJean seemed more distracted than usual, and less communicative. I was used to that; but there was something new in his silence. A kind of vagueness. The studio was finished. The workmen's litter had long since been cleared away. There was no longer any reason for GrosJean to be outside supervising affairs, and to my dismay he reverted once again to his usual apathy, worse now than ever before, sitting staring out of the window or drinking coffee in the kitchen, waiting for the boys to come home.

Those boys. They were the only reason he ever left that somnolent, indifferent state. He came alive only when they were there, and it filled me with anger and pity. Pépère Gros Bide, they called him behind his back. Old Man Fat Belly. They aped him in secret, mimicking his dragging walk, sticking out their feet and their little round tummies in monkeyish glee. To his face they were prim and giggly, eyes downcast, hands outstretched for gifts of money or sweets. There were more costly gifts too. New sweatsuits—Franck's red, Loïc's blue—worn once and then left carelessly bundled up in the back garden among the thistles. Numerous toys—balls, buckets, and spades, electronic games that he must have sent for from the mainland, as none of our children could have afforded such things. It would be Loïc's birthday in August, and there was talk of a boat.

Partly to alleviate my anxiety, I painted faster and with more enthusiasm than ever before. I had never felt closer to my subject: I painted Les Salants and the Salannais; lovely Mercédès in her short skirts; Charlotte Prossage bringing in the washing against a blue-black bank of storm clouds; young men, stripped to the waist, working on the salt marshes, the cones of stark white salt rising around them like an alien landscape; Alain Guénolé, sitting at the prow of his *Eleanore 2* like a Celtic chieftain; Omer with his earnest, comic face; Flynn with his collecting bag at the water's edge, or with his little single-sailed boat, or lifting lobster pots out of the water, his hair tied back with a piece of sailcloth, one hand over his eyes to shield them from the sun. . . .

I have a good eye for detail. My mother always said so. I painted mostly from memory—no one really had time to pose for me—and I piled the stretched canvases against the wall of my room to dry before framing. When she came over from La Houssinière, Adrienne watched me with a growing interest that, I felt, was not entirely benevolent.

"You're using a lot more color than you used to," she remarked. "Some of those pictures look quite garish."

It was true. My earlier paintings were bleak in comparison, the colors often limited to the soft grays and browns of an island winter. But summer had come to my palette now as it had to the whole village, bringing with it the dusty pinks of the tamarisk, the chrome yellow of broom, gorse, and mimosa, the hot whites of salt and sand, the orange of the fishing buoys, the stark blue sky, and the red sails of the island boats. This new work too was bleak in its way, but it was a bleakness I loved. I felt I had never done better work.

Flynn said as much, with a curt little nod of admiration that made me hot with pride. "You're doing well," he said. "You'll soon be ready to set up on your own someday."

He was sitting in profile to me, his back against the *blockhaus* wall, his face half-hidden beneath the brim of his floppy hat. Above his head, a small lizard flicked against the warm stone. I tried to capture his expression—the curve of his mouth, the shadow slanting down from his cheekbone. Behind us on the summer blue dune, came the *chirr* of crickets. Flynn saw me drawing him and sat up.

"You moved," I complained.

"I'm superstitious. We Irish believe pencils steal away a portion of the soul."

I smiled. "I'm flattered you think I'm that good."

"Good enough to open up a gallery of your own. In Nantes, perhaps, or Paris. You're wasted here."

"I don't think so."

Flynn shrugged. "Things change. Anything might happen. And you can't hide away here forever."

"I don't know what you mean." I was wearing the red dress Brismand had given me; the silk was almost weightless against my skin. It felt strange after so many months of trousers and sailcloth shirts, almost like being in Paris again. My bare feet were dusty from the dune.

"Oh yes, you do. You're talented, smart, beautiful—" He broke off, and for a moment he looked almost as nonplused as I was. "Well, you are," he said finally, with a touch of defensiveness.

Far below us, La Goulue was alive; dozens of little boats flecked the water. I recognized them by their sails: the *Cécilia*; the *Papa Chico*; the *Eleanore 2*; Jojo's *Marie Joseph*. Beyond them, the vast blue sweep of the bay.

"You're not wearing your lucky bead," I noticed suddenly.

Flynn touched his throat in an automatic gesture. "No," he said indifferently. "I make my own luck." He looked back across the bay. "It looks so small from up here, doesn't it?"

I did not answer. Inside me something had begun to clench like a fist, leaving me breathless. I put my hand in my pocket. The bead I had picked up at Les Immortelles was there, no bigger than a cherry stone. Flynn put his hand in front of his face and closed his fingers over La Goulue.

"These little places," he said gently. "Thirty houses and a beach. You think you can hold out against them. You're careful. You're clever. But it's like getting your finger caught in one of those Chinese tubes, where pulling only squeezes tighter. Before you know it, you're involved. At first it's only little things. You think they're not important. And then one day, you realize that the little things are all there is."

"I don't understand," I told him, moving closer. The smell of the dune was strong now—dune pinks and fennel and the apricot scent of broom warmed by the sun. Flynn's expression was still half-hidden by that ridiculous floppy hat; I wanted to push it away and see his eyes, touch the spray of freckles across the bridge of his nose. . . . In the pocket of my dress my fingers tightened once more over the bead, then relaxed again. Flynn thought I was beautiful. The idea was astonishing, like a volley of fireworks.

Flynn shook his head. "I've been here too long," he said gently. "Mado, did you expect me to stay forever?"

Perhaps I had; in spite of his restlessness I had never imagined him leaving. Besides, it was high season; Les Salants had never been as busy.

"You call this busy?" said Flynn. "These seaside places, I've seen them before—lived in them before. Dead in winter, a handful of people in summer." He sighed. "Little places. Little people. It's depressing."

His mouth was all I could see now of his shadowed face. I was fascinated by its shape, its texture; the fullness of the top lip; the tiny smile lines at the corners. My astonishment still lingered like the imprint of the sun on my retinas; Flynn thought I was beautiful. In comparison the words he was speaking seemed insubstantial, bright nothings designed to decoy me from a larger truth. I reached out gently, firmly, and took his face between my hands.

For a moment I felt him hesitate. But his skin was as warm as the sand at my feet; his eyes were the color of mica; and I felt different, somehow, as if Brismand's gift had contained some vestige of the man's charm, making me, for that moment, someone else.

I sealed Flynn's protest with my mouth. He tasted of peaches and

wool and metal and wine. All my senses seemed suddenly heightened—
the smell of the sea and the dunes; the sounds of the gulls and the water
and the distant voices from the beach and the small popping sounds of
grass growing; the light. It overwhelmed me. I was spinning, too fast for
the center of me to hold. I felt that at any moment I might explode like
a rocket, scrawling my name in stars across the dazzling sky.

It should have been clumsy. Maybe it was; but to me it seemed effort-
less. The red dress slipped from me almost by itself. Flynn's shirt joined
it; beneath it his skin was pale, barely darker than the sand itself, and he
was returning my kisses the way a man gulps water after days of being
lost in the desert; avidly, without pausing to take breath until the
moment at which consciousness founders. Neither of us spoke until our
thirst was slaked, and from a kind of daze we emerged to find ourselves
lying clothed in sand and sweat, with the dry dune grasses swaying over
our heads and the hot white wall of the *blockhaus* and the shimmering
sea beyond it like a mirage.

Still entwined, we watched it in long, complicated silence. This
changed everything. I knew it, and yet I wanted to retain the moment
for as long as possible, lying with my head on Flynn's stomach and one
hand slung casually around his shoulders. There were a thousand questions I wanted to ask, but I knew that to ask them would be to admit the
change, to confront the fact that he and I were no longer simply friends
but something infinitely more dangerous. I sensed that he was waiting
for me to break the tension, perhaps to take his cue from me; above us a
gyre of gulls wheeled and protested.

No one spoke.

4

The midmonth tides had brought heat storms, but since these were mostly limited to extravagant displays of sheet lightning and a few hard night showers, trade remained unaffected. We celebrated our success with a fireworks display arranged by Flynn and paid for by Aristide with the cooperation of Pinoz, the mayor. It wasn't the kind of huge spectacle you might see on the coast, but it was certainly the first time Les Salants had ever had such a thing, and everyone came out to see it. Three giant Catherine wheels rode the Bouch'ou, accessible only by boat and designed to shimmer across the water. There were Bengal lights on the dune. Rockets garlanded the sky with fat fiery blossoms. The whole display lasted no more than a few minutes, but the children were enthralled. Lolo had never seen fireworks before, and while Laetitia and the other tourist children were less easily impressed, everyone agreed that it was the best fireworks display the island had ever seen. Capucine and Charlotte made celebration cakes to be handed around as a treat, little *devinnoiseries* and twisted rolls, fried pastries lathered in honey, and griddled pancakes dripping salt butter.

My father was absent from the celebration. Adrienne came, and her boys with her, though they seemed bored by the treats, which delighted the other children. I saw them later by one of the bonfires. Damien was with them, looking dissatisfied and angry: I gathered from Lolo that there had been some kind of falling-out between them.

"It's about Mercédès," confided Lolo forlornly. "He'd do anything to impress her. That's all he cares about."

Certainly Damien had changed. His natural sullenness seemed to have taken over completely, and he now avoided his old friend altogether. Alain too was having trouble with him. He admitted as much, with a mixture of annoyance and reluctant pride.

"We've always been like that, you know," he told me. "The Guénolés. Head full of rocks." Still, I could tell he was concerned. "I can't do anything with the boy," he said. "He doesn't talk to me. He and his brother used to be close as crabs, but even Ghislain can't get a smile out of him, or a word. Still, I was just the same at his age. He'll grow out of it."

Alain thought that perhaps a new moped would take Damien's mind off his troubles. "Might keep him away from those Houssins too," he added. "Bring him back to the village. Give him something new to think about."

I hoped so. I'd always liked Damien in spite of his reserve. He reminded me a little of myself at his age—suspicious, resentful, brooding. And at fifteen, a first love is summer lightning; white-hot, fierce, and quickly over.

Mercédès, too, was causing concern. Since her engagement had been announced, she had become more temperamental than ever; spending hours in her room; refusing to eat; in turns cajoling and berating her hapless betrothed so that Xavier no longer knew what to do to please her.

Aristide put it down to nerves. But it was more than that; I thought the girl looked ill as well as nervous, smoking too much and ready to snap or cry at the most trivial thing. Toinette revealed that Mercédès and Charlotte had quarreled over a wedding dress and were now no longer speaking to each other.

"It belongs to Désirée Bastonnet," explained Toinette. "An old lace dress, nip-waisted, very fine. Xavier wanted Mercédès to wear it."

Désirée had kept the dress, lovingly stored away in lavender-scented sheets, since her own wedding. Xavier's mother had worn it too, the day she married Olivier. But Mercédès had refused outright to wear it, and when Charlotte timidly persisted, had thrown an epic tantrum.

Malicious rumors that Mercédès had only refused the dress because she was too fat to get into it did nothing to restore peace to the Prossage household.

During that time, Flynn and I had settled into a kind of routine. We did not speak of the change that had occurred between us, as if to admit its existence might somehow compromise us more deeply than either of us wanted. As a result there was a deceptively carefree quality to our intimacy, like that of a holiday romance. We existed within a webwork of invisible lines that neither of us dared cross. We talked, we made love, we swam together at La Goulue, we went fishing, we grilled our catches over the little barbecue that Flynn had built in a hollow behind the dune. We respected the boundaries we had set ourselves. Sometimes I wondered whether it was my cowardice that had set these limits, or his. But Flynn no longer spoke of leaving.

❦

No one had heard any more rumors about Claude Brismand. He had been seen a few times, with Pinoz and Jojo-le-Goëland, once on La Goulue and once in the village. Capucine said they had been hanging around near her trailer, and Alain saw them outside the *blockhaus*. But as far as anyone could tell, Brismand was still too busy damp-proofing Les Immortelles to be planning anything new. Certainly there had been no mention of a new ferry, and most people were inclined to believe that the *Brismand 2* thing had been someone's—maybe Ghislain's—idea of a joke.

"Brismand knows he's lost the game," said Aristide gleefully. "High time those Houssins got a taste of the underdog for a change. Their luck's turned, and they know it."

Toinette nodded. "We've got the Saint our side."

☙

Her optimism was premature. Only a few days later I came back from the village with some mackerel for GrosJean's lunch and found Brismand sitting under the parasol in the yard, waiting for me. He was still wearing his fisherman's cap but had chosen to dignify the occasion by wearing a linen jacket and a tie. His feet, as usual, were bare in faded espadrilles. There was a Gitane crooked between his fingers.

My father was sitting opposite him, a bottle of Muscadet close at hand. There were three glasses waiting.

"Why, Mado." Brismand raised himself with difficulty from his chair. "I hoped you'd be along soon."

"What are you doing here?" Surprise made me abrupt, and he looked pained.

"I came to see you, of course." Behind the rueful expression, something like amusement. "I like to keep abreast of what's going on."

"So I've heard."

He poured himself another glass of wine, then another for me. "You Salannais have had rather an unusual run of luck, haven't you? You must be pleased with yourself."

I kept my tone neutral. "We manage."

Brismand grinned, his gangster's mustache bristling. "I could use someone like you at the hotel. Someone young and energetic. You should think about it."

"Someone like me? What could I do?"

"You'd be surprised." His tone was encouraging. "An artist—a designer—could be very useful to me right now. We could sort something out. I think you'd find it profitable."

"I'm happy as I am."

"Maybe so. But circumstances change, heh? You might welcome a little independence. Safeguard the future." He grinned widely and pushed the glass toward me. "Here. Have some wine."

"No thanks." I indicated my packet of fish. "I need to get these in the oven. It's getting late."

"Mackerel, heh?" said Brismand, getting up. "I know a wonderful way of doing them, with rosemary and salt. I'll help you, and we can talk some more."

He followed me into the kitchen. He was more deft than his bulk suggested, slitting and gutting the fish in a single swift movement.

"How's business?" I asked, lighting the oven.

"Not bad," said Brismand, smiling. "In fact, your father and I were just celebrating."

"Celebrating what?"

Brismand gave his enormous smile. "A sale."

They'd used the boys, of course. I knew my father would do anything to keep the boys close by. Marin and Adrienne had played on his fondness; spoken of investments; encouraged GrosJean to borrow beyond his capacity to repay. I wondered how much of the land he had already signed away.

Patiently Brismand waited for me to speak. I could feel his huge and chilly amusement as he waited, his slate-colored eyes intent as a cat's. Presently, without asking me, he began to prepare the marinade for the fish, with oil, balsamic and salt, and shoots of rosemary from the bushes beside the front door.

"Madeleine. We should be friends, you know." His look would be mournful, I knew—drooping jowls and sad mustache—but there was laughter in his voice. "We're really not so different. Both fighters. Both businesspeople. You shouldn't be so prejudiced about joining me. I'm sure you'd be a success. And I sincerely do want to help, you know. I always have."

I did not look at him as I salted the fish and wrapped them in foil papillotes, then slid them into the hot oven.

"You forgot the marinade."

"That's not the way I do it, Monsieur Brismand."

He sighed. "A pity. You would have enjoyed it."

"How much?" I said at last. "How much did he give it to you for?"

Brismand tutted. "*Give* it to me?" he said reproachfully. "No one has given me anything. Why should they?"

The legal papers had been drawn up on the mainland. My father was slightly in awe of the arcane business of seals and signatures. Legal terminology bewildered him. Though Brismand was vague with the details, I gathered he had accepted to take land as collateral on a loan. As usual. This was simply a variation on his old technique: short-term loans to be paid off in property at a later date.

After all, as Adrienne would have said, the land was useless to my father. A few kilometers of dune between La Bouche and La Goulu, a derelict boatyard; useless, at least, until now.

All my worst suspicions had been confirmed. The repairs to the house, the presents for the boys, the new bicycles, the computer games, the sailboards—

"You paid for all that. You lent him the money."

Brismand shrugged. "Of course. Who else?" He dressed a green salad with vinaigrette and *salicorne*, the fleshy island herb often used in pickles, and put it into the wooden bowl as I began to slice tomatoes. "We should have shallots with these," he observed in the same mild tone. "They bring out the flavor of a ripe tomato like nothing else. Tell me, where do you keep them?"

I ignored him.

"Ah, here they are, in the vegetable bin. Lovely fat ones too. I can see Omer must be doing good business down at the farm. It's been a golden year all around for Les Salants, hasn't it? Fish, vegetables, tourists—"

"We've done all right."

"So modest. Heh. It's almost a miracle."

He sliced shallots with a swift, practiced hand. The scent was pungent, like the sea. "And all thanks to that nice beach you've stolen. You and your clever friend, Rouget."

I put down the knife gently on the tabletop. My hand was shaking a little.

"Careful. You don't want to cut yourself."

"I don't know what you mean."

"I mean you should be more careful with that knife, Mado." He chuckled. "Or are *you* trying to tell me you don't know anything about the beach?"

"Beaches move. Sand moves."

"Yes, it does, and sometimes it even moves of its own accord. But not this time, heh?" He held out his hands, still bloody from the fish, in a wide gesture. "Oh, don't think I bear you any grudge. I'm full of admiration for what you've done. You've brought Les Salants out of the sea again. You've made it a success. All I'm doing is standing up for my own interests, Mado, making sure I get to enjoy my share. Call it compensation, if you like. You owe me that."

"You're the one who started the flooding in the first place," I told him angrily. "No one owes you anything."

"Oh, but they do." Brismand shook his head. "Where did you think the money was coming from, heh? The money for Angélo's café, Omer's windmill, Xavier's house? Who do you think provided the capital? Who laid the foundations for all this?" He gestured toward the window, sweeping La Goulue, the village, the sky, the sparkling sea into his grimy palm.

"Maybe you did," I said. "But that's over now. We're holding our own. Les Salants doesn't need your money anymore."

"Shh." With exaggerated concentration Brismand poured marinade over the tomatoes. It was tempting and aromatic. I could smell how it would be on the hot fish, how the rosemary vinegar would evaporate, the olive oil sizzle. "You'd be surprised at how things alter when there's money to be made," he said. "Why be content with a couple of tourists in a back room when, with a little capital, you could convert a garage into a holiday flat, or build a row of chalets on some waste ground? You've had a taste of success, Mado. Do you really think people will be so easily satisfied?"

I thought about it in silence for a while. "You may be right," I said at last. "But I still don't see what you're going to get out of it. You can't build much on my father's bit of land."

"Madeleine." Brismand's shoulders slouched expressively, reproach etched into every line of his body. "Why must there always be an ulterior motive? Why not simply accept that I want to invest in Les Salants?" He spread his hands in appeal. "There's been so little trust between our two communities. So much antagonism. Even you have been drawn into it. What have I ever done to earn your suspicion? I advance money to your father in exchange for land he doesn't need—suspicion. I offer you a job at Les Immortelles—more suspicion. I try to mend the bridges between our communities for the sake of my family—greatest suspicion of all. Heh!" He threw up his arms dramatically. "Tell me. What do you suspect me of now?"

I did not reply. His charm, fully unfurled, was palpable and immense. Even so, I still knew I was right to mistrust him. He had some plan—I thought of the *Brismand 2*, half-completed six months before, now ready to launch, and I wondered once again what it might be. Brismand sighed heavily and tugged at his collar to loosen it.

"I'm an old man, Mado. And a lonely one. I had a wife. A little son. Both sacrificed to my ambition. I admit that once I valued money over everything else. But money gets old. It loses its shine. Now I want the things money can't buy. A family. Friends. Peace."

"Peace!"

"I am sixty-four years old, Madeleine. I sleep badly. I drink rather too well. The machine begins to run down. I ask myself whether it was worthwhile, whether the making of money has made me happy. I ask myself these things more and more often." He glanced at the oven. The timer was on zero. "Madeleine, I think your fish are cooked."

Using the gloves, he brought the mackerel out of the oven. He unwrapped them from the foil and poured the rest of the marinade over them. It smelled as I had imagined, sweet and hot and delicious. "I'll leave you to enjoy your dinner in peace, heh." He sighed theatrically. "I usually eat at my hotel, you know. I can choose any table I like, any dish from the menu. But my appetite—" He patted his stomach ruefully. "My appetite isn't what it once was. Perhaps the sight of all those empty tables—"

I still don't know why I asked him. Perhaps because no Devinnois ever refuses to offer hospitality. Perhaps because his words had struck a chord. "Why not eat with us?" I suggested impulsively. "There's enough to go around."

But Brismand laughed suddenly and hugely, his belly shaking with his giant mirth. I felt my cheeks redden, knowing I had been manipulated into showing sympathy where none was needed, and that my gesture had amused him.

"Thank you, Mado," he said at last, wiping tears from his eyes with the corner of his handkerchief. "What a kind invitation. But I must be on my way, heh? Today I have other fish to fry."

5

When I passed by the *blockhaus* the following morning, Flynn was nowhere to be seen. The shutters were closed, the generator was off, and there were none of the usual signs of his presence. Looking through the window, I could see no breakfast dishes in the sink, no coverlet on the bed, no clothes. A quick glance inside—few people lock their doors in Les Salants—revealed nothing but the unaired smell of an empty house. Worse still, the little boat that he kept at the top of the *étier* had gone.

"He's probably gone fishing," said Capucine, when I called at her trailer.

Alain agreed, saying he thought he'd seen Flynn's boat going out early that morning. Angélo too seemed unworried. But Aristide looked concerned. "Accidents happen," he told us dourly. "Remember Olivier—"

"Heh," said Alain. "Olivier always was unlucky."

Angélo nodded. "Rouget's more likely to be making trouble than getting it. He'll land on his feet, wherever he is."

But as the day wore on and Flynn did not reappear, I began to feel a little anxious. Surely he would have told me if he'd been planning to be away for long?

When he had not returned by noon I went to check in La

Houssinière, where the *Brismand 1* was just about to set off. A line of tourists waited out of the sun beneath the awning of the Chat Noir; cases and rucksacks lined the gangplank. Automatically I found myself scanning the line for a man with red hair.

Of course Flynn was not among the departing tourists. But as I was about to turn back toward the esplanade I noticed a familiar figure waiting in line. Her long hair obscured her face, but there was no mistaking the tight jeans and the burnt orange halter top. A big rucksack lay at her feet like a dog.

"Mercédès?"

She turned at the sound of my voice. Her face was pale and clean of makeup. She looked as if she had been crying. "Leave me alone," she said, and turned back toward the *Brismand 1*.

I looked at her, concerned. "Mercédès? Are you all right?"

Without looking at me, she shook her head. "This is nothing to do with you, La Poule. Don't interfere." I did not move, but stood silently at her side, waiting. Mercédès tossed her hair. "You've always hated me. You should be happy to see the back of me. Now just leave me alone, won't you?" Her face was an unhappy blur beneath the curtain of hair.

I put my hand on her thin shoulder. "I never hated you. Come with me, and I'll buy you a coffee, and we can talk. And after that, if you still want to go—"

Mercédès gave a furious sob under her hair. "I *don't* want to go!"

I picked up her bag. "Then come with me."

"Not the Chat Noir—" said Mercédès quickly, as I turned toward the café. "Some other place. Not there."

I found a small snack bar at the back of the Clos du Phare, and ordered coffee and doughnuts for both of us. Mercédès still sounded brittle and close to tears, but the antagonism was gone.

"Why did you want to run away?" I asked at last. "I'm sure your parents are worried about you."

"I'm not going back," she told me stubbornly.

"Why not? Is this about that silly wedding dress?"

She looked startled. Then, reluctantly, she smiled. "That's how it started, yes."

"But you can't run away because a dress didn't fit," I said, trying not to laugh.

Mercédès shook her head. "That's not why," she said.

"Why then?"

"Because I'm pregnant."

I managed to get the story from her, with some coaxing and another pot of coffee. She was a strange mixture of arrogance and little-girl naïveté, appearing by turns much older, and at the same time much younger, than her years. I imagine this was what attracted Joël Lacroix to her in the first place, that flirtatious show of confidence. But in spite of her short skirts and sexual bravado, she remained an island girl at heart, touchingly, alarmingly ignorant.

Apparently she had trusted to the Saint for contraception. "Besides," she said, "I thought it couldn't happen the first time." It had only happened once, I gathered. He'd made her feel as if it were her fault. Before, there had been nothing but kisses, secret rides on his motorbike, a feeling of delicious rebellion.

"He was so nice at first," she said wistfully. "Everyone else assumed I was going to marry Xavier and be just a fisherman's wife, and get fat, and wear a scarf around my head like my mother." She wiped at her eyes with the corner of the napkin. "Everything's ruined now. I said we could run away, to Paris maybe. We could get a flat together. I could get a job. And he just—" She pushed back her hair listlessly. "He just laughed."

She had told her parents straightaway, on the advice of Père Alban. Surprisingly it had been quiet, fussy Charlotte who had raged the most; Omer La Patate had simply sat down at his table like a man in shock. Xavier would have to be told, Charlotte had said; there had been a contract that could now no longer be honored. Mercédès sobbed quietly and hopelessly as she told me about it. "I don't want to go to the mainland. But I'll have to now. No one will want me here, after what's happened."

"Omer could talk to Joël's father," I suggested.

She shook her head. "I don't want Joël. I never did." She wiped her eyes with the back of her hand. "And I'm not going back home," she said tearfully. "They'll make me see Xavier if I go back. And I'd rather *die*."

In the distance came the sound of the ferry's whistle. *Brismand 1* was leaving.

"Well, you're here until tomorrow, at least," I said crisply. "Let's try and find you somewhere to stay."

6

 I found Toinette Prossage in her garden, hoeing bulbs of wild garlic out of the sandy soil. She nodded to me in a friendly fashion as she straightened up, her face shaded not by the *quichenotte* this morning, but by a wide straw hat tied at the side of her head with a red ribbon. On the turf roof of her cottage, a goat was cropping grass.

"So, what do you want?"

"Do I need an ulterior motive?" I brought out the big bag of pastries I had bought in La Houssinière and held it out to her. "I thought you might like some *pain au chocolat*."

Toinette took the bag and inspected the contents greedily. "You're a good girl," she declared. "It's a bribe, of course. Go on, you've got my attention. At least for as long as it takes me to finish this."

I grinned as she started on the first *pain au chocolat*, and as she ate I told her about Mercédès. "I thought you might be able to look after her here for a while," I said. "Till the dust settles."

Toinette considered a cinammon-sugar roll. Her black eyes shone keenly under the brim of her hat. "Such a tiresome girl, my granddaughter," she said, with a sigh. "I knew she'd be trouble from the day she was born. I'm too old for all that now. These cakes are very nice, though," she added, biting into the roll with gusto.

"You can have them all," I told her.

"Heh."

"Omer wouldn't have told you about Mercédès," I ventured.

"Because of the money, heh?"

"Maybe." Toinette lives frugally, but there are rumors of hidden wealth. The old woman does nothing to confirm or deny these, but her silence is generally taken as a kind of admission. Omer loves his mother dearly, but is secretly dismayed at her longevity. Toinette is aware of this, and plans to live forever. She cackled gleefuly. "Thinks I'll disinherit him if there's a scandal, heh? Poor Omer. There's more of me in that girl than there is of anyone else, I'll tell you. I was the bane of my parents."

"You've not changed much, then."

"Heh!" She inspected the paper bag again. "Nut bread. I always liked nut bread. Good thing I've got all my teeth, heh? It's better with honey, though. Or a little goat's cheese."

"I'll bring some over."

Toinette looked at me for a moment with cynical amusement. "Bring the girl over here with you, while you're at it. I expect she'll wear me to a splinter. At my age I need all the rest I can get. The young don't understand that. All they think about is their own affairs."

I wasn't fooled by this pretense at frailty. Within ten minutes of her arrival I imagined that Mercédès would be put to work cleaning, cooking, and tidying the house. It would probably do her good.

Toinette read my thoughts. "I'll soon take her mind off things," she announced imperiously. "And if that boy comes sniffing round—heh!" She made an airy gesture with the nut loaf, looking like the world's oldest fairy godmother. "I'll give him what for. I'll show him what a Salannaise is made of."

I left Mercédès with her grandmother. It was past one o'clock, and the sun was at its hottest. Les Salants was deserted in its glassy glare: shutters closed, only the tiniest sliver of shadow at the foot of the white-washed walls. I would have liked to lie down quietly in the shade of a parasol, perhaps with a long drink, but the boys would be home—at least until the games arcade opened again—and after Brismand's visit, I did not trust myself near my father. So instead I turned toward the dunes. It would be cooler above La Goulue, and at this time of day, free of tourists. The tide was high; the sea brilliantly clear. The wind would clear my head.

I could not help looking in at the *blockhaus* on my way. It was deserted as before. But La Goulue was not entirely deserted. A single figure stood by the water, a cigarette clamped between his teeth.

He ignored my greeting, and when I came to stand beside him he turned his face away, though not quickly enough to hide his reddened eyes. The news about Mercédès had traveled fast.

"I wish they were dead," said Damien in a low voice. "I wish the sea would just come in and swallow the whole island. Wash everything clean again. No people at all." He picked up a stone from between his feet and pegged it as hard as he could at the oncoming waves.

"It may feel like that now—" I began, but he interrupted me.

"They should never have built that reef. They should have left the sea to it. They thought they were being so clever. Making money. Laughing at the Houssins. All of them too wrapped up in thinking about money to see what was going on right under their noses." He kicked at the sand with the toe of his boot. "Lacroix would never have looked at her twice if it hadn't been for all this, would he? He'd have been gone by the end of the summer. There wouldn't have been anything to keep him here. But he thought he could make *money* out of us." I put my hand on his shoulder, but he shook it off. "He pretended to be my friend. Both of them did. Using me to send messages. Spying for them in the village. I thought if I could do something for her—then maybe she—"

"Damien. It isn't your fault. You weren't to know."

"But it *is*—" Damien broke off suddenly and picked up another stone. "Oh, what do you know, heh? You're not even a proper Salannaise. You'll do all right, whatever happens. Your sister's a Brismand, isn't she?"

"I don't see what—"

"Just leave me alone, okay? It isn't your concern."

"Yes it is." I took his arm. "Damien, I thought we were friends."

"That's what I thought about Joël," said Damien sullenly. "Rouget tried to warn me. I should have listened to him, heh?" He picked up another stone and threw it at the oncoming surf. "I tried to tell myself it was my father's fault. I mean, that business with the lobsters and everything. Taking up with the Bastonnets. After everything they'd done to our family. Pretending things were all right again, just because of a good catch or two."

"And then there was Mercédès," I said gently.

Damien nodded.

"The motorcycle gang," I said. "Was that you? Did you tell them about the money? To hit back at the Bastonnets? Because you were jealous of Xavier?"

Damien nodded miserably. "Xavier wasn't supposed to get hurt, though. I thought he'd just hand over the cash. But after what happened, Joël said I might as well throw in with his gang; I had nothing left to lose."

No wonder he'd looked so unhappy. "And you've kept this to yourself all this time? You didn't tell anyone?"

"Rouget. You can tell him stuff, sometimes."

"What did he say?"

"He told me to come clean with my dad and the Bastonnets. Said things would just get worse if I didn't. I said he was crazy; my dad would have kicked the crap out of me if I'd told him the half of what I'd done."

I smiled. "I think maybe he was right, you know."

Damien shrugged listlessly. "Maybe. It's too late now."

I left him on the beach and returned the way I came. When I looked back, the lone figure was kicking sand into the sea with a furious energy, as if by so doing he might force all of the beach back onto La Jetée, where it belonged.

7

When I got home, Adrienne was there with Marin and the boys, just finishing lunch. They looked up as I came in. GrosJean did not; instead he kept his head lowered over his plate, finishing his salad with slow, methodical movements.

I made coffee, feeling like an intruder. There was silence as I drank it, as if my presence had killed the conversation. Was this what it was going to be like from now on? My sister and her family, GrosJean and his boys, and myself, the outsider, the unwanted guest whom no one quite dared eject? I could feel my sister watching me, her blue island eyes narrowed. From time to time, one of the boys whispered something too low for me to make out.

"Uncle Claude said he'd spoken to you," said Marin at last.

"I'm glad he did," I said. "Or were you planning to tell me in your own time?"

Adrienne glanced at GrosJean. "It's up to Papa to decide what he does with his own land."

"We'd discussed it before," said Marin. "GrosJean knew he couldn't afford to develop the property. He thought it would make more sense to let us do that."

"Us?"

"Claude and I. We've been discussing a joint venture."

I looked at my father, seemingly absorbed in mopping oil from the bottom of the salad bowl. "Did you know about this, Father?"

Silence. GrosJean gave no sign of even having heard.

"You're just upsetting him, Mado," murmured Adrienne.

"What about me?" My voice was rising. "Didn't anyone think to consult me? Or was that what Brismand meant when he said he wanted me on his side? Is that what he wanted? To make sure I turned a blind eye when you signed away the land for nothing?"

Marin gave me a meaningful look. "Maybe we could discuss this some other—"

"Was it for the boys, is that it?" Anger fluttered inside me like a bird in a cage. "Is that what you bribed him with? GrosJean and P'titJean, back from the dead?" I glanced at my father, but he had gone away inside himself, staring placidly into space, as if none of us were there.

Adrienne looked at me reproachfully. "Oh Mado. You've seen him with the boys. They're therapy for him. They've done him so much good already."

"And the land was no use," said Marin. "We all thought it would make more sense to concentrate on the house, to make it into a proper family summer home, for all of us to enjoy."

"Think of what it would mean to Franck and Loïc," said Adrienne. "A lovely holiday home by the seaside—"

"And a sound investment," added Marin, "for when—you know."

"An inheritance," explained Adrienne. "For the children."

"But it isn't a holiday home," I protested, feeling a little sick.

My sister leaned toward me, her face shining. "We hope it will be, Mado," she said. "The fact is, we've asked Papa to come home with us in September. We want him to live with us all year round."

I left as I had come, with my case and my art folder, but this time I did not make for the village. Instead I took the other path, the one that led to the *blockhaus* above La Goulue.

Flynn still wasn't there. I let myself into the house and lay down on the old cot, feeling suddenly very isolated, very far from home. At that moment I would have given almost anything to be back in the Paris flat with the brasserie outside and the noise from the Boulevard Saint-Michel drifting up on the hot gray air. Perhaps Flynn had been right, I thought. Perhaps it was time to think of moving on.

I could see quite clearly now how my father had been manipulated. But he had made his choice; I would not stop him. If he wanted to live with Adrienne, he could. The house in Les Salants would become a holiday home. I would be welcome to stay whenever I liked, of course, and Adrienne would feign surprise when I stayed away. She and Marin would spend every holiday there. Maybe they would rent it out-of-season. I had a sudden image of myself and Adrienne as children, quarreling over some toy, breaking its limbs between us, its stuffing shedding unheeded as we fought each other for possession. No, I told myself. I didn't need the house.

I put my art folder against the wall and my case under the packing-crate bed, then went out again onto the dune. By now the sun had mellowed a little, and the tide was going out. Far across the bay, a single sail wavered against the sun's reflection, far away beyond the protective ring of La Jetée. I could not make out its shape with any accuracy, or imagine who could be sailing so far out at this time. I began to make my way down toward La Goulue, occasionally glancing at the distant sail. Birds yarked at me as they wheeled. It was difficult in the troubling light to identify it correctly, no one from the village in any case. No Salannais would be so ham-handed with his steering, tacking feebly, losing the wind, finally ending up adrift, sail loose and flapping, as the current bore the craft away.

As I came closer to the side of the cliff I saw Aristide watching from his usual place. Lolo was sitting next to him with a cooler of fruit for sale and a pair of binoculars around his neck.

"Who is that, anyway? He'll end up on La Jetée at this rate."

The old man nodded. Disapproval lined his face. Not for the careless sailor—in the islands you have to learn to look after yourself, and to ask for help is a shameful thing—but for the good boat left adrift. People come and go. Property endures.

"You don't think it's someone from La Houssinière?"

"Neh. Even an Houssin knows not to go out that far. Some tourist, perhaps, with more money than sense. Or something adrift. You can't be sure at this distance."

I looked down onto the crowded beach. Gabi and Laetitia were there. Laetitia was sitting on one of the old pilings at the side of the cliff.

"D'you want a melon slice?" suggested Lolo, looking enviously down at Laetitia. "I've only got two left."

"Okay." I smiled at him. "I'll take them both."

"Zen!"

The melon was sweet and good against my dry throat. Away from Adrienne, I found my appetite had returned, and I ate slowly, sitting in the shade of the winding cliff-side path. I thought the unidentified sail looked a little closer now, though that was probably a trick of the light.

"I'm sure I know that boat," said Lolo, squinting through his binoculars. "I've been keeping an eye on it for ages."

"Let me see," I said, taking a few steps toward him. Lolo handed over the binoculars and I looked through them at the distant sail.

It was typically red, quadrangular, and bore no visible markings. The boat itself—long and slim, little more in fact than a skiff—was low in the water, as if it had been flooded. My heart gave a sudden lurch.

"D'you recognize it?" urged Lolo.

I nodded. "I think so. It looks like Flynn's boat."

"Are you sure? We could ask Aristide. He knows all the boats. He'll be able to tell for sure."

The old man looked through the binoculars in silence for a few moments. "It's him, heh," he declared at last. "Far out, and drifting, but I'd lay money on it."

"What's he want out there?" asked Lolo. "He's right out on La Jetée. D'you think he's run aground?"

"Neh." Aristide snorted. "How could he? All the same"—he got to his feet—"it looks like trouble."

The identification of the craft had changed things. Rouget was not some unknown tourist, drunk in charge of a hired boat. Within a few minutes a small group had gathered on the top of the cliff, watching the distant boat with anxious curiosity.

Aristide wanted to take his *Cécilia* out straightaway, but Alain beat him to it in the *Eleanore 2*. He wasn't the only one. Word reached Angélo's that there was a problem at La Goulue, and ten minutes later there were half a dozen people at the beach, armed with hooks, poles, and lengths of rope. Angélo himself was there—selling shots of *devinnoise* at fifteen francs each—and Omer, Toinette, Capucine, and the Guénolés. Farther down the beach, a few tourists watched and speculated. From the cliff the sea was silver-green and crepey, barely moving.

It took more than an hour to reach La Jetée. It felt like longer. Rouget's little skiff had gone beyond the sandbanks, too close to the shallows for the bigger boats to reach it easily. Alain had to maneuver the *Eleanore 2* into position around the jutting sandbanks while Ghislain pulled in Flynn's boat, using hooks and poles to keep it a safe distance from *Eleanore 2*'s hull, then together, haul the rescued craft out toward the open sea. Aristide, who had insisted on coming too, held his place at the rudder, voicing his pessimism at intervals. The wind was strong outside the bay, the sea was riding high, and I had to stand beside Alain at the stern of the *Eleanore 2* to control the swaying boom as the little boat pitched and rocked. So far there had been no sign of Flynn at all, either in the boat or in the water.

I was glad no one commented on my presence. I had been the one to recognize the sail in the first place. That gave me a kind of right, in their eyes, to be there. Alain, sitting at the prow of the *Eleanore 2*, had the best view of the proceedings, and kept up a running commentary as Ghislain maneuvered Flynn's boat into range. He had fastened a couple of old car tires to the side of the *Eleanore 2* to protect the hull from a possible shock.

Aristide was typically gloomy. "I knew there was trouble," he declared, for the fifth time. "I'd had that feeling, just like the night the storms took my *Péoch ha Labour*. A kind of doomed feeling."

"Indigestion, more like," muttered Alain.

Aristide ignored him. "We've had too much good luck, that's what it is," he said. "It was bound to turn eventually. Why else would this happen to Rouget, of all people? The lucky one?"

"It may be nothing," said Alain.

Aristide threw up his hands. "I've been sailing for sixty years, and I've seen it happen twenty times or more. Man goes out alone, gets careless, turns his back on the boom—wind changes—good night!" He put his finger on his throat in an expressive gesture.

"You don't know that happened," Alain said stubbornly.

"I know what I know," replied Aristide. "Happened to Ernest Pinoz in 1949. Swept him right over the side. Dead before he hit the water."

At last we got the little boat within range of the *Eleanore 2*, and Xavier jumped aboard. Flynn was lying motionless at the bottom. He must have been lying there for hours, Xavier guessed, because there was a stripe of sunburn across the side of his face. With some difficulty Xavier lifted Flynn under the arms, struggling to move him within reach of the rocking *Eleanore 2* while Alain tried to secure the boat. Around them the little skiff's useless sail flapped and slapped, the loosened ropes flying dangerously in all directions. Though he did not recognize it, Xavier knew better than to touch the thing—something that looked like the soggy remains of a plastic bag—wrapped around Flynn's arm and trailing pieces of itself in the water.

At last, after several attempts, the boat was secure.

"Told you, heh?" announced Aristide with grim satisfaction. "Takes more than a lucky red bead to save you, once your time's come."

"He's not dead," I said in a voice I did not recognize.

"No," panted Alain, hauling Flynn's unresponsive body from the waterlogged skiff into the *Eleanore 2*. "Not yet, anyway."

We laid him down in the stern of the boat, and Xavier put up the warning flag. With unsteady hands I kept busy with the *Eleanore 2*'s sails until I could trust myself to look at Flynn without shaking. He was already burning up. His eyes opened occasionally, but he did not respond when I spoke to him. Through the semitransparent thing that clung to his skin, I could see red lines of infection shooting up his arm. I tried to keep the tremor from my voice, but even so I sounded screamy to myself, dangerously close to hysteria. "Alain, we have to get that thing off him!"

"That's a job for Hilaire," said Alain shortly. "Just let's get the boat back to the shore as quickly as we can. Keep him out of the sun. Trust me; there's nothing more we can do here."

It was good advice, and we obeyed, Aristide holding a piece of sailcloth over the unconscious man's face while Alain and I maneuvered the *Eleanore 2* as quickly as we could into La Goulue. Even so—and with the good west wind at our backs—it took almost an hour. By then there were more would-be helpers waiting on the shore, people with flasks, ropes, blankets. Rumors were already flying. Someone ran to fetch Hilaire.

No one could be certain what the thing—still wrapped around Flynn's arm—could be. Aristide thought it was a box jellyfish, washed up the freakish trail of the Gulf Stream from warmer seas. Matthias, who had come over with Angélo, dismissed the likelihood with scorn.

"It's not," he snorted. "Are you blind? It's a Portuguese man-of-war. Remember the time we had them off La Jetée? 1951, it must have been, heh, hundreds of them riding the edge of the Nid'Poule. Some of them came all the way to La Goulue, and we had to drag them up away from the shoreline with rakes."

"Box jellyfish," said Aristide stoutly, shaking his head. "I'd lay money on it."

Matthias took him up on that, to the tune of a hundred francs. Several other people followed suit.

Whatever the thing was, it was no easy task to remove. The tentacles—if indeed those feathery, frondlike ribbons were tentacles—adhered to bare skin wherever they had touched it. They clung there, defying all attempts to remove them cleanly.

"It must have looked like a plastic bag, heh, floating in the water," speculated Toinette. "He leaned over to scoop it up—"

"Lucky he wasn't swimming, heh. It would have been all over him. Those tentacles must be a couple of meters long, at least."

"Box jellyfish," repeated Aristide with grim satisfaction. "Those marks are from the blood poisoning. Seen it before."

"Man-of-war," protested Matthias. "When d'you ever see a box jelly-fish this far north, heh?"

"Cigarettes. That's what you use for leeches," said Omer La Patate.

"Maybe a shot of *devinnoise*," suggested Angélo.

Capucine thought vinegar.

Aristide was fatalistic, saying that if the thing was indeed a box jelly-fish then Rouget was done for anyway. There was no antidote to that poison. He gave him twelve hours, maximum. Then Hilaire arrived with Charlotte, who was carrying a bottle of vinegar.

"Vinegar," said Capucine. "I said that would do it."

"Let me through," grumbled Hilaire. He was gruffer than usual, hiding his anxiety behind a mask of irritation. "People think I've nothing better to do, heh. I've got Toinette's goats to see to, and the horses from La Houssinière. Can't people pay attention? Do they think I enjoy this kind of thing?" Anxiously the little group watched as Hilaire removed the clinging tentacles with tweezers and vinegar.

"Box jellyfish," said Aristide under his breath.

"Head full of rocks," replied Matthias.

❦

They took Flynn to Les Immortelles. It was the most sensible place, insisted Hilaire, with beds and medical supplies. An adrenaline injection, administered on the scene, was all Hilaire could give, and he was reluctant at this stage to make a prognosis. From his surgery he rang the coast, first for a doctor—a rapid motorboat was available in Fromentine in case of emergency—then to the coast guard to issue a jellyfish warning.

So far no more of the creatures had been spotted at La Goulue, but the old measures were already in place at the new beach, with a cord and floaters stretched across the swimming area, and a net to filter out any unwanted visitors. Later, Alain and Ghislain would sail across to La Jetée to check there. It was a procedure sometimes used after the autumn storms.

I lingered on the outside of the little group, feeling superfluous now that there was nothing useful left for me to do. Toinette volunteered to go to Les Immortelles with Rouget. There was talk of calling Père Alban.

"Is it that bad?"

Hilaire, who was not familiar with either of the disputed jellyfish types, could not say for sure. Lolo shrugged. "Aristide says by tomorrow we'll know one way or another."

8

I don't believe in omens. In that I am not a typical islander. And yet the air was filled with them that evening; they rode the waves like gulls. A tide was turning somewhere, a dark one. I could feel it on the turn. I tried to imagine Flynn dying; Flynn dead. It was unthinkable. He was ours—the island's—a piece of Les Salants. We had shaped him, and he us.

As evening approached I went to Sainte-Marine's shrine on the Pointe, spattered now with candle wax and guano. Someone had left a plastic doll's head with the offerings on top of the altar. The head was very pink; the hair blond. There were candles burning there already. I put my hand in my pocket and took out the red coral bead. I turned it in the palm of my hand for a moment, then placed it on the altar. Sainte-Marine looked down, her stone face more ambiguous than ever. Was it a smile on the blunt features? Was that arm raised in a blessing?

Santa Marina. Take back the beach, if that's what you want. Take anything you like. But not this. Please. Not this.

Something—a bird, perhaps—screamed in the dunes. It sounded like laughter.

Toinette Prossage found me still sitting there. She touched my arm and I looked up; behind her, coming up the Pointe toward me, I could see more people. Some carried lanterns; I recognized the Bastonnets, the Guénolés, Omer, Angélo, Capucine. Behind them I could see Père Alban with his driftwood staff, and Soeur Thérèse and Soeur Extase, their *coiffes* bobbing against the sunset like birds.

"I don't care what Aristide says," Toinette told me. "Sainte-Marine has been here longer than any of us, and there's no knowing what other miracles she can perform. She brought us the beach, didn't she?"

I nodded, not trusting myself to speak. Behind Toinette the villagers were arriving in a line, some carrying flowers. I saw Lolo following at a distance, and in the village, a few tourists watching curiously.

"I never said I *wanted* him to die," protested Aristide. "But if he does, he'll have earned his place in La Bouche. I'll find him a plot next to my own son."

"There's no call for any of this talk of dying and burials," said Toinette. "The Saint won't allow it. She's Marine-de-la-Mer and she's the Salannais' special Saint. She won't let us down."

"Heh, but Rouget isn't a Salannais," pointed out Matthias. "Sainte-Marine's an island saint. Maybe she doesn't care for mainlanders."

Omer shook his head. "The Saint may well have brought us the beach, but it was Rouget built the Bouch'ou."

Aristide grunted. "You'll see," he said. "Bad luck's never far away in Les Salants. This proves it. Jellyfish in the bay, after all these years. Don't tell me that will improve trade, heh?"

"Trade?" Toinette was indignant. "Is that all you care about? Do you think the Saint cares for it?"

"Maybe not," said Matthias, "but it's a bad sign all the same. Last time that happened was in the Black Year."

"The Black Year," repeated Aristide darkly. "And luck turns like the tide."

A few days earlier, his doom-laden tone might have made me smile. But I found that I had almost begun to believe in omens again. Once more I glanced at the Saint, trying to read her expression.

"Our luck has *not* turned!" protested Toinette. "We make our own luck in Les Salants. This proves nothing."

Père Alban shook his head disapprovingly. "I don't know why you all wanted me to come here anyway," he said. "If you want to pray, go to a church that's still standing. If not—heh! All this superstitious carrying on. I should never have encouraged it."

"Just a prayer," urged Toinette. "Just the *Santa Marina.*"

"All right, all right. Then I'm going home, leave you here to catch your deaths if you like. It looks like rain."

"I don't care what you say," muttered Aristide. "Trade matters. And if she's our Saint, then she should understand that. That's the luck of Les Salants."

"Monsieur Bastonnet!"

"All right, heh, all right."

We bowed our heads like children. Island Latin is pig-Latin, even by church standards, but all attempts to update the service have been rejected. There is magic in the old words, something that would be lost in translation. Père Alban has long since stopped trying to explain that it is not the words themselves that hold the power, but the sentiment behind them. The idea is incomprehensible to most Salannais, even a little blasphemous. Catholicism has naturalized here in the islands, reverting to its pre-Christian origins. Charms, symbols, incantations, rituals are what remain most strongly rooted here, in these communities where so few books—even the Bible—are read. The oral tradition is strong, details added with each retelling, but we like miracles better than numbers and rules. Père Alban knows this, and plays along, knowing that without him the church might soon become altogether redundant.

He left as soon as the prayer was finished. I heard the crunching sound of his fishing boots in the sand as he left the little circle of lanterns. Toinette was singing in a high old-lady's voice; I caught a few words, but it was in an old island patois, which like the Latin, I did not understand.

The two old nuns had remained, and standing on either side of the driftwood altar they supervised the prayers. Quietly, the villagers waited in line. Several people—Aristide among them—removed the lucky bead from around their necks and placed it on the altar beneath Sainte-Marine's dark, ambivalent stare.

Leaving them to their prayers I made my way down toward La Goulue, spread out wide and red in the sun's afterglow. Far, far out toward the water's edge, almost lost in the gleam from the flats, a figure was standing. I walked out toward it, enjoying the cool of the wet sand beneath my feet and the soft lapping of the receding tide. It was Damien.

He looked at me, his eyes filled with the red pandemonium of the sun. Beyond it, a dark line across the sky promised rain to come. "You see?" he said. "Everything's coming apart. Everything's finished."

I shivered. Far behind us came the eerie warble of Toinette's singing.

"I don't think it's going to be that bad," I said.

"Don't you?" He shrugged. "My father went out to La Jetée with the *platt*. He says he saw more of those things out there. Storms must have brought them up the Gulf Stream. My grandfather says it's an omen. Bad times coming."

"I never thought you were superstitious."

"No. But it's what they cling onto, when there's nothing else left. It's what they do to pretend they're not afraid. Singing and prayers and garlands on the saint. As if any of that was going to help Rou—Roug—" His voice broke at the last word, and he stared at the water with renewed fierceness.

"He'll be all right," I said. "He always is."

"I don't care," replied Damien unexpectedly, without raising his voice. "He's the one who started all this. I don't care if he dies."

"You don't mean that!"

Damien seemed to be speaking to something on the horizon. "I thought he was my friend. I thought he was different from Joël and Brismand and the others. Turns out he was just a better liar."

"What do you mean?" I demanded. "What's he done?"

"I thought he and Brismand hated each other," said Damien. "That's what he always pretended. But they're *friends*, Mado. Him and the Brismands. They're all working together. He was working for them yester-day, when he had the accident. That's why he'd gone out so far. I heard Brismand say so!"

"Working for Brismand? Doing what?"

"He's been doing it all along," said Damien. "Brismand's been pay-ing him to string us all along. I heard him talking to Marin about it out-side the Chat Noir."

"But, Damien," I protested. "Everything he's done for Les Salants—"

"What *has* he done, heh?" Damien's voice cracked; suddenly he sounded very young. "Built *that* thing in the bay?" He gestured at the distant Bouch'ou, where I could just see the two warning lights winking like Christmas baubles. "What for? Who for? Not for me, that's certain. Not for my father, in debt up to the eyes and still hoping for the big break. Thinks he'll make a fortune out of a few fish, how stupid can you get? Not for the Guénolés, or the Bastonnets, or the Prossages. Not for Mercédès!"

"That's not fair. The beach isn't responsible for that. And neither is Flynn."

The sun had set. The sky was a bruise, pallid at the edges. "And that's another thing," said Damien, looking at me. "His name isn't Flynn. It's not Rouget, either. It's Jean-Claude. After his father."

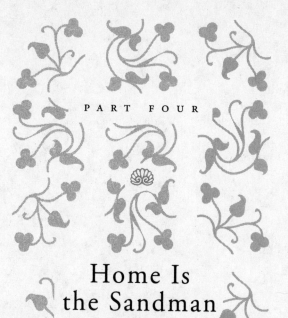

PART FOUR

Home Is
the Sandman

I raced up the cliff-side path, my thoughts rattling inside my skull like seeds in a gourd. It made no sense. Flynn, Brismand's son? It was impossible. Damien must have misheard. And yet something in me cried out in recognition; my sense of danger, finally alerted, ringing out its warning louder than La Marinette.

It told me that there had been clues to find, if I'd chosen to see them: the clandestine meeting, the embrace, Marin's hostility, his divided loyalties. Even his nickname, Rouget, the Red One, reflects that of Foxy Brismand. Island-fashion, they share the same name.

But Damien was only a boy, after all; a boy in the throes of teenage infatuation. Hardly the most reliable informant. No, I had to know more before I convicted Flynn in my heart. And I knew the place to go.

The lobby of Les Immortelles was deserted except for Joël Lacroix, who was sitting with his cowboy boots up on the reception desk, smoking a Gitane. He looked disconcerted at seeing me.

"Heh, Mado." He smirked halfheartedly and stubbed out his cigarette in the ashtray. "You looking for accommodation?"

"I heard my friend was here," I said.

"The *Angliche?* Yeh, he's here." He lit up again with a flourish, puffing out the smoke in a long lazy stream, like in the movies. "The doctor said he shouldn't be moved. You wanna see him, heh?"

I nodded.

"Well, you can't. Monsieur Brismand said no one, and that, *ma belle*, includes you." He winked at me and moved a little closer. "The doctor came by special boat, maybe an hour ago. Said it was some kind of Portuguese jellyfish sting. Nasty."

So Aristide's gloomy prognosis was wrong. A reluctant relief washed over me.

"Not a box jellyfish, then?"

Joël shook his head, I thought with regret. "Neh. But nasty, all the same."

"How nasty?"

"Bof. What do these doctors know about anything, heh?" He dragged at his Gitane. "Doesn't help that he was passed out in the sun for hours. Sunstroke can be a real bitch if you're not careful. Trust a mainlander not to know that." Joël's tone implied that he, Joël, was far too tough to be affected by such things.

"And the jellyfish?"

"Stupid bastard went and picked it up out of the water, didn't he, heh?" Joël shook his head in disbelief. "I mean, would you believe that? The doc says the poison should last twenty-four hours." He grinned. "So, if your friend's still here tomorrow morning, heh—" He winked again and moved a little closer.

I sidestepped him. "In that case I need to see Marin Brismand. Is he here?"

"Heh, what is it with you?" Joël looked aggrieved. "Don't you like me?"

"I like you at a distance, Joël. Think of it as fishing rights. Territorial waters. Just keep out of mine."

Joël grunted. "Thinks she's Santa Marina," he muttered. "Marin went out an hour ago. With your sister."

"Where?"

"God knows."

❊

I eventually found Marin and Adrienne in the Chat Noir. By that time it was getting late, and the café was filled with smoke and noise. My sister was sitting at the bar; Marin was playing cards at a table full of Houssins. He looked surprised to see me.

"Mado! We don't often see you here. Is something wrong?" He narrowed his eyes at me. "It's not GrosJean, is it?"

"No, it's Flynn."

"Oh?" He looked startled. "He's not dead, is he?"

"Of course not."

Marin shrugged. "That would have been too much to hope for."

"Stop playing games, Marin," I told him sharply. "I know about him and your uncle. Your business together."

"Oh." He grinned. I could tell he was not entirely displeased. "Right. We'll go somewhere a little more private. Keep it in the family, heh?" He threw in his hand and stood up. "I was losing anyway," he said. "I don't have your friend's luck at cards."

We went outside onto the esplanade where it was cooler and less crowded. Adrienne followed us. I sat down on the seawall and turned to them both, my heart beating hard though my voice was calm. "Tell me about Flynn," I said. "Better still, tell me about Jean-Claude."

"It was going to be me, you know." Marin's face was sour under the smile. "I was the old man's only remaining relative. I've been more than a son to him. At least more than *his* son ever was. It was going to be mine. Les Immortelles. The business. Everything."

For years Brismand had led him to expect as much. A loan here, a small gift there. He had kept Marin in sight, just as he had done with me, keeping his options open; planning for future possibilities. He avoided any mention of his estranged wife, his missing son. He'd led Marin to understand that he'd washed his hands of them both, that they'd moved to England, that the boy didn't even speak French, was no more a Brismand than any other *Angliche* on that big island of *rosbif* and bowler hats.

But of course, he had lied. Foxy Brismand had never once lost hope. He had kept in touch with Jean-Claude's mother; sent money for schooling; played a double game for years as he bided his time and waited. It had always been his intention, once the time came, to pass on his business to Jean-Claude. But his son had been uncooperative, more than ready to accept the money Brismand sent, but less enthusiastic when he mentioned his joining the business. Brismand had been patient, letting the boy sow his wild oats, trying not to think of time running out. But by now Jean-Claude was over thirty, and still his plans—if he had any—remained unclear. Brismand was beginning to think his son would never return at all.

"That would have been it," said Marin smugly. "Claude may be obsessed with family, but he would never have left his money to someone who hadn't earned it. He made it clear that if Jean-Claude wanted to see a penny of his inheritance, he'd have to come here first."

Of course, Brismand had not voiced any of his concerns to Marin and Adrienne. During this uncertain time he'd needed more than ever to keep Marin sweet. Marin was his insurance, his second string in case Jean-Claude did not reappear. And Marin was a valuable contact, after all, married as he was to GrosJean's daughter.

"He wanted closer ties between himself and Les Salants. He especially wanted to buy GrosJean's house and the land that went with it. But GrosJean refused to sell. There was some kind of quarrel between them—I never knew what. Or maybe it was just his stubbornness."

However, with Adrienne and Marin in line to inherit when the time came, all Brismand needed to do was bide his time. He had been more than generous with the young couple, had set them up in business with a substantial sum.

I could see Adrienne becoming increasingly restless as Marin spoke. "Wait a minute. Are you saying that your uncle *bribed* you to marry me?"

"Don't be absurd." Marin looked uncomfortable. "He just used an opportunity, that's all."

Land prices in prosperous La Houssinière were prohibitive. Les Salants was still cheap. A foothold there would be immensely valuable to Brismand. GrosJean's house with its stretch of land going all the way to La Goulue would be a considerable asset for the man clever enough to exploit it. And so Brismand had been good to Marin and Adrienne. He had sent presents for the boys. They had waited in comfortable expectation of an eventual share in his wealth, and had lived far beyond their means for years.

Then, Flynn had arrived.

"The prodigal son," said Marin venomously. "Thirty years late, almost a foreigner, but he turned the old man's head completely. You'd have thought he could walk on water."

Suddenly Marin was only a nephew again. Now that his son was back, the business in Tangiers no longer interested Claude, and the loans and investments upon which Marin and Adrienne depended were withdrawn.

"Oh, he didn't tell us the reason at once. Les Immortelles needed repairs, he said. New sea defenses to protect the beach. Improved facilities. And after all, it was in *our* interest too, because *we'd* inherit Les Immortelles eventually."

No public mention had as yet been made of Jean-Claude. Brismand's natural caution had taken over early, and he was disinclined to lay his affairs open to scrutiny until he was certain the prodigal was indeed his son. Preliminary investigation seemed to confirm it. Jean-Claude's mother had returned to her old home in Ireland when she left Le Devin. Remarried now, with another family, she had told Brismand that Jean-Claude had left some years previously, and that she had had little contact with him since then, although she had always passed on Brismand's checks to him. This already confirmed Flynn's story to some extent. More important, there were letters written by Brismand, photographs of his estranged wife with Jean-Claude, birth documents. More than that, there were anecdotes that only Jean-Claude and his mother would have known. Marin had advised a blood test. But Brismand knew in his heart; there was no need for confirmation. Flynn had his mother's eyes.

He enlisted him to help him with his erosion problem, hinting that if he proved himself at Les Immortelles, he would earn an eventual partnership in the business. It was a means of keeping an eye on him, and of sounding him out.

"There are no flies on my uncle," said Marin with sour satisfaction. "Even if Jean-Claude was who he claimed to be, it was obvious why he'd come back. He wanted money. Why else would he have waited all this time before showing his face?"

It was a situation that Brismand, like all Devinnois, knew well. Deserters are welcomed with open arms but closed purses, in the knowledge that what returns does not always remain. "He found him a job. Said that if he was going to inherit the business he'd better start from the bottom." Marin laughed. "The only thing that gives me any satisfaction in this whole affair is the thought of that bastard's face when my uncle told him he had to earn his name."

There had been an argument. Marin's expression brightened as he remembered it. "The old man was spitting feathers. Jean-Claude realized he'd gone too far, and tried to calm him down, but by that time it was too late. My uncle told him that unless he earned his place he'd never see a penny, and packed him off to Les Salants."

But it had been a controlled outburst on both sides. Jean-Claude had given his father time to cool down while working to regain his favor. Little by little, Brismand had begun to understand some of the advantages of having a spy in Les Salants.

"He heard everything. Who was short of cash, whose business was doing badly, who was seeing whose wife, who was in debt. He has a knack for getting in with people. They trust him."

Within a few months Brismand knew every secret in Les Salants. Thanks to his work at Les Immortelles the currents had shifted. Fishing had ceased. Several people were already in his debt. He could pull them in whenever he wanted.

GrosJean was among these. Flynn had adopted him from the start, and had become his friend in a number of small ways, acting as a go-between to enable him to borrow the money he needed when his savings finally ran out. Brismand was enthusiastic about the plan. If GrosJean could be bought, then within a year or two Les Salants—what was left of it—could be his.

"Then you came back," said Adrienne.

That had changed everything. GrosJean, formerly so tractable, stopped cooperating. My interference had been too blatant. Flynn's subtle spadework had been ruined.

"So he changed direction," said Adrienne, with a malicious smile. "Instead of targeting Papa, he started to concentrate on you. To find out your weaknesses. He flattered you—"

"That's not true." I said quickly. "He helped me. Helped us."

"He helped himself," said Marin. "He let Brismand know about your reef as soon as the sand began to show at La Goulue. Think about it, Mado," he said, seeing my expression. "You didn't think he was doing it for you, did you?"

I looked at him bleakly. "But Les Immortelles," I protested. "If he knew what he was doing to Claude's beach from the start—"

Marin shrugged. "That can be reversed," he said. "And a little pressure at Les Immortelles was exactly what Rouget needed to force my uncle's hand." Marin looked at me with bitter amusement. "Congratulations, Mado," he said. "Your friend's earned his name at last. He's a Brismand now, with a company checkbook to prove it and a fifty percent share in Brismand & Son. And it's all thanks to you."

3

Les Immortelles was dark. A small light shone in the lobby, but the door was locked, and it was only after ringing the bell repeatedly for five minutes that I finally got an answer. Brismand was in his shirt with the sleeves rolled up, a Gitane at the corner of his mouth. His eyes widened a fraction as he saw me through the glass, then he took a bunch of keys from his pocket and unlocked the door.

"Mado." He sounded tired, and there was fatigue in his posture, in the mournful jowls, the drooping mustache, the eyes almost closed. His shoulders were hunched beneath his shapeless *vareuse*, and he looked more primitive and boulderlike than ever, a statue of himself in old granite. "I'm not so sure this is a good time, heh?"

"I understand." Anger rolled over me like a hot rock, but I pushed it away. "You must be devastated."

I thought I saw his eyes flicker momentarily. "The jellyfish, you mean? Bad for business, heh. As if business could get worse."

"Well, obviously the jellyfish must be a problem," I said. "But I meant the accident to your son."

Brismand observed me mournfully for a few seconds, then gave one of his enormous sighs. "That was careless of him," he said. "A stupid mistake. No true islander would have made it." He smiled. "But I told you I'd get him back one day, didn't I, heh? It took time, but he came back in the end. I knew he would. At my age a man needs his son beside him. Someone to lean on. Someone to run the business when I've gone."

I thought I could see the resemblance now; something in the smile, the posture, the mannerisms, the eyes. They have the same color eyes, Brismand and Flynn; not summer-sea blue like my father's but slate colored, narrow and subtle. That was what finally convinced me. Those slaty eyes.

"You must be very proud," I remarked, feeling sick.

Brismand cocked an eyebrow. "I like to think there's something of me in him, yes."

"But why the pretense? Why hide it from the rest of us? Why did he help us—why did *you* help us—if he was on your side all the time?"

"Mado, Mado." Brismand shook his head dolefully. "Why must this be a question of sides? Is there a war, heh? Must there always be an agenda?"

"Good by stealth?" I mocked.

"That hurts me, Mado." His posture echoed his words, back rounded and half-turned from me, hands digging into his pockets. "Believe me, I only want what's best for Les Salants. That's all I ever wanted. Look what your stealth has achieved so far—growth, trade, business, heh! Do you think they would have let *me* give them all that? Suspicion, Mado. Suspicion and pride. That's what's killing Les Salants. Clinging to the rocks, growing old, so afraid of change that they'd rather the sea swept them away than make a sensible decision—show a little enterprise." He spread his hands. "It's such a waste! They *knew* it was useless, but no one would sell. They'd let the sea go over their heads before they'd see sense."

"Now you even sound like him," I said.

"I'm tired, Madeleine. Too tired to be interrogated like this." Suddenly he looked old again, his energy dispersed. His jowls dropped. "I like you. My son likes you. We would always have made sure you were all right. Now go home and get some rest," he advised gently. "It's going to be a long day."

4

So that was what I'd been searching for without even know-ing it. Brismand and his long-lost son. Working together in secret on either side of the island, planning—planning what? I recalled Brismand's sentimental talk of growing old. But could it be possible that Flynn had somehow persuaded him to make amends? Could it be that they really were working for our side? No. I knew it. In the deepest part of me, where nothing is hidden, I understood that I had known all along.

I ran all the way to the *blockhaus*. There was a feeling of remoteness inside me that I recognized vaguely; I'd felt it once before, the day my mother died. It was as if a subtle mechanism designed only for these moments of crisis had begun to operate, distancing me from everything but the business at hand. I would pay for it later, with grief, maybe with tears. But for now I was in control. Flynn's betrayal was something that had happened in someone else's dream; an eerie calm passed over my heart like a wave over something written in the sand.

I considered GrosJean, and the newly built studio. I thought of all the Salannais who had taken out loans to pay for their improvements, their new businesses, all the little investments we had made in our new future. Behind the clean paintwork, the new gardens, the stalls, shiny shop counters, refurbished fishing boats, stocked larders, new summer dresses, bright shutters, flowery planters, cocktail glasses, barbecue pits, lobster tanks, buckets and spades lay the hidden gleam of Brismand money, Brismand influence.

And the *Brismand 2*, half-completed six months before. It must be ready now; ready to join the plan; Jean-Claude's share in the Brismand enterprise. I could see Flynn's place now—a vital point in the Brismand triumvirate. Claude, Marin, Rouget. La Houssinière, Les Salants, the mainland. There was an inescapable symmetry there—the loans, the reef, Brismand's interest in flooded land. I had seen some of his plans early in the game; all I had needed to complete the equation was the news of Flynn's betrayal.

In my place, my demonstrative mother would have spread her news at once; but there was too much of GrosJean in me for that. We are more alike than I realized, he and I; we nurse our grudges in secret. We look at ourselves from the inside out. Our hearts are as prickly and tightly layered as artichokes. I would not cry out. I would learn the whole truth. I would examine it calmly and analytically. I would make a diagnosis.

But I needed to talk to someone. Not Capucine, to whom I would normally have gone first; she was too trusting, too comfortable. Suspicion was not in her nature. Besides, she adored Rouget, and I was not going to alarm her needlessly—at least not until I had determined the extent of his betrayal. He had lied to us; yes. But his motives were still unclear. He might yet, miraculously, be proved innocent. I wanted that, of course. But the truthful part of me—the GrosJean part—worked inexorably against it. Later, I told myself. There would be time for that later.

Toinette? Her age had made her peculiarly aloof: she watched the rivalries in Les Salants with a lazy indifference, having long since ceased to find anything new to amuse her. In fact it was possible that she had even recognized Rouget for who he was but had kept silent for the sake of her own inscrutable enjoyment.

Aristide? Matthias? One word of this to either of the fishing families and the truth would be all over Les Salants by morning. I tried to imagine the reactions. Omer? Angélo? Equally impossible. Certainly I needed to confide in someone. If only to convince myself I wasn't going crazy.

I could hear the night sounds of the dune through the open window. Off La Goulue came a scent of rising salt, of cooling earth, of a million small things coming alive under the stars. GrosJean would be in the kitchen now, a cup of coffee at his elbow, watching the window as he always did, in silent anticipation. . . .

Of course. I would tell my father. If he couldn't keep a secret, who could?

He looked up when I came in. His face looked puffy and strained, and he lolled heavily on the little kitchen chair like a figure made of dough. I felt a sudden surge of love and pity for him, poor GrosJean with his sad eyes and his silences. This time it was all right, I thought to myself. This time all I needed him to do was listen.

I kissed him before I sat down at the table opposite. It was a long time since I'd done that, and I thought I saw a shadow of surprise cross his face. I realized that since my sister's arrival I had barely spoken to my father at all. After all, he hardly ever spoke to me.

"I'm sorry, Papa," I said. "None of this is your fault, is it?"

I poured coffee for us both—sugaring his automatically, the way he liked it—and leaned back on my chair. He must have left a window open, because there were moths fluttering under the lampshade, making the light flicker. Far away I could smell the sea, and knew the tide was turning.

I'm not sure how much of it I said aloud. In the boatyard days we sometimes spoke without words, with a kind of empathy, or so I told myself. A movement of the head, a smile, the lack of a smile. All those things could be so telling to someone who cared to read the signs. As a child his silence was mystic to me, almost divine. I read his leavings like entrails. The placement of a coffee cup or a table napkin could signify favor or displeasure; a discarded crust of bread could change the course of a day.

That was over now. I'd loved him; I'd hated him. I'd never really seen him. Now I did, a sad, silent old man at a table. What fools love makes of us. What savages.

My mistake was thinking it has to be earned. Deserved. That's the island in me talking, of course; the idea that everything costs, everything has to be paid for. But merit has nothing to do with it. Otherwise we would only ever love saints. And it's a mistake I've made so many times. With GrosJean. With my mother. With Flynn. Even, perhaps, with Adrienne. Most of all with myself, working so hard to deserve, to be loved, to earn my place in the sun, my fistful of earth, that I overlooked what mattered most.

I put my hand over his. His skin felt smooth and worn, like old driftwood.

My mother's love was exuberant; mine has always been furtive, obstinate. That's the island again, the GrosJean in me. We dig ourselves in like clams. Openness alarms us. I thought of my father on the top of the cliff, watching the sea. So many hours spent waiting for Sainte-Marine to make good her promise. GrosJean had never quite believed P'titJean was gone forever. The body recovered with the *Eleanore* at La Goulue, smoothed and featureless as a skinned seal's, could have been anyone. His vow of silence—was it a pact with the sea, some kind of offering, his voice for his brother's return? Had it simply become a habit, a permanent kink in him until, at last, speech had become so difficult that in moments of stress it was almost impossible?

His eyes fixed mine. His lips moved soundlessly.

"What? What was that?"

I thought I heard it then, a rusty wisp of sound, barely a word. *P'titJean.* His expressive hands clenched in frustration at the reluctance of his tongue.

"P'titJean?"

He was red with the effort of trying to tell me, but no more would come. Only his lips moved. He indicated the walls, the window. His hands fluttered nimbly, mimicking the pattern of the incoming tide. He mimed with his uncanny accuracy, dug his hands into his pockets, slouched. *Brismand*. Then he indicated the air on two levels, insistently. *Big Brismand, little Brismand*. Then a sweep toward La Goulue.

I put my arms around him. "It's all right. You don't have to say anything. It's all right." He felt like a wooden figure in my arms, a cruel caricature of himself made by a careless sculptor. His mouth worked against my shoulder in huge and incomprehensible distress, his breath acrid with Gauloises and coffee. Even as I held him I could still feel his big hands fluttering at his sides, strangely delicate, as he tried to communicate something too urgent for words.

"It's all right," I repeated. "You don't have to say aything. It's not important."

Again he mimed; *Brismand. P'titJean*. Again the sweep toward La Goulue. A boat? *Eleanore?* His eyes were imploring. He tugged at my sleeve, repeated the gesture more insistently. I had never seen him so agitated before. *Brismand. P'titJean. La Goulue. Eleanore.*

"Write it down if it matters so much," I said at last. "I'll get a pencil." I rummaged in a kitchen drawer and finally found a stub of red crayon and a scrap of paper. My father looked but did not take them. I pushed them toward him across the table.

GrosJean shook his head.

"Go on. Please. Write it."

He looked at the paper. The stub of crayon looked ridiculously small between his big fingers. He wrote with application, awkwardly, with none of the nimbleness he had once had when stitching sails or making toys. I knew what he'd written almost before I looked. It was the only thing I remember ever seeing him write. His name; *Jean-François Prasteau* in large, shaky script. I'd even forgotten his full name was Jean-François. He'd always been GrosJean to me, as he was to everyone. Never a reader, preferring fishing magazines with color pictures, never a writer—I recalled the unanswered letters from Paris—I'd always assumed my father simply wasn't interested in writing. Now I realized he didn't know how.

I wondered how many other secrets he had managed to keep from me. I wondered whether even my mother had known. He sat motionless, as if the effort of writing his name had taken up all his remaining energy, his hands hanging loosely by his side. I understood that his attempt at communication was over. Defeat—or indifference—smoothed his features into Buddha-like serenity. Once again he gazed out toward La Goulue. "It's all right," I repeated, kissing his cool forehead. "It isn't your fault."

Outside, the long-expected rain had begun at last. In seconds, the dune behind us was prey to a thousand rumors, hissing and whispering through small gullies in the sand toward La Bouche. The drifts of dune thistles gleamed, crowned with rain. On the far horizon, night showed its single black sail.

Summer nights are never quite dark, and the sky was already lightening as I walked slowly back toward La Goulue. I picked my way across the dune, the fluffy rabbit-tails of the grasses bobbing against my bare ankles, and climbed up onto the *blockhaus* roof to watch the tide coming in. On the Bouch'ou two lights blinked—one green, one red—to mark the position of the reef.

It looked so secure. Anchored safely, and the whole of Les Salants with it. And yet now everything was changed. It wasn't ours anymore. It had never truly been ours. Brismand money had built it.

But why had they done it?

Brismand had suggested as much: to take over Les Salants. Land is still cheap here; properly exploited it could be profitable. Only the inhabitants remain an embarrassment, clinging so stubbornly.

Debts are sacred on Le Devin. To repay them is a matter of honor. To fail, unthinkable. The beach had swallowed what savings we had, the rolls of coins hidden under floorboards and the tins of notes set aside for rainy days.

Once more I thought of the "metal pig" in the Fromentine boatyard, and remembered Capucine asking me why Brismand would be interested in buying flooded land. Maybe it wasn't *building* land that interested him, I thought suddenly. Maybe *flooded* land was what he had wanted from the beginning.

Flooded land. But why would he want it? What possible use could it be to him?

Then it came to me. "A ferry port."

If Les Salants was flooded—better still, if it was cut off from La Houssinière at La Bouche—then the creek could be expanded to allow a ferry to enter and dock. Level the houses and flood the entire area. There would be space for two ferries, maybe more. Brismand could run a service to all the islands down the coast, if he liked, making sure of a steady stream of visitors to Le Devin. A shuttle service to and from the ferry port would mean that premium space in La Houssinière would not be wasted.

I looked out again at the Bouch'ou, its lights winking calmly across the water. Brismand owned that, I told myself. Twelve modules of used car tires and airplane cable, concreted into the ocean bed. It had once seemed so permanent to me; now I was appalled at its fragility. How could we have placed so much trust in such a thing? Of course, that was when we believed Flynn was on our side. We thought we'd been so clever. We'd stolen our piece of Les Immortelles from under Brismand's nose. And all the time Brismand had been consolidating his position, watching us, drawing us out of ourselves, gaining our trust, raising the stakes so that when he made his move. . . .

Suddenly, I felt very tired. My head was aching. Somewhere below La Goulue I heard a sound—a thin drone of wind between the rocks, a change in the air's note—a single resonant sound that might almost have been that of a drowned bell, then, in the caesura between waves, an eerie lull.

Like all inspired ideas, Brismand's plan was really very simple. I could see now how our prosperity had become the means to manipulate us.

The air was warm from the west and smelled of salt and flowers. Below me I could see the *grève* shining in the false dawn; beyond it the sea was a dark gray stripe a little lighter than the sky. The *Eleanore 2* was already out there, the *Cécilia* setting out far in her wake. They looked dwarfed by the bank of cloud above them, stilled by distance.

I thought of another night, long ago, the night we had put the reef into place. Our plan then had seemed impossibly grandiose, awe-inspiring in its scale. To steal a beach. To change a coastline. But Brismand's plan—the idea underlying everything—dwarfed my small ambitions by far.

To steal Les Salants.

All he had to do now was to move his final piece, and the place was his.

6

"I can guess why *you're* coming by here so early," said Toinette.

I was passing her house on my way into the village. Fog had rolled off the sea as the tide came in, and there was a haze across the sun that might turn to rain later. Toinette was wearing her thick cape and gloves as she fed vegetable scraps to her goat. The goat lipped impudently at the sleeve of my *vareuse*, and I pushed it away with some irritation.

Toinette chuckled. "Sunstroke, my girl, that's all it is now, and even that can be nasty, with that thin northern blood of his, but not fatal, heh. Not fatal." She grinned. "Give him a day or so, and he'll be back as slippery as ever. Does that set your mind at rest, girl? Is that what you came to ask me?"

It took me a moment to understand what she meant. In fact I'd been so preoccupied with my thoughts that Flynn's illness had receded—now that I knew he was safe—to a kind of dull ache at the back of my mind. Having it brought back to me so unexpectedly took me by surprise, and I felt my cheeks grow hot.

"Actually, I wanted to see how Mercédès was doing."

"I'm keeping her busy," confided the old woman, with a glance back at the house. It's a full-time job. And there's the visitors to cope with—

young Damien Guénolé creeping around at all hours, and Xavier Bastonnet who won't stay away, and her mother coming around screaming like hell's own furies—I swear, if that woman sets foot anywhere near here again . . . But what about you?" She gave me a keen glance. "You don't look well. You're not sickening for something, are you?"

I shook my head. "I didn't sleep much last night."

"I can't say I did myself. But they say red-haired men are luckier than the rest of us. Don't you worry. I wouldn't be surprised if he came home tonight."

"Hey! Mado!"

The call came from behind me; I turned, grateful for the interruption. It was Gabi and Laetitia with the day's provisions. Laetitia waved imperiously to me from the brow of the dune. "Seen the big boat?" she chirped.

I shook my head. Laetitia made a vague gesture in the direction of La Jetée. "It's *zen!* Go and see!" Then she skipped off toward the beach, dragging Gabi in her wake.

"Give my love to Mercédès," I said to Toinette. "Tell her I'll be thinking of her."

"Heh." I thought Toinette looked suspicious. "Perhaps I'll walk with you a way. See the big boat, heh?"

"All right."

From the village we could see it clearly—a long, low shape only half-visible in the white fog off Pointe Griznoz. Too small to be a tanker, the wrong shape for a passenger boat, it might have been some kind of factory ship, except that we knew every vessel that passed this way, and it was none of these.

"In trouble, perhaps?" suggested Toinette, looking at me. "Or waiting for the tide?"

Aristide and Xavier were cleaning nets in the creek, and I asked their opinion.

"It's probably something to do with the jellyfish," declared Aristide, picking a big *dormeur* crab out of one of his pots. "It's been there since we went out. Just off the Nid'Poule, a big thing, heh, machinery and all kinds of things. From the government, or so Jojo-le-Goëland says."

Xavier shrugged. "Seems a bit much, just for a few jellyfish. It's not as if the world was coming to an end."

Aristide gave him a dark look. "A few jellyfish, heh? You've no idea. The last time this happened—" He bit off the remark sharply and returned to his net.

Xavier gave a nervous laugh. "At least Rouget's going to be all right," he said. "Jojo told me this morning. I sent a bottle of *devinnoise*."

"And I told you not to go blabbing to Jojo-le-Goëland," said Aristide. "I wasn't *blabbing*—"

"You'd do better minding your own business. If you'd done that in the first place, you might still be in with a chance with the Prossage girl."

Xavier looked away, flushing beneath his glasses.

Toinette lifted her eyes heavenward. "Leave the boy alone, heh, Aristide?" she said in a warning tone.

"Well," grunted Aristide. "I thought my son's boy would have had more sense."

Xavier ignored them both. "You talked to her, didn't you?" he said to me quietly as I turned to go. I nodded. "How did she look?"

"What does it matter how she looks, heh?" demanded Aristide. "She's made *you* look like a prize idiot, that's for certain. And as for her grandmother—" Toinette stuck out her tongue at Aristide with such sudden petulance that I had to smile.

Xavier ignored them both, his shyness gone in the face of his anxiety. "Was she all right? Will she see me? Toinette won't say."

"She's confused," I said. "She doesn't know what she wants. Give her time."

Aristide snorted. "Give her nothing!" he spat. "She's had her chance, heh. There'll be other girls better than that one. Decent girls."

Xavier said nothing, but I saw his expression.

Toinette bridled. "Not decent, my Mercédès!"

Quickly I put my arm around her shoulders. "Come on. This is pointless."

"Not until he takes that back!"

"Please. Toinette. Come on." I glanced again at the boat, an oddly threatening presence on the pale horizon. "Who are they?" I said, almost to myself. "What are they doing here?"

🐚

Everyone in the village seemed uneasy that morning. Going into Prossage's shop for bread I found the counter untended, and heard raised voices from the back room. I took what I needed, leaving the money beside the till. Behind me Omer and Charlotte continued to argue, their voices carrying eerily in the still air. Ghislain and Damien's mother was scrubbing lobster pots by the vivarium, a rag tied around her head. Angélo's was empty except for Matthias, sitting alone over *café-devinnoise*. There were few tourists to be seen, perhaps because of the fog. The air was oppressive and smelled of smoke and the coming rain. No one seemed to feel like talking.

On the way back home with my provisions I passed Alain. Like his wife he looked drawn and colorless. His teeth were clamped on the stub of a Gitane. I greeted him with a nod. "No fishing today?"

Alain shook his head. "I'm looking for my son," he told me. "And when I find him I swear he'll wish I hadn't." Apparently Damien hadn't been home all night. Anger and worry had gouged deep lines between Alain's eyebrows and around his mouth.

"He can't have gone far," I said. "How far can he go on an island?"

"Far enough," replied Alain in a bleak voice. "He's taken the *Eleanore 2*."

They had left her moored off La Goulue, he explained. Alain had planned to go to La Jetée with Ghislain in the morning to check for jellyfish.

"I thought the boy might like to come too," he said bitterly. "Thought it might take his mind off other things."

But when they had arrived at the beach the *Eleanore 2* had already gone. There was no sign of her at all, and the little *platt* that they used for access at high tide was moored alongside the marker buoy.

"What's he think he's doing?" demanded Alain. "That boat's too big for him to handle alone. He'll wreck her. And where the hell's he taken her on a day like this?"

I realized I must have seen the *Eleanore 2* from my vantage point outside the *blockhaus* that morning. What time had that been? Three? Four? *Cécilia* had been out too, though only to check the lobster pots out in the bay; even then the fog had been closing in, and the Bastonnets knew better than to risk the sandbanks in such conditions.

Alain paled when I told him. "What's the boy playing at, heh?" he moaned. "Oh, when I find him—you don't think he's done something *really* stupid, do you? Like trying to get to the mainland?"

Surely not. It takes nearly three hours for *Brismand 1* to reach us from Fromentine, and there are some rough places between there and us. "I don't know. Why should he?"

Alain looked uncomfortable. "I told him a few truths. You know boys." He studied his knuckle for a moment. "I may have gone a bit far. And he's taken some of his things with him."

"Oh." That sounded more serious.

"How was I to know he'd be such a fool?" Alain exploded. "I tell you, when I get my hands on him—" He broke off, sounding tired and old. "If something happened to him, Mado. If something happened to Damien. You'll tell me if you see him, heh?" He looked at me sharply from eyes pinched by worry. "He trusts you. Tell him I won't be angry. I just want him to be safe."

"I will," I promised. "I'm sure he won't have gone far."

7

By midday the fog had lifted a little. The sky had veered to stonewashed gray, the wind had risen, and the tide had turned again. I walked slowly to La Goulue, feeling more anxious than my optimistic farewell to Alain had let show. Since the day of the jellyfish, it seemed that everything was on the verge of coming apart, even the weather and the tides conspiring against us. As if Flynn were the Pied Piper, going away and taking our luck with him.

When I reached La Goulue the beach was almost deserted. For a moment that surprised me, then I recalled the jellyfish warnings and saw the frill of white at the water's edge, too thick to be foam. The tide had left dozens of them there, opaquing as they died. Later we would have to organize a clean-up operation with rakes and nets. Knowing how dangerous the things were, the sooner it was done the better.

Just above the tide line I could see somebody watching the water in almost exactly the same spot as Damien had the night before. It might have been anyone—faded *vareuse*, the face shielded beneath a wide-brimmed straw hat—an islander, in any case. But I knew who it was.

"Hello, Jean-Claude. Or do we call you Brismand 2 now?"

He must have heard me coming, because he was ready. "Mado. Marin told me you knew." He picked up a piece of driftwood from the beach and poked at one of the dying creatures with it. I noticed that his arm was bandaged under the *vareuse*. "It's not as bad as you think," he said. "No one's going to be left out in the cold. Believe me, everyone in Les Salants will come out of this better off than they were before. Do you really think I'd let anything terrible happen to you?"

"I don't know what you'd do," I said bleakly. "I don't even know what to call you anymore."

He looked hurt at that. "You can call me Flynn," he said. "It was my mother's name. Nothing's changed, Mado."

There was enough gentleness in his voice to bring me close to tears. I closed my eyes and let the coldness take me again, feeling glad that he hadn't tried to touch me.

"Everything's changed!" I heard my voice rise and was powerless to stop it. "You lied to us! You lied to *me!*"

His expression hardened. I thought he looked sick, his face pale and pinched. There was a graze of sunburn across his left cheekbone. His mouth was slightly downturned. "I told you what you wanted to hear," he said. "I did what you wanted. You were happy enough with the result at the time."

"But you weren't doing it for us, were you?" I couldn't believe he was trying to justify his betrayal. "You were looking after number one. And it's paid off, hasn't it? A Brismand partnership, with a bank balance to match?"

Flynn kicked at one of the faded creatures at his feet with sudden viciousness. "You have no idea what it was like," he said. "How could you? You've never wanted anything but this place. It never bothered you that you were living in someone else's house where nobody cared about you, that you had no money of your own, no proper job, no future. I wanted more than that. If I'd wanted to live like that I'd have stayed in Kerry." He looked down at the stranded jellyfish and kicked it again. "Filthy things." He looked up at me suddenly, and I saw a challenge in his expression. "Tell me the truth, Mado. Didn't you ever ask yourself what you'd do if things were different? Weren't you ever tempted, just a bit?"

I ignored the question. "Why Les Salants? Why not just stay quietly in La Houssinière and mind your own business?"

His mouth twisted. "Brismand isn't easy. He likes to have control. He didn't just welcome me with open arms, you know. All that took time. Planning. Work. He could have kept me hanging on for years. That would have suited him just fine."

"So you let us look after you while you used us to bring him around."

"I paid my way!" He sounded angry now. "I worked. I don't owe you people anything." He made an abrupt gesture with his uninjured arm, driving a burst of gulls yarking into the air. "You don't know what it's like," he repeated in a softer voice. "I spent half my life being poor. My mother—"

"But Brismand sent you money," I protested.

"Money for—" He bit off the end of the phrase. "Not enough," he finished in a flat voice. "Not nearly enough." He met my look of contempt with defiance.

Silence, like clouds.

"So." I made my voice expressionless. "When is it going to happen? How soon are your people going to dismantle the Bouch'ou?"

That caught him unawares. "Who told you that was going to happen?"

I shrugged. "It's the obvious thing to do. Everyone owes Brismand money. Everyone's counting on a healthy profit this season. Plenty of money to pay him back. But without the reef, people are forced to sell out at rock-bottom prices to pay their debts; a year later Brismand moves in. Then all he has to do is wait for the tides to reassert themselves, and start building his new ferry port. Am I close?"

"Close enough," he admitted.

"You bastard," I said. "Was it your idea or his?"

"Mine. Well, yours, actually." He shrugged. "If you can steal a beach, then why not a village? Why not a whole island? Brismand owns half of it already. He virtually runs the rest. He's already making me a partner. And now—" He saw my expression and frowned. "Don't look at me like that, Mado," he said. "It's not as bad as you think. There's a choice, for anyone who wants to take it."

"What choice is there?"

Flynn turned to face me, his eyes gleaming. "Ah, Mado, do you really

think we're monsters?" he said. "He needs workers," he continued.
"Think what a ferry port might mean to the island. Jobs. Money. Life.
There'll be jobs for everyone in Les Salants. Better than anything they
have now."

"For a price, I suppose." We both knew Brismand's terms.

"So?" At last I thought I could hear defensiveness in his voice.
"What's the problem there? Everyone at work—good money, good
trade. Everything's disorganized here, everyone pulling in different
directions. There's land here not being used because no one has the
enterprise or the financing to use it. Brismand could change all that. You
all know it; only pride and stubbornness keep you from admitting it."

I stared at him. I couldn't help it; he sounded as if he really believed
in what he was saying. For a second he almost convinced me. And it was
appealing—order out of chaos. It's a cheap trick, that casual charm, like
the brief gleam of sunlight on water that catches the eye—just for an
instant, but long enough to distract, sometimes fatally—from the rocks
ahead.

"What about the old people?" I'd spotted the flaw in his reasoning.
"What about those who can't contribute—or who won't?"

He shrugged. "There's always Les Immortelles."

"They won't accept it. They're Salannais. I know they won't."

"Do you think they'll have the choice?" Flynn saw my expression and
smiled. "We'll find out soon enough, anyway," he told me gently.
"There's going to be a meeting at Angélo's tonight."

"Better do it soon, while the coastal inspectors are still here."

He gave me an appreciative glance. "Oh, you saw the ship, then."

"You're hardly going to take out the Bouch'ou without it," I said
scornfully. "But as you once said to me, it's an illegal construct. It's
unplanned. It's done damage. All you have to do is drop a word in the
right ear, sit back and let the bureaucrats do your work for you." I had to
admit that it was elegant. Salannais are fearful of bureaucrats, overawed
by authority. A clipboard succeeds where dynamite would fail.

"We hadn't planned on acting straightaway, but we would have had to find a reason to call them in eventually," Flynn told me. "Jellyfish warnings seemed like a good enough excuse. I only wish I hadn't been the victim." He winced and indicated his bandaged arm.

"Will you be at this meeting tonight?" I asked, ignoring this.

Flynn smiled. "I don't think so. I might go back to the mainland; run my side of the business from there. I don't think my presence will go down too well in Les Salants when Brismand tells them who I am."

For a moment I was sure he was about to ask me to come with him. My heart flip-flopped like a dying fish; but Flynn had already turned away. I was conscious of a dim feeling of relief that he hadn't asked; at least he'd ended it cleanly, without any further pretense.

The silence was between us like an ocean. Far across the flats I could hear the *hishh* of the waves. I was amazed that I felt so little; I was as hollow as a piece of dried driftwood, light as foam. The hazy clouds made a bright band across the sun. Squinting into that deceptive light I thought I saw a boat, far out on La Jetée; I thought of *Eleanore 2* and looked closer, but already there was nothing to see.

"It's going to be all right, you know," said Flynn. His voice jolted me back into myself. "There'll always be work for you. Brismand's talking about setting up a gallery for you in La Houssinière, or even on the mainland. I'll make sure he finds you a nice house. You'll be better off than you ever were in Les Salants."

"What do you care?" I spat. "*You're* all right, aren't you?"

He looked at me then, and his face closed. "Yes," he said at last in a hard, bright voice. "I'm fine."

8

I turned up late at the meeting. At nine o' clock it was all over but the shouting, of which there had already been plenty. I could hear raised voices and the sounds of stamping and table slamming from as far as the Rue de l'Atlantique. When I looked through the window I could see Brismand standing at the bar with a *devinnoise* in his hand, looking like an indulgent schoolteacher with a group of turbulent pupils.

Flynn wasn't there. I hadn't expected him to be—his presence would no doubt have turned an already chaotic gathering into a riot or a massacre—but I was aware of a strange pang at his absence. I shook it away, angry at myself.

There were a few other faces I didn't see; the Guénolés and the Prossages were missing—probably still searching the island for Damien—as well as Xavier, GrosJean. Otherwise, most of Les Salants seemed to be present, even the wives and the children. People were standing cramped against one another; the door was wedged open to make more room; tables wobbled against a tide of legs; the bar was six deep. No wonder Angélo looked dazed; this evening's takings would surely be a record.

Outside, the tide was almost high; a squally scribble of purple cloud obscured the horizon. The wind had changed slightly too; veering south as it often does before a storm. There was a chill in the air.

Even so, I lingered at the window, trying to make out individual voices, reluctant to go in. I could see Aristide close by with Désirée holding his hand; beside them I noticed Philippe Bastonnet and his family—even Laetitia and the dog Pétrole. Though I did not see Aristide actually speak to Philippe, I thought there was something less aggressive in his posture, a kind of slackening, as if a vital support had been removed. Since the news about Mercédès, much of the old man's assurance had gone, and he looked bewildered and pitiful beneath his gruffness.

Suddenly I heard a sound at the creek behind me. I turned and saw Xavier Bastonnet and Ghislain Guénolé coming down the dune together at top speed, their faces set. They did not see me but made at once for the *étier*, now swollen with high-tide seawater, where the *Cécilia* was moored.

"You're surely not taking her out tonight?" I called, seeing Xavier beginning to take in the moorings. Ghislain joined him, looking grim. "There's been a boat seen off La Jetée," he told me shortly. "Can't be sure with this mist till we go out there."

"Don't tell my grandfather," said Xavier, struggling with the *Cécilia*'s engine. "He'd go mad if he thought I was going out there with Ghislain on a night like this. He's always saying it was a Guénolé's recklessness that killed my father. But if Damien's out there and can't get back—"

"What about Alain?" I asked. "Shouldn't there be someone else with you, at least?"

Ghislain shrugged. "Gone to La Houssinière with Matthias. Time's short. And if we can get the *Cécilia* out there before the wind rises too far—"

I nodded. "Good luck, then. Be careful."

Xavier gave me a shy smile. "Maybe someone could give the message that we're on the way to Alain and Matthias in La Houssinière."

The little engine growled and came to life. While Ghislain held the *Cécilia*'s boom, Xavier steered the little boat between the wood-shored banks and carefully out toward La Goulue and the open sea.

9

Preferring not to explain the disappearance of Xavier and the *Cécilia* in front of Aristide, I decided to deliver the message to Alain myself. It was almost dark by the time I reached La Houssinière. It was cold too; what had been a squally wind in the hollow of Les Salants caused wires to squeal and flags to rattle on this, the southernmost part of the island. The sky was tumultuous, the pale strip above the beach already half-engulfed by gaudy purple thunderheads; the waves bore chevrons of white; birds settled in expectation. Jojo-le-Goëland was leaving the esplanade carrying a placard saying that due to weather warnings, the evening's return trip to Fromentine aboard *Brismand 1* had been canceled; a couple of glum-looking tourists with suitcases followed him, protesting.

There was no sign of either Alain or Matthias on the esplanade. I stood at the seawall and squinted out over Les Immortelles, shivering a little, regretting not having brought a coat with me. From the café behind me came a sudden surge of voices, as if a door had been opened.

"Why, it's Mado, *ma soeur*, heh, come to pay us a call."

"Little Mado, looking cold, heh, looking veryvery chilly indeed."

It was the ancient nuns, Soeur Extase and Soeur Thérèse, both coming out of the Chat Noir with cups of what looked like *café-devinnoise*.

"You should come inside, heh, Mado? Have a hot drink?"

I shook my head. "Thanks. I'm all right."

"It's the bad south wind again," said Soeur Thérèse. "That's what brought back the jellyfish, Brismand says. There's a plague of them every—"

"Thirty years, *ma soeur*, when the tides run from the Gulf. Nasty things."

"I remember the last time," said Soeur Thérèse. "He waited and waited at Les Immortelles, watching the tides—"

"But she never came back, though, did she, *ma soeur?*" Both nuns shook their heads. "No, she never did. Nevernever. Not at all."

"Who do you mean, *she?*" I asked.

"That girl, of course." The two nuns looked at me. "He was in love with her. Both of them were, those brothers—"

Brothers? I stared at the nuns, baffled. "Do you mean my father and P'titJean?"

"Summer of the Black Year." The sisters nodded again and beamed. "We remember it perfectly. We were young then—"

"Younger, anyway—"

"She said she was leaving. She gave us a letter."

"Who did?" I asked, confused.

The sisters fixed their black eyes on me. "The girl, of course," said Soeur Extase impatiently. "Eleanore."

❦

The name took me so much by surprise that the sound of the bell scarcely registered at first; it clanged flatly across the harbor, the sound ricocheting off the water like a stone. A few people came crowding out of Le Chat Noir to see what was happening. Someone knocked against me; a drink spilled; when I looked up again, the momentary confusion had dispersed, and Soeur Thérèse and Soeur Extase had vanished.

"What's Père Alban up to, ringing the church bell at this time?" asked Joël lazily, a cigarette hanging from his lip. "There's no mass, is there?"

"I don't think so," said René Loyon.

"Maybe it's a fire," suggested Lucas Pinoz, the mayor's cousin.

People seemed to think fire was the likeliest possibility; on a small island like Le Devin there are no emergency services to speak of, and the church bell is often the quickest way to sound an alarm. Someone shouted *Fire!*, and there was some confusion, with more drinkers hustling one another at the café entrance, but as Lucas pointed out, there was no red glow in the sky and no smell of burning.

"We rang the bell in '55, heh, when the old church got hit by lightning," declared old Michel Dieudonné.

"There's something off Les Immortelles out there," said René Loyon, who had been standing on top of the seawall. "Something on the rocks."

It was a boat. Easy enough to see it now we knew where to look, a hundred meters out, grounded on the same snarl of rocks that had done for the *Eleanore* the previous year. My breath caught. With no visible sail, and at that distance, it was impossible to say whether it was either of our Salannais boats.

"It's a hulk," said Joël with authority. "Must have been out there for hours. No reason for anyone to panic now." He stubbed out his cigarette beneath his boot.

Jojo-le-Goëland was unconvinced. "We should try shining a light out there," he suggested. "Might be something to salvage. I'll bring the tractor."

Already people were assembling under the seawall. The church bell, its warning work done, fell silent. Jojo's tractor made its way unsteadily across the uneven beach toward the sand's edge; its powerful headlight shone aross the water.

"I can see it now," said René. "It's whole, but not for long."

Michel Dieudonné nodded. "Tide's too high to get to her now, even with the *Marie Joseph*. And with a squall blowing—" He spread his hands expressively. "Whoever she belongs to, she's finished now."

"Oh God!" It was Paule Lacroix, Joël's mother, standing above us on the esplanade. "There's someone out there in the water!"

Faces turned toward her. The spotlight from the tractor was too bright; only the dark hull of the crippled boat was visible among the reflections.

"Turn off the light!" yelled Mayor Pinoz, who had just arrived with Père Alban.

It took a moment for our eyes to adjust to the darkness. The sea looked black now, the boat a shade of indigo. Straining our eyes, we tried to make out a pale blur among the waves.

"I see an arm! There's a man in the water!"

Someone screamed some distance to my left, in a voice I recognized. I turned around and saw Damien's mother, her face shapeless with distress beneath a thick island scarf. Alain was standing on the seawall with a pair of binoculars, though with the south wind in his face and the growing height of the waves, I doubted whether he could see anything more than the rest of us could. Matthias was standing by his side, looking helplessly at the water.

Damien's mother saw me and ran down the beach toward me, her coat flapping in the wind. "It's the *Eleanore 2!*" She clung to me breathlessly. "I know it is! Damien!"

I tried to calm her. "You don't know that," I said as calmly as I could. But she was beyond comfort. She began to make a high keening noise, half-wail, half-words. I caught her son's name several times, but nothing more. I realized that I hadn't mentioned the fact that Xavier and Ghislain had taken the *Cécilia;* but it occurred to me that to speak of it now might simply make things worse.

"If there is someone out there, we have to make an effort to reach them, heh?" It was Mayor Pinoz, half-drunk but trying gamely to take command of the situation.

Jojo-le-Goëland shook his head. "Not in my *Marie Joseph*," he said adamantly.

But Alain was already racing down the path from the esplanade toward the harbor. "Just try stopping me," he yelled.

The *Marie Joseph* was certainly the only vessel with enough stability to maneuver close to the stranded boat; even so, the operation would be almost impossible in this weather.

"There's no one there!" wailed Jojo indignantly, starting up the beach after Alain. "You can't take her out on your own!"

"Then go with him!" I said urgently. "If that boy's out there—"

"If so, he's finished," muttered Joël. "There's no sense in joining him."

"Then I'll go!" I took the steps up to the Rue des Immortelles two at a time. There was a boat on the rocks; a Salannais was in danger. In spite of my anxiety my heart was singing. A fierce joy engulfed me—*this* was how it feels to be an islander; this was how it feels to belong—no other place commands such loyalties, such stony, steadfast love.

There were people running alongside me—I saw Père Alban and Matthias Guénolé, who I'd guessed could not be far away; Omer was lumbering after them as fast as he could; Marin and Adrienne were staring from the lit window of La Marée. Groups of Houssins watched us run, some confused, others incredulous; I didn't care. I ran for the harbor.

Alain was already there. People gaped at him from the jetty but few seemed inclined to join him in the *Marie Joseph*. Matthias was calling from the street; I heard more raised voices behind him. A man in a faded *vareuse* was taking in the *Marie Joseph*'s sails with his back turned to me; as Omer caught up, out of breath, the man turned around and I recognized Flynn.

There was no time for me to react. I saw him catch my eye, then he looked away, almost with indifference. Alain was already settling himself at the helm. Omer was struggling with the unfamiliar engine. Père Alban, standing on the jetty, was trying to calm Damien's mother, who had arrived out of breath a few minutes after the rest. Alain spared me a brief glance, as if appraising whether I was fit to help, then he nodded.

"Thank you."

People were still crowding around us, some trying to help where they could. Objects were thrown—almost randomly, it seemed—into the *Marie Joseph;* a boat hook, a coil of rope, a bucket, a blanket, an electric flashlight. Someone handed me a flask with brandy in it; someone else gave Alain a pair of gloves. As we pulled away from the jetty Jojo-le-Goëland threw me his coat. "Try not to get it wet, heh?" he said gruffly.

Getting out of the harbor was deceptively easy. Although the boat pitched a little, the harbor was almost completely sheltered, and we steered with little difficulty through the narrow central channel toward the open sea. Buoys and dinghies bobbed around us; I leaned forward in the bow to push them out of the way as we passed.

Then the sea hit us. In the short time it had taken us to get organized, the wind had risen; now it moaned through the wires, and the spray was as hard as gravel. The *Marie Joseph* was a good little workhorse but not built for heavy weather; she sat low in the water, like an oyster boat; waves crashed across her bow. Alain cursed.

"Do you see her yet, heh?" he yelled at Omer.

Omer shook his head. "I see something," he shouted against the wind. "I still don't know if it's the *Eleanore 2*."

"Bring her around!" I could barely hear his voice. Water blinded me. "We have to take it face on!" I could see what he meant. Steering straight into the wind was tricky; but the waves were high enough to tip us right over if we let them push us aside. We moved with sickening slowness, riding one wave only to have the next slap us down. The *Eleanore 2*—if it was she—was barely visible but for the wild ruffles of foam around her. Of the figure we thought we had glimpsed in the water, there was no sign.

Twenty minutes later I was not sure whether we had made even a few dozen meters; at night distances are deceptive, and the sea took all our attention. I was vaguely conscious of Flynn in the bottom of the boat, bailing water, but there was no time to think about that, or to remember the last time we had been in a similar situation together.

I could still see lights on Les Immortelles; from a great distance I thought I heard voices. Alain shone the flashlight out to sea; the water looked gray-brown in its weak light, but at last I could see the crippled boat, closer now and recognizable, broken almost in two across a spine of rock.

"It's her!" The wind had stolen the anguish from Alain's voice; it sounded thin and distant to me, a whistle through reeds. "Get down!"

This to Flynn, who had moved so far forward that he was almost hanging from the *Marie Joseph*'s nose. For a second I glimpsed something in the water, something pallid that was not foam. It was visible for an instant, then seemed to roll with the wave.

"I see someone!" yelled Flynn.

Alain sprang for the bow, leaving Omer to control the boat. I grabbed a rope and flung it; but a vicious cat's-paw of wind blew it back in my face, dripping wet, and lashed me savagely across the eyes. I fell back, my eyes closed and streaming. When I was able to open them once more I found the world oddly out of focus; in a blur I could just make out Flynn and Alain, one holding onto the other in a desperate trapeze while beneath them the sea hitched and plummeted. Both were soaking; Alain had lashed a rope around his ankle to keep himself aboard; Flynn, who was carrying a looped rope, had gone even farther and was actually leaning out, one foot wedged in the pit of Alain's stomach and the other pressing against the side of the *Marie Joseph*, both arms spread wide into the turbulence below. Something white flashed by; Flynn dived for it and missed.

Behind us Omer struggled to keep the boat's nose to the wind. The *Marie Joseph* pitched sickly; Alain staggered; a wave rolled over both men and pulled the boat to the side. Cold water crashed onto all our heads. For a second I feared that both men had been knocked overboard; the *Marie Joseph*'s bow sagged, barely a centimeter from the sea. I did what I could to bail water while the rocks surged into view, shockingly close. Then there was a terrible sound on the boat's hull, a grating noise and a crack like a lightning strike. We tensed in anticipation—but it was the *Eleanore 2* that had given way, her spine finally broken, falling into two pieces on the creaming rocks. Even so, we were far from safe, drifting as we were toward the floating debris. I felt something judder against the boat's side. Something seemed to catch underneath—but then a wave lifted us, and the *Marie Joseph* cleared the rock just in time, with Omer using the boat hook to push us free of the wreckage. I looked up; Alain was still holding his position in the bow, but Flynn was gone. Only for a moment, though; with a hoarse cry of relief I saw him emerge again from beneath a wall of water with something—a loop of rope—in his hands. Something bobbed briefly into view as he and Alain began to haul it in. Something white.

Much as I longed to know what was going on I had to keep bailing; the *Marie Joseph* was as full as she could take, and we were all fully occupied. I heard shouts and dared to glance up, but Alain's back stopped me from seeing very much. I bailed for five minutes at least, or until we were out of range of those terrible rocks. I thought I heard a distant, ghostly cheer from Les Immortelles.

"Who is it?" I yelled. My voice was snatched from my mouth by the wind. Alain didn't turn around. Flynn was struggling with a sheet of tarpaulin from the bottom of the boat. The tarpaulin obscured my vision almost completely.

"Flynn!" I knew he had heard me; he looked back at me quickly, then turned away. Something in his expression told me it wasn't good news. "Is it Damien?" I yelled again. "Is he alive?"

Flynn pushed me back with a hand still partly wrapped in dripping bandage. "It's no use," he called, barely audible above the sound of the wind. "It's over."

With the tide at our stern we had made good headway toward the harbor; already it seemed to me that I could feel a lull in the waves. Omer sent a questioning look at Alain; Alain replied with one of dismay and incomprehension. Flynn didn't look at either of them; instead he picked up a bucket and began to bail water, although by then the need for that had passed.

I grabbed Flynn's arm and made him look at me. "For pity's sake, Flynn, tell me! Is it Damien?"

All three men glanced at the tarpaulin, then back at me. Flynn's expression was complex, unreadable. He looked down at his hands, which were raw from handling the wet ropes. "Mado," he told me at last. "It's your father."

10

I remember it as a painting, a violent Van Gogh with swirling purple skies and blurry faces; in silence. I remember the boat lurching like a heart. I remember holding my hands up to my face and seeing the skin pale and puckered with seawater. I think maybe I fell.

GrosJean was lying half-covered by the tarpaulin sheet. For the first time I was truly aware of his hugeness, his dead and lumpen weight. He had lost his shoes somewhere along the way, and his feet looked small in comparison with the rest of him, almost delicate. When you hear about death you're often told that the dead look asleep, at peace. GrosJean looked like an animal who has died in a trap. His flesh had the rubbery feel of a butcher shop's pig, his mouth open; a snarl drawing his lips up to reveal yellow teeth, as if at the last moment, in the face of death, he had finally found a voice. I didn't feel that numbness of which so many of the bereaved speak; that merciful sense of unreality. Instead I felt a surge of terrible anger.

How dared he do this? After everything we had been through together, how *dared* he? I'd trusted him, I'd confided in him, I'd tried to make a fresh start. Was this what he'd thought of me? Was this what he'd thought of himself?

Someone took my arm; I was pounding my fists against my father's clammy body; it felt like meat. "Mado, please." It was Flynn. My anger surged again; without thinking, I whipped around and hit him across the mouth. He recoiled; I stumbled backward and fell onto the deck. Briefly I saw the Dog Star from behind a scud of cloud. The stars doubled, trebled, then filled the sky.

I heard later that they'd found Damien hiding in the goods hangar of *Brismand 1*, cold and hungry but unharmed. Apparently he had been trying to stow away on the mainland ferry when the trip was canceled.

Ghislain and Xavier had never reached Les Immortelles. They had spent hours trying, but eventually they had been forced to land *Cécilia* at La Goulue, and returned to the village just as the volunteers from La Houssinière were coming home.

Mercédès was waiting. She had met Aristide in the village, and there had been a fine screaming match between them, all inhibitions flung aside. Her meeting with Xavier and Ghislain was more restrained. Both young men were exhausted, but strangely euphoric. Their efforts at sea had not borne fruit; but it was clear that a new understanding had been reached between them. Where once they had been bitter rivals, now they were close to being friends again. Aristide began to berate his grandson for taking the *Cécilia*, but for the first time Xavier did not seem at all overawed. Instead he took Mercédès aside, with a smile very different from his usual shy manner, and though it was too early to speak of a reconciliation between them, Toinette secretly hoped for a favorable outcome.

I caught a chill on the *Marie Joseph*, which turned overnight to pneumonia. Maybe that's why I remember virtually nothing of what happened—a couple of stills, that's all, in faded sepia. My father's body being lifted in a blanket sling onto the quayside. The undemonstrative Guénolés hugging one another with a fierce and unrestrained passion. Père Alban waiting patiently, his soutane hitched up over his fishing waders. Flynn.

It was almost a week before I was truly conscious of what was going on around me. Till then things had been blurry, colors heightened, sounds absent. My lungs were filled with concrete; my fever soared.

I was moved to Les Immortelles at once, where the emergency doctor had remained. Gradually, as my fever ebbed, I became conscious of my room with its white walls, of flowers, of presents left like offerings at the door by a constant stream of visitors. At first I barely paid attention. I felt so sick and weak that it was an effort to keep my eyes open. Breathing required conscious effort. Even the memory of my father's death was secondary to my body's distress.

Adrienne had been filled with panic at the thought of nursing me and had fled with Marin to the mainland as soon as the weather permitted. The doctor declared that I was on the mend, and left Capucine to watch over me, with the grumbling Hilaire to administer antibiotic injections. Toinette made herb infusions and forced me to drink them. Père Alban sat by me, Capucine said, night after night. Brismand kept his distance; no one had seen Flynn.

It was perhaps good for him that they hadn't; by the end of the week his role in events had been made clear to everyone, and the hostility against him in Les Salants was phenomenal. Surprisingly, there was less against Brismand; he was a true Houssin, when all was said. What could you expect? But Rouget had been one of us. Only the Guénolés dared defend him—after all he had gone out to the *Eleanore 2* when no one else would. Toinette refused to take the matter seriously at all, but many Salannais spoke darkly of revenge. Capucine was convinced that Flynn had gone back to the mainland, and shook her head mournfully over the entire business.

The plague of jellyfish was under control, with nets stretched across the sandbanks to prevent any more from entering the bay, and a coast guard boat to collect the ones that remained. The official explanation was that freak storms had brought them up the Gulf Stream, perhaps from as far away as Australia; village gossip preferred to take it as a warning from the Saint.

"I always said it was going to be a Black Year," affirmed Aristide with glum satisfaction. "See what happens when you don't listen?"

In spite of his anger against Brismand, the old man seemed resigned. Weddings cost money, he remarked, if his young fool of a grandson continued to persist in his stubbornness. . . . He shook his head. "Still, I won't live forever. Good to think the boy may have something to inherit after all, other than quicksand and rot. Maybe the luck will turn at last."

Not everyone thought so. The Guénolés held fast against the Brismand project—as well they might. With five to support, one a schoolboy and one an old man of eighty-five, money had always been short. Now they were in crisis. No one knew exactly how much they had borrowed, but it was widely thought to be upward of a hundred thousand. The loss of the *Eleanore 2* had been the final blow. Alain had spoken out fiercely after the meeting, saying that it wasn't fair, that the community had a responsibility, that because of Damien's disappearance he hadn't been party to the discussion; but his objections went mostly unregarded. Our precarious sense of community had been ruptured; once again it was every Salannais for himself.

Matthias Guénolé refused to go into Les Immortelles, of course. Alain supported his decision. There was talk of their leaving the island. The Guénolé-Bastonnet hostilities had resumed; Aristide, sensing weakness and the possible departure of their biggest fishing rival, had apparently done all he could to turn the rest of Les Salants against them.

"They'll wreck it all with their stubbornness, heh! Our one chance. It's selfish, that's what it is, and I won't let Guénolé selfishness wreck my boy's future. We've got to salvage something from this mess now, otherwise we all go under!"

Many had to admit that he had a point. But Alain's rage, when he learned what had been said, was explosive. "So that's it?" he roared. "That's how we look after our own in Les Salants? What about *my* boys? What about my father, who fought in the war? Are you going to give up on us now? And for what? Money? Rotten Houssin profit?"

A year ago it might have been a more forceful argument. But now we had had a scent of that money. We knew it better. There was silence, and some red faces. But few were moved. What was a single family when a whole community was at stake? Better the Brismands' ferry port than nothing, after all.

My father was buried while I lay in Les Immortelles. Corpses don't keep well in summer, and islanders have little to do with the mainland rituals of postmortem and embalming. We had a priest, didn't we? Père Alban did his office out at La Bouche, as always, in his soutane and fishing waders.

The gravestone is a lump of gray-pink grantite from Pointe Griznoz. They used my tractor trailer to drag it. Later, when the sand has settled, I will have an inscription carved onto it—Aristide might do it for me, if I ask him.

"Why did he do it?" I found my anger was unchanged since the night on the *Marie Joseph*. "Why did he take the *Eleanore 2* that day?"

"Who knows?" said Matthias, lighting a Gitane. "All I know is that we found some damn funny things in her when we finally brought her back—"

"Not when the girl's sick, you idiot!" interrupted Capucine, intercepting the cigarette with a deft pinch of the fingers.

"What things?" I demanded, sitting up in bed.

"Ropes. Crampons. And half a box of dynamite."

"What?"

The old man shrugged and heaved a sigh. "I don't suppose we'll ever be sure what he was doing. I only wish he hadn't chosen the *Eleanore* to do it in."

The *Eleanore*. I tried to recall exactly what the nuns had said to me the night of the storm. "She was someone they knew," I said. "Someone both he and P'titJean cared about. This Eleanore."

Matthias shook his head disapprovingly. "You don't want to believe those magpies. They'll say anything." He glanced at my face, and I thought he blushed a little. "Nuns, heh! They're the worst gossips there are. Besides that business—whatever it was—happened such a long time ago. How could that have anything to do with how GrosJean died?"

Not *how* he died perhaps, but *why*. I couldn't help thinking about it; the connection with his brother's suicide thirty years ago; his suicide in the *Eleanore*. Had my father done the same? And why was he carrying dynamite?

I fretted so long that Capucine decided it was affecting my recovery. She must have spoken about it to Père Alban, because the dry old priest turned up to see me two days later, looking as mournful as ever.

"It's over, Mado," he said. "Your father's at peace. You should let him rest now."

Physically, I was feeling much better by then, though still very tired; propped up against the pillows I could see the stark August sky behind him. It would be a fine day for fishing. "Père Alban, who was Eleanore? Did you know her?"

He hesitated. "I knew her, but I can't discuss her with you."

"Was she from Les Immortelles? Was she one of the nuns?"

"Believe me, Mado, she's best forgotten."

"But if he named a boat after her—" I tried to explain how important that had been to my father; how he had never done that again, not even for my mother. Surely it was no accident that he had chosen that particular boat. And what could be the significance of what Matthias had found in her?

But Père Alban was even less talkative than usual. "It means nothing," he repeated, for the third time. "Let GrosJean rest in peace."

11

By then I had been in Les Immortelles for over a week. Hilaire recommended another week's rest, but I was growing impatient. The skyscape through the high window taunted me; gilded motes filtered down to my bed. The month was almost at an end; in a few days the moon would be full and it would be time once more for Sainte-Marine's festival on the Pointe. I felt as if all these familiar things were taking place for the last time; every second was a final farewell I could not bear to miss. I prepared to go home.

Capucine protested, but I overrode her arguments ruthlessly. I'd been away too long. I had to face Les Salants at some time. I hadn't even seen my father's grave.

La Puce gave way in the face of such determination. "Stay in my trailer for a while," she suggested. "I'm not having you in that empty house alone."

"It's all right," I promised her. "I'm not going back there. But I do need to be on my own for a while."

I did not go back to GrosJean's house that day. I was surprised to discover that I felt no curiosity about it, or any desire to look inside. Instead I went to the dunes above La Goulue and overlooked what remained of my world.

Most of our summer people had gone. The sea was silk; the sky crude and blue as a child's painting. Les Salants faded silently under the late-

August sun as it had for so many years before: the window boxes and gardens, lately neglected, had withered and died; stunted fig trees gave up small, mean fruit; dogs loitered outside shuttered houses; rabbit-tail grasses went white and brittle. The people too had reverted to type: Omer now spent hours in Angélo's, playing cards and drinking cup after cup of *devinnoise;* Charlotte Prossage, who had been so sweetened by the arrival of the summer children, once more hid her face behind earth-colored head scarves; Damien was sullen and argumentative. Within twenty-four hours of my return I could see for myself that the Brismands hadn't simply broken Les Salants; they had eaten it whole.

Few people spoke to me; it was enough that they had shown their concern with presents and cards. Now that I was well again I sensed a kind of inertia among them, a return to the old ways. Greetings were once more abbreviated to a single nod. Conversations flagged. At first I thought perhaps they resented me; after all, I was related to Brismand. But after a while I began to understand. I saw it in the way they watched the sea; one eye perpetually fixed on the floating thing out there in the bay, our Bouch'ou, our very own sword of Damocles. They weren't even aware of doing it. But they did watch it, even the children, paler and more subdued than they had been all summer. It was all the more precious, we told ourselves, because sacrifices had been made. The greater the sacrifice, the more precious it became. We'd loved it once; we hated it now; but to lose it was unthinkable. Omer's loan had compromised Toinette's property, even though it had not been his to stake. Aristide had mortgaged his house far beyond its value. Alain was losing his son—perhaps both his sons, now that the business was in decline. The Prossages had lost their daughter. Xavier and Mercédès were talking about leaving Le Devin for good, of settling down somewhere like Pornic or Fromentine, where the baby could be born without scandal.

Aristide was devastated by the news, though he was far too proud to say so. Pornic isn't far, he would repeat to anyone who would listen. It's a three-hour ferry ride twice a week. That isn't what you'd call far, is it, heh?

Rumors were still flying about GrosJean's death. I heard them second-hand from Capucine—village protocol demanded that at this time I should be left alone—but speculation was rife. Many believed he had comitted suicide.

There was some reason to believe it. GrosJean had always been unstable; maybe the realization of Brismand's treachery had pushed him over the edge. And so close to the anniversary of P'titJean's death and Sainte-Marine's festival . . . History repeats itself, they said in lowered voices. Everything returns.

But others were less easily convinced. The significance of the dynamite in the *Eleanore 2* had not escaped notice; it was Alain's belief that GrosJean had been trying to demolish the breakwater at Les Immortelles when he lost control of the boat and was thrown onto the rocks.

"He sacrificed himself," Alain had repeated to anyone who would listen. "He knew before any of us that it was the only way to stop Brismand's takeover."

It was no more far-fetched than any of the other explanations. An accident; suicide; a heroic gesture . . . The truth was that nobody knew; GrosJean had told no one of his plans, and speculation was all we had. In death, as in life, my father kept his secrets.

I went down to La Goulue the morning after my return. Lolo was sitting with Damien by the water's edge, both of them silent and unmoving as rocks. They seemed to be waiting for something. The high tide was on the turn; dark commas of wet sand marked its passage. Damien had a new bruise on his cheek. He shrugged when I commented about it. "I fell over," he said, not bothering to make it sound convincing.

Lolo looked at me. "Damien was right," he said glumly. "We should never have had this beach. It's messed everything up. We were better off before." He said it without resentment, but with a deep weariness, which I found even more disturbing. "We just didn't know it then."

Damien nodded. "We would have survived. If the sea had come too close we'd just have rebuilt farther up."

"Or moved."

I nodded. Suddenly, moving didn't seem like such a terrible alternative after all.

"It's just a place, after all, isn't it, heh?"

"Sure. There are other places."

I wondered if Capucine knew what her grandson was thinking. Damien, Xavier, Mercédès, Lolo . . . At this rate by next year there wouldn't be a young face left in Les Salants.

Both boys were looking out toward the Bouch'ou. Invisible now, it would begin to show in five hours or so, when the tide uncovered the oyster beds.

"What if they took it, heh?" There was an edge to Lolo's voice.

Damien nodded. "They could have their sand back. We don't need it."

"Neh. We didn't want Houssin sand anyway."

I was shocked to find myself half-agreeing with them.

❀

In spite of that, since my return I found the Salannais spent more time on the beach than ever before. Not swimming or sunbathing—only tourists do that—or even in comfortable conversation, as we so often had earlier that summer. This time there were no cookouts or bonfires or drinking parties at La Goulue. Instead we crept there in secret, early in the mornings or at the turning tides, running the sand through our furtive fingers and not meeting one another's eyes.

The sand fascinated us. We saw it in a different way now; no longer gold dust but the debris of centuries: bones, shells, microscopic pieces of fossilized matter, pulverized glass, vanquished stone, fragments of unimaginable time. There were people in the sand; lovers, children, traitors, heroes. There were the tiles of long-demolished houses. There were warriors and fishermen, there were Nazi planes and broken crockery and shattered gods. There was rebellion and there was defeat. There was everything, and everything there was the same.

We saw that now; how pointless it all was: our war against the tides, against the Houssins. We saw how it would be.

12

It was two days before Sainte-Marine's festival when I finally decided to visit my father's grave. My absence at the funeral had been inevitable, but I was back now, and it was expected of me.

The Houssins have their own neat, grassy churchyard, with a park keeper to tend all the graves. At La Bouche, we do our work ourselves. We have to. Our gravestones look pagan compared with theirs; monolithic. And we tend them with care. One very old one is the grave of a young couple, marked simply GUÉNOLÉ-BASTONNET, 1861–1887. Someone still puts flowers on it, though surely no one is old enough to remember its occupants.

They had placed him next to P'titJean. Their stones are almost twins in size and color, though P'titJean's is older, its surface furred with lichen. As I came closer I saw that clean gravel had been raked around the two graves, and that someone had already prepared the earth for planting.

I had brought some lavender cuttings to plant around the stone, and a trowel to dig with. Père Alban appeared to have done the same; his hands were covered with earth, and there were red geraniums freshly planted under both stones.

The old priest looked startled to see me, as if caught out. He rubbed his gritty hands together several times. "I'm glad to see you looking so well," he said. "I'll leave you to your farewells."

"Don't go." I took a step forward. "Père Alban, I'm glad you're here. I wanted—"

"I'm sorry." He shook his head. "I know what you want from me. You think I know something about your father's death. But I can't tell you anything. Let it go."

"Why? I demanded. "I need to understand! My father died for a reason, and I think you know what it is!"

He looked at me severely. "Your father was lost at sea, Mado. He went out in the *Eleanore 2* and was swept overboard. Just like his brother."

"But you do know something," I said softly. "Don't you?"

"I have—suspicions. Just as you do."

"What suspicions?"

Père Alban sighed. "Let it go, Madeleine. I can't tell you anything. Whatever I may know is bound by the confessional, and I can't speak to you about it." But I thought I heard something in his voice, an odd intonation, as if the words he spoke were at variance with something else he was trying to convey.

"But someone else can?" I said, taking his hand. "Is that what you're saying?"

"I can't help you, Madeleine." Was it my imagination, or was there something in the way he said "*I* can't help you," a little stress on the first syllable? "I'm going back now," said the old priest, gently prying my hand from his. "I have to sort out some old records. Birth and death registers, you know the kind of thing. It's a job I have been putting off for a long time. But I have a responsibility. It preys on my mind." There it was again, that peculiar intonation.

"Papers?" I repeated.

"Registers. I used to have a clerk. Then, the nuns. Now I have no one."

"I could help." I wasn't imagining it; he *was* trying to say something to me. "Père Alban, let me help you."

He gave a smile of peculiar sweetness. "How kind of you to offer, Madeleine. That would be a great relief."

⁂

Islanders mistrust paperwork. That's why we set a priest to guard our secrets, our strange births and violent deaths, to tend our family trees. The information is public, of course, at least in theory. But shadows of the confessional lie over it, buried as it is beneath the dust. There has never been a computer here, nor will there be. Instead there are ledgers, closely written in reddish brown ink, and mushroom-colored folders containing documents crisp with age.

The signatures that sprawl or scurry across these pages contain entire histories; here an illiterate mother has stuck a rose petal onto the birth certificate of her child; there a man's hand has faltered on the entry for his wife's death. Marriages, stillbirths, deaths. Here two brothers, shot by the Germans for smuggling black market goods from the mainland; there an entire family died of influenza; on this page a girl—another Prossage—gave birth to a baby "father unknown." Opposite, another girl—a child of fourteen—died giving birth to a deformed infant, which did not survive.

The endless variations were never dull; strangely enough I found them rather uplifting. To continue as we do in the face of everything seems oddly heroic, knowing that in the end it all comes to this. The island names—Prossage, Bastonnet, Guénolé, Prasteau, Brismand— marched across the pages like soldiers. I almost forgot why I was there.

Père Alban left me alone. Perhaps he did not trust himself. For a time I lost myself completely in the histories of Le Devin until the light began to fail and I remembered why I had come. It took me a further hour to find the reference for which I was searching.

I was still not entirely sure what I was looking for, and I wasted time on my own family tree—my mother's signature bringing tears to my eyes as I came across it by chance at the top of a page, with GrosJean's careful illiterate's script next to it. Then GrosJean's birth and his brother's, on the same page though years apart. GrosJean's death and his brother's—*Lost at sea*. The pages, closely written to the point of being almost illegible, took long minutes to scan. I began to wonder if maybe I had misunderstood, and there was nothing for me after all.

And then, suddenly, there it was. A notice of marriage between Claude Saint-Joseph Brismand and Eleanore Margaret Flynn, two signatures in purple ink—a curt *Brismand* followed by an exuberant *Eleanore,* with a loop on the *l* that goes on almost forever, intertwining like ivy with the names above and below.

Eleanore. I said it aloud, with a catch in my voice.

I'd found her.

"So she has, *ma soeur.*"

"I knew she would if she kept at it."

It was the two sisters. Both of them were standing in the doorway, smiling like apple dolls. In the dim light they looked almost young again, their eyes shining. "You remind us of her, just a little, doesn't she, *ma soeur?* She reminds us of—"

"Eleanore."

After that it was easy. Eleanore was where it began and *Eleanore* was where it ended. We unraveled the tale, the nuns and I, in the records room of the church, lighting candles to illuminate the old papers as the light began to fail.

I had already guessed a part of the story. The sisters knew the rest. Maybe Père Alban had let something slip, when they were helping him with the registers.

It's an island story, bleaker than most, but then we are so used to clinging to these rocks that we have developed a resilience—some of us have, at least. It begins with two brothers, close as crabs, Jean-Marin and Jean-François Prasteau. And of course, the girl, all fire and temperament. There was passion too; it was in the way her signature looped and sprawled across the page, a kind of restless romance.

"She wasn't from here," explained Soeur Thérèse. "Monsieur Brismand brought her back from one of his trips abroad. She had no parents, no friends, no money of her own. She was ten years younger than he was; barely out of her teens—"

"But a real beauty," said Soeur Extase. "Beautiful and restless, the dynamite combination—"

"With Monsieur Brismand so busy making money that after the wedding he hardly seemed to notice her at all."

He'd wanted children; all islanders do. But she'd wanted more. She found no friends among the Houssin wives—she was too young and foreign for their taste—and took to sitting alone at Les Immortelles every day, watching the sea and reading books.

"Oh, she loved stories," said Soeur Extase. "Reading them and telling them—"

"Knights and ladies—"

"Princes and dragons."

That was where the brothers first saw her. They had come to pick up a delivery of supplies for the boatyard they ran with their father, and she was waiting there. She had been on Le Devin for less than three months.

The impulsive P'titJean had been instantly smitten. He started to visit her in La Houssinière every day, sitting next to her on the beach and talking to her. GrosJean looked on stolidly, amused at first, then curious, a little jealous, then finally, fatally ensnared.

"She knew what she was doing," said Soeur Thérèse. "It was a game at first—she liked games. P'titJean was a boy; he would have got over her eventually. But GrosJean—"

My father, a silent man of deep emotions, was different. She sensed it; he drew her. They met in secret, in the dunes or by La Goulue. Gros-Jean taught her to sail; she told him stories. The boats he built at the yard reflected her influence, those fanciful names from books and poems he would never read.

But by now Brismand had grown suspicious. It was mostly P'titJean's fault; his adoration had not gone unnoticed in La Houssinière, and although he was so young, he was much closer to Eleanore in age than her husband. Claude never seriously suspected him; but for Eleanore there were no more trips alone to Les Salants, and he made sure that there was always a nun out at Les Immortelles to watch over her. Besides, now Eleanore was pregnant, and Claude was overjoyed.

The boy was born a little prematurely. She named him after Claude—island tradition demands it—but with typical perversity she inserted another, more secret name there, on the birth certificate, for anyone to see.

No one made the connection. Not even my father—that complex, looping script was far beyond his skill to decipher—and for a few months Eleanore found her restlessness curbed by the infant's demands.

But Brismand had become more possessive now that he had a son. Sons are important on Le Devin—more so than on the mainland, where healthy children are so common. I imagined how he had been, how proud of his boy. I imagined how the brothers watched him, in scorn and guilt and envy and desire. I'd always assumed my father hated Claude Brismand because of something Brismand had done to him. Only now did I understand that the ones we hate most are those we ourselves have wronged.

And what of Eleanore? For a while she really tried to devote herself to her baby. But she was unhappy. Like my mother, she found island life unendurable. Women eyed her with suspicion and envy; men dared not speak to her.

"She read and read those books of hers," Soeur Thérèse told me, "but nothing helped. She got thin—she lost her shine. She was like some wildflowers you should never pick, because they droop and fade in a vase. She talked to us sometimes—"

"But we were too old for her, even then. She needed life."

Both sisters nodded, their sharp eyes gleaming. "One day she gave us a letter to deliver to Les Salants. Veryvery nervous, she was—"

"But laughing fit to split—"

"And the next day—*Pfft!* She and the baby were gone."

"No one knew where or why—"

"Though we can guess, can't we, *ma soeur,* we don't hold confession, but—"

"People tell us things, all the same."

When had P'titJean guessed the truth? Did he find out by accident, or did she tell him herself, or did he see it, as I had thirty years later, written on the child's birth certificate in her own exuberant hand?

The sisters looked at me expectantly, both smiling. I looked down at the birth certificate on the desk in front of me; the purple ink, the name written in that now-familiar looped, elaborate script. . . .

Jean-Claude Désiré St.-Jean François Brismand.

The boy was GrosJean's son.

13

I know guilt. I know it very well. That's my father in me, the bitter core of him I inherited. It paralyzes; it stifles. When P'titJean and his boat were washed up at La Goulue, that's how he must have felt. Paralyzed. Sealed shut. He had always been the silent one; now it seemed that he could never be silent enough. P'titJean alive must have caused him enough heartache; P'titJean dead was an obstacle that could never be removed.

By the time my father thought to contact Eleanore, she had already gone, leaving behind the letter, which he found, opened, addressed to himself, in the pocket of his brother's coat, hanging by a hook behind his bedroom door.

I found it, you see, as I made my final search through my father's old house. It is from the letter that I was able to piece together the final details; my father's death; P'titJean's suicide; Flynn.

I don't pretend to understand it all. My father left no other explanation. I don't know why I expected him to; in life he never gave any. But we discussed it for a long time, the sisters and I, and I think we may have come close enough to the truth.

Flynn was the catalyst, of course. Without knowing it, he had set the machine in motion. My father's son; the son he could never acknowledge, because to do that, he would have to admit his responsibility for the suicide of his brother. Now I could understand my father's reaction when he learned who Flynn was. Everything returns; from Black Year to Black Year, Eleanore to *Eleanore,* the cycle was complete; and the bitter poetry of this ending must have appealed to the romantic in him.

Perhaps Alain had been right and he had not intended to die, I told myself. Perhaps it had been a desperate gesture, an attempt at redemption, my father's way of making amends. After all, the man responsible for all of this was his son.

The sisters and I returned the papers and registers to their original place. I was silently grateful for their presence, their incessant chatter, which kept me from examining too closely my own part of the tale.

Night had fallen, and I walked slowly back to Les Salants, listening to the crickets in the tamarisk bushes and looking at the stars. From time to time a glowworm shone sickly between my feet. I felt as if I had given blood. My anger had gone. My grief too. Even the horror of what I had learned seemed terribly unreal, as remote as stories I'd read as a child. Something in me had been cut loose, and for the first time in my life I felt that I might be able to leave Le Devin without that dreadful sensation of *drifting*, of weightlessness, of flotsam on an alien tide. At last, I knew where I was going.

My father's house was silent. However I had a peculiar feeling that I was not alone. It was something in the air, a scent of stale candle smoke, an unfamiliar resonance. I was not afraid. Instead I felt oddly at home, as if my father had simply gone night fishing, as if my mother were still there, maybe in the bedroom, reading one of her tattered paperback romances.

I hesitated for a moment at my father's door before pushing it open. The room was as he had left it, perhaps a little neater than usual, with his clothes folded and his bed made. I felt a pang at the sight of GrosJean's old *vareuse* hanging from a peg behind the door, but otherwise I was calm inside. This time I knew what to look for.

He kept his secret papers in a shoe box, as such men do, tied up with a piece of fishing twine, at the back of his wardrobe. A small collection; as I shook the box I could tell that it was barely half full. A few photo-

graphs—my parents' wedding, she in white, he in island dress. Beneath
the flat-brimmed black hat his face was achingly young. A few snapshots
of Adrienne and me; several of P'titJean at various ages. Most of the
other papers were drawings.

He drew on butcher's paper, mostly in charcoal and thick black pencil, and the passing of time and the friction of the papers against one
another had blurred the lines, but even so I could see that GrosJean had
once had an extraordinary talent. Features were represented with a
sparseness that almost matched his conversation, but every line, every
smudge was expressive. Here his thumb had traced a fat line of shadow
around the contour of a jaw; there a pair of eyes peered with strange
intensity from behind a mask of charcoal.

They were all portraits; every one of the same woman. I knew her
name; I'd seen the elegant scrawl of her writing on the church register.
Now I saw her beauty too: the arrogance of her cheekbones, the cock of
her head, the curve of her mouth.

These were his love letters, I realized, these drawings of her. My
silent, illiterate father had once found a beautiful voice. From between
two sheets of butcher's paper a dried flower slid; a dune pink, bleached
yellow with age. Then a piece of ribbon that might once have been blue
or green. Then a letter.

It was the only written document. A single page, breaking open at the
seams from having been so many times folded and unfolded. I recognized her handwriting at once, the looping scrawl and the violet ink.

My dear Jean-François,
Maybe you did well to stay away from me so long. I resented it at first,
and I was angry; but now I understand it was to give me time to
think.

I know I don't belong here. I'm made of a different element; for a
while I thought we might change each other, but it was too hard for
both of us.

I've decided to leave on tomorrow's ferry. Claude won't stop me;

he's gone to Fromentine on business for a few days. I'll wait for you on the jetty until 12.00.

I won't blame you if you don't come with me. You do belong here, and it would be wrong of me to force you to leave. But all the same, try not to forget me; maybe one day our son will come back, even if I never do.

Everything returns,
Eleanore

I folded the letter carefully again, and replaced it in the shoe box. There it was, I told myself. The final confirmation, if one was needed. How it had come into P'titJean's possession, I did not know; but for an impressionable and melancholic young man, the shock of his brother's betrayal must have been terrible. Had it been suicide, or a dramatic gesture that went wrong? No one was certain, except perhaps for Père Alban.

GrosJean would have gone to him, I knew. An Houssin, a priest, only he was far enough from the center of the affair to be trusted to decipher Eleanore's letter. It was confession enough for the old priest; and he had kept the secret well.

GrosJean had told no one else. After Eleanore's departure he had become increasingly withdrawn, spending hours at Les Immortelles, looking out to sea, retreating further and further into himself. For a time it had seemed that perhaps his marriage to my mother might draw him out of himself, but the change had been short-lived. Different elements, Eleanore had said. Different worlds.

I put the lid back on the shoe box and carried it out with me into the garden. As the door closed behind me I was struck by a feeling of certainty; I would never set foot inside GrosJean's house again.

"Mado." He was waiting by the boatyard gate, almost invisible in his black jeans and jumper. "I thought you'd come if I waited long enough."

My hands tightened around the shoe box. "What do you want?"

"I'm sorry about your father." His face was in shadow; shadows leaped in his eyes. I felt something tighten inside me. "My father?" I said harshly.

I saw him wince at my tone of voice. "Mado, please."

"Don't come near me." Flynn had reached out his hand to brush my arm. Though I was wearing a jacket, I imagined I could feel his touch burning through the heavy fabric and felt a sick horror at the desire that uncoiled like a snake at the pit of my stomach. "Don't touch me!" I cried, lashing out. "What do you want? Why did you come back?"

My blow had caught him across the mouth. He put a hand to his face, watching me calmly. "I know you're angry," he said.

"Angry?"

I'm not usually a talker. But this time my anger had a voice. A whole orchestra of voices. I gave him everything: Les Salants, Les Immortelles, Brismand; Eleanore; my father; himself. At the end I stopped, breathless, and thrust the shoe box into his hands. He made no move to retain it; it slipped onto the ground, spilling all the sad trivia of my father's life into a drift of papers. I kneeled to pick them up, my hands trembling.

His voice was blank. "GrosJean's son? His *son?*"

"Didn't Eleanore tell you? Wasn't that why you were so eager to keep it in the family?"

"I had no idea." His eyes narrowed; I sensed he was doing some very quick thinking. "It doesn't matter," he said at last. "This doesn't change anything." He seemed to be speaking to himself rather than to me. He turned toward me again with a rapid movement. "Mado," he said urgently. "Nothing's changed."

"What do you mean?" I was close to striking him again. "Of course it's changed. Everything's changed. You're my *brother*." I could feel my eyes beginning to burn; my throat was raw and bitter. "My brother," I said again, my fists still full of GrosJean's papers, and went off into a harsh scream of laughter that ended in a long, painful bout of coughing.

There was a silence. Then Flynn began to laugh softly in the darkness.

"What now?"

Still he laughed. It should not have been an unpleasant sound, but it was. "Ah, Mado," he told me at last. "It was going to be so easy. So beautiful. The biggest trick anyone had ever pulled. It was all there; the old man, his money, his beach, his desperate need to find someone to inherit. . . ." He shook his head. "It was all in place. All it needed was a little time. More time than I'd expected, but hey, all I had to do was to let events take their course. Spending a year in a sink like Les Salants was no great price to pay." He gave me one of his dangerous, sunlight-on-water smiles. "And then," he said, "along you came."

"Me?"

"You with your big ideas. Your island names. Your impossible plans. Stubborn, naive, utterly incorruptible you." He touched the nape of my neck briefly; I felt static in his fingertips.

I pushed him away. "Next you'll be saying it was me you did it for."

He grinned. "Who did you *think* I was doing it for?" I could still feel his breath on my forehead. I closed my eyes, but his face seemed to be imprinted onto my retinas. "Oh, Mado. If only you knew how hard I tried to keep you away. But you're like this place; slowly, insidiously, it gets to you. And before you know it, you're getting involved."

I opened my eyes. "You can't," I said.

"Too late." He sighed. "It would have been great to have been Jean-Claude Brismand," he said ruefully. "To have money, land, to do whatever I liked—"

"You still can," I told him. "Brismand need never know—"

"But I'm not Jean-Claude."

"What do you mean? It's there, on the birth certificate."

Flynn shook his head. His eyes were unreadable, almost black. Fireflies danced there. "Mado," he said, "the guy on that birth certificate isn't me."

❀

I listened in growing confusion as he told his story. This was his secret, the space into which I had never been invited, flung wide open at last. A story of two brothers.

They were born a thousand miles and a little less than two years apart. Though they were only half-brothers, they favored their mother, and as a result looked strikingly alike, although in every other way they were very different. Their mother had poor taste in men, and changed her mind often. As a result, John and Richard had had many fathers.

But John's father was a wealthy man. Although he lived abroad, he continued to support the boy and his mother, staying in touch, even though he never came in person. As a result the two brothers came to see him as a benevolent, if shadowy, figure; one to whom they might turn in time of need.

"That was a joke," said Flynn. "I learned that the hard way, the day I started school." John had been sent, two years earlier, to a grammar school where he learned Latin and was in the cricket First Eleven; but Richard went to the local comprehensive, where differences—intelligence above all—were exposed without mercy and subjected to a number of ingenious and brutal persecutions.

"Our mother never told him about me. She was afraid that if she told him about her other men, he might cut the support money." As a result, Richard's name was never mentioned, and Eleanore took pains to give Brismand the impression that she and John were living alone.

Flynn went on. "When there was money, it was always for my brother. School trips, school uniform, sports kit. No one said why. John had a savings account at the post office. John had a bike. All I had was the stuff John was tired of, or had broken, or was too stupid to figure out how to use. No one ever thought I might want something of my own." Briefly I thought of myself and Adrienne. Almost without knowing it, I nodded.

After school John had been sent to university. Brismand had agreed to finance his studies providing he chose something that would prove useful to the business; but John had no skill in engineering or in management, and resented being told what to do. In fact, John resented the idea of having to work at all, having been indulged for so long, and dropped out of university in his second year, living on his savings and hanging around with a group of disreputable—and perpetually bank-rupt—friends.

Eleanore covered for him as long as she could. But John was beyond her influence now, making his money the easy way, selling stolen car radios and contraband cigarettes, and constantly boasting, after a few drinks, of his wealthy father.

"It was always the same. Someday he'd get a job; the old man would fix him up; not to worry; plenty of time. Secretly I think he was hoping Brismand would die before he had to make a decision. John's never been much good at sticking to anything, and the idea of moving to France, learning the language, giving up his mates and his easy life—" Flynn gave an ugly laugh. "As for me, I'd been working in dockyards and building sites for long enough, and the role of Jean-Claude was vacant. Golden Boy didn't seem to be in any hurry."

It had seemed the perfect opportunity. Flynn had enough documentary and anecdotal evidence to pass for his brother, as well as more than a passing resemblance to John. He had left his job with a building company and used his few savings to get a ticket to Le Devin.

At first his plan had simply been to take Brismand for whatever cash he could get his hands on before making his escape. "A gold card would have been nice to begin with, or maybe a trust fund. Not an unusual arrangement between father and son. But islands are different."

He was right; islanders have no trust in funds. Brismand wanted more commitment. He wanted help. First with Les Immortelles. Then with La Goulue. Then Les Salants. "Les Salants clinched it," said Flynn with a touch of regret. "It would have made me. First the beach, then the village—then the whole island. I could have had it all. Brismand was ready to retire. He would have put me in charge of the bulk of the business. I would have had complete access to everything." He sighed. "It would have been nice," he said regretfully. "To have been wanted, for a change. To have somewhere of my own."

I stared at him. "But not now."

He grinned and touched my cheek with his fingertips. "No Mado. Not now."

From afar I could hear the *hisshh* of the incoming tide from La Goulue. Even farther away, a yarking of seagulls as someone disturbed a nest. But the sounds were distant, muffled by the huge beating of my blood. I struggled to understand Flynn's story; but it was already slipping away from me. My temples throbbed; there seemed to be an obstacle in my throat that made breathing difficult. It was as if everything else had been overshadowed by one single, giant reality. Flynn was not my brother.

"What's that?" I pulled away almost without knowing I'd heard it. A warning sound, something deep and resonant, just audible above the sound of the sea.

Flynn shot me a glance. "Now what?"

"Shh!" I put my finger to my mouth. "Listen."

There it was again, barely a drone in the still evening air, the pulse of a drowned bell throbbing against our eardrums.

"I can't hear anything." Impatiently, he made as if to put an arm around my shoulders. I stood up and pushed him away, more forcefully this time. "Can't you hear what that is? Don't you recognize it?"

"I don't care."

"Flynn, it's La Marinette."

14

That's how it ends, as it began. The bell—not the fabled Marinette, as it happened, but the church bell from La Houssinière, ringing the alarm for the second time that month, in a voice that carried its message clear across the marshes. At night a bell has a tone different from the one it has in daytime; dark urgency was in its ringing now, and I responded to it with an instinctive haste. Flynn tried to stop me, but I was in no mood for interference; I sensed a disaster maybe even worse than the loss of the *Eleanore 2*, and I was running down the dune toward Les Salants before Flynn realized where I was going.

The village was the only place he couldn't follow me, of course; he stopped at the brow of the dune and let me go. Angélo's was open, and a group of drinkers had gathered outside, alerted by the sound of the bell. I saw Omer there, and Capucine, and the Bastonnets. "Thass the alarm, heh," said Omer in a thick voice. He had already drunk enough *devinnoise* to slow him down considerably. "Thass the Houssin alarm."

Aristide shook his head. "It's none of our business, then, is it, heh? Let the Houssins have the crisis for a change. It's not as if the island's sinking, is it?"

"Someone ought to find out, all the same," suggested Angélo uncomfortably.

"Someone ride out onna bike, heh," said Omer.

Several people agreed with this, though no one volunteered. There were a number of wishful suggestions as to the nature of the emergency, ranging from more jellyfish warnings to Les Immortelles being carried away by a freak cyclone. This possibility found favor with the majority of the assembly, and Angélo suggested another round of drinks.

It was then that Hilaire rounded the Rue de l'Atlantique, waving his arms and shouting. This was unusual enough, for the doctor was undemonstrative at the best of times, without his peculiar state of dress; in his haste he seemed to have thrown on his *vareuse* over his pajamas, and on his feet he wore only a pair of faded espadrilles. For Hilaire, usually very correct even in the hottest weather, this was beyond unusual. He was shouting something about a radio.

Angélo had a drink set up for him when he arrived, and the first thing Hilaire did was swallow it quickly and with grim relish. "We'll all need one," he said tersely, "if what I've just heard is true."

He'd been listening to the radio. He liked to hear the international news program at ten o' clock before going to bed, although islanders rarely follow the news. Papers on Le Devin usually arrive out-of-date, and only Mayor Pinoz really claims to take an interest in politics or current affairs; in his position it's expected.

"Well this time I heard something," said Hilaire, "and it isn't pretty!"

Aristide nodded. "No surprises there," he said. "I've told you, it's a Black Year. It was due."

"A Black Year! Heh!" Hilaire grunted and reached for his second *devinnoise*. "And by the sound of it, it's about to get a lot blacker."

❦

You will have read about it, I imagine. A broken oil tanker off the coast of Brittany, disgorging hundreds of gallons of oil a minute. It's the kind of thing that captures the public imagination for a few days, maybe for a week. The television stations show pictures of dead seabirds; indignant students protest against pollution; a few volunteers from the cities hone their social consciences by cleaning up a beach or two. Tourism suffers for a time, though the coastal authorities usually take measures to clean up the more profitable areas. Fishing, of course, suffers for longer.

Oysters are sensitive; even a slight taint of pollution can wipe them out. Crabs and lobsters are the same; and as for mullet, it's almost worse. Aristide remembers mullet in 1945 with bellies bloated with oil; all of us remember the spillage in the 1970s—much, much farther away than this one—which had us scraping great gouts of black tar from the rocks at Pointe Griznoz. By the time Hilaire had finished his explanations, a number of other people had arrived at Angélo's bar with conflicting or corroborating information, and we were in a state of near panic; the ship was less than seventy kilometers away—no, make that fifty—she was carrying crude diesel, the worst possible thing; already the slick was kilometers long, and completely out of control. A few of us went to La Houssinière to see Pinoz, who might have more information. Many of the rest stayed to see if they could find out more details from the television channels, or pulled out old maps from their pockets to speculate on the eventual movements of the slick.

"If it's here," said Hilaire glumly, indicating a spot on Aristide's chart, "then I can't see how it could miss us, heh? This is the Gulf Stream—"

"There's nothing to say whether the slick has reached the Gulf Stream," said Angélo. "They might catch it before it does. Or it might go around here, around the nearside of Noirmoutier, and miss us altogether."

Aristide was unconvinced. "If it hits the Nid'Poule," he intoned, "it could sink right down there and poison us for half a century."

"Well *you*'ve been doing that for nearly twice the time," remarked Matthias Guénolé, "and we've still survived."

There was nervous laughter from everyone else. Angélo served another round of *devinnoise*. Then someone called for silence from inside the bar, and we joined the little group of drinkers clustered around the old television. "Shh, everyone! Here it is!"

Some news can only be received in silence. We listened like children, eyes widening as the screen broadcast its message. Even Aristide was silent. We remained stunned, pinned to the television screen and the little red cross that marked the scene of the wreck. "How close is it?" asked Charlotte anxiously.

"Close," said Omer in a low voice, his face very white.

"Bloody mainland news," exploded Aristide. "Can't they use a proper map, heh? That stupid diagram makes it look like it's twenty kilometers away! And where are the *details?*"

"What happens if it comes here?" whispered Charlotte.

Matthias tried to sound unmoved. "We'll think of something. We'll pull together. We've done it before."

"Not like this!" said Aristide.

Omer muttered something under his breath.

"What was that?" demanded Matthias.

"I said I wish Rouget was still here."

All of us looked at one another. No one contradicted him.

15

That night, powered by *devinnoise*, we began what work we could. Volunteers were gathered to spend shifts in front of the television and the radio, to collect any new information about the spillage. Hilaire, who had a telephone, was nominated as our official mainland contact. His job was to liaise with the coast guard as well as the shipping services, so that we could be forewarned. Watchers were posted at three-hour intervals at La Goulue; if there was anything to be seen, said Aristide grimly, it would begin there. Moreover, the creek was being dredged and blocked off from the open sea, using rocks from La Griznoz and leftover cement from the Bouch'ou. "At least if we can keep the *étier* clean we'll have something," said Matthias. Aristide, for once, agreed without complaint.

Xavier Bastonnet appeared at about midnight—apparently he and Ghislain had gone out twice in the *Cécilia*—with the news that the coast guard ship was still out beyond La Jetée. It seemed that the disabled tanker had been in danger for some time, but that the authorities had only released the news during the past few days. The projections, Xavier reported, were not optimistic. There was a south wind due, he said, which, if it held, would drive the oil straight toward us. If that happened, only a miracle could save us.

The morning of Sainte-Marine's festival found us in poor spirits. There had been some progress made along the *étier*, but not enough. Even with the proper materials, said Matthias, it would take at least a week to contain it properly. At ten in the morning, reports of a black residue spotted some kilometers off la Jetée had reached the village, and we were brittle and apprehensive. The sandbanks were black with it already, and although it had not yet reached the shore, it would surely do so within twenty-four hours.

Nevertheless, as Toinette pointed out, it would not do to neglect the Saint on her festival day, and in the village the usual preparations were already under way: the repainting of the little shrine, flowers on the Pointe, the brazier lit next to the ruins of the church.

Even with binoculars it was still not clear what the residue was, but Aristide reported that there was a hell of a lot of it, and with the tide coming back that night and the wind from the south, it was likely to wash up onto La Goulue at any time. The next high tide would be due at about ten that evening, and by afternoon a number of the villagers were already watching from Pointe Griznoz, with offerings and flowers and effigies of the Saint. Toinette, Désirée, and many of the older villagers were inclined to believe that the only solution was prayer.

"She's done miracles before," declared Toinette. "There's always hope."

The Black Tide had been visible to the naked eye since late that afternoon. Glimpses under a wave, something rolling from the sandbanks, an unusual buoyancy in the shadows of a rock. There was as yet no sign of any oil on the water, however, not even a film, but as Omer said, this could be a special kind of oil, a bad kind, even worse than we'd had in the past. Instead of floating on the surface it clotted, sank, rolled to the bottom, poisoning everything. Technology could do terrible things, heh? Heads were shaken over this, but no one really knew. It was not our area of expertise, and by early evening tales of the Black Tide had proliferated. There would be two-headed fish, claimed Aristide, and poisonous crabs. Simply to touch it would be to risk dreadful infection. Birds would go mad, boats would be dragged under by the weight of the congealing sludge. For all we knew it could even have been the Black Tide that had brought the jellyfish plague. But in spite of all this—perhaps because of it—Les Salants stood fast.

The Black Tide had brought us this, at least. We had a direction again, a common purpose. The spirit of Les Salants—the hard core at the heart of us, the thing that I had glimpsed in the pages of Père Alban's books—was back again. I could feel it. Old grievances were once more forgotten. Xavier and Mercédès had abandoned their plan to leave—at least for the present—and had turned their attention to helping out. Philippe Bastonnet, who had been waiting in La Houssinière for the next ferry, returned with Gabi, Laetitia, and the baby to Les Salants, where, despite Aristide's dwindling protests, he was determined to stay and help. Désirée had found room for them in the house, and this time, Aristide had not objected.

As dark fell and the tide rose, more people began to congregate at La Griznoz. Père Alban had been too busy in La Houssinière, where a special service was being held at the church, but the old nuns were there, bright and alert as ever. Braziers were lit; red, orange, and yellow lanterns flared around the foot of the ruined church; and once again the Salannais, strangely touching in their island hats and Sunday dresses, lined up at the feet of Sainte-Marine-de-la-Mer to pray and to plead aloud with the sea.

The Bastonnets were there with François and Laetitia; the Guénolés, the Prossages. Capucine was there with Lolo; Mercédès was there, holding Xavier's hand, a little shyly, one hand on her stomach. Toinette sang the "Santa Marina" in her quavery voice; and Désirée, standing between Philippe and Gabi at the foot of the Saint, looked as rosy and contented as if it were a wedding. "Even if the Saint chooses not to intervene," she said serenely, "just having my children here makes it worthwhile."

I stood apart from the rest, on the brow of the dune, listening and thinking back to last year's festival. It was a still night, and the crickets were loud in the warm grassy hollows. The hard sand was cool under my feet. From La Goulue, the *hisssh* of the incoming tide. Sainte-Marine looked down in her stony isolation, her features brought to life by the leaping flames. I watched as the Salannais drew close to the shore, one by one.

Mercédès was first, dropping a clutch of flower petals into the water. "Sainte-Marine. Bless my baby. Bless my parents and keep them safe."

"Santa Marina. Bless my daughter. Keep her happy with her young man, and close enough to visit us once in a while."

"Marine-de-la-Mer, bless Les Salants. Bless our shores."

"Bless my husband and my sons—"

"Bless my father—"

"Bless my wife."

Slowly I became conscious that something extraordinary was happening. Salannais linking hands in the firelight—Omer with his arm around Charlotte; Ghislain linking arms with Xavier; Capucine and Lolo; Aristide and Philippe; Damien and Alain. People were smiling in spite of their anxiety; instead of the sullen, bent heads of last year I could see bright eyes and proud faces. Head scarves were thrown back; hair loosened; I could see faces illuminated by something more than the firelight; dancing figures throwing handfuls of flower petals and ribbons and sachets of herbs into the waves. Toinette began to sing again, and this time more people joined her; the voices merging little by little into one voice—the voice of Les Salants.

I found that if I listened carefully I could almost hear GrosJean's voice among them; and my mother's; and P'titJean's. Suddenly I wanted to join them; to step out into the firelight and pray to the Saint. But instead I whispered my prayer from the dune, very quietly, almost to myself. . . .

"Mado?" He can move absolutely silently when he wants to. That's the islander in him—if there *is* an islander beneath all the pretense. I turned abruptly, my heart leaping.

"Jesus, Flynn, what are you doing here?" He was standing behind me on the dune-side path, out of sight of the little ceremony. He was wearing a dark *vareuse*, and he would have been almost invisible except for the skein of moonlight in his hair.

"Where have you been?" I hissed, looking back nervously at the Salannais, but before he could answer, there came a great cry from the lookout at Pointe Griznoz, echoed a second or two later by a wail from La Goulue.

"*Aii!* The tide! *Aii!*"

At the shrine, the singing stopped. There was a moment of confusion; some Salannais ran out to the edge of the Pointe, but in the uncertain light of the lanterns there was nothing much anyone could make out. *Something* was riding the waves, a dark, semibuoyant mass, but no one could tell precisely what it was. Alain grabbed a lantern and began to run; Ghislain did likewise. Before long, a trail of lanterns and flashlights were bobbing across the dune toward La Goulue, and the Black Tide.

Flynn and I were lost in the confusion. The crowd passed right beside us, shouting and questioning and swinging lanterns, but no one seemed to notice either of us. Everyone wanted to be first at La Goulue; some grabbed rakes and nets from the village as they passed, as if to begin the clean-up operation at once.

"What's going on?" I asked Flynn as we let the crowd carry us along.

He shook his head. "Come and see."

We had reached the *blockhaus*, always a good vantage point. Below us La Goulue was alive with lights. I could see several people standing in the shallows with lanterns, like a string of light-fishers. Around them I could see black shapes, dozens of them, half-buoyant, half-submerged, rolling under the waves. From afar I could hear raised voices, and— surely that was laughter? The black shapes were too unclear in the light of the lanterns to be recognizable, but for a moment I thought I glimpsed a regular pattern, too geometric to be natural.

"Watch this," said Flynn.

Below us the raised voices had grown louder; more people had gathered at the water's edge, some were in the sea up to their armpits. Light from the lanterns skated across the water; from above, the shallows were an unreal, lurid green.

"Keep watching," said Flynn.

It was definitely laughter; down on La Goulue I could see people splashing in the shallows. "What's going on?" I demanded. "Is it the Black Tide?"

"In a way."

Now I could see Omer and Alain rolling dark objects out of the surf. Others joined them; the objects were about a meter in diameter and regular in shape. From a distance I thought they looked like car tires.

"That's exactly what they are," said Flynn quietly. "That's the Bouch'ou."

"What?" I felt as if something in me had been cut adrift. "The Bouch'ou?"

He nodded. His expression was strangely illuminated by the glow from the beach. "Mado. It was the only thing to do."

"But what for? All our work—"

"Right now, we have to stop the drift toward La Goulue. Get rid of the reef, and the currents move with it. That way, if the oil comes as far as Le Devin, it might bypass Les Salants. At least this gives you a chance."

He had gone out at low tide. He had used bolt cutters on the airplane cables that held the modules together. Half an hour's work; the tide did the rest.

"And are you sure this will do it?" I said at last. "We'll be safe now?"

He shrugged. "I don't know."

"You don't know?"

"Ah, Mado, what did you expect?" He sounded exasperated now. "I can't give you everything!" He shook his head. "At least you can fight back now. Les Salants doesn't have to die."

"What about Brismand?" I asked dully.

"He's too busy with his own side of the island to pay much attention to what's going on here. The last I heard, he was racking his brains to try and figure out how to move a hundred-ton breakwater in twenty-four hours." He smiled. "It seems maybe GrosJean had the right idea about that, after all."

For a moment his words were incomprehensible to me. I had been so absorbed in my thoughts of the Black Tide that I'd actually forgotten about Brismand's plans. I felt a sudden joyous, savage surge inside me. "If Brismand takes down his defenses too, it could all stop," I said. "The tides would go back to the way they were before."

Flynn laughed. "Little cookouts on the beach. Three guests in a back bedroom. Three francs a head to look at the Saint. Counting pennies. No money, no expansion, no future, no fortune, nothing."

I shook my head. "You're wrong," I told him. "There'd be Les Salants."

He laughed again, rather wildly. "That's right. Les Salants."

16

I know he can't stay in Les Salants. It's stupid of me to expect it. There are too many lies and deceptions to trip him up. Too many people hate him. And he is a mainlander at heart. He dreams of cities and lights. However much he may want to, I don't see how he could stay. Similarly I will not leave; that's the Gros-Jean in me, the island in me. My father loved Eleanore, but in the end he did not go with her. The island finds a way to keep you. This time it's the Black Tide; the slick is ten kilometers from us now, on the Noir-moutier side. No one knows whether it will hit us or pass us by—not even the coast guard. Already there is devastation down the Vendée coast; the television brings us images of our possible future in exasperat-ingly grainy, garish colors. No one can quite predict what will happen to us; by rights the slick should follow the Gulf Stream, but it is a matter of kilometers now, and it could go either way.

Noirmoutier will almost certainly get it. The Île d'Yeu is still uncer-tain. The savage currents that separate us are already battling for control. One of us—maybe only one—will get the oil. But Les Salants has not lost hope. Indeed, we are working harder than ever before. The creek is secure now, the vivarium well stocked. Aristide, whose wooden leg pre-vents him from more active duties, scans the television broadcasts for news while Philippe helps Xavier. Charlotte and Mercédès are running

Angélo's, providing food for the volunteers. Omer, the Guénolés, and the Bastonnets spend almost all of their time at Les Immortelles. Brismand has enlisted anyone who will help him—Houssins or Salannais—to help with the slow dismantling of the breakwater at Les Immortelles; he has also changed his will in favor of Marin. Damien, Lolo, Hilaire, Angélo, and Capucine are still clearing La Goulue, and we plan to reuse the old car tires to construct protective barriers against the oil, if it makes it to our beaches. We have already collected supplies of cleaning equipment for this eventuality. Flynn is in charge.

Yes, for the moment, he remains. Some of the men are still cool toward him, but the Guénolés and the Prossages have accepted him back wholeheartedly in spite of everything, and Aristide played chess with him yesterday, so maybe there's hope for him yet. Certainly this is no time for useless recriminations. He works as hard as any of us—harder, even—and on Le Devin that's really all that matters now. I don't know why he stays. Still, it is oddly comforting to see him every day, in his usual place at La Goulue, poking with a stick at the things the sea brings in, rolling the endless tide of car tires up into the dunes for disposal. He has not yet lost his sharp edges—perhaps he never will—but I think he seems softened, smoothed, partly reclaimed, almost one of us. I have even begun to like him—a little.

Sometimes I wake up and look out of the window at the sky. It is never quite dark at this time of year. Sometimes Flynn and I creep out to look over La Goulue, where the sea is glaucous with the strange phosphorescence peculiar to the Jade Coast, and sit out there on the dune. There are tamarisks growing there, and late pinks, and rabbit-tail grasses, which flicker and bob palely in the starlight. Across the water we can sometimes see the lights of the mainland: a warning beacon to the west, the winking *balise* to the south. Flynn likes to sleep out on the beach. He likes the small sounds of insects from the cliff side above his head, and the *oyat* grass that whispers. Sometimes we stay there all night.

Epilogue

Winter has come, and still the Black Tides have not reached us. Île d'Yeu has been somewhat affected; Fromentine is under oil; the whole of Noirmoutier badly ravaged. And still it rises; following the coast northward, fingering its way into shallows and across promontories. It is still too soon to say what will happen here. But Aristide is optimistic; Toinette has consulted the Saint and claims to have seen visions; Mercédès and Xavier have moved into the little cottage on the dunes, much to old Bastonnet's unspoken delight; Omer has hit an unprecedented winning streak at belote; and I'm certain that the other day I saw Charlotte Prossage smile. No, I wouldn't say our tide has turned. But something else has come back to Le Devin. A kind of purpose. No one can turn back the tide, at least not forever. Everything returns. But Le Devin holds fast. In flood, in drought, come Black Year or Black Tide, it holds. It holds because we do; the Devinnois—Bastonnets, Guénolés, Prasteaus, Prossages, Brismands—even perhaps, more recently, the Flynns. Nothing can keep us down. Might as well spit in the wind as try.

![Perennial] Perennial

Novels by Joanne Harris:

COASTLINERS
ISBN 0-06-095801-4 (paperback)

After ten years in Paris, Madeleine has returned to her home in a small island village off the coast of France. But when she arrives she finds that her father—who once built fishing boats that fueled the town's livelihood—has withdrawn into a world where no one can reach him. His decline seems reflected in the town itself, for when the only beach in Les Salants washed away, what little tourism existed drifted to the rival village of La Houssinière. Now, almost against her will, Madeleine finds herself united with the other lost souls of her childhood home in the struggle to survive.

"This novel...flows as rhythmically as the waves that wash upon Le Devin, the tiny French island where the story takes place." —*New York Daily News*

FIVE QUARTERS OF THE ORANGE
ISBN 0-06-095802-2 (paperback)

As a child, Framboise Dartigen and her family were driven from their small Loire village because of a tragedy that took place during the German occupation—an event that still haunts the town. Now, as an adult, Framboise will find the terrible truth of that long-ago time hidden among the newspaper clippings, herbal cures, and cherished recipes that fill the pages of the scrapbook her mother bequeathed to her.

"Unexpectedly sweet and powerful." —*New York Times Book Review*

BLACKBERRY WINE
ISBN 0-380-81592-3 (paperback)

As a boy, writer Jay Mackintosh spent three golden summers in the ramshackle home of Joseph "Jackapple Joe" Cox. Then one fall, Joe disappeared without warning. Years later, Jay's life is stalled with regret and ennui. He impulsively heads to a small village where he finds a strange yet oddly familiar place—and in the dark, guarded secrets of a reclusive woman and her young child, Jay Mackintosh begins to find himself again.

"A charming fairy tale for grown-ups." —*Kirkus Reviews*

Don't miss the next book by your favorite author.
Sign up for AuthorTracker by visiting *www.AuthorTracker.com*.

Available wherever books are sold, or call 1-800-331-3761 to order.

(((Listen to)))

COASTLINERS
A Novel

by Joanne Harris

PERFORMED BY
VIVIEN BENESCH

*"[Vivien Benesch's] subtle, controlled
inflections bring the colorful characters alive."*
—Audio File

ISBN 0-06-051783-2 • $39.95 ($59.95 Can.)
12½ Hours • 8 Cassettes • UNABRIDGED

Available wherever books are sold, or call 1-800-331-3761 to order.

HarperAudio *An Imprint of* HarperCollins*Publishers*
www.harperaudio.com

William Morrow

MY FRENCH KITCHEN
A Book of 120 Treasured Recipes

For the first time, this beloved novelist offers a hand-picked selection of classic French recipes from her *grandmère, maman,* and others. With the assistance of food writer, editor, and chef Fran Warde, Joanne Harris throws open wide the door to her French kitchen inviting readers to share the good food, treasured memories, and time-honored traditions that are the true pleasures of the table.

ISBN 0-06-056352-4 (hardcover)
FULL COLOR PHOTOS THROUGHOUT

Coming Fall 2003 from
Joanne Harris and Fran Warde